Summer
Stalk

Summer
Stalk

Bentley Lyon

ST. MARTIN'S PRESS NEW YORK

Design by Judy Christensen

Production Editor: Suzanne Magida

Production Manager: Marni Siskind

Library of Congress Cataloging-in-Publication Data

Lyon, Bentley.
    Summer stalk / Bentley Lyon.
    New York : St. Martin's Press, 1992.
    "A Thomas Dunne Book."
    ISBN 0-312-08312-2
    I. Title.
    PS3562.Y44487S86   1992
    813'.54—dc20   92-27465
                                                   CIP

FIRST EDITION: December 1992

10 9 8 7 6 5 4 3 2 1

TO TAHIRIH

*for her humor, her love,
and her adolescence*

Acknowledgments

T hanks to Lawrence M. Whitfield, former Regional Forester, U. S. Forest Service, also attorney-at-law, for his help with California law, and also for having been a great guy to work for. Thanks to Dennis Ensign, fire prevention specialist, retired, Los Padres National Forest, for technical material and counsel, and for his on-the-job diligence through the years. I also express my gratitude to the many other fine people of the Forest Service who, indirectly and without their knowledge, made this story possible. None of the characters in this book are intended to represent specific former or current employees of the service.

Special thanks to my wife Liz for her help in brainstorming and proofreading, and to Destiny for being such a pushy agent, not to mention lovable daughter, and to her partner, Jack Albert. And finally, thanks to my editor Ruth Cavin, whose counsel has proven most helpful and reliable.

WARNING: the language of some of the story characters is obscene at times, and is only included to reflect the way many of these people really spoke. Please keep in mind that if you are offended, it's their fault, not mine.

Summer
Stalk

Prologue

M y story really begins in 1957, but it has taken me all these years to find a way to tell it. I haven't driven this highway for so long, the sights along the way seem only vaguely familiar, and I wonder now and then if I am on the right road.

At Redding I turn eastward to leave the scalding Sacramento Valley, where by early June the browned annual grasses quit trying at ankle height and the streambeds struggle to show water along their stony surfaces. The baking foothills of the Sierra Nevada offer little comfort of their own, the dusty manzanitas and live oaks providing only enough shade for a few thirsty jackrabbits and the coyotes who live from them. But an hour's drive brings me beneath the cool canopy of the towering pines, firs, and cedars that softens the rugged contours of these mountains and provides shelter for its streams, soils, and wildlife.

Each new vista triggers a sequence of images I once owned but that have since escaped me. It's why I am here. I make mental notes and keep driving, still not knowing why I waited so long to do what I always knew would have to be done—come to grips with what happened here, justify it on my own terms, then learn to live with some facts that will never change. To do these things I must write the story.

The tale is about justice, or more precisely, the lack of justice, and the frustration that comes from this. It's nothing new. The lives of all of us have been touched by this problem: the inability of our society to unfailingly provide us with moral outcomes for the immoral acts—the outrages—that threaten our sanctity of life.

As a young police officer on the streets of Los Angeles, I carried with me an improbable idealism. I accepted the imperfections of our judicial system in the belief that they were, in reality, the strengths of the system. If the system failed to provide justice, then society would strengthen the system in response, and we were obliged to accept the occasional failure to earn the longer term good.

But experience can change behavior and convictions, and it did so for me. This did not happen gradually over a period of years, but in a matter of only a few hours.

Since then I've had about thirty-three years to reconsider. And now, at the outset of writing this story, my view is that people who steadfastly accept what the system gives them do so simply because it best suits their purposes, because they fear the law—or the morality of society—more than they do their own con-sciences, or because their reverence for the law was never fully tested by emotion.

I hope I am wrong, because I don't really want to live in a world where the rule of vigilantism prevails.

Chapter 1

1957

When the phone rang that morning I figured it for Belinda, because she had the nasty habit of calling each morning just as I would be leaving to go on shift, or just as I was getting home and needed to use the bathroom. God knows how many times she called when I wasn't there.

My reaction to her calls was a symptom, of course. I really didn't care much for her and hadn't yet faced up to it. When I finally gave it some thought, I realized she was becoming less a girlfriend to me and more something like a sticky parasite. But she thought of herself as my lover and tried to prove it by tightening the vise on me day by day. The more I tried to ease things off by ignoring her, the more aggressively she preyed on me. Nothing I'd said to her so far had dampened her pushiness in the least, and I thought I'd been pretty blunt at times.

I was running late, and when the phone rang I practically snarled into the receiver. But it turned out to be my father, calling from his home in Sunland.

"Oh, sorry, Dad, I thought it was somebody else."

"Son, it's about Heath."

My father's voice sounded all wrong, too high-pitched, too tense, too charged with emotion. My brother? What could have happened to produce this effect on my father? A wave of anxiety hit as I tried to anticipate what might follow. I tried to maintain a cheerful tone. "Well, come on, Dad. What is it?"

He cleared his throat. "We just got a call from the Forest Service in Winchester; you know, near where Heath was working."

When he said *was,* I began suspecting the worst news a brother can hear. "Yes, what is it, Dad? . . . Dad?"

"They say . . ." He sighed heavily. "They say he was killed fighting a fire."

It hit me like a locomotive smashing into a car at a grade crossing. I was suddenly catapulted into a world in which time raged backward to stage a lightning-fast slide show of familiar scenes, but in which the shapes were hideously distorted, the accompanying music a vibrating crescendo of discordant percussion crashes. It felt like my head was imploding, and I fought hard to focus on the horror confronting me.

"Who says, goddamnit? *Who* says?" I roared into his ear. "How do they know?"

"The forest supervisor called me, Gene. He said they made a positive identification. He told me . . . he told me . . . I'm sorry, son. He told me Heath died trying to save a man that was trapped in the fire."

I struggled to control my emotions. As a police officer I dealt with death often, trauma and panic the daily fare on the streets of L.A., and I'd long ago learned to think coolly in the midst of chaos. But this was new. This was about my little brother, the kid who wanted more than anything else to be a forest ranger. Why Heath? Why not some slimy scumbag dope peddler on Western Avenue, or some rotten pimp who made a fat living destroying runaway kids? I kicked a wooden chair clear across the room in my rage.

"Gene? You still there?"

"Yeah," I sobbed, the tears now beginning to stream down my face. "How's Mom?"

"Not so good, son. Can you come over?"

"Have you told Alice yet?" She was Heath's fiancée.

"No. Would you mind, son?"

4

At my father's direction, the Forest Service had Heath's body delivered to a mortuary in Sunland, where they staged one of those insipid, commercial package funerals that benefit the owners of the store substantially more than the emotions of the bereaved. The experience so flattened my mom and dad, they declined making the long trip north to Cedar Valley, where the people of the town had arranged a memorial service. I would have gone but for a critical courtroom appearance I was unable to get delayed. I wanted to see where my brother had worked, what kind of people lived there, maybe talk to some of his friends. And I suppose I wanted the sympathy and compassion due a close relative of someone who had died performing a heroic act.

When I next saw my father and mother, they had received a letter from Don West, the district ranger in Cedar Valley, telling them about the memorial service. The letter also told how Heath had sacrificed his life trying to save a tractor operator trapped in the fire. Unforseeably, the tractor operator had escaped moments before Heath arrived at the scene. An arsonist had apparently caused the fire, West wrote, and the crime was under investigation.

Under investigation, to my police officer ear, meant they had no leads and possibly didn't even know where to begin. But I didn't trouble my mom and dad with that interpretation. They were having enough problems trying to deal with the tragedy and assumed the responsible person would soon enough be brought to account. I didn't know anything about forest fires, but in homicide cases, every day that goes by without isolating a primary suspect reduces the chances of solution by about fifty percent. I had little confidence they'd find the perpetrator.

A month went by, one I really don't remember much about. I went to work, saw Belinda a lot less often than she wanted, and tried to be with my dad and mom as much as I could. The idle times were the worst, the times spent alone replaying again and again my recollections of Heath.

I was the elder by five years, and so we had different friends, went to different schools, had different interests. Perhaps that's what made the bonding so strong. We didn't compete in games, or for the attention of our parents or friends. We had nothing to fight about. He saw me as a protector, a coach, a loyal friend and role model, and aware of this, I saw myself that way too. There was nothing we couldn't comfortably discuss, nothing too much or too little to ask of each other.

It's impossible to set something like that aside, to simply forget about it and move on to other things. At least, I couldn't do it, not until all the nails had been hammered into place.

It bothered me that my folks had received no further news of the fire investigation, so I made a few phone calls. The Forest Service people in Cedar Valley told me they had been instructed to refer questions about the investigation to their regional fiscal agent in San Francisco. Not surprising, I thought. The government lawyers were already on the job, doing what they do best— keeping people from talking to one another.

When I finally got through to somebody familiar with the case, I learned they hadn't yet identified a suspect. A Mr. Graves, who called himself the law enforcement branch chief, told me that a special agent had made an investigation. This investigation revealed that the Pegleg fire, as he called it, had been incendiary and possibly one of a series of such fires in that area.

"What's the current status of the investigation?"

"Well, we keep the case file open indefinitely, Mr. Murphy, in case anything develops. But to answer your question, we've ended the field investigation, for all practical purposes."

"In other words, you've just quit, given up on it, even though my brother was killed?"

"Look, Mr. Murphy, I feel deeply about your concern. But at the same time I won't pull any punches. I put our best investigator on that job and left him there a week. He damn well might have found out some things that will mean something when somebody comes forward, or when the guy who did this tries it again. We're ready to move on that when it happens. But in the meantime, we've got a hell of a lot of other cases pending, and only three investigators in the whole state to do the work."

"Yeah, I understand. I'm not trying to give you a hard time. It's just rough sitting on my hands waiting for something to happen. Would it be possible for me to get a copy of the investigation report? I'd like to know more about the circumstances of my brother's death than just the few comments in the autopsy report."

"Mr. Murphy, I'll personally do everything possible to make that report available to you when it's been released by legal counsel."

"When do you think that will be?"

"As soon as, in his opinion, there is no longer any problem about the investigation being compromised by releasing information prematurely."

"I don't understand. You told me the investigation was pretty well wrapped up for the present. What's the problem?"

"Look, Mr. Murphy, my hands are tied. If you'd like to speak directly with the USDA regional attorney, I can give you his number."

"Thanks anyway. Perhaps you can put me in touch with the agent who made the investigation."

There was a sigh on the other end. "You need to understand he's not authorized to give any specific information on the case."

"Fine. I'd like to ask him some general questions—that is, unless he's not authorized to answer those either. Look, Mr. Graves, Tommy Billings indicated to me you folks would be cooperative with me, but I'm not yet getting the impression you are." I had not, in fact, talked with Regional Forester Thomas P. Billings and only knew his name by asking it of a telephone operator. But the ploy worked, and I got an appointment with the investigator.

About a week later I showed up in the headquarters of the Tahoe National Forest in Nevada City, California. Here, Special Agent Anselmo A. Adams had office space to do his paperwork and take his phone calls. A matronly receptionist with bulging varicose veins in her calves hobbled down a corridor ahead of me and gestured me into an unimposing office toward the rear of the building.

"Please sit down, Officer Murphy," she said. "Mr. Adams will be with you in a moment."

When I began looking at the clutter in this room, the word

chaos came to mind. How could anyone possibly find any specific item among the random stacks of papers and folders on the desk, the table, and all those shelves? What Martian organizational scheme governed the placement of books, magazines, and papers protruding at odd angles from the bookcase? And why did this man keep on display all of those jagged chunks of metal, pieces of exhaust pipes, broken hand tools, framed pencil notes, and a dozen or more items I couldn't even identify?

Eight or ten crumpled pieces of paper, having missed their mark, lay near a wastebasket. A broken crutch leaned against an empty dynamite box in a corner. And all by itself on a high shelf stood an unopened bottle of Jim Beam whiskey, curiously out of place in a government office. A handwritten sign taped to the front of the desk advised JANITOR, PLEASE DO NOT MOVE THINGS AROUND. I began having misgivings about the awesome investigative might of the federal government.

A man of about sixty to sixty-five entered with a slight limp. "Officer Murphy? Adams. 'Selmo Adams." He had a friendly smile.

I got to my feet. At six foot two, I towered over the balding man. "It's Gene Murphy, sir. I didn't come here on behalf of the city of Los Angeles."

He looked me up and down from behind rimless glasses. "All this way to see me? You took a chance. I'm usually not here."

"I called your office in San Francisco. Your boss said you'd be expecting me."

"Oh shit—Murphy! Of course. About the Pegleg fire. Sit down. Coffee?"

I waved it off.

"Your brother, wasn't it? That's a rough one, no saying it any other way. How're the folks taking it?"

"Better than I am, I think."

Adams nodded. "That's what I figured when Graves called me. He said he had a hard time getting you off his hands."

"I asked to read the investigation report, but he indicated that would be impossible. He said something about the investigation being compromised."

"That's bullshit. What they're really worried about is lawsuits.

8

For example, if you found out we were negligent fighting the fire, well, you know the routine from there."

"You think that's why I came?"

Adams withdrew a knife from his pants pocket and began carving out the inside of a pipe he took from his coat pocket, carefully pouring the scrapings into a brass ashtray. "I doubt it. More likely, you'd like to know what we're doing about finding the guy who started the fire."

"Mr. Graves told me the field investigation was over."

"He pulled me off the case when I was unable to report progress. It made sense. We found no evidence. Sometimes it takes a while for somebody to come forward. Case stays open, far as I'm concerned."

"You really think there's a chance after all this time?"

"In an arson case, definitely."

"How do you know it was arson? You said you found no evidence."

"That's why. We'd have found something otherwise."

"What about lightning?"

"Lookouts reported no recent strikes within five miles. Anyway, there'd have been a scar on a tree, or some other marks."

"Spontaneous combustion?"

"No such thing, at least not without man's intervention, and then again, we'd have found something."

"How were you able to locate the exact place where the fire started?"

Adams began filling his pipe from a paper pouch of Sir Walter Raleigh tobacco. "That part is easy. Wind spreads the fire, and we look at the char patterns. For example, a tree will show char higher on the leeward side than the windward side, because the flame was leaning downwind. That gives us an arrow pointing back toward the point of origin. It's a bit more complicated than that, but that's the general idea."

"Did this fire start near a road?"

"No. Along a road or a railroad, we'd have looked for large carbon particles from an engine or brake shoe. But this place was out in the boonies. No reason for anyone to be there, not loggers, hunters, fishermen, or even the Forest Service guys."

"You checked out the rangers?"

Adams chuckled. He fired up his pipe with a three-inch flame from a butane lighter. "First ones we look at. I guess your outfit doesn't have any problems like that, right?"

It made me laugh, and I began to like the man. "Where did you take it from there?"

"Fire records." The old man reached into the center of a pile of folders almost without looking and as if by magic pulled one out, which he handed me. "You can see my summary there in front. Can't prove it, but I think a lot of those were set by the same guy."

I looked at the data, not getting much out of them. "Mr. Adams, these fires are all labeled *incendiary* fires."

"It's our term for arson fires."

"Well, do these notes identify the reason for the arson in each case?"

He smiled. "Wish to hell they did. Problem here is that unless we find the guy responsible, there's no way to know for sure. Could be pyromania, nothing to gain but self-gratification. These are the jokers we find jacking off behind trees while they watch the fire. Or could be a grudge fire, or to get a job fighting the fire, or maybe to force a salvage sale of timber, improve hunting conditions, whatever."

"You check out the rangers. What might be their motivation?"

"To become an instant hero. You light the fire, then discover it, report it, fight it."

"Makes sense. Cedar Valley's not a big town. Is there any such thing as a profile of an arsonist that might help?"

"Not that I know of. The sociologists have spent a bundle on that question—taxpayer money, of course—and haven't come up with shit."

"You said *guy* a moment ago."

"Not a woman's thing, we know that much."

"Anybody around the town with a motive?"

"Probably dozens. The cattlemen are unhappy about their permits being cut back. Loggers want more trees marked for cutting, or maybe they got cited for contract violations. Somebody got fired from the Forest Service and wants to get even.

10

Could be a personal beef with a ranger over a woman. That sort of thing goes on all the time in those towns."

"Have there been some arson fires in town as well?"

"Needs looking into. I couldn't get much out of the local volunteer fire chief, and they don't keep fire records."

"What else is there left to do?" I asked.

"The ranger district guys are keeping their eyes open. If they run onto anything interesting, I'll hear about it. Until then, I've got about eighteen other cases to work on. I wish I could tell you something better than that."

"I appreciate your being candid, Mr. Adams. Can I ask you one more question?"

He leaned back in his chair. "Please."

"If your total priority were to get to the bottom of this case, how would you go about it?"

"Fair question. You see, we have a small town here, one where everybody knows everybody else's business, public and private. Most of the people who live there are smart. Not educated, mind you, but country smart. They watch and listen and calculate and guess and gossip. There's not a whole helluva lot that escapes their notice. What I'm saying is that in a town like Cedar Valley, there's *somebody* who either knows who it is or who has a strong suspicion about it."

"The problem being to find out what they know or suspect."

"That's right. They might even discuss it among themselves, but there's not much chance they'd cough it up to some fire investigator, or to any other outsider, for that matter."

"What about the local Forest Service guys?"

"They might as well be from the moon."

"So you'd have to get on the inside?"

He pointed at me with the stem of his pipe. "It wouldn't be as easy as you think, young man. Those folks don't take readily to strangers. Matter of fact, some of them are downright nasty."

He'd already figured me out. "How nasty can they be?" I asked.

"One of them took a shot at me one night." He puffed on his pipe, studying my reaction.

"Warning shot?"

"Harassment, I'd say. Missed me by five or six feet. Nobody around there could miss that bad with a two-seventy."

"You got the slug, then."

"Dug it out of a telephone pole the next morning."

"Did you report it?"

Adams chuckled, shaking his head. "No, I'd already had a slight run-in with the local sheriff's deputy, fella named Dhrymes. He wasn't at all happy to have some fed nosing around his bailiwick, and he let me know about it. Anyway, I'd rather keep it between myself and the shooter."

I didn't have to ask why, and stored the bit away. "What would it take to get you to go back there? More fires of the same apparent origin?"

"A pattern isn't enough; we've already got that. I'd need some solid evidence, or a witness, or maybe some unusual circumstances." He set his pipe down and folded his gnarled hands in his lap.

I couldn't think of any other questions. "I'm glad I came here, Mr. Adams. You know, my brother and I were very close. Every time I read that autopsy report, I feel the heat of those flames on my own body. Then I die a little more myself." I felt myself beginning to choke up. "It's just not right that some son of a bitch . . ." My throat knotted up and I could feel tears coming.

Adams rose and stuck out his hand, and we shook. Then as I turned away he said, "Murphy . . . good luck."

It wasn't much of a send-off, but at least the old man didn't tell me to forget about it. I decided to give the Forest Service some more time to do their job.

I shut off the alarm clock and just lay in the dark for several minutes, trying to figure out whether it was Wednesday or Thursday. But what difference did it make? The shift would go on at eight, and there would come another day of writing up traffic accidents, responding to burglary complaints, breaking up domestic squabbles, hauling in drunks, and finally taking a ration from the sergeant over one thing or another.

I'd drunk too much again, stayed up too late again, and couldn't even remember if I'd skipped supper. I'd ignored two phone calls, probably from Belinda wondering with whom I was sleeping.

I rolled out of bed and sort of rocked my way to the sink. My body looked muscular, but suddenly slimmer. The scale told me my weight had plummeted to one seventy, a twenty-pound loss in five months. But the face in the mirror had gained about ten years in the same time. I quit thinking about it and went through the motions of washing and shaving, not caring if I missed a few spots or nicked a few others.

Then I dug around in the closet, searching for my clean uniform, finally realizing I'd failed to pick it up from the cleaners. Now it would take me a half hour to do something about the one I'd tossed in a heap the night before. And then the phone rang.

"Gene, where were you last night? I called and called."

"I was here, Belinda. Didn't feel like talking. Look, I'm—"

"Are you all right? I'm worried about you . . . about us."

"Yeah, well, I'm down right now . . . need to work things out. I need to do it alone. You understand?"

"I'm not sure I do. You've been acting like this for a long time. I could understand it at first, but it shouldn't be going on like this. Don't you think—"

"I'm late, Belinda. I've got to get going."

"Can we talk tonight, like over dinner somewhere? We really need to talk, darling."

"Uh, I don't know. I really need—"

The phoned clicked, then went to dial tone. I'd pissed her off again. Why did she keep coming at me? Why didn't I just get it over with, tell her to go plow a field or something? That idea made me smile, even through my hangover. The mental image was one of a carefully coiffured and cosmeticized Belinda sinking into the mud up to her asshole as she struggled to control a team of giant draft horses farting steam at her through the cold morning air.

Ron Burford worried about me too. Patrol partners for the last year and a half, we knew each other pretty well. We knew how to cope when one of us got down. I admired Ron's perfectionism: everything by the book, everything up front, no hanky-panky on the job. When I found him sullen or morose, the explanation would lie in his dissatisfaction with his own performance. But he would accept my occasional inadequacies, kidding me about them, always in a constructive way.

Ron laid off me for the first month after Heath's death. He took the tough jobs and was careful not to let me feel guilty about it. But since then there had seemed to be a growing uneasiness on his part about my emotional condition. He made me talk about Heath, what my brother had meant to me, and asked me endless questions about our experiences together. He wasn't that interested, it was just that he wanted his partner back—full time.

Another month went by, and my sergeant called me in. We talked about my "situation," eventually getting around to the departmental offer of free psychological counseling. There was no refusing the invitation, it was a take-it-or-good-luck-on-your-next-job sort of thing.

Apparently Ron had reported to the sergeant that I seemed to be taking unnecessary risks during pursuits, almost to the point of seeming to have a death wish, and that I used excessive force during confrontations, because those were the first things the "designated psychologist" got into. I thought the reason for my behavior was obvious, and that I soon would be able to bring it under control. But the shrink seemed uninterested in Heath's hideous death, dwelling incessantly on my early relationship with my mother and all that other Freudian bullshit. The guy even asked me if, in my infancy, I'd finger-painted on the floor with my own feces. I asked him if he'd like to see a demonstration of it right there on his Persian carpet. We didn't get along at all well, and his report strongly suggested I be assigned to "nonstressful" duties, pending further evaluation.

I fought off the reassignment, arguing that the psychological counseling had been immensely helpful to me in coming to understand the source of my problems, and that my whole outlook toward life and my job had been transformed. That was a pile of crap, of course, and within about a week, Ron told me things weren't getting any better, and he was asking to be assigned a new partner.

"What's the problem?" I asked. "Anything the matter with my driving, with the way I'm handling suspects, or what?"

He didn't say anything for a while as he headed the squad car down Figueroa. Pretty soon he pulled into a spot by a fireplug and looked at me.

"Can you tell me one item on today's hot sheet?"

I glanced down at the clipboard between us, but he was covering it with his hand. I drew a blank.

"When was the last time you saw Henry Tafoya?"

"When we picked him up and booked him a couple of weeks ago on grand theft auto."

Ron snorted. "We just passed him two blocks back, standing on the corner—on your side."

"But—"

"Got out on bail the next day. You didn't know that?"

I was silent. He wasn't through with me yet. "What was the address on that last burglary-in-progress call?"

"It got by me."

"Do you even recall what fucking town it was in?"

"I'm making progress. Just give me a little time."

"A little time? Jesus Christ, Gene, it's been over five months! I'm riding around with a goddamn zombie, and we're not getting our job done because you're in a perpetual fucking trance. Know what? I want to be a detective. Want it in the worst way. I came in second on test results. But with the record of arrests we've piled up lately, which is microscopic at best, I'll be on the lower half of the list. Know why? Because I'm baby-sitting a chronic crybaby, one who finds himself unable to pick up the fucking pieces of something that sooner or later happens to most all of us, and we're able to get over it. But are you able to get over it? No. You'd rather live in a quagmire of self-pity and grief. When the hell are you going to get a grip on yourself?"

"Is it that bad, Ron?"

"You need help, Gene. You need it bad."

A week or so later I was the new man on the evidence custody detail at our precinct house. It was a slot for losers, for officers considered unreliable for duty possibly involving life-threatening situations, or who might make an unfavorable impression in public, such as at schools or at meetings. The slow pace of the job gave me even more time to dwell on my problems, to count the hours until I could get smashed into oblivion again.

At times like these, you can really sort out your friends—or I should say, acquaintances, because I found out the difference. One group keeps trying to help, the other figures you've got leprosy or something.

Dad and Mom were concerned, because they couldn't understand my grief. It was they, the parents, who were solely entitled. As merely a brother, I had no vested interest, no right to share in the loss. They made me feel like a foreign invader of their private terrain, someone who was stealing something that belonged only to them. As for Belinda, she felt cheated by my brother's death. The deterioration of our relationship was Heath's fault, and she began to hate his memory. When she began to vocalize that feeling, it made it easy for me to recommend the farm work.

About the only thing that really made me feel better was learning to hate the arsonist. Everything that had gone sour in my life came back to the arsonist and what he had done to Heath. So what if Heath's death was an accident, something that happened while he was doing his job? Like his older brother, Heath had selected a hazardous job and wanted to do it to the utmost. He had accepted full responsibility for his men and had proved it by giving up his own life when it came down to a choice.

But why did he have to die, when this scumbag arsonist was still walking the streets, getting his kicks?

At least a dozen well-meaning friends told me that hatred was eating me alive, that it would destroy me, that I had to get it out of my system. God, I got sick of hearing that line. Yes, hatred was eating me alive, yes, it might destroy me, yes, I had to get it of my system. I knew all that. But nobody told me *how* to get it out of my system. What does one do, begin reading the Bible? Go to confession? Do the finger paintings?

The only consistent advice I received was to forgive the arsonist. "Forgiveness: the sweetest revenge," said Isaac Friedman. "The fragrance the violet sheds on the heel that has crushed it," wrote Mark Twain. "God's command," said Martin Luther. Who was I to question such wisdom? And yet . . .

Christmas came and went with no more meaning for me than if it were Groundhog Day. Over the winter months I learned to mask my feelings, to concentrate on my job, to make a good impression again. I quit getting sloshed, started taking better care of myself, and even worked my way back out onto the streets of L.A., this time with a rookie partner who thought I was God. His youthful idolatry did more for my self-esteem than the combined efforts of the LAPD, their house shrink, and all my friends and relatives.

But life was still hollow, still incomplete. It took a little nudging, but Belinda finally got off my case. I think she really became disenchanted when I began farting audibly in her presence. Funny how the little things seem to count the most.

Mom and Dad became more and more reclusive, and I began to realize that Heath's death was going to hurt them more than I had imagined. It shouldn't have surprised me, for I'd long recognized he was their special star from the day of his birth. The last few times I visited them, I was made to feel almost as if they resented my survival.

The estrangement from Belinda, from Mom and Dad now, and from most of my acquaintances somehow gave me a strange sense of power over my own destiny. Whereas I used to draw strength from family and friends, now I was drawing strength from my solitude. I kept asking myself where I should go from here, knowing the answer, refusing to say it to myself. Each time I would bring my true need to the surface, a voice would tell me it was wrong. Or I would hear Mark Twain reminding me about the violet. It went on like that for most of the spring.

At the end of May, I applied for and was granted an indefinite leave of absence from the department. I stated the reason simply: ". . . to regain control of my life following the death of my younger brother."

But that wasn't all I had in mind.

Chapter 2

E ver try to get a night's sleep on the front seat of a '51 Ford, your head wedged up against one door, feet pushing on the other? It should have been easy after the tiring two-day drive from Los Angeles, but it didn't exactly work out.

My evening had begun pleasantly enough, rolled up in a blanket beneath a big pine tree, but a cold rain had driven me into the shelter of the car, where I listened to the rat-a-tat-tat of hailstones on the roof and hood. Soon a gusty wind began lashing the trees along the creek, and violent downdrafts of frigid air started rocking the Ford.

Then came the lightning, dazzling displays—frighteningly close—punctuated by thunderous explosions. It reminded me of Korea, of being crouched in a bunker taking the concussion of a battery of 155-mm howitzers firing over my head. I marveled at the brilliance of the lightning as it continued its dance across the sky, and counted the seconds between flashes and the booming ripostes from the thunderclouds. If I could have spoken to my brother during those moments, I would have told him the celestial fireworks were in his honor. The storm moved slowly away, and sleep finally came.

★　★　★

A slow drip on my cheek awakened me, rainwater having pooled up on the fabric portion of the car top, finally working its way through the beading. I got uncoiled from my cramped position and climbed out to find it almost full daylight already, even though the sun had not yet appeared from behind a ridge to the east. I'd come up this road from the highway in the dark and now discovered myself surrounded by tall pines, firs, and cedars. The trees and shrubs still dripped from the rain, and the reddish dirt road had a cap of mud an inch thick. A cold breeze carried the deliciously clean smells of the mixed conifer forest, something new and pleasant to me.

A creek ran parallel to the road, and I clambered down the bank and washed my face and hands in shockingly icy water. I probably could have used a full bath, but this definitely wasn't the time, and I settled for a quick shave using my Norelco battery-powered shaver.

Somehow my old Ford slithered its way through the mud to the blacktop, and I headed back to the little town I had passed through the night before, my destination for months. I wondered how long I would be there, how long it would take to get my job done.

I slowed to read the sign at the edge of town:

CEDAR VALLEY

Elevation 4142

Population 502

Several bullet holes decorated the face of the metal sign, each one surrounded by a circular brown area where rust had eaten away the enamel from below. The road swung southward, where a sawmill dominated the whole north end of the town, its pungent-smelling pond of barely floating logs bordering the highway for an eighth of a mile.

Then the road turned eastward, becoming the main street

through town. I drove slowly, inventorying the place. I saw two gas stations, two grocery stores, a post office, a bar, and a cafe, all on the main street. On the left loomed the community church, probably the one where they'd held Heath's memorial service. On a side street I spotted a fire station and a sheriff's substation. Then I came to a repair shop, some houses, the ranger station, more houses, then at the south end of town, the Starlight Motel. A sign in the office window said CLOSED FOR REPAIRS. I'd seen that in dismay the night before.

I made a U-turn and started back. Lombardy poplars lined the street on both sides, mitigating the harshness of the drab structures, crisscrossing electrical wires, and the absence of other landscaping. Nobody was in sight along the road, but cars and pickup trucks parked helter-skelter kept the place from looking like a ghost town. The pickups all had gun racks in their back windows, and all the vehicles appeared uniformly mud-spattered and weather-beaten. Two mammoth logging trucks, a Peterbilt and a Kenworth, their dollies piggybacked, waited outside The Cedars Cafe while their drivers sipped coffee inside.

I'd last had a bite in Redding, some sixteen hours earlier, and felt ravenous. I parked and went inside. A cowbell attached to the inside of the door announced my entry, and the eight or nine patrons inside the place all twisted their necks to give me about a four-second size-up.

I glanced at the empty booths along the wall, then picked out a stool at the counter between two beefy men dressed in rugged wool shirts, Frisco jeans, and high-topped boots. Loggers, probably. The waitress, a blondish woman of about forty, wearing a pin saying "Lucille," set her cigarette down on the edge of the counter, grabbed the coffee pot, socked a china mug down in front of me, and poured it full all in one quick, splashing stroke. Most of the coffee went into the cup. Her long dangling rainbow-trout earrings oscillated wildly.

"Breakfast, or have you been here before?" she asked, keeping a straight face.

"I'll take a chance. How are the hotcakes?"

"Stack!" she screeched without even turning her head toward the kitchen. "Eggs with that, honey, or just the neoprene?"

"Whatever you've got."

Lucille glanced at me sidewise. "Think you could handle it?"

I was saved having to answer that one by the guffaws from the guys sitting next to me. I just hoped Lucille didn't see me blushing.

"Where you headin'?" asked the guy on my right, his ruddy face the texture of an old baseball mitt, three days' growth of whiskers poking out from his chin.

"Not sure yet. I'm looking for work."

He glanced down at my street shoes, then at my hands. He took a swallow from his coffee mug. "Where you from, L.A.?"

The question jabbed me. L.A. was over six hundred miles from there. "I didn't think it showed."

He laughed good-naturedly. "Just lucky that time. What kind of work you do?"

"I'm not particular. Anything that would keep me out of the city."

He lit a cigarette. "Jobs are hard to come by. That is, anything steady and that pays good. Around here, there's the mill, the woods, the forestry, an' that's about all. Anything else you almost got to be kin." He gestured with a thumb at one of the logging trucks parked outside. "Had that rig for a year now. If I miss two payments on it, it's gone." He laughed. "Then I'd be in the same fix you're in. Course, then I could go to loggin' . . . riggin' or skinnin' cat like I was before. You probably never worked in the woods, though."

"Not yet, anyway."

"Why you lookin' here? There's a lot more work in the valley."

"I like the looks of the country around here. I've always liked small towns."

"Well, good luck to you. Say your name?" He stuck out his hand.

"Sandow. Harper Sandow." It felt strange pronouncing aloud my new name for the first time. After he told me his name, Bill Epson laid a dime on the counter and walked out, the cowbell clanging behind him.

The hotcakes were doughy, the syrup cold, and the eggs runny, but my hunger and Lucille's wry humor got me through it with only minor indigestion. She'd overheard my conversation with Epson, obviously, because she suggested I ask at the post office about jobs.

"Her name is Vivian Crump," Lucille said of the postmistress. "She can tell you anything you ever wanted to know. If Vivian don't know about it, it hasn't happened yet."

I paid my tab of a dollar twenty, left fifteen cents for Lucille, then headed for the post office. Not that I thought I needed Vivian's help in finding a job, but I did want her help in letting everyone in this town know why I was here. Anybody that knew as much as she reportedly did was bound to do a lot of talking herself. But I didn't yet know how communicative she really was.

The Cedar Valley post office stood by itself between the bar and one of the grocery stores. Its dull-textured gray-concrete-building-block construction gave it a somewhat governmental look, even without the American flag that flew overhead. The main room inside accommodated a large glass-topped table, a bulletin board, five or six rows of post office boxes, a couple of stamp vending machines, and a service window. Behind the window waited Vivian Crump.

"Good morning, Mr. Sandow." Her greeting rattled me. At least she didn't say Murphy.

"But . . ."

"Good news travels fast." She had a pretty smile and sparkling eyes.

"You're very good," I said, trying to figure out whether it was the trucker or the waitress who had passed the word so quickly.

"We do try. You're looking for work, I understand."

I nodded.

"What can you do?"

"I'm willing to try anything, and I learn fast."

"What did you work at in Los Angeles?" Her eyes twinkled as she asked it.

I felt like I was in a job interview already, but what the hell, I had prepared myself for the question. "Manufacturing. Boring stuff. I want to work outdoors if possible."

"They're looking for a swing shift setter at the mill, but if

23

you've never done that before they wouldn't even talk to you. Then, one of the graders quit the other day, but you'd have to pull green chain for at least a year before you're even eligible for training."

I didn't even know what she was talking about. "What about jobs that don't require experience?"

"New guys usually start out on the pond."

I vividly recalled the stench of the pond when I'd driven by it that morning. "What about the forestry?"

"Well, they hire quite a few seasonals for the fire crews at this time of year, but most of them are forestry students from around the country. You could give that a try, though, because they don't all show up."

"Uh, while I'm looking around, where is there to stay?"

"Starlight should be opening today. They've got the fire damage repaired now. You can get a room there for four fifty, or twenty-five per week. If you need something for longer than that, there's several rental rooms available."

I thanked Vivian Crump, making a mental note not to tell anyone in Cedar Valley anything I didn't want generally known throughout the western world.

The sign in front of the sawmill office said BOARDMAN LUMBER COMPANY. I went inside, and a middle-aged man in a white shirt, open at the neck, and red suspenders got up from his desk and came to the counter.

"Can I help you, sir?"

"I'm looking for work." The four people in the office hunched over desks all glanced up at me. That seemed normal, of course, but one of the women, a very attractive brunette, tensed up in her chair. She seemed startled to see me. Could she have detected a likeness between me and my brother? I never thought we looked much alike, but others said so. Or could it have been my voice? Friends had sometimes confused us on the phone. Had Heath known this young woman? He'd never mentioned it to me, or to our folks, as far as I knew.

"You have any experience in mill work?"

"No, sir, I don't. But—"

houses, a pump house, a paint house, a hose-drying rack, and a materials storage area. On the north side of the road was a barracks building, three more employee houses, and a weather station enclosed within a chain link fence. I pulled into the visitor parking area in front of the office, got out, and looked around. A freshly painted white picket fence enclosed this part of the compound, and a new lawn and young shrubs accomplished the landscaping. On the front porch lay a large black dog with tan muzzle and legs, long drooping ears, and long tail. He didn't look at all menacing.

An eerie feeling crept over me as I approached the front door. It had been the better part of a year since Heath had worked here, but I could somehow sense his presence. Heath's enthusiastic and lengthy letters about his experiences here had created visual images that were already beginning to prove amazingly accurate. For a fleeting moment I wondered if he were watching me, wondering how I would carry out my plan. I shook off the illusion and stepped inside the office.

"Good morning," said a smiling, rust-haired young woman.

I explained my need for a job, any job, and she said there was nobody there now for me to talk to but offered to have me fill out an application. She introduced herself as Lois Hart and said she was the district clerk.

I stood there at the counter and filled out a Standard Form 57, Application for Federal Employment. It didn't bother me at all to enter my faked-up job history, but when it came to signing my name below the ominously worded warning concerning giving false information, I did hesitate. My "references" down south would corroborate what I put down on the form, I knew, but the phony social security number could cause problems. If anything came up, I decided, I'd have to claim error on the number or work some other stall.

While I filled out the four-page form, Lois Hart stayed busy issuing campfire permits to visitors, answering telephone and radio calls, and retrieving papers from the files for some of the rangers working in the office. I was worried she might have guessed I was Heath's brother, but if she had, there was no indication.

"Do you think there's any chance I may get a job here?" I asked when she had a free moment.

She shrugged and smiled. "Gosh, I have no idea. Felton Shackle, he's the DFCO, he does all the hiring for crews. Sometimes somebody quits unexpectedly, or fails to show up, and there's an opening. After he reads your application you could come in and talk to him about it."

"I'll probably do that. Would tomorrow or the next day be too soon?"

"Tomorrow should be fine. And your name is . . . ?"

I almost said Murphy. "Sandow," I got out. "Harper Sandow. Have you been here long?" I wanted to know if she'd known my brother.

"This is my first year in the office; that is, full time. I did two summers on a lookout first. Frankly, I liked the lookout work better, but my husband got a job with a logger here, so it works out better for the two of us. He was crawling the walls in the lookout, especially while he was trying to quit smoking."

She hadn't really answered my question yet. "I haven't had any experience fighting fires. Is it a very dangerous job?" She blinked several times, almost a flutter, then looked away. She started to speak, then stopped herself.

"Felton can tell you about that," she said finally.

I didn't press her; my guess was that she must have known Heath.

My next stop was at Booth's Repairs, a small shop only a block from the ranger station. Outside of one rototiller and a lawn mower, the front part of the place was filled with chain saws either awaiting repair or ready to be reclaimed. In a minute or so a good-looking, square-faced man of about thirty-five came out of the back of the shop to wait on me. The sleeves of his khaki shirt were rolled above the elbows to reveal strong forearms.

"I'm looking for work. You know anybody that might be hiring?"

"No, not offhand," he said, running a grease-stained hand over his straight dark hair. "You checked with Donovan? He might be looking for a swamper."

"No, I don't know anybody here. This is my first day in town."

"Donovan's a gyppo. Does salvage sales and hauls it to Boardman's. You'd have to catch him at his place tonight, most likely. He lives on Dogwood, a brown place about the middle of the block."

"What about the forestry? I heard they might have some openings on their fire crews."

"I wouldn't know. Why don't you go ask them?"

He didn't elaborate, but I noticed a trace of bitterness in his voice and made a mental note of it. I introduced myself and found out his name: Ned Booth. I thanked him and left.

I decided to spend the night at the Starlight, the only motel for the forty-mile stretch of state highway between Purple Pond and Powder Cache. That wasn't a difficult choice for someone whose back was still in a knot from sleeping in his car the night before. Anyway, one more day without a shower wouldn't do much for my job prospects.

"You're the first since the fire," was my greeting from the middle-aged woman behind the office counter. "I hope the smell of the new paint won't bother you. We had to repaint everything, even in the units that weren't smoke-damaged. It just smelled so bad, you know." She placed a registration card and pen in front of me.

"What happened?"

"Oh, Clyde thinks it was the electric heater, bad wiring or something. But I don't know. That unit was so badly burned I don't see how you could tell."

"Clyde is the owner?"

"No, I own the place. Clyde is Clyde Krafft. He's the fire chief here in town. Trouble is, it was of a Saturday night, and they were all at the dance at the ladies club hall. I think it was about fifteen minutes before they got the truck here, and by that time it was really going good."

"Nobody hurt, I hope."

"No, thank God for that. We got everybody out, not that there were that many. How long you be staying?"

"I don't know yet. Depends on whether I get a job here."

"Well, I'll put you in number four, Mr. Sandow. You can pay now if you like, then let me know by noon tomorrow if you're staying over. Who are you thinking about going to work for?"

"Probably either at the mill or the forestry. There doesn't seem to be much else around here."

"You might check back with Vivian again next day or two. She's already told folks you're looking."

I gulped some air. "You mean the postmistress, I guess."

She laughed. "Yes. She takes care of unemployment, social security, the census, legal problems, advice to the lovelorn. Whatever you might want. And you might check with her husband, Chubby, who owns the gas station next door to the post office. He may know of something."

"Well, she sure was helpful to me today, just like most of the people I've met here. But that deputy sheriff didn't seem to take kindly to me at all. Is he that way to all strangers?"

"Oh, don't pay too much attention. He thinks that's his job. Wyatt Earp or somebody. But he's really good-hearted when you get to know him. Thing is, nobody's ever got to know him."

I expected her to laugh, but she didn't. I think it was her way of giving him the benefit of the doubt. She led me to number four, opened the door, and handed me the key.

"It's plain," she said, "but at least it's clean. Let me know if you need anything."

I brought a suitcase from the car and set it on the bed. She was right about the room on both counts. There was no carpet, no draperies, no radio, no desk, no closet, no ice bucket, not even a Gideon Bible. But it was clean, and would do nicely for what I had in mind. I pulled down the shades, poured about four ounces of Jack Daniel's whiskey into a glass, added some water from the tap, kicked off my shoes, then sat down at the little table in the corner to make some notes. Inasmuch as I came here to solve a most difficult puzzle, I wanted no information to get lost, insignificant as it might seem at the time.

With that little chore behind me, I stretched out on the bed, looking forward to a long night's sleep. But that was not to be. At about nine, the late trade began arriving. First nights in a strange place had always been a problem for me, and in this case, with the slamming doors, muted laughter, headboards banging against the walls, beer cans hitting the floor, then more slamming doors and car engines revving, it was a long night.

Somewhere between two and three, things died down and I finally got to sleep. It was at four thirty, I believe, when the first logging truck roared by the motel, rattling the windows and shaking the earth beneath me. Trucks apparently were dispatched from the mill every fifteen minutes, and I counted ten trucks. It was then almost seven, and only a matter of minutes, I calculated, until the first diesel-powered behemoth returned from the woods with its giant cargo of pine and fir logs destined for Boardman's pond. It turned out to be only seconds, however, and the vibrations almost jolted me out of the bed. It was obviously time to get up.

I stepped into the shower to get the next little surprise: no hot water. Well, she said it was plain, and as I mentioned, the price was right. It didn't take long to get the job done.

While getting dressed I thought over my two job prospects. I figured I'd be able to get on either at the mill or the Forest Service. Working at the mill would provide the advantage of my not being associated with the feds, and thus it might be easier to get acquainted with people around town. Also, I'd be under less suspicion from my quarry. On the other hand, a forestry job would put me more in contact with the fire situation and the people involved. I reasoned that by participating in whatever community affairs might be going on, I could make friends with almost anybody and might be able to gain their confidence. I decided to try for a job with the Forest Service.

I had breakfast with Lucille again, just coffee and toast this time, then headed back to the ranger station. Lois Hart was there, and she led me to one of the rear offices and introduced me to Felton Shackle, the DFCO, as she called him: the district fire control officer.

He shook my hand, pointed at a chair in front of his desk, then sat down himself. "Sandow, is it?" he asked, shuffling through the papers on his desk for my application form. The rugged-looking young man in boots, jeans, and a ranger shirt looked curiously out of place behind a desk.

"Harper Sandow."

"Yeah, here it is. I read through it last night when I came in. You're from L.A.? What brings you clear up to a place like this?"

I was ready for the question. "My brother got killed in a motorcycle accident there. I can't drive down Wilshire Boulevard anymore. I can't go to any of the places we went together. It was tearing me up. I thought the best thing would be to get completely away from it, go to some different kind of place, do some different kind of work." I went on and on, really getting into it, making the artificial account of my brother's real death convincing enough that I almost choked up telling this young man about it. Ordinarily it would make me feel awful to lie like that, but I had it rationalized to the point where I felt morally justified.

Shackle nodded sympathetically. "Well, this place is different, all right. You realize, I suppose, we don't pay the kind of wages here you were getting down there. In fact, starting jobs here would only pay about half of that."

"I wasn't even going to ask. It's not important to me."

"Ever had any outdoor jobs, worked with long-handled tools?"

"I worked summers on a ranch. I think that's on the application. Then I guess you could call Korea outdoors."

"Any health problems?"

"None."

"Married?"

"No."

"You're about ten years older than most of our applicants. A lot of them are college students. They don't mind living out in tents, batching and all that."

"I've done that before. I know what it's like."

"You're probably interested in a yearlong job, rather than just for the summer."

"Sure. But I'd accept anything to get started. I learn fast and do good work. I figure when you get to know me you'll want me full time."

32

That remark seemed to impress him, but he wasn't sold yet. "We check up on the employment history you put down on the application, and also with the police departments where you've lived. If there's any problem about that, you'd best tell me about it now."

I'd done a lot of homework before leaving L.A. One of my best friends in the department was a homicide detective, and he pulled some strings and got me a pair of unlisted license plates, corresponding vehicle registration certificate, and a fake operator's license. That was strictly illegal, but he was confident I'd never admit he was involved. Through my father I'd arranged for corroboration as to my previous (phony) employment. I doubted whether I'd get tripped up on a routine check. "You're welcome to check. There's no problem."

He spent some time looking through some sheets of paper and mumbling to himself. Then he pushed the papers aside. "I'd like to hire you, but the only opening I have at the moment is on the Buzzard Lake crew. It's about thirty-five miles from here, and they're camped out by a lake whose main product is heavy-lift mosquitos. I usually save those jobs for forestry students so they can find out if they really want to do this kind of thing for a living. But I don't really recommend it for regular human beings."

I held my tongue. His description of it wasn't all that inviting, and it didn't sound like I could really accomplish what I came there for if I went to Buzzard Lake.

"And the foreman's just a twenty-year-old kid," he went on. "I don't think that would be the right place to put you. There is one other possibility. We have a student leaving the Cedar Valley crew in a week. If you'd be interested in waiting that long, I'll put you in his slot."

I felt truly elated. "That's sounds great."

"Okay, tell you what. Get a form from Lois for a physical, and take it to Dr. Brainyard in Winchester. He's the designated physician. When you get back, I'll turn you over to Punky Swiftbird, your foreman, and he'll put you up in the barracks across the street. Your room and board will be deducted from your first check, but that'll be about a month from now. Does that sound all right?"

33

"Better than all right. You won't be sorry."

"And while you're in Winchester, you'll need to pick up some decent work boots. Get high top lace-ups with lug soles, similar to these. And pick up a couple of khaki shirts, long-sleeved ones, and some blue jeans. You'll also need a warm jacket and some work gloves. Have enough money for all that stuff?"

"No problem, and thanks again."

Punky Swiftbird's head came up to about the middle of my chest, so I figured he was about five feet even or a fraction under. His skin was of a walnut hue, unwrinkled except at the corners of his large brown eyes, and he displayed the most dazzling white teeth I had ever seen. He carried himself erect as a tower, and while he had the aura of somebody of authority, there was no cockiness or arrogance about him. His complexion was so smooth and his doleful expression so youthful it seemed impossible to judge his age, but I decided it must be early forties. He walked me across the road and up the path toward the barracks.

"You been here long?" I asked.

"Came here in 'fifty-one from Oklahoma looking to get rich," he said with a chuckle, "but ever since then I could never get enough money together to even leave this place."

"So you're Cherokee?"

"Choctaw. Shoot, *you* could be a Cherokee. They're not real Indians, they're too watered-down." He gave me a flashing smile. "This is the barracks," he said as we entered what I took to be the living room. "It's not fancy, but we try to keep it clean."

I glanced around at what passed for the furnishings: a faded, threadbare green sofa and matching easy chair, a heavy oak table and several chairs in need of refinishing, torn window blinds of the pull-down variety, and an oil-burning space heater. A framed document with the legend FIRE PLAN served as the sole wall decoration, and a stack of outdated magazines lay on the table. The air carried a strong scent of mustiness combined with an assortment of animal smells and cooking odors. The linoleum floor looked clean and damp, as if it had just been mopped.

"We redid the kitchen in stainless steel," Swiftbird said as we moved into an adjoining room. "There is a cook, but everybody who stays here has to do the cleanup."

We walked down a hallway past a half dozen closed doors.

"Two men per room except for me. I share my room with Donald." He gestured at the black and tan coonhound I'd seen on the porch the day before. "He showed up here one day and just sort of adopted me. Now he's even got me buying food for him." He laughed and patted the dog on the head.

"This'll be your room here," he said, opening one of the doors.

It looked like a large closet, but I wasn't about to make the remark. An iron cot with a thin mattress stood against each longer wall, with a large chest of drawers between. A small table and chair seemed to be tightly wedged between the foot of one bed and the wall next to the door. The room stank of stale perspiration, and the bed with bedding on it was unmade, the sheets badly soiled and well-wrinkled.

"Who's my roommate?"

Swiftbird shook his head and smiled, seemingly at a loss for words.

"That bad, huh?"

He laughed softly. "Well, let's just say he's a little different than most guys. But you might like him."

"What's wrong with him?"

"See that footlocker?" He pointed beneath the bed. "Know what's inside?"

I shrugged.

"Manuscripts, he calls them. I understand one of them is on the subject of political assassins. The other one has to do with the great diseases that wiped out populations at different times during history."

"Wow. Sounds like he's had a lot of education somewhere."

"Yeah, Orange, or Brown, or someplace like that. He told the ranger he had an advanced pedigree in politics or something."

"What's he doing here?"

"Beats me. One day the ranger found him along the highway like he was lost or something. Brought him and his footlocker here and gave him a job."

"How does he get along with the other guys here?"

"They give him a hard time. You'll see. Anyway, make your-self at home. Supper will be at six."

I dropped by the post office to rent a box, and Vivian Crump had already filled out the application card with my name and fake social security number. She obviously maintained close contact with the ranger station. My box number was ninety-one. I de-cided to be extremely careful whom I'd let write to me here, and how the mail would be addressed. The last thing I could risk would be letting this woman figure out exactly what I was doing in Cedar Valley. On the other hand, I wasn't precisely sure of it myself, at least, not yet.

Chapter 3

I made a quick trip to Winchester for my exam, and while there, I bought the clothes and boots Shackle had recommended. Then I returned to Cedar Valley, where I attacked my new living quarters.

After locating the broom and mop, it took about two hours to clean the tiny room and get it aired out. That was really not completely possible, given my roommate's smelly clothing hanging from hooks on the inside of the door, but at least I made the effort. His things occupied the top two dresser drawers, and I glanced into them: some personal belongings, but mostly books, borrowed, I presumed, from some library. A biography of someone I'd never heard of lay on top of dirty underwear and socks.

Late that afternoon some vehicles pulled up outside, and soon there came the tromping of booted feet through the building. Our door swung open and my roommate came in. I greeted him, sticking out my hand.

"Hello. Punky assigned me to this room. Harper Sandow."

"Oh, hello. I'm Albert Carlisle. Do you smoke?"

I shook my head.

"That's good. It's full of smoke around here. These kids are going to die of black lung. I've never smoked. I don't believe in it. I left home because my mother smoked."

Already I wondered why his mother hadn't left first. As he spoke, he took off his khaki shirt and shook it, allowing a shower of sawdust and pine needles to rain down on my formerly clean floor. From his emaciated neck down across his sunken chest, his skin was the color of milk, providing a marked contrast with his battleship gray underwear.

"What happened to your eye?" I couldn't decide which was the one that didn't track.

"You're the first one here to ask me that." He put the shirt back on. "It happened during puberty. My parents never let me associate with girls or even be exposed to anything with sexual connotations. They checked on me constantly to make sure I wasn't masturbating. The pressure from all this gradually caused a loss of muscular control."

By this time he had his boots off and began emptying them onto the floor. "I just cleaned the floor," I said. "Thought you'd appreciate it."

"My parents thought the eye would correct itself if I adopted more Christian thoughts and clean living," he went on, ignoring my comment.

"That didn't help?"

"I don't know. I never tried it."

"Which do you mean?"

"I'm an atheist, and nobody has ever clearly defined clean living."

"What about surgery?"

"I've learned to live with it." He stretched his lanky body out on the bed, his sweaty socks almost beneath my nose. "The kids here think it's pretty funny, but it doesn't bother me. All they're really interested in is sex, drinking, eating. . . ."

"You mean . . . there's something else?" I asked, trying to get him to lighten up a bit. He didn't even smile, seeming more intent on scratching his scalp through the close-cropped hair that stood out from his head like unevenly mowed grass on a hilly lawn.

Pretty soon somebody rang a bell, one of those large iron triangles that hang from a rope, and I again heard the sounds of tromping feet. I washed up and entered the dining room, where nine or ten other men had already gathered to sit down at the long table. I introduced myself to them, missing most of their names. Punky Swiftbird stood by me, telling me which ones belonged on the fire crew and which on what he called the TSI crew. I found out later TSI stood for timber stand improvement.

I noticed one guy, somewhat older than I, who made no move toward me, so I went to him and offered my hand. "Harper Sandow," I said, beginning to get used to the sound of it already.

"Stan Turpin."

No smile. But Turpin looked me over from head to toe. One glance at his shoulders, arms, and waist told me: all muscle and bone. I'd also got the impression he'd tried to break my hand when we shook.

"Haven't I seen you around somewhere?"

"No, I'm new here."

He turned away and headed for his place at the table. Then I got my first look at the cook as she carried serving dishes of food in. Sophie, they were calling her. Sophie had eaten too much of her own cooking during the past thirty years or so; when she stood in the doorway to the kitchen it was almost like a watertight seal across the opening. She served the food family style, and the men began hungrily scraping the chunks of meat and the mashed potatoes and carrots onto their plates, washing it all down with gallons of whole milk.

"TSI does dishes tonight," one man said gleefully. His name was Jurgenson, I recalled. He was obviously on the fire crew. "That includes you, doesn't it, Albert, or are you off for another walk down the highway?"

Carlisle glowered at the younger man. "I do my share."

"Yeah," another guy chimed in, glancing around to make sure Sophie was in the kitchen. "I bet you do your share of cockwalloping, too." Everybody laughed.

"You know, what you really need is a good piece of ass, Albert," one of them said. "We'll even chip in and buy it for you."

"Shit," said another, "he couldn't make out in a whorehouse with a twenty-dollar bill taped to his forehead. I think he's still a virgin. How old are you, Albert, thirty-five? Forty?"

"I'm thirty-three," Carlisle said, trying to stay cool.

"Thirty-three and never yet dipped his wick," said Jurgenson. "Must be some kind of a record. Are you going to write yourself up in that book you're working on? Hey, that's good. I can see it now: Obscure Writer Dies of Perpetual Hard-on While Crouched in Footlocker."

The image was pretty compelling, all right, and I had to struggle not to laugh along with the others. Then Jurgenson turned his attention to me.

"Say, Harper, what do you think of a guy like this, never had a piece of ass in his whole life?"

All the young studs looked my way, eager for this first shot at taking my measure. Except for Swiftbird and Turpin, they were all kids, untested in life, looking for thrills, ready to attack, wanting come across as one of the strong ones, unmerciful in the business of detecting weakness and pouncing on it. I didn't want any of it, and least of all now.

"I admire his patience and understanding," I said loud enough for everyone to hear. "I think if any of you talked like that to me, we'd come to an understanding real soon." I said it calmly, and in the most professional police voice I could muster, glancing around to make eye contact with each man. Nobody smirked or had anything to say. That pleased me, because the last thing I wanted was to get into a fight with one of these kids, especially on my first day there. The topic of conversation switched abruptly, and the meal ended without turmoil. But it stuck in my mind that each time I glanced toward Stan Turpin, I caught him studying me, still trying to figure out, I supposed, where he might have seen me before. But it was the trace of hostility in his expression that was most vivid to me.

Later in the evening, Swiftbird invited me to go to Kelley's, the bar for a beer and some conversation with the locals, and I quickly accepted. We got into his prewar Packard sedan and started down the gravel drive. An earthy smell in the car caused me to glance into the back seat. It was Donald, a contented expression gracing his jowls.

"This guy Turpin," I said. "What's his job here?"

"Stan is the improvement foreman. He takes care of the buildings, telephone lines, generators, fences and all that. He doesn't stay in the barracks, just eats supper there."

"He seemed hostile. Is he usually that unfriendly?"

"No, he just likes to act that way sometimes. And I guess he's a little moody. You know, mad at the outfit."

"He thinks he should have a better position?"

"Well, when the fire prevention officer job last came open, he wanted it real bad and he was probably as qualified as anybody. But they gave it to another guy named Bill Marklee. Stan's been kind of sore about it ever since."

"When was that?"

"About five years ago."

"Long time to stay mad about something like that."

"Well, a girl he was going with dropped him for a new guy who worked here. That didn't help either. And to make it worse, the guy was a forester—you know, college educated—while Stan was just a technician."

"Are they still going together, the forester and the girl?"

Swiftbird shook his head slowly. "He was killed last summer in a fire near here. You probably haven't heard about that yet. Anyway, after that she stayed cool towards Turpin, so he's a little touchy about it."

My head began spinning. Heath had had an affair here? I kept my emotions under control. "Who was the girl?"

"I never did know her name, but she was married before to a guy who got killed in the mill, and then they gave her a job there in the office. A real good-looking woman."

That had to be the young woman I'd noticed in the sawmill office. So now I understood her reaction to me and wondered if she'd figured it out yet. Meantime, we'd arrived at Kelley's, and Swiftbird parked right in front between two pickup trucks. I mentally catalogued them, not knowing whether by habit from police work or because of what was going on in the back of my mind. Heath's remarks about hostilities between the Forest Service people and the locals came back to me, and I'd now get a chance to sample that.

We went in. Booze smells. A ground fog of tobacco smoke.

Red, blue, green neon signs advertising brands of beer. Silhouettes of men sitting at the bar. A melange of male voices. Animal heads mounted on the wall: two mule deer and a pronghorn antelope. A clock with all fives on the dial. A dish of hard-boiled eggs and a jar of Polish sausages on the bar, along with a rack of beer nuts and beef jerky.

"Hey, Punky, how ya doin'?" called a voice from the dimness. Beckoning arms gestured us to seats at a table near the back of the room, and without asking, one of the men brought bottles of beer to set in front of us. Swiftbird introduced me to Clyde Krafft and Bill Donovan, names I'd already written down in my notebook, and to Ned Booth, the guy I'd met in his repair shop the day before. Krafft, the volunteer fire department chief, had an open bottle of bourbon in front of him, and he poured some into a tumbler, straight. Donovan was the logger; he looked big and strong enough to pick up a whole tree by himself. Booth was drinking a beer.

"You must have found yourself a job," Booth said. "I told Bill here there was a guy lookin'. But I thought you were too smart to go with the feds."

"Well, I heard so many bad things about them, I thought I'd see if it was all true," I said.

"It's all true," Swiftbird said, "but he failed to ask me."

"You'd better be careful, Punky," said Donovan. "Maybe he's one of these undercover guys checking up on you."

"I hope so," the Indian said. "Then maybe I'll find out what's wrong with me for working for the outfit this long."

"Shit, nothin' wrong with you a trip down to the Green House won't cure," said Krafft.

Swiftbird laughed and shook his head. "No, I've given that up for Lent."

"Lent," said Donovan. "Hell's fire, that was two months ago."

"Yeah, that's why I picked it," Swiftbird said.

The banter went on and on, and I looked at the backs of the men sitting at the bar, recognizing a familiar shape, that of Deputy J. P. Dhrymes. He sipped Coke from a bottle and turned now and then to listen in on our conversation. I caught his eye once and winked at him. I think it really rattled him.

42

"Where you from?" Krafft asked me from behind thick glasses. Grease stains outlined the nails on his square fingertips.

"L.A.," I said, barely loud enough to be heard across the table, expecting some derisive remarks.

"You going to be working in town?"

"Watch out," said Donovan. "He's trying to get you on his fire department already."

"Well, shit, he looks big and strong enough. Maybe he's had some experience."

They all looked at me. "Sorry, never been in a fire department. But I wouldn't mind learning."

"Okay. Come on over to the fire hall some Sunday morning about eight. We get together to have some drills, and we can talk about it."

Then Donovan and Booth started talking about chain saws, and Krafft went over to the bar to talk to somebody. Swiftbird gestured toward the door as if we should leave, so I finished my beer and we walked out.

"I didn't mean to rush you, Harper," Swiftbird said. "That cowboy in there at the end of the bar, name is Steve Christian. He's okay when he's not drinking, but right now, he's drinking."

"What happens?"

"He gets nasty, and is quick to pick a fight. When it's with anybody from our outfit, he lands on us about putting out fires."

"What's his beef with that?"

"Beef is a good word for it. He and most of the other cowboys around here believe the range needs to be burned off every once in a while to clear out the brush and make the grass grow better. It's a real sore point with some of them."

"This guy Christian, he owns a ranch around here?"

"No, just hires on. He plays a guitar and sings in one place or another. Always had a problem with drinking, I guess. When he's working he's working, and when he's drinking he's fighting."

"Thanks for telling me."

"Come on," he said, gesturing at the Packard. "I'll give you a mini-tour."

We drove around the area in the fading light, and the foreman pointed out places of interest and told me some things about the history of the town. "About four years ago a guy got slicked right over there in that quarry."

"Slicked?"

"Yeah, a guy from Powder Cache. He was long-cocking a guy named Talbot who works at the mill here. Talbot laid for him and spotted his wife coming out of the motel with the guy. He forced them off the road in this quarry, jerked the guy out of his car and cold-cocked him, then sliced off his privates with a jackknife."

"God damn," I said, shuddering.

"Talbot's wife got the guy to the hospital, and then she went back to look for his pecker but couldn't find it. Magpies probably got it. When he got better, he got a lawyer and got Talbot charged with mayhem. Talbot's wife testified against her husband. It was a jury trial."

"Did they convict him, Talbot?"

"He walked free. People started calling him the Cedar Valley Barber after that."

"They're still married? I don't suppose there's too many guys fooling with his wife anymore."

"Yeah. And the guy that got slicked isn't fooling around much anymore either."

I told Swiftbird I wanted to go to work, even though my job on the crew wouldn't begin until next week. He told me Stan Turpin needed help the next day on a phone line problem and said he'd arrange it. I thought it an excellent opportunity to find out more about my brother's former adversary.

Turpin looked at me skeptically through his wide-set gray eyes, quickly appraising the new outdoor clothing and boots I'd bought the day before in Winchester. I thought it looked like pretty authentic stuff, but his withering gaze was the kind I'd get if I showed symptoms of some communicable disease. He wore a plaid wool shirt, blue jeans, and engineer's field boots. "Let's go," he said simply, gesturing at the dark green pickup truck. His movements were strong and purposeful, his attitude all business.

"This is a metallic circuit." He pointed at the overhead wires as we drove along on a road out of town. "When we get to the Scarface cutoff, it'll be ground line all the way to Coyote Peak."

"Ground line?"

He glanced at me with what I took to be a look of mild contempt, as if I should have already known all about fucking ground lines. "Ground return circuit. One wire. Tree line," he instructed.

I still didn't know what he was talking about, but wasn't about to ask. We rode along in silence for a while, Turpin busy craning his neck out the pickup window, looking upward at the telephone line.

He glanced at me again. "You sure I don't know you from somewhere?"

"Don't think so. Maybe I just remind you of somebody."

"Maybe. I'll figure it out sooner or later."

The tone of each thing this man said radiated a touch of animosity. I could readily imagine him hating my brother, but the image of his stealthily igniting a forest fire was hard to conjure up. He seemed more the type to slug you in the face.

Soon the road began zigzagging its way up the side of a mountain, only occasionally passing beneath the telephone line, which followed a straight course to the summit. At the summit stood a lookout tower, and a woman standing at the rail gave us a wave.

"We'll start here and work down. You walk the line and I'll tie in with you everywhere it crosses the road."

"What am I looking for?"

"There shouldn't be anything touching the wire except insulators." What more could I possibly have needed to know?

While walking the third segment I found the problem, a tree down across the line. Turpin was waiting for me where the line crossed the road, and I told him what I'd found and where it was.

"Get in. Be closer to where the line crossed above, and no sense carrying the gear uphill."

We drove back up and then he parked, climbed into the back and opened the jockey box, behind the cab, pulling out a knapsack labeled TELEPHONE GEAR. He handed it down to me as if it were light, but when I took it in hand the weight nearly jerked me off my feet, and that got an unsmiling chuckle from Stan.

"What've you got in this thing, barbells?"

He snorted. "Everything I might need, no more, no less."

I slung the sack over my shoulders and we headed down the hill to the downed tree, where Turpin grabbed the sack away from me and began pulling out the equipment. He quickly severed the line where it lay pinned to the ground, then, using a sleeve and a crimping device, spliced it above the tree, meanwhile holding the loose ends with come-alongs.

"Pulled that insulator out," he said, pointing to a nearby tree. "You want to make the climb?"

I told him no thanks. He strapped on a set of long-bladed climbing spurs—he called them "tree hooks"—and put on a lineman's belt, then attached to it a twenty-four-foot climbing rope, one with a steel core in it. He handed me the free end of the rope and I passed it around the trunk of the big pine tree and gave it back to him. In less than a minute, he was twenty-five feet up the tree, reattaching the insulator. Then he told me to send up the field telephone on a grunt line, and as soon as I figured out how to do that, no help from the strong silent one, he checked the line and found it working.

"I'm impressed," I told him. "You operate like a real pro up there. How did you learn all that?"

"Ned Booth. Best damned telephone man on the forest. Nobody ever had to troubleshoot his work."

"He's the one who has the repair shop in town, isn't he?"

"He's also a locksmith, gunsmith, and general handyman. He can fix anything, and do it right."

"So he used to work for the Forest Service?"

"Until about six years ago."

Turpin got a smirk on his face, as if the recollection of whatever happened then was amusing to him. He didn't seem ready to elaborate, and I wanted to know more.

"He figured there was more money in working for himself?"

Turpin thought about it a few moments before answering. "Well, let's just say he and the organization had a falling-out. Matter of fact, he had a falling-out with his wife about then also, and he left town. They got divorced. Worked for about a year in Winchester. That's where he learned about all there is to know about chain-saw repair."

"Did she stay in town?"

His face darkened perceptibly, or maybe it was just my imagination. "Yeah. She got married to a guy who worked in the mill. But a while later he got killed. He was trying to dislodge a chunk of wood from a jammed conveyor belt with a pike pole. The top of the pole came into contact with a twenty-thousand-volt feed line overhead, and it blew the bottoms of his feet right off." Turpin chuckled.

"And that killed him?"

"Not that instant. But none of the dumb shits there knew how to get him breathing again, and he died on the way to the hospital."

"I heard somebody saying something about that. They gave his wife a job in the mill office, right?"

"Yeah."

I waited for more about this, recalling Swiftbird's comments about the woman's snubbing Turpin in favor of Heath, but he seemed done with it for now.

On the way back down the mountain, I asked him how long he'd been the improvements foreman.

"I took over from Booth when he left. That was in '53. I wanted to get back into fire, but nothing was open. When the district fire prevention job came open, they gave it to that numbnut Marklee. He'd been working telephone lines and didn't know fire prevention from sour owl shit at that time, and still doesn't. Politics—that's the polite term for brownnosing. I came close to telling them to shove it."

"You're still interested in that job, though?"

"It'd be a good stepping-stone toward district fire control officer, which was always a goal of mine since I first worked on a fire crew. But shit, after all this time on this job, maybe my best route would be C and M foreman at the forest level. Between the army and this outfit I've got about eighteen years in, so I guess I'll stick it out."

Turpin had loosened up a little, so I decided to take a bit of a chance, touch a tender nerve. "Would it be possible for you to work up to a district ranger job?" I already suspected the answer but wanted to hear his version of it.

"It would have been, some years ago. But now they have this

policy from Washington that you've got to be a college graduate, as if that had any fucking bearing on anything." His voice began to get louder as he got into the subject. "While I'm off defending the country when I could have been going to college, they figure out that some young punk from a forestry school back east is better qualified than me to be a ranger. You wouldn't believe the incompetent idiots they give me to teach how to wipe their asses, and then before you know it, I'm taking orders from them."

He carried on with this theme for several minutes, and it's the same one you can hear in almost any line of work: an embittered person laying the blame in the wrong place. So I told him, "I know a lot of guys who came out of the service and went to college on the GI Bill. You could have done that. You still could if you wanted to."

He must have known I was right but couldn't seem to come up with a suitable defense.

"You have all the answers, don't you?" he finally said. "You must be a college boy yourself. It must be terrific to be so smart. How come you're only making a dollar sixty-five an hour, then?"

He was really beginning to piss me off, so I decided to give him some business. "No, I didn't go to college, for whatever that's worth. But if I do, I think I'll study psychology. You ever heard that word before?"

"Yeah, I heard it. You think I'm an idiot or what?"

"That's why I'd study it. Then I'd be able to figure out what makes guys like you idiots."

Turpin slammed on the brakes, and the pickup rattled to a halt, enveloping us in a cloud of brown dust. "You want to settle this right now?"

"Settle what? Whether you're an idiot or not? You're already proving it."

Turpin's eyes were like fireballs, and his strong hands looked as if they were about to rip the steering wheel off the column. For a moment I thought he would explode, but then he seemed to control it.

"You talk like that, you better be able to back it up."

"Back what up? You took a shot at me, I took one at you. You'll find out that's what I'm like."

"Some people would call you yellow."

"And some people would call you an asshole."

He sat there smoldering for several seconds, then put the pickup in gear and drove on toward town. Not another word was spoken nor a glance exchanged the rest of the way back.

It was still early, so I walked down to Mona's Groceries and General Merchandise to pick up some personal items. A giant, gravel-voiced female, perhaps in her late fifties, with a cigarette hanging out of the corner of her mouth tended the cash register. That had to be Mona, I decided. She immediately noticed me and gave me the smile probably used on newcomers and invited me to look around.

I noticed a young woman, back turned to me, putting tomatoes into a bag. She upset the stack and the tomatoes began rolling off the shelf. I swooped in to try to catch them, and we bumped together awkwardly. She started to laugh, but when she turned her face toward me she went white—it was the dark-haired young woman from the sawmill office. She looked on the point of fainting, and I grabbed her arm to steady her, but she quickly regained her composure and pulled her arm free.

"I'm sorry, miss. That's twice I've managed to startle you. Do you know me from somewhere?"

She stared straight at me, her brown eyes wide and her mouth slightly open, revealing a line of beautifully white teeth. "No. . . . No, I don't think so. It's just that . . . for a moment you reminded me of someone else, someone who—died several years ago, in Korea." She blinked rapidly, not carrying it off at all well.

"It's really strange," I said. "I get mistaken for somebody else quite often."

"You mean here in town?"

I laughed. "No, you're my first victim in Cedar Valley. My name is Harper Sandow." I offered her my hand, watching her reactions closely. Her face revealed nothing.

"I'm Nora Jeffers. You're new here, aren't you?"

I nodded.

"And you came here from?"

I immediately understood Heath's attraction to her; why he fell

49

for her despite being engaged to Alice. Nora was devastatingly alluring. She had the kind of rustic good looks that can't much be improved upon with makeup and an elegant hairdo. Her plain blue jeans, denim jacket, flannel shirt, and western boots looked like they were designed especially for her. She wore no rings.

"You found a job, then?"

She obviously hadn't been to the post office in the last two days. "I'm going to be working on the fire crew here with the Forest Service."

She stood there studying me for long moments, and I knew she held back some questions she wanted to ask. "Well, welcome to Cedar Valley, then. I'll try not to fall apart next time I see you." She gave me a reserved yet enticing smile.

"I'll be disappointed if you don't." I kept her in sight until she'd finished shopping and paid her bill. Then she went out and got into a red Jeep with a canvas top and drove away. I had two exceptionally strong feelings at that moment: Nora Jeffers had information that would prove highly valuable to me, and I was pretty sure I had just fallen in love.

Chapter 4

The day after I met Nora Jeffers, Punky Swiftbird told me I'd start on the payroll the next day, a Sunday, the beginning of a new pay period. Seven of us comprised the fire crew, and we worked staggered tours of duty, with at least four of us on duty every day of the week and six on Saturdays and Sundays, the days of greatest fire occurrence. I would have Thursdays and Fridays off except during fires and extreme fire danger.

During the next three days I got a lot better acquainted with the rest of the crew and had a lot of training pumped into me concerning use of the different fire-fighting tools and how to operate the portable and truck-mounted water pumps and other equipment.

The other crewmen seemed bored with the training; they'd had most of it already and itched for a real fire call. Fred Sweeney, the tank truck operator, had worked on the crew the summer before, as had Tim Jurgenson. Myself, Vaughan Day, Larry Banks, and Ardis Corbin made up the rest of the crew. Day and Corbin, eastern forestry students, spent their summers working for the Forest Service, but this was their first one on a fire crew. Banks, the son of a local rancher, said he was in it for the money.

Swiftbird, Sweeney, and Jurgenson, I found out, had all been on the Pegleg fire the year before. Heath Murphy's death on that fire hadn't yet come up in conversation, but each time somebody mentioned the fire, I could sense an aura of awareness concerning what happened.

On Wednesday a thunderstorm moved into the area, and we could see lightning dancing between dark clouds and the mountains around Cedar Valley. Swiftbird decided against leaving for his days off, telling us all to expect a lot of work before the day ended, and that nobody had permission to leave the station. He'd earlier told us that in the event of a big fire or a lightning bust that all other district work would be suspended and that all the men, including maintenance workers, the TSI crew, and the ranger's staff would be expected to be available for fire duties. While at work in the warehouse-garage building at the rear of the compound, we listened to the truck's VHF radio receiver and could hear the four lookouts on the district reporting strikes throughout the northern and eastern portions of the area. Several of the outlying fire crews were already on the way to fires, and we all wondered when our turn would come.

It didn't take long. Felton Shackle came out the back door of the dispatcher's office and into the warehouse and told us to gather around. He held a clipboard in his hand.

"So far, we've had twenty-eight smokes reported out of this storm, and I'm sure there'll be a lot more before sundown. We've declared a lightning plan, which means we're breaking the crews into small units in order to man all the fires while they're still small. For everybody here at this station, that means two-man crews. The new men here will go out with district staff as follows:

"Vaughan, you'll go with Stan Turpin. Larry Banks, I'm sending you out with Bill Marklee, and Sandow, you go with Ray Owens. He'll come and get you. You'll all head out in pickup trucks with hand tools. The rest of you will man the tanker and move up immediately to the Cedar Creek junction and stand by there."

I hadn't yet met Ray Owens, but Shackle had no more than left when a burly and severe-looking man of about forty-five came up and introduced himself to me. He gave me a list of things to put into two knapsacks, then headed back toward the dispatcher's office. In a few minutes a pickup pulled up outside the ware-house, and he leaned out the driver's-side window and beckoned for me to get in. When I tossed the knapsacks in the back I noticed an assortment of fire-fighting tools there.

We'd got less than a half mile down the road when Owens pulled over to the side and said, "You drive. I want to look at the map."

"I don't have a government license yet, Mr. Owens."

He came around the front of the pickup, swung open the right door, and almost sat in my lap, forcing me to scoot over. "Call me Ray, and start driving." He didn't need to ask a second time. As we drove along he studied the map, pointing out the turns as we came to them. He kind of reminded me of a bear, sort of barrel-shaped, with hairy arms, and hair showing at the open neck of his shirt, his speech more like growls than human sounds. His hands looked like industrial tools, and I doubted he would often have need for a wrench or pliers.

"Where we heading?"

"Manzanita Creek. You the guy from L.A.?"

"Yeah, sorry. How many fires did they give us?"

"Just one, but it's a long way from the nearest road."

"I don't mind hiking."

"Why did you come here?"

"Thought I'd like it. What's your job on the district?"

"Cows and sheep, mainly. You married?"

"Haven't got around to it."

"Just as well. Cedar Valley's not what most wives have in mind for a place to live and raise kids."

"Your wife doesn't like it here?"

"Better than where we were, on a ranch in Idaho, where I grew up. Wilma's from L.A. Couldn't tolerate the routine. You know, like the barn burns down, there's no doctor around, kids ride the bus an hour to get to school, winter's too long, all that stuff."

"But there's no high school here either, is there?"

"It's a mistake to try to figure women out. I guess it's okay for the kids to ride forty-five miles from one town to another, but evidently not from a ranch to a town. Anyway, I think she

53

basically wanted to move to a more civilized place where she could fart against silk and look wise. Turn left here."

We drove up an unsurfaced road lined with shrubs he told me were sagebrush and rabbitbrush, and this vegetation soon gave way to sparse stands of ponderosa pine, incense cedar, and white fir. He called out the species for me, understanding that I had no idea what they were. It began raining, which made the road slick and hard to negotiate.

"Has this country burned off before?"

"Sure, like everywhere else. But not much since we started putting out all the fires. The cattlemen don't like it. They'd rather see it burn off every three or four years."

"Better for grazing?"

"Burning brings in better grass, and it kills off the older shrubs. Then when they sprout back they're more tender and nutritious."

"Then you agree with the ranchers?"

"To a point. Like everything else, you can overdo it. This used to be good bunchgrass country. But it was overgrazed and burned too often, and now all you can see are the undesirable species. On the other hand, the Forest Service doesn't permit any controlled burning, except under conditions so restrictive as to be ridiculous."

"Would the ranchers prefer to see fires just burn out of control once in a while?"

He smiled. "Sure, depending on which way the wind is blowing. They don't want their fences and barns burned down in the process."

"You think they ever kind of take matters into their own hands?"

"If they did, you'd never catch them at it." His face didn't reveal anything further.

"Is the restriction on burning a problem for sheepmen as well as for cattle ranchers?"

"To some extent, but they keep sheep on the move, so that you'd have to burn the whole damn countryside to benefit them for long. Why so interested?"

"Just curious. It's all new to me. You must work closely with the ranchers in your job. Are they pretty much down on the Forest Service?"

"We try to get along. They have permits to graze their stock on the national forest part of the time and depend on it to help support their herds. Our job is to see that the land doesn't get abused in the process, and that's the source of a lot of our conflicts."

"They want to run more cattle than the range can support?"

"No, not really. But traditionally, they've figured the land is theirs, and I think they just naturally resent our being around to quibble about the way they use it. Besides that, they don't think we know much about it."

"But you grew up on a ranch."

"I had a lot of fun when I first got here. Those guys were expecting another schoolbook-range-management type who didn't know a salt log from a dugout canoe. It took me a while working with them, gathering stock, helping on the branding, castrating and all that, meantime pretty much keeping my mouth shut. When they began to see I knew the cattle business, they started asking me what I thought about this and that. Over the course of a couple of years I proved to them how they could spend less money and put more weight on their stock, and pretty soon they quit talking about what a bunch of assholes we were. We still are a bunch of assholes, of course, but at least they stopped talking about it."

"You ever think about getting back into ranching again?"

"About every day. That is, if the right opportunity ever came along."

"But what about Wilma?"

"Wilma who?"

He said it without laughing, and I wondered if he half meant it. I also wondered just how sympathetic with the ranchers' desires to see the range burned off he might be.

"You know this fellow Steve Christian?" I asked.

"Christian? Sure. Where'd you meet him?"

"Punky Swiftbird pointed him out to me in Kelley's. Said he works on a ranch out here somewhere."

"Yeah, the Circle R. Decent fellow when he's not drinking.

55

Fact, he plays in my band sometimes. Hard guy to figure. Good-looking, good musician, has this sexy-looking girlfriend. Then just when everybody figures they're about to get married, he gets drunk and kicks the shit outta her."

"And she puts up with it, I suppose."

"Yeah, one of those women who seem to thrive on it. Wish my old lady was like that, 'cause God knows, she could sure use a good kick in the ass now and then."

At about dark we stopped on a ridge. The rain had stopped, but the trees still dripped rain and a fog had settled in. Owens carried a portable radio up the ridge to a higher point nearby and checked in with the fire dispatcher and one of the lookouts. He came back in a few minutes and told me we would stay put until things cleared up enough to get a compass shot on Manzanita lookout, so we could determine our location with respect to the reported smoke.

The fog made us chilly, so we built a small fire and sat down on rocks to eat some rations and enjoy the warmth. I decided to find out what I could about the circumstances of the Pegleg fire, specifically things that weren't included in the official report.

"Did you know the firefighter that was killed last summer?"

"Heath Murphy," he said. "Yeah, I knew him. I had him out several times to help on readiness checks, utilization checks, fence surveys. Nice kid. Good sense of humor, and very bright. He seemed to have a natural knack for getting along well with people, even belligerent ones. I think he would have gone a long way in this outfit."

"How did the fire start?"

"Incendiary, just like some others we've had in the past several years. Except this time, somebody got killed. Manslaughter, pure and simple." He poked at the fire with the toe of his boot, fishing in his shirt pocket for a cigarette. "They investigated it, of course, but couldn't turn up anything, not even one piece of evidence."

"And nobody around town had any idea who might have done it?"

"That part fascinated me," he said, lighting a Camel. "Normally, the town folks would just snicker about somebody setting a fire and getting away with it. But Heath's death got their attention. People around town don't have much use for Forest Service guys, especially junior foresters like this kid. But they liked Heath a lot, and what happened shocked them. It was like they felt partly responsible or something. They suddenly seemed ashamed that something like that could happen here."

"Because he tried to save the life of a non–Forest Service employee?"

"Maybe partly. But I think the basic unfairness, the absence of a good reason for it better explains their feelings. They saw that a petty crime, for whatever reason, led to the death of an innocent person. It all came out at the memorial service they held in town. I've never witnessed anything quite so moving. At least a dozen people from the town got up and said how much their association with Heath had meant to them in all kinds of ways. They carried on so, when it finally came time for the district ranger to speak, there remained nothing for him to say."

The darkness kept Owens from seeing my tears. When I found my voice, I asked, "And after all that, nobody came to the Forest Service with any rumors or ideas about who might have done it?"

"No, and around town nobody even talked about intentional sets for weeks later."

"You think that might have put an end to the arson, then?"

Owens puffed on his cigarette for a few moments. "I doubt it. See, the guy probably has a sick streak. He rationalized it. Figured the kid fucked up, so tough shit. I'd bet a paycheck the son of a bitch will surface sooner or later, because whatever problem led to this hasn't gone away."

"I don't know anything about fires, but it seems to me that a good investigator might establish a pattern that would help get to the bottom of it."

"You'd sure think so, but as far as I know, no evidence has ever been found for any of the sets, and that's highly unusual."

"Yeah. Sick but plenty smart."

He pointed. "There. You can see it now, that light across the canyon."

"That's Manzanita lookout?"

"Yeah. Let's take a look," he said, aiming his compass at the light. "Hit it almost on the money. If we move down the ridge about a quarter of a mile, we can head directly back along his line of sight and intercept the fire. At least that's the general idea."

We drove back along the ridge and parked. Owens made another compass sighting on the light in the tower and seemed satisfied. We then slung our knapsacks over our shoulders and grabbed tools. He carried a shovel and the portable radio, and I carried a Pulaski, half axe and half grubbing tool, and a six-foot falling saw. Owens started down the hill first, stopping now and then to take compass readings on the silhouettes of trees, and I followed along behind, stumbling over rocks and beating my way through the dense underbrush. After about an hour we were only about a mile and a half down the hill and soaked to the skin from the sopping foliage.

"Let's take a break," Owens finally said, and we both sort of collapsed onto the trunk of a fallen tree. We ate some more of the dry rations, surplus stuff left over from World War II.

"This stuff is terrible, Ray. This outfit lives in the dark ages."

"It's not so bad, Harper. Beats Wilma's cooking. Anyway, if we eat enough of it then it'll be all gone and we can start in on the Korean War surplus rations. I figure that'll be in about four or five years." He lit a Camel and asked me how I liked the Forest Service so far.

"I think I'm going to like it a lot. But I hear guys like Ned Booth kind of bad-mouthing the outfit. It seems strange to me because Stan Turpin said he thinks very highly of Booth, that he does real good work."

"Booth? Yeah, he does good work all right, but I'd just as soon not have to listen to his steady stream of bullshit. According to him, nobody else in the whole outfit ever did any work worth a shit except himself."

"Why did he quit?"

"Quit? Turpin said that?"

"I guess he said Booth and the Forest Service had a parting of the ways."

Owens laughed heartily. "They had a parting of the ways, all right. Ned got caught screwing the former district ranger's wife, and the old man offered him the opportunity to resign."

"In exchange for?"

"Something they never talked about, but which both obviously understood."

"Was Booth married at the time?" I felt deceitful asking for information I'd already obtained, but needed the verification, along with whatever other tidbits he might throw in.

"Yeah, and that kind of ended it right there. Since then he hasn't had a single decent word for the outfit."

"Understandable. But you don't think he'd go out and start fires to get back at the Forest Service, do you?"

"Naw, not Ned. He just likes to build himself up by picking away at us. You keep coming back to that fire, Harper. Know something? You come on like an investigator. You working on something?"

He said it with a grin, but watched my reaction. "Me? I wouldn't know where to begin. But it does intrigue me. I sure hope they catch the guy."

"Well, I'll tell you what. If that happened to somebody in my family, sooner or later I'd find out who did it, and nobody except me and him would ever know about it."

It startled me for a moment when he made the remark about family. Had he figured me out already? Then I thought not; he was just reflecting on the situation. I sat there in the dark measuring his words. What he had suggested revealed acceptance of criminal means to right a wrong. That was contrary to what I'd been taught, what I'd been trained to practice as a lawman. And yet, how would *I* see things when the time came?

By about midnight we'd reached the canyon bottom and took off our packs. By walking a short distance up Manzanita Creek we could see the light of the gasoline lantern in the lookout. Owens radioed the lookout, a relief man, and had him sight on Owens's flashlight.

"That's it, right there," said the lookout. "That's exactly where I saw the smoke."

Owens got a skeptical expression on his face. "Okay. If it's here, we'll find it. We won't need you till morning."

We spent about an hour searching for some sight or smell of a smoke, or at least evidence of a recent lightning strike, but there was none.

"Nuts," Owens said. "I'd bet my dog against a sack of fresh cat shit that kid was looking at a fog pocket last night. You game to hike up to the lookout so we can take a look for ourselves at first light?"

We picked up the pack and tools, then fought our way uphill through the wet brush for three hours before reaching the road that led to the lookout. There was a small campground along the way, and we stopped there to build a fire, dry out, eat some more of the insipid rations, and get an hour's sleep. Uncomfortable as I was, I kept my mouth shut, as I had learned to do in the marines, and kept my eye on Owens. He was taking it all in stride, but I judged from his comments that when we arrived at the lookout, we'd better be able to see a smoke.

At dawn we put out our little campfire and pushed on up the road to the base of the lookout tower, where we were surprised to find two cars parked at the bottom. We shed our packs and tools and stared up at the cab of the lookout, but could see nobody out on the catwalk. Owens put his ear up against one of the steel legs of the tower, and a wry smile came over his weather-beaten face.

"You know, Harper, I think Horace has company."

He gave me a beckoning motion, then began clomping up the first of the eight flights of meshed steel stairs. When we got to the catwalk, Owens flung open the steel trap door with a clang, and, peering through the glass, we found ourselves looking at a skinny young girl, her long hair flying in huge arcs, bouncing up and down astride a supine and equally naked young man whose eyes were rolling white like a wild stallion's. On a card table nearby were dirty dishes, cups, glasses, and an unfinished half gallon bottle of cheap red wine.

"Jesus, ain't youth great?" asked Owens, banging his big fist against the glass door.

Two unbelieving faces turned toward us in a moment of stunned silence as the oscillations abruptly ceased. Then panic set in, and there was a flurry of nakedness flailing wildly about in search of something to hide behind, under, or inside of.

"Oh shit! Oh shit!" was all Horace Broadwink could think to say, while the young lady, whose name we never inquired about, came up with something like, "Damn you, Horace, I *told* you this was going to happen."

Owens didn't give them any breathing room. He gestured with his gnarled thumb at the Osborne firefinder, an aiming device mounted on a high table in the center of the lookout cab and said, "All right, Horace, show us exactly where you saw that smoke last night."

Broadwink jumped into position behind the device, his blanket slipping off his shoulders to the floor, and he stood there, one hand over his privates, the other on the firefinder. "Right there," he gasped, still out of breath. "Right there in the bottom of the canyon. See! Right now! There's a puff of smoke!"

Meantime the girl was off in a corner struggling with a pair of panties, the main problem being she had managed to get both legs into the same hole.

Owens squinted through the sights of the firefinder. Then he glanced at Broadwink, and he wasn't smiling. "Where's your goddamn binoculars?" he growled.

The pimply-faced young man whirled around and started pawing desperately through the things on the shelves of the firefinder stand. Then, one hand still protecting his rectitude, he rummaged through stuff on all the shelves along the sides of the cab below the windows. Finally he unearthed a leather binoculars case and handed it to Owens.

"You mean you didn't use these last night?"

"I couldn't find them," the young man answered lamely.

There was a terrible crash, as the girl, one foot still caught in the crotch of the panties, lost her balance and fell against the heavily laden card table, collapsing two of its legs and sending it to the floor with her on top of it. Broadwink, in a gesture of misplaced gallantry, attempted to help her up, but now the panties were around both ankles, and all she could do was writhe around like a fish on the dock. Broadwink did have the presence of mind to jerk a blanket off the rumpled bed and throw it over her, head and all.

I was holding myself up against the refrigerator suffering parox-

61

ysms of hysteria, and through tears, caught Owens's eye. He was trying to come across as fierce and outraged, but I could see he was having trouble doing that. He jerked the binoculars out of the case and focused them on the canyon bottom, then surveyed the area for a full minute.

"Who sent you up here as relief lookout?" he demanded.

"Mr. Parker," Broadwink said, referring to the Powder Cache district fire control officer. "This is my first time."

"That so? And what kind of instructions did he give you?"

"To report any smokes I saw, and call him if I had any questions."

"Well, did you have any questions for him last night?"

"He told me not to call after nine."

Owens simply shook his head in disbelief.

"Listen, Mr. Owens," Broadwink said, struggling into a pair of jeans, "I'm awful sorry about this. Isn't there a fire down there?"

"Don't sweat it, Horace. Just tell John Parker when you see him that next time he lets one of his ace relief lookouts send me out all night chasing fog pockets, he's going to wind up with a Pulaski up his ass."

The young man's face was white as an eggshell. "What are you going to tell him about . . ."

"I'm going to tell him you have a helluva lot to learn."

Owens then grabbed the radio and called for a Cedar Valley district pickup to give us a ride back to his rig, then said, "Harper, let's get out of here before I get sick."

We clambered back down the stairs.

"I think you've got that poor kid worried, Ray."

"I sure hope so. He should have his ass kicked."

"For having that girl—"

"Hell no. Would've done the same thing myself. I mean running us around in the wet brush all night chasing fog. At my age I don't need it."

"What are you going to tell his district about the girl?"

"Nothing. The kid will go crazy waiting for the axe to fall."

"Think he'll get confused and tell on himself?"

"I don't think he'll get *that* confused."

We got back to the station in time to turn around and go out after another fire, a real one this time, and as it turned out, a small one. We got a line around it in a couple of hours, then mopped it up, finishing about eight that night.

A hot shower and a change of clothes made me feel refreshed, but Albert Carlisle's snoring plus the gas from whatever he'd eaten for supper drove me out into the cool night air. I soon found myself strolling down the main street, where the only thing open was Kelley's. So I walked in, sat down on a stool, and ordered a beer. Several other men sat at the bar, talking and drinking and studying themselves in the mirror.

The bartender, Kelley Puckett, moved back and forth along the bar trying hard not to miss a word of any of the several conversations going on. He looked to be about sixty, and he was small and wiry. His dark eyes looked like eight-balls behind his thick spectacles, and his obviously dyed hair was slicked back like that of an old-time gangster. He was offering comments on every subject, and from his authoritative tone and the finality of his statements, he sounded like the ultimate regional authority on all of them. Either that or he was full of shit. Most of the topics had to do with hunting and fishing, about which I knew little, and so as a newcomer, I decided to reserve judgment.

At one point in a conversation with two of the beerdrinkers, Puckett extended his audience to take in the full bar, just as if they all were privy to what had already been said. "And this flatlander tells me he has a doe permit, and wants to know where to go to shoot one. So I sent him up Silver Canyon."

Several of the men laughed knowingly.

"Where's Silver Canyon?" asked a logger in red suspenders.

"About fifty miles from here, out in the middle of the biggest lava flow in the state," Puckett said, chuckling derisively.

I recognized a gravelly voice, then noticed Deputy Dhrymes on the end stool, laughing along with the others.

"Well, that new county supervisor, what's his name . . . Bigelow?" said another logger, this one still wearing his hard hat. "At that meeting in Winchester the other night he said he agreed with fish and game's policy. He said studies showed that too many does were overbrowsing the range, and it was hurting the whole herd."

"He's an asshole," stated Puckett, wiping the bar. "What's hurting the deer herd is the fire suppression policy of the Forest Service. That and too many flatlanders from L.A. and Frisco coming up here and shooting at anything that moves."

"If you ask me," said Red Suspenders, "the either-sex hunts ought to be outlawed. What sense does it make to shoot a doe?"

The man on the stool next to me suddenly looked up from his beer. He was decked out as a fly fisherman and looked as if he'd had at least one too many. "What the fuck difference does it make whether it's male or female?" he gushed. "You guys go out and shoot Canada geese of either sex because they all look alike. So what's the big deal about sex?"

Everybody spun around on their stools to look at the fisherman, apparently a transient.

"Geese are different," said Puckett. "They all fly the same, and the goose is as hard to hit as the gander. It's not the same as plugging some tame doe in a meadow."

"That's absolutely right," said Hard Hat, staring at the fisherman's image in the bar mirror. "As far as I'm concerned, anyone who shoots at a doe is nothing but a useless *cunt* who doesn't know a buck from a white giraffe."

"Well, I put in for a doe permit this year," said the fisherman. "You calling me a cunt?"

At this point, all peripheral conversation came to a sudden halt, all attention focused on the probable highlight of the evening.

"Well now, why don't you just take down your panties, flatlander, and we can check that out?"

The silence was awesome. I glanced at Puckett, then at Dhrymes. Both were savoring it, neither making a move to intervene. By this time Hard Hat and the fisherman had eased off their stools and stood facing one another. The logger's muscles rippled, even beneath his clothing, and the fisherman, obviously tipsy, looked flabby and overmatched from the outset. The fisherman's move was next. He had to either back off and depart in humiliation or exacerbate a worsening situation. He took one step backward with his right foot and doubled his fists.

"Eat shit, you egotistical cocksucker," he said through clenched teeth.

Uh-oh, I said to myself. While I admired the man's courage, he was obviously suicidal, forcing the logger's hand in his own back yard. Then I saw Red Suspenders move quickly up behind the fisherman and grab both his arms from behind. In a half second Hard Hat got in a clean shot to the fisherman's mouth. He was winding up for his next punch when instinct and training took over, and I found myself squarely between them, wrapping my arms around the logger. "Hold it, hold it!" I was shouting.

Hard Hat struggled to get free, so I pushed his left elbow upward with my right hand and slipped quickly behind him in a wrestling maneuver called a go-behind. From there, I forced his right arm into a hammerlock. Then everything went black.

When my eyes opened, the deputy had me by the shirtfront. He pulled me to my feet and held me up in front of him. His out-of-focus image shimmered before me, and I heard my ears ringing. I figured out he must have slugged me from behind. He pulled me close; I could smell his onion breath.

"Listen, junior," he said. "I don't know who the fuck you think you are, but we don't really appreciate your assistance in settling local arguments. You understand that?"

I concentrated hard, my mind clearing now, the anger rising like a tide. "I understand you just assaulted me without due cause," I said, pulling my shirt loose from his big hands.

"Did I do that?" he said, leering around at the other patrons. "Anybody see me do anything like that?" He turned back to me. "Listen, sonny," he went on, reveling in his performance, "give me any more of that kind of crap and you're in the slammer. Now I suggest you get outta here while you still can."

"No," I said, surprising myself. "I didn't cause the disturbance, and I haven't violated the law. I have a right to remain on the premises unless asked by the management to leave."

Everybody swung around to look at the management, in the dubious corpus of Kelley Puckett. The light reflected off his glasses, and I could see him smiling. He remained mute, clearly enjoying the show.

Dhrymes looked confused. Maybe nobody had never put it to

65

him like that before. I could read his thoughts: *Who is this guy, a lawyer, or what?* Then he looked around, only to find everyone else looking back at him expectantly.

Finally he responded. "All right, you smart-ass. I'm running you in for disturbing the peace, obstructing justice, assaulting an officer of the law."

"Like hell you are," said a voice from the other end of the bar. A man pushed past the loggers and the fisherman and came to face the deputy: Clyde Krafft, chief of the volunteer fire department. "I saw the whole thing. You take him in and I'm going straight to the DA."

The thick veins in the deputy's neck began twitching noticeably. "You and who else?" he asked, looking around from face to face.

"And me," said the fisherman, whose mouth was bleeding badly.

"And me," said a woman's voice from a dark corner of the room.

Dhrymes's face turned gray, then kind of purple. His lips quivered but his voice was inaudible. I seized the offensive. *"You* get out, or tomorrow morning I'll have you charged with felonious assault."

Dhrymes began laughing, but it sounded hollow and contrived, and nobody laughed with him. He knew he'd lost, at least for this night, and scooping up his trooper's hat from a barstool, he faced me once more, his voice now low and dry. "You son of a bitch, you make one mistake in this town and I'm having your purple ass."

On the way out he said something menacing to Krafft that I couldn't hear. But everybody heard the rear wheels of the patrol car screeching as Dhrymes roared away into the night. The fisherman stumbled out, leaving the loggers with their beers and a few laughs. A few people patted me on the back, and then I left too.

Krafft caught up with me outside and I thanked him for intervening.

"My pleasure, Harper," he said, clearly pleased. "He had no

right to jump you like that. But you'd better keep an eye open. He can be nasty at times."

"Thanks. Say, who was the woman who spoke out?"

"That was Nora Jeffers. I was good friends with her husband before he got killed in the mill."

"And who was that guy she was with?"

"You don't know him? He works for the same outfit you do. Name is Turpin. Stan Turpin."

"Oh. They're a steady pair?"

Krafft laughed. "I don't rightly know, but you'd think so, as nasty as he gets whenever she shines on to anybody else."

The evening had been ugly up until then, but the thought of Turpin and Nora together made it hideous. Swiftbird's comments had made it sound like things were all over between them, but maybe things weren't as simple as I'd have liked them to be.

Chapter 5

The rain began before I reached the barracks, and all during the night I could hear hail pelting down on the roof and against the window. At times I thought the glass would surely shatter, but Carlisle slept through the whole thing. At breakfast, Swiftbird told us the rain had covered the whole district, and that it would be unlikely any smoke would show up until it had dried again. That was fine with me, having awakened with a headache of monumental proportions and a very sore neck.

By noon the story about my kicking the deputy out of Kelley's had spread all over town, and worse, all over the ranger station. When Swiftbird told me he'd heard about it at the post office, I expected a command visit to the office, and said so to the foreman.

"Felton told me Mr. West was upset about it. He doesn't like any of his people getting crosswise with the locals, that there's enough problems already. Felton told him it wasn't your fault, so don't sweat it. My advice would be to just lay low for a while and maybe stay out of Kelley's for a few weeks."

"This guy Dhrymes is no admirer of the Forest Service, I guess."

"You could say that. I think it goes back to a couple of years ago when he tried to get into the volunteer fire department but was blackballed by our former district ranger. Dhrymes found out about it."

"Why did the district ranger vote against him?"

"Mr. Nelson was a stickler for principle, I guess. He apparently thought it would be a conflict of duty. When there's a fire in the town, the law enforcement officer shouldn't be involved in fighting the fire."

"You think Dhrymes will be laying for me?"

"He won't take it lightly, but I doubt if he'll do anything rash. But you'd better look out for that cowboy Steve Christian. Bein' famous now, you're on his list for sure."

I took his advice seriously, but at the same time, the investigation was what was most important to me. I had to keep making progress, if only by continuing to get acquainted and finding out about the people who lived in this town. If that meant a run-in with somebody, I'd just have to deal with it. The tiff with Dhrymes made getting to know folks easier, as it provided a focal point, a conversation starter. And I gathered most of the town people approved of the outcome and had taken my side. Little by little, they started opening up to me.

I should qualify that a bit. One segment of Cedar Valley society, maybe half the town, didn't drink or go to the bar or to dances, and they probably disapproved of anyone who did. Inasmuch as their total knowledge of me came from news of the barroom incident, I suppose they viewed me as an outcast, one of the undesirables, and as such, unapproachable.

The idea of attending church services went through my mind—at high speed—but then, how could I? I had to work Sundays. I added this to my growing list of problems to work out.

For the next five days, things moved along a smooth track, but still, I hungered for progress. It seemed to me that sooner or later I'd have to get a look at where some of the incendiary fires had started, to get a real feel for the problem. How could I do this without creating suspicion? Clearly, I'd have to study the fire reports and find out where the blazes had started, then go to the sites and look at them. How I might accomplish this stumped me for some time, but finally I got lucky.

Punky Swiftbird asked one morning if I'd be interested in taking the weather observations for Lois on her days off. I knew this would involve going into the office several times a day, and I immediately said yes. The next day I reported to Lois for instructions, and she led me across the highway to the little fenced-in weather station. There she showed me how to read and record the maximum and minimum temperatures and reset the thermometers, then how to figure the relative humidity and the wind speed and direction and measure any rain that had fallen. The willowy redhead manipulated the sturdy instruments with meticulous care, as one would handle priceless and fragile art objects.

"To get the fuel moisture," she told me, holding her pencil sideways in her mouth, "grab that set of fuel moisture sticks over there on that little rack. Wait! Not with your hands. Use these tongs. If the sticks get greasy we'll get an inaccurate reading."

"I have greasy hands?"

"Nothing personal. We don't want dogs urinating on them either. Oh, sorry, that didn't sound so good either. Anyway, hang the sticks on this little scale and put this hundred-gram weight on the counterbalance."

"Okay, it reads seventeen. That's the fuel moisture?"

"Right. The lower the number, the hotter things burn."

"What do you do with all these data?"

"Some of it's for the U.S. Weather Bureau records. We use the rest of them to figure the current fire danger, and to predict the fire danger for the next day. That will vary enormously from day to day, especially if the fire weather forecasters in Redding predict strong winds. With a prediction of higher fire danger, we put more men on duty. I'll show you how we do it when we get back to the office. Don't mind the clutter," she said merrily. "This is payroll day, and we're also getting out a cutting report."

"You're the entire work force in here?"

"I'm it. Thank God we don't have any fires to worry about right now." She began explaining how to calculate the fire danger just as Ned Booth came in the front door. He told Lois he'd completed work on some Forest Service chain saws and wanted to get the vouchers signed. While she attended to that matter, the radio began crackling, and one of the lookouts reported a smoke. Booth looked on as she pulled out the azimuth string on the large wall map to indicate the lookout's reading. In moments another lookout reported a sighting, providing a cross-reading that, by intersection of the two strings, established the smoke's map location, a spot near Rucker's Ridge.

By this time Don West, the district ranger, and Bill Marklee, the fire prevention officer, were at Lois's elbow, monitoring the situation. She had already dispatched the two nearest crews by radio.

"What's going on up there, Bill?" West asked Marklee as they both stared at the map. I hadn't met West, but he nodded at me. I guessed him to be about forty, and about my height. "There's no salvage logging going on right now, is there?"

Marklee wrinkled his brow, his nostrils twitching rapidly like a rabbit smelling its food. "Not that I know of, Don. And if those readings are good, it's not even near a road. Must be a mile from the Rucker's Ridge road." He turned, grabbed a desk mike, and instructed incoming crews to get ID on any vehicles seen exiting the area. "There's only one road into the area," he went on. "Maybe we can nail this one, for a change."

"Better roll Cedar Valley also," West told Hart.

When I heard him say that, I headed out the back door toward the warehouse-garage, not wanting to miss my ride to this fire. Fred Sweeney had already rolled the 1948-model Marmon-Harrington truck out of the garage, and the crewmen scrambled to get aboard. I jumped onto the crew seat with Vaughan Day and Ardis Corbin, and in moments we found ourselves heading southward out of town on the main highway. The crew seat faced forward, and as we raced along the paved two-lane road we all scanned the mountains to the south, eager to be first to spot a column of smoke on Rucker's Ridge. Day and Corbin vibrated with excitement. So far they had only fought a few lightning fires; this "real" blaze would test their mental and physical toughness under battle conditions.

I well remembered the sensation and thoughts from my first

few weeks as a cop in L.A. While hating the idea of crime, I had lusted after it. All the training had prepared us for crime fighting, and this mission naturally dominated our thinking and behavior. I'd thought it ironic at the time: being taught to do a job that discouraged crime, then hoping to hell we'd get involved in a lot of it. And now I found myself amidst a bunch of firefighters with the same kind of thing going on. It made me think again about Anselmo Adams's remark that the firemen deserved to be the first looked at in an investigation.

I coupled those thoughts with a recollection of the comments by West and Marklee minutes earlier, the ones indicating that this fire might have suspicious origins. These circumstances provided me with a double dose of adrenalin, as I psyched myself up for the fire itself, and the question of who might have started it, and why. Nobody on this truck felt more keyed-up than I did.

"There it is!" shouted Corbin, pointing at a bluish column of smoke some five miles distant. Looking into the rear window of the cab, I could see Sweeney and Swiftbird craning their necks in that direction too. In moments we slowed and turned from the highway onto a dirt road that led southward past a farmhouse and up the side of the mountain. Soon the terrain obscured the smoke, and I started keeping watch for vehicles coming the other way but saw none.

After about twenty minutes of eating dust and bracing ourselves for bumps and curves, we saw Felton Shackle standing in the road waving us to a stop. He stepped up onto the running board on the right side and leaned in so he could give instructions to Swiftbird. I could see no fire or smoke from there.

"The Willow Creek crew is on top to keep it from crossing the road up there," Shackle said. "Scarface crew is on the way up to the bottom of the fire. They'll start flanking the east side."

"And we've got the west side?" asked Swiftbird.

"Right. Tie in with their line at the bottom." Shackle jumped down and headed up the steep slope toward the fire.

While Sweeney parked the rig, Swiftbird assigned us tools. "Okay, two Pulaskis, two McLeods, two shovels, one back pump, and a crosscut saw." He handed me a shovel and a McLeod tool, half rake, half hoe. Each of us slung gallon canteens onto our backs, and we set out up the slope, weaving our way through a maze of manzanita, mountain mahogany, and buckbrush shrubs beneath a sparse canopy of Jeffrey pine, incense cedar, and white fir.

The hot afternoon and steep slope made it tough going, but the excitement kept us moving at a steady pace. In about twenty minutes we reached the base of the fire, where we stopped to catch our breath. I immediately saw where the fire had started, as the blackened area extended from this lowest point up the slope in a widening pattern. We could see only smoldering duff and twigs here, but from the look of the smoke column visible above us, the fire burned intensely up the hill from our location.

Swiftbird told us to stay clear of the area around the very bottom of the fire so as not to destroy any evidence. I looked hard from where I stood but could see nothing to indicate how the fire might have started. Nor could I deduce why somebody might pick this spot to kindle a blaze. It looked like Bill Marklee would have his hands full again.

As I stood there trying to memorize the scene, Marklee showed up, puffing and perspiring and clutching an attaché case that looked entirely inappropriate for use in the mountains. I surmised it contained his investigative equipment and wondered whether he would find anything. The blank expression on his face along with the incessant twitching of his nostrils told me he hadn't seen anything yet. I would have given my paycheck to work with him on the investigation but could think of no way to even suggest it. Merely offering might make it look like I was trying to avoid doing the heavier work of building fireline.

"Leave the can and the whip," Swiftbird told us, referring to the back pump and the crosscut saw. "Start building the line right here, and all of you stay ten feet apart and keep one foot in the burn. Don't work out away from the edge of the fire unless I say so."

Fred Sweeney grabbed the shovel I'd carried up the hill and moved ahead, throwing dirt onto the hotspots. Vaughan Day went next, chopping out saplings and shrubs with his Pulaski. Ardis Corbin and I fell in behind with our McLeod tools, raking the litter and duff aside to form a narrow trail along the smoldering edge of the fire. Swiftbird, carrying a shovel, moved ahead up the hill scouting the edge of the fire.

In about a half hour we had overtaken the flaming edge of the blaze, and the work got a lot harder and a lot hotter, forcing us to build the line several feet away from the three-foot-high flames. When the wind would shift toward us, we were enveloped in a blanket of acrid smoke that forced us to flatten ourselves against the ground just to find a few breaths of clean air. Then when it would lift, we'd get back on our feet and hack away at the fireline again.

Swiftbird came back down the line telling each of us to watch for "spots" outside the line, which we must extinguish immediately, and that in case of a serious flare-up or wind shift, we were to jump through the flaming edge and take refuge inside the burned area. I took a look in that direction and judged it a pretty hostile environment but figured he must have known what he was talking about, not realizing I'd get the chance to find out in only moments.

The head of the fire raged well upslope from us yet, but we could hear it roaring as clumps of trees "crowned out" in great candles of flame that rocketed skyward in prolonged bursts. From more than a hundred yards away I could feel the heat on my face and wondered what it would be like up close. I bent to my task, hacking at stubborn roots with the cutting edge of my McLeod tool, cursing the rocks that dulled the blade at each stroke. Then I heard the crackling behind me and turned to see three or four spots of fire some twenty feet outside the line. Tiny firebrands were landing everywhere now, each one kindling a new little fire. I ran among them, pounding them out with the flat bottom of my tool, all the while hollering for help from the other crewmen. But they were all too busy on their own little spot fires to give me a hand.

For a few moments I thought I'd be able to smother them all, but then the breeze intensified, and in moments I found myself all but surrounded, the dozens of spot fires now coalescing into a couple of huge ones. The main fire, moments ago quite subdued along our little fire trail, now raged across the trail, hungry for any unburned fuel in its path. I was trapped, but it all happened so fast there wasn't even time to try to figure things out.

Swiftbird's instructions flashed through my mind, and without hesitation I charged the main fireline, throwing my body through the wall of flames, landing atop a jackstraw pile of smoldering tree limbs and downed saplings. Blinded by the acrid smoke, I got to my feet and clambered through the debris away from the worst heat until I collapsed, gasping, on what felt like unburned ground. My lungs screamed for clean air, but the harder I sucked in, the more smoke I got. I was gagging on a mixture of ashes and mucus, I could see nothing but red streaks on a yellow field, and arrows of pain darted around inside my head. For a few moments I thought I was dying.

Suddenly I became my brother. Lying there in the smoke, the images came readily. My mind created a sort of movie sequence of Heath's last few minutes of life, the mental pictures based, I suppose, on what I'd read in the fire report and heard said about it, my imagination doing the rest.

An unexpected wind shift carries firebrands downslope from the fire, cutting off the escape route of a tractor operator building line there. Heath, in charge of that sector, perceives the man to be unaware of his plight, and decides to find him and lead him out.

The young forester rips a shovel out of the brackets on the side of his pickup, pulls down the chin strap on his hard hat, then plunges down the mountainside, half running, half skiing toward the trapped dozer operator. He moves rapidly through the burned-out hillside, dodging burning logs and stumps, trying to avoid the heaviest concentrations of smoke. He can barely see and stops several times to rub his eyes and listen for the purring of the Cat's big diesel engine.

He comes up on a rise and sees the yellow Cat through a wall of fire four or five feet high. The machine is motionless but idling at a high throttle setting. Where is the operator? Why isn't the machine moving, he asks himself. He works his way around below the tractor, where the flames are less intense, and begins throwing dirt with his shovel to smother a way through the fire's edge. With his head down and his face protected against the worst radiation by the blade of his shovel, Heath jumps through the fire front and runs to the tractor. He finds nobody.

He can't see fifty feet through the dense smoke. He calls out "Yo!" and gets no answer. The operator must have headed back afoot along his new fireline, he reasons. He starts in pursuit at a lope, tracking bootprints in soft dirt. Suddenly, a swirling mass of flames, smoke, dust, and firebrands halts his advance. He turns to retreat, now beginning to feel the adrenalin taking hold. But now a sheath of flames from below the Cat trail shoots across in front of him, igniting the vegetation on the unburned, uphill side. A fire-storm traps him.

Heath runs back and forth in his shrinking island, looking futilely right, left, ahead, back. He sees only yellow, feels only heat. All firefighters fear this nightmare. He realizes in an ugly flash that he is about to be killed. He has no time to think about loved ones, about good times, about what might have been. He has time only to try in desperation to produce a miracle, and almost by instinct, bends all effort to this task.

He digs out a shallow trench on the uphill side of the cat-line, then lies face down in it just as the flames roar over him. As he feels the skin on his neck burning he jerks up his shirt collar, then quickly jams his bare hands back under his chest. He takes a deep breath, pushes his face hard down into the dirt. In a few seconds, tiny firebrands burn a dozen holes in his khaki shirt, and his jeans start smoldering. But he doesn't feel this, the pain of the radiation from above overwhelming other sensations. He feels the skin on his ears burning, begins to realize his clothing is on fire.

Finally, panic-stricken, he jumps from his tiny refuge, and driven now only by an instinct to survive, runs without knowing or caring in what direction. He knows it's all over and for a split second sees an image of himself with his family on a picnic by a creek some-where. There is no time even to call out, "I love you Mom, Dad, Gene!" He sucks in a deep breath of hot gases that sear his lung tissues, then drops unconscious to the ground like a bird shot out of flight. The unrelenting flames play overhead like a low stormcloud, quickly reducing the handsome young man to a charred and rigid hulklike ember.

The man he goes there to save, unaware either of Heath's terrible fate or his selfless valor, escapes unhurt.

A hand clapped me on the shoulder and I heard Swiftbird's voice. "Harper! You all right?"

I was. I was lying there near the fire line, my face in my hands. I looked up at the foreman's sweaty face. "Yeah. Yeah, I'm okay. Too much smoke, I guess."

We controlled the Rucker's Ridge fire that night and got it mopped up two days later, the Fourth of July. On the sixth, a Sunday, I took the weather observations and ran into Bill Marklee in the office. I asked how his investigation had turned out.

"Somebody's fucking us around," he answered while searching through a file folder. "Verna didn't see any dust come up on that road all day until we responded to the fire." Verna, I had already learned, was Bill's wife and the lookout on Grouse Hill.

I waited for more information, then finally asked. "Somebody on foot, then?"

"He'd have to like walking a lot. Must be about a five-hour hike through the brush to where you could park a car out of sight and not meet us coming in."

"And you've ruled out a lightning holdover?"

"It's been over two weeks since the last storm that passed over that area. The only big tree near the point of origin was a Jeffrey pine, and I looked it over pretty close for lightning scars. Anyway, a pine wouldn't hold fire that long this time of year. A rotten white fir, maybe."

"And no sign of a device, I gather."

Marklee gave me a snort and an irritated look, as if I needn't have asked that one. "It's just like the others," he said, walking away toward his office.

I'd looked at the district map several times and speculated about how somebody might sneak into the area, start the fire, then get out undetected. We'd met nobody coming out of the area as we went in, and I began wondering if we'd perhaps missed someone who'd come out just before we made the turn off the main highway. I remembered the farmhouse by the turnoff and figured that Marklee hadn't thought to check with whoever lived there. So I skipped supper and drove down there to find out.

On driving into the yard in front of the farmhouse, my car was attacked by four large dogs, who kept me from setting foot on the ground until their master came out and called them off. The middle-aged man gave my car a suspicious once-over through squinting eyes, his downturned mouth revealing no friendliness.

"Good evening, sir," I said. "I'm from the Forest Service in Cedar Valley, and we're trying to figure out how that fire got started up the mountain last Wednesday. We wondered whether maybe you'd seen any strange vehicles going by before the fire."

He turned away to spit some tobacco juice. "Don't you guys talk to each other over there?"

I gave him a blank look and waited.

"Bill Marklee already came asking me that question, and I told him the same as I'm telling you, there wasn't anybody I didn't know who it was."

"Sorry, I guess he forgot to tell me he'd already asked you. Thanks a lot for your help. We appreciate it." I hoped I was coming across as a member of the official investigation, however inept.

I had started back toward my car when he said, "Only rig I seen that made me curious was one last night, but then you ain't interested in that."

"Yes, sir, I am interested."

"Girl in a red Jeep. Went past about five last evening and came back out around seven thirty."

I got him to describe the Jeep, thanked him, then drove back to the main highway, wondering why Nora Jeffers might have gone up that road. Instead of turning back toward Cedar Valley, I decided to go to Purple Pond for something to eat and a change of scenery.

The name Purple Pond made the town sound more picturesque than it was, the dusty streets and drab houses, most without landscaping, lending little charm to the mountain-valley setting. It seemed only a place to sleep, gas up your car, and buy no-nonsense groceries. I saw some children playing ball in a little park and wondered where they went to school.

I parked on the main street, went into what looked like the only bar, a place called the Rainbow Tavern, drank a beer, then entered the restaurant a few steps away. I slid into a booth and looked around at the other customers, people I'd never seen before. I checked out the down-to-basics menu and gave my order to the waitress, a girl with a decidedly Texas accent.

Something outside caught my eye and I turned to see. Three people stood talking on the sidewalk. One of them was a woman in a plaid jacket whose back was turned to me, but I recognized one of the others: the cowboy, Steve Christian. He was with an attractive blond woman I'd not seen before.

I vaguely heard the door open and close, and suddenly a woman in blue denim and a plaid jacket plumped down in the seat opposite me. Maybe the way her long dark hair was tied back stumped me; it took a moment for me to realize it was Nora Jeffers. I looked at her in amazement. "Where did you come from?"

"From Mars, where did you think?" she asked, her eyes twinkling.

"No, I don't mean originally, but just now."

"I saw you come out of the bar. Didn't you get enough excitement in Kelley's? Or did you need to get into another fight tonight?"

"I am embarrassed. Barroom brawls are definitely not my specialty."

"What really *is* your specialty, then?"

"Afraid I don't have one right now. I was an instrument-calibrating specialist, but now I'm not sure what I am."

"Oh, yes, with Becker Industries, didn't you say? But why the fire-fighting thing. Is there really a future in it?"

The waitress showed up to take Nora's order, and she asked for coffee. I could remember every word of our conversation in the grocery store, and I'd said nothing about Becker Industries. I had mentioned it only on the job application form. How did she find out about that, and why had she made note of it?

"Well, mainly, I had to get out of L.A., and this seemed like a good place to try out something different. By the way, thanks for your timely support in Kelley's that night. You and Clyde Krafft came through when I really needed some friends."

She seemed pleased I'd found out it was she who'd spoken up. I thought maybe she'd have something to say about my tiff with Stan Turpin earlier, but she changed the subject.

"So why the big rush to get out of L.A.?"

"My brother's death." I watched her blink several times, but her expression didn't change. "A drunk blew a stop sign on Wilshire Boulevard and hit his motorcycle."

"My God," she said, looking stunned.

"That started it. Everything went downhill from there . . . my job, my friends. I was drinking too much. It got so I couldn't stand that place any longer." While going through all this bullshit, I wondered how I'd do as an actor. She seemed to believe every word.

"Tell me about your brother."

I did a good job of describing Heath to her, but of course changed his name and physical characteristics. The transferral of my feelings about Heath happened during the description, and I found myself choking back tears just talking about a character I'd made up.

"I understand completely," she said, reaching across the table to touch my cheek. "Did your crew go on that fire up toward Rucker's Ridge last Wednesday?" she asked out of nowhere, changing the subject abruptly. She had a way of squinting slightly when she asked a question, and every new line I saw in her face added to her charm.

"Yes, we did. For most of us, it was our first real fire."

"How did it start?"

Her straight-to-the-point query jolted me. "Arson."

She tilted her head to one side. "How do you know that?"

"I'm just repeating what Bill Marklee said. All I did was help fight it."

"Well, did they find some evidence, or see somebody, or what?" she persisted.

I'd played this kind of game with suspects before and decided to check her reaction with a bit of shock treatment. "Well, I can tell you this much. A red Jeep was seen heading up that road yesterday. You know, like returning to the scene of the crime."

Her face quickly pinkened, but her voice was steady. "Now you're teasing me. There are several red Jeeps around here."

"With beautiful dark-haired women drivers?"

Her expression was still gay, teasing, but now her eyes seemed to drill into me, assessing my motives.

"Just kidding," I said, forcing a laugh. "One of my weaknesses, a bad sense of humor. No, really, I don't think they found a damned thing. Typical Forest Service investigation, from what I'm beginning to learn."

She didn't seem to buy it, at least from what I could judge by her reactions. It made me conclude it was indeed she who'd driven the red Jeep up the Rucker's Ridge road. I changed the subject, and after a while she seemed to calm down. We talked about life in Cedar Valley until my meal arrived. She got up and thanked me for the coffee.

"Heading back to town?"

"Not tonight, . . . Harper." Hearing her say my name for the first time, even my phony name, gave me a pleasant little zing. "I'm staying over here with my aunt. She broke her hip, and several of us are taking turns helping out."

"That's nice of you. Hope some day when I break my hip you'll still be around."

"You wouldn't like it. The broken-hip part, anyway."

"It would definitely be worth it."

She smiled, then turned and walked out.

Driving back toward Cedar Valley, I pondered our conversation, wondering if I shouldn't have pushed harder, tried to find out more about Nora. I needed to know more about her relationship with Heath, with Ned Booth, with Stan Turpin—and . . . with myself. Why had she gone to such apparent lengths to find out about where I'd worked in L.A. and then been deceptive about it? How could I find out for sure if she knew or suspected my real identity? And the most intriguing question of all: what had she been doing in the area of the Rucker's Ridge fire?

Headlights approaching fast from behind broke my train of thought. As the dark-colored vehicle came abreast, it slowed somewhat to match my speed, then lurched sharply toward me as if to force me off the road. I hit the brakes hard to avoid being struck, but the maneuver put me into a four-wheel slide along the shoulder. I gave it the gas and almost pulled my car out of the skid, but the slope of the shoulder took me off the road, where I bounced to a dusty halt among grapefruit-size rocks and sagebrush bushes. When I tried to get going again, I discovered the right front tire had blown. I shut off the engine and doused the headlights.

I couldn't find my flashlight, but did locate the tire tools and began jacking up the front of my car. The more I replayed it, the surer I became that the other driver had intentionally forced me off the road. But why? It had all happened too fast for me to get a fix on the vehicle, but I remembered it as a dark-colored pickup with a man driving alone.

I had the wheel about off when I looked up and saw the silhouette of a pickup truck moving slowly back along the road in my direction, its headlights extinguished. It made my scalp tingle. I quickly got back into the car and took out the revolver I had hidden in a special bracket beneath the dashboard. Staying low, I moved away from the car, obscuring my silhouette behind that of the car.

When the pickup got to within a hundred feet of my car, it stopped, and I lay down in the low cover of bunchgrasses and rocks. In a few seconds a powerful spotlight snapped on and its beam began playing over the area around my car. I avoided looking directly at the beam. When the light snapped off I quickly raised my head and got a glimpse of a man getting out the driver's side of the pickup. He had something long and thin in one hand—probably a rifle, I guessed—and a shorter object in his other hand. That had to be a flashlight.

As I lay there clutching my little snub-nose .38, I heard one of the most unmistakable, most menacing of all sounds, the metallic clatter of a cartridge being pumped into the chamber of a shotgun. This guy meant business, and I had to act fast.

At the risk of giving away my position, I got to my feet and quietly put another hundred feet between me and my car, then crouched down and looked back. The man was heading down the bank in the direction of my car. In moments I lost his silhouette against the shadow of the road bank.

For the next two minutes I could hear nothing but my own breathing and heartbeat. Then the flashlight came on right by the car. The guy looked around inside and out, playing the light around the general area. I calculated my chances of doing a sort of end run and sneaking back to his car before he got there but decided that be taking too great a chance of being detected.

After a minute or so of absolute silence, an ear-shattering boom stunned me. The noise was followed by the tinkling of glass. I kept my head down. Shortly, I heard the pickup start. Getting to my feet, I saw the rig make a U-turn and head toward Cedar Valley. I wasn't at all surprised to find the windshield of my Ford smashed to smithereens.

I got back to work changing the tire and tried adding up what I'd just learned. Somebody was out to do me in, or at least to strongly discourage me. That meant he probably knew who I was and why I was there—which was a lot more than I had on him. It occurred to me that if I could find the cartridge casing that would have been ejected when he fired the shotgun, that might tell me something more about this guy. So I crawled around in the grass near the car, looking and feeling, but couldn't find anything. My recollection was that his flashlight hadn't come back on after I heard the shotgun blast, which would mean he hadn't picked up the casing. I would remember the place and come back in daylight to look again.

By the time I had the car back on the road, I began to feel strangely elated, even knowing my quarry might make another run at me. At least now I had reason to believe there indeed was a quarry, and very likely it was the son of a bitch who killed my brother.

Driving back through the chilly mountain air with a smashed windshield dampened my elation a bit, but it didn't keep me from thinking about Nora, and that came altogether too easily. I had to be cautious, advising myself not to get mushy over somebody who might be deeply involved in this whole thing. But then, how

could somebody like her be involved in this, especially consider-
ing her relationship with Heath?

I could hear the gravelly voice of Anselmo Adams saying, "Not
a woman's thing, we know that much."

Chapter 6

I parked my car in a remote spot behind the barracks and pulled a tarp over the front end, having decided the smashed windshield would, at least for now, remain a secret between me and the guy who did it. With luck, I thought, it could be kept out of sight until I got a chance to get into Winchester to have it replaced. If anybody asked me about the tarp, I was ready to tell them it was to keep rainwater from leaking in and around the top of the windshield.

Lois Hart quickly gained confidence in my ability to record the weather observations and calculate the fire-danger indexes, and she soon invited me to do it regularly. This fit my plans perfectly, as it gave me routine access to the office, and a valid reason to ask about the fire reports. I had decided to do my own survey of all suspiciously caused fires that had occurred in the past several years and quickly found out how to decipher the coded forms kept on file for each fire.

Each evening I would borrow the folder of human-caused fire reports for a particular year and take it to my room, where I would extract data of interest to me.

"What are you working on?" asked Albert Carlisle, who lay on his bed, his work boots still on.

I had expected such questions. "It may turn into a book on the social aspects of fire prevention."

"Sounds interesting. Could I help you with it?"

"Thanks, Albert. You'd surely be better at this sort of thing than I would, but as you know, personal fulfillment demands individual performance."

"All right. But I've studied a lot of behavioral psychology. You won't get very far into fire prevention without delving into that. And sooner or later you're going to have to deal with the motivation for intentionally setting fires. Like a lot of kids, I did that as a child. One problem is, some kids keep doing it. Let me know if you'd like to do some brainstorming on it."

"May take you up on it, Albert. Meantime, think I'll just get started on a statistical analysis and see where it leads me."

The reports offered more surprises than I'd expected. I managed to identify fifteen fires, all of which had at least twelve things in common, and eleven of which had fifteen things in common. The pattern soon became clear: these fires were being set under conditions that ensured that they would be difficult to discover early, burn rapidly, be hard to get to and suppress quickly, and finally, offer no clue as to the cause.

The fire reports offered few clues either as to motivation for the sets, and I found myself trying to explain whether the fire in each case would improve grazing or hunting conditions, lead to a salvage sale of timber, provide fire-fighting jobs for locals or overtime pay for Forest Service men. And when the motive was determined to be "pyromania," how was that known? I had a lot of uncertainties to deal with.

The next night I plotted the fifteen suspect fires on a district map. All of them fell within a belt ten to twenty-one miles outside town. I sketched in the two concentric circles, then noted a striking fact: every fire was accessible only by a dead-end road. Adams had figured they were all probably started by the same person, and this added credibility to the idea. But why a dead-end road, a tactic making one's exit from the scene more detectable? Could it be a sort of taunting of the Forest Service?

I colored in those roads, then took stock. Within the belt, there were only three areas accessible only by dead-end roads where human-caused fires had not yet been reported. These three areas also met the "in-common" criteria of being on southwest-facing slopes and out of the direct line of vision of one of our lookout towers. I reasoned it was only a question of time until we'd get fires there.

Another factor the fires had in common was that all of them had been discovered on days falling between Tuesday and Friday. And they all had been discovered during days of either "very high" or "extreme" fire danger. I immediately concluded that the situation lent itself neatly to a stakeout. That seemed logical from a police standpoint, but would the Forest Service go for it? Should I suggest it to Bill Marklee? I needed to think that one over.

On Thursday, one of my days off, I drove to Winchester and got the windshield replaced. Nobody had noticed it was smashed. Friday was off too, so I gathered up my map of fire locations, compass, and camera, then set off to check out my list of fires. But I'd underestimated the difficulty of locating them. The fire reports merely identified the quarter-quarter section, or forty-acre plot of the section (square mile) in which the fire occurred. The first problem was just finding that square mile of national forest!

It took a while, but I figured out how to read the "cruiser tags" that were nailed up on trees along the roads. These tags, placed where section lines from the old land surveys crossed roads, could be used to find the section corners. The "forty"—one sixteenth of a section—I deduced, could be found by pacing along a compass course from a section corner. But over steep terrain littered with down trees, giant boulders, and dense thickets of thorny brush, that is not quite as easy as it sounds.

To make matters even more confounding, most of the burns were more than a year old, and over much of their surfaces they had only burned along the ground and not up the trunks or into the canopies of standing trees. After the winter rains and snows, the spring "green-up" pretty well masked their presence, and I found I had to stumble directly onto one to even recognize it as the burn I sought. I gained a new appreciation for how big a forty-acre parcel really was.

But even after locating one of the burns, I had to find the point of origin, and found myself wishing I had listened more closely to Anselmo Adams's pointers on that subject. The steep slopes simplified that task, however, because fire generally spreads rapidly uphill, and only very slowly downhill.

It took me three days to find nine of the fifteen fires. At each point of origin, I made a careful search and found precisely nothing of value to my investigation, other than the fact I'd found nothing. I took photos of each scene, vaguely thinking it might save a hike back if I began wondering about something. I decided to hell with the other six fires.

One of my trips took me past the place where my windshield had been shot out, and I stopped and managed to find the shotgun cartridge, a twenty-gauge Winchester round. I placed it in my dresser drawer in the barracks and forgot about it.

My trips into the forest aroused little curiosity from the other crewmen, and when asked about it I said I liked to go hiking. They already thought I was a bit strange, I suppose, and seemed to accept the story.

Clyde Krafft, impressed by my performance in Kelley's that night, got me approved for membership in the Cedar Valley Volunteer Fire Department, providing, as he put it, I survived the initiation ceremonies to be held on the next Wednesday evening. I had participated in two of their Sunday morning training sessions, along with some other prospective members, and we were told we were technically qualified but that the main test would be forthcoming. We suspected it was all a lot of hype, but Krafft and the others let us know that only one or two of the five of us would get by the trials. He told us to wear old clothes so that the members could properly evaluate us, whatever that meant.

I got to the fire hall a little before eight that evening and was escorted up a stairway to a large room filled with folding chairs and wooden benches. Along the walls hung framed photos of fire engines, groups of men standing in front of the station, and large portrait photos of past chiefs of the department. A curtain shielded one end of the room.

Two of the original five candidates failed to appear, leaving myself, Sid "Sugar" Maples, and Acton Price. Maples, a huge blond man, was a faller for a logging outfit, and Price was the local Baptist minister. Krafft told the three of us to take seats on a bench in front, facing the members.

By ones and twos the volunteer firefighters entered the hall and stood around talking to one another until Krafft told them to sit down so he could start the meeting. I counted thirty-three men, of whom I knew only a dozen.

Krafft announced that the minutes of the preceding meeting had been lost, and that old business was open for discussion. Nobody said anything, so he moved on to new business.

"Let's get on with the initiation," yelled one man from the rear. Two or three other men shouted their agreement.

"All right," Krafft said, and the members settled down. "Back in 1938," he began, whereupon several groans were heard, as if they'd been exposed to this routine before. Krafft laboriously went through his story about how one winter night a fire had been ignited by a faulty stove, and three children were burned to death in their beds because there was no fire department. He related how money had been raised, the first fire engine obtained and outfitted, and on and on, dragging out the details mercilessly. He was just getting into a bit about how important bravery was to fire fighting when the group's patience came to an end.

"Get on with it, Clyde," shouted one man in the rear.

"Yeah, let's get the wheel out here," shouted another.

"All right, all right," said Krafft. "Bring out the wheel."

The curtain was pulled partway back to reveal a large wooden wheel on a spindle, similar to devices I'd seen in carnival shows in which a woman is spun round and round as knives are thrown at her. This one had the spread-eagled silhouette of a man painted on it, and was complete with little steps for the feet, and leather straps for the waist, arms, and legs. The audience registered no surprise on seeing the device, so I figured this was a regular part of the initiation.

"This is the test of courage," Krafft announced proudly. "We strap you on here, blindfold you, then throw axes at you, coming as close as possible without actually hitting you. The object of the test is to undergo it without screaming, even if you get nicked a little."

There was general laughter from the department members, and such remarks as, "We've never missed a new man yet!"

Krafft went on. "Okay. Get your tickets out. Who's got number fifty-one? Big John? Well, didn't you get lucky tonight! Okay. Here's your axe, John, we just had it balanced. You get three practice throws before we put the first candidate on the wheel."

Ned Booth stepped up and gave the wheel a spin, and the silhouette figure began rotating. Big John, a simple-looking man with a low hairline, took aim from about twenty feet back, reared back, and threw the axe. The weapon sailed through the air and stuck at least two inches into the wooden table—the axe head buried neatly in the middle of the silhouette's chest. A roar went up from the crowd.

"Okay, not bad," said Krafft. "But try to miss him next time."

John took another shot, this time merely whacking the silhouette in the lower leg.

"Much better," said the chief, "but room for improvement."

On his third try, John, who wielded the axe as if he'd had a lot of experience, managed to miss the silhouette, sticking the axe between the legs only inches below the crotch and drawing wild cheers from the audience and a simultaneous gasp from the three of us.

"All right, John is ready," proclaimed Clyde Krafft. "Who wants to go first of you three brave candidates?"

I knew it was a game, but it looked like a scary one. Was Big John really an expert who was part of this scheme to scare us to death? I decided not to volunteer for anything.

"The preacher! The preacher!" howled the mob, impatient for action.

Acton Price, his face white as a new drumhead, got up and headed for the door, but strong men grabbed him and dragged him to the wheel, where he was strapped over the silhouette and blindfolded.

"All right," Krafft directed, "get these other two men put into their coffins—er, I mean boxes. We don't want them to see anything in case Big John messes up like Elmer did the last time we tried this."

The curtain was opened the rest of the way, and I saw three wooden coffins near the wheel. They looked like they'd already been used a few times. Each lid was outfitted with a strong hasp and a padlock, and there were several air holes in the lid of each box.

Sid Maples and I were helped into our coffins. I had the feeling it was a big mistake allowing it but nonetheless decided to go along with the gag, hoping nothing would go wrong.

The lids were closed on us, and the hasps latched. But with all the noise in the room, I couldn't tell whether they'd locked the padlocks, or merely slipped them through the hasps. In either case, we were securely imprisoned until somebody chose to let us out. Krafft asked us if we were all right and told us it wouldn't be long before it was our turn on the wheel. I heard Maple's muffled voice saying he couldn't wait.

Then Krafft asked the preacher if he had any last requests, just in case anything went wrong.

"I changed my mind," he said. "I don't think you boys better do this to me. Something might not work out right. Please, take me off of this thing."

"It's too late, Acton. You signed the paper, just like everybody else. Now you got to take the test. You've already got a point against you for whining. Ned, spin the wheel."

I heard Booth grunt as he got the wheel turning, and the creaking noise of its axle sounded ominous.

"Get back farther, John," Krafft was shouting. "You have to be back of the line." Somebody else hollered out something about getting the ambulance ready, that the last time they couldn't get it started. The taunting went on and on, and I heard Ray Owens's voice asking the preacher if he now had a better idea of what hell might be like.

The preacher's whining soon turned into groans of despair, then nausea. It was a pretty good show, even if I couldn't see it.

Then there came a loud *thunk* and a roar of approval from the audience.

"You'll have to get closer, John," I heard Krafft holler out.

"You missed him by a good eight inches that time. Two more tries, John."

The creaking of the wheel and the preacher's moaning went on,until another *thunk* could be heard, this one muted, as if the axe had hit something softer than the wood of the wheel. The preacher screamed out and the crowd gasped.

"Oh, shit!" two or three men said. There was a moment of stunned silence, and then it sounded like everybody was on their feet stomping around, swearing at each other, arguing about what to do, telling someone to get the ambulance started, others saying it was too late. I listened hard for muffled laughter but could hear none. They were doing a superb acting job, good enough to send chills up and down my spine.

Sid Maples was buying it, as I could hear his muted voice shouting to let him out of his coffin and then his banging on the sides and lid. I figured as big and strong as he was, if he couldn't break out, there was little use in my even trying.

The show must have lasted a good ten minutes and had all the sound effects of first aid being given in vain, and a body being put in the third coffin and carried out. Then there were the sounds of cleaning up whatever mess might have been made.

Finally, they held some kind of an impromptu meeting in hushed tones; I could make nothing out of it. Then I could hear them all leaving the hall and descending the stairway, and the lights were extinguished.

"You still there, Sid?"

"Yeah. Where the fuck else would I be. You think they killed the preacher?"

"I think it's a game. Can you break out of your coffin, you think?"

"I been trying. It's built like a brick shithouse, and I'm stuck in here too tight to get any leverage."

I lay there wondering what these overage juvenile delinquents had figured out for the remainder of the evening, and decided they'd let us think the worst to see how we'd react. But what was the delay getting the rest of the show going? After about a half hour, still nothing, and my body was getting very cramped. Sid, a bigger man, must have felt even worse, and pretty soon he said he'd figured out what he was going to do to each of the crazy bastards that had locked us in these things.

Eventually we heard faint footsteps on the stairway, and I could see through the air holes that the lights had been snapped on.

"Acton? Acton? Are you in here?" called out a woman's voice.

Maples and I both started yelling and banging on the lids of our coffins.

Footsteps approached. She opened Maple's box first, the padlock not having been clicked closed.

"You're Sid Maples. I recognize you from church. Where is Acton? He's needed right away at the medical clinic in Purple Pond."

"I don't rightly know, Mrs. Price," I heard Maples tell her. "He was here a little while ago, but they took him away."

Maples let me out of my coffin.

"Where did they take my husband?" she asked me, her face lined with concern. I judged she was not part of the performance. Rather, I hypothesized, they would soon be back to cart us in our coffins away for a mock burial, or something similar.

"It's some kind of a prank, ma'am. We're also being initiated this evening, and we have no idea where they took your husband. Maybe the sheriff can help you locate him."

Mrs. Price said some unkind things about the Cedar Valley Volunteer Fire Department, then strode out purposefully.

"What now?" Maples wanted to know.

I told him what I suspected and asked if he might be interested in playing our own trick on these guys, and he immediately agreed.

We went down the stairway and outside the fire hall, where I had earlier noticed a stack of sandbags. We carried eight of them up the steps and placed four in each coffin, closed the lids, and snapped the padlocks shut. Then we exited the hall, turning off the lights on our way out.

We got ourselves hidden in the shrubbery nearby just in time to avoid being seen by the errant firemen when they returned to the hall, climbing out of their cars and pickup trucks and trooping up the stairway. It struck me as a bit ominous that they weren't talking or having fun; it seemed all serious business. Could this bunch of elderly would-be fraternity boys actually have been dumb enough to risk a man's life throwing axes at him while he was spinning around on a carnival wheel? That seemed preposterous, even in a town like Cedar Valley.

In a couple of minutes we could hear them carrying the coffins down the stairs, bumping against the walls and having trouble maneuvering around the corners. They carried the coffins toward one of the pickup trucks parked in front of the hall.

One of the men chuckled and said, "These guys think they're real cute, actin' like they're unconscious. Just wait'll they hear us throwin' the dirt on top of 'em."

I elbowed Maples, giving him a grin. But he glanced at me wide-eyed, all serious.

We watched in fascination as eight of the men hoisted the coffins onto the bed of the truck and closed the tailgate.

"Where to?" I heard Booth ask Clyde Krafft.

"Same place. Might as well put all three of them in the same graveyard."

"You really think this is necessary?" Owens asked. "These guys never did anything to deserve anything like this. I'm sure we could swear them to silence, just like the rest of us."

"Absolutely not," Krafft said. "What'd happen to the rest of us if anybody found out what really happened in there tonight? Why we'd be tarred and feathered, and just for starters."

"Yes, but they never saw it happen. We could claim the preacher just ran off. Nobody's ever going to find him out there in that old graveyard."

"I'm against it," said a guy I didn't know. "If they told what they heard, there'd be a big investigation, and it'd be hell to pay. I say let's get rid of them too."

The acting was so good it was almost convincing. Of course, they thought we were listening from inside the coffins, and they were laying it on thick.

"Jesus Christ," Maples whispered to me. "They're talking about that old graveyard just off the county road up on Haskin's Hill. You think they buried the preacher there?"

"We'll find out," I whispered back. "Is your rig anywhere close?"

He pointed back over his shoulder to a pickup truck. We watched the men get back in their cars and trucks. When the last one pulled out, we got into Maples's rig and followed them, just like we were part of the procession. Along the way, Maples told me the graveyard was near an abandoned mining town that had flourished around the turn of the century, and that many of the graves had been pillaged over the years.

It took about thirty minutes to reach Haskin's Hill, where all the vehicles parked. We stopped about a hundred yards back down the road, turned the rig around, and stayed in the truck until the men had unloaded the two coffins. It was so dark we could barely discern their silhouettes as they trudged up the hill toward the old cemetery.

"How far is it to the graveyard?" I asked.

"About two hundred yards. What do you want to do, sneak up there after them?" Maples asked.

I told him my plan, and he bought in right away. We gave them a couple of minutes, then walked up the road to where all their vehicles were parked. One by one, we quietly got the hoods opened and collected the rotors from the distributors, replacing the distributor cap each time. Then we methodically let the air out of every tire on every vehicle, including all the spares for good measure. Meanwhile we could hear the men talking at the graveyard, apparently discussing where to dig the graves. Then we could hear them going to work with shovels.

We were walking back down the road to Maples's pickup joking about how we turned the tables on them when Maples said, "The dirty bastards probably killed the preacher after all."

"I don't know. I hope not. There has to be something fishy about this whole thing. Anyway, they're all in for a hell of a long hike home tonight."

"Well, if they didn't really kill the preacher, where would he be?"

"I'd be right about here," said a voice from the shadows next to Maples's pickup truck.

Dumbfounded, we looked into the face of Acton V. Price, who appeared calm and collected and smiled broadly at us.

"Why you dirty cocksucker," Maples began, catching himself

97

too late. "Uh, I mean, Reverend, how could you be a part of all this bullsh—uh, nonsense?"

"Yes, boys, I confess to playing a role in it. They made me do it as my part of the initiation. I saw your rig back down here and wondered who it was. I thought you were still in the coffins."

"What were they going to do to us up there at the cemetery?" I asked.

"They didn't tell me, but one of them said they'd know by morning how brave you were. That fellow Turpin said he didn't think you'd pass, Sandow, that you were basically yellow. He said he had a special test figured out for you. How'd you boys get out of your coffins?"

"Your wife. She came looking for you. Said you were needed urgently at the medical clinic in Purple Pond. Come on, we'll give you a lift back to town."

"But the others will wonder where I am. Perhaps I'd better tell them."

"They'll have other things to worry about," Maples said, tossing the bag of rotors into the back of his truck. "Better come along with us. You'll get there a lot faster."

We got back to town about ten thirty, dropped the preacher off at his house, and went to Kelley's for a beer. Kelley was alone in the place and had already had quite a few of his own drinks by the time we'd arrived.

"You boys aren't in on the initiation party tonight, I take it?"

"No, what's going on?" Maples asked.

"Ned Booth and Stan Turpin cooked it up. They've got a couple a dumb shits they're putting in coffins. Takin' 'em up to bury 'em on Haskin's Hill to scare the shit outta 'em. Then while they're freezin' their asses off up there the whole night, the rest of them'll be in here drinkin' it up."

"Sounds pretty good," I said. "Who they got lined up for this gag?"

Kelley sucked in about two ounces of straight bourbon whiskey. "Oh, lessee. I heard it was some idiot from the forestry and a dumb-ass logger works for Boardman. Ned Booth told me a sheepherder was supposed to dig them up in the morning, but that neither one of them had sense enough to find their way back to town. Haw haw haw haw."

"Yeah, well I bet they'll have some good stories to tell about this tomorrow," Maples said.

"You can count on that," Kelley said. "They should be here any minute."

"When they get here, will you give them a message from Mona?" I asked.

"Okay. What is it?"

"Just tell them she's having a special on rotors at her store tomorrow."

"Rotors? What the fuck you talking about?"

"Try to get it straight, Kelley. Rotors at Mona's tomorrow."

Kelley looked a little perplexed. "Motors at Rona's tomorrow, right?"

"Almost. It's rotors, not motors. Tomorrow, at Mona's."

"Got it. Rotors tomorrow, not motors at Mona's."

"Close enough. Only one other thing, Kelley."

"Yeah?"

"They won't be here tonight anyway, so might as well just forget it."

"Whyzat?"

"No rotors."

"Just motors," Maples added.

On the next Sunday, Felton Shackle caught up with me in the warehouse and asked if I'd be interested in filling in for the lookout on Coyote Peak while she and her husband attended a family funeral in Oregon. I immediately accepted, sensing another chance to find out things I needed to know. I'd already found out none of the recent arson fires were within direct view of any of the lookouts, so I thought it unlikely I'd get to discover one from Coyote Peak. But maybe I'd get lucky. And it was also another chance to get away from the putrid odors and crude jokes of the barracks for a few days. Shackle told me to be ready to go at seven the next morning, and to bring along things I'd need for the next three days.

That night I went to the telephone booth outside Chubby

Crump's gas station to call my parents. My father answered. He knew my mission and asked about progress. I tried to keep it vague enough so that some nosy telephone operator wouldn't catch on and do something with the information. Then my father gave me some news.

"Son, Phil's people got a call on you over at Becker Industries. Somebody wanted to know if you still worked there in the instrument calibration department. They gave the caller the agreed-on response, that you had quit in May and left town."

I figured it was Lois, a routine check. "Did they say why she called?"

"It was a man. He said it was a job reference check for the federal government. But then right after the call, the operator got Becker Industries back on the line and asked who had made the call, because the caller owed another seventy-five cents for overtime, like he might have called from a phone booth."

I stashed that in my head to think over later. "Okay, got it. Anything from the LAPD?"

"No, but I tested them myself. Called one day and asked how I could contact you, and they let me know that no such information would be made available by phone."

"That's good. It's working."

"So then I asked if they had an officer by your name in the department. The lady had me contact a Sergeant Perkins in community affairs. Perkins wanted to know why I wanted the information, and I told him I was old school friend lining up a reunion. He took my number and said if there were such an officer in the department, he'd be given the message and would decide himself whether to call back."

"You do good work, Dad. How's Mom doing?"

"She's out at the moment, playing cards. She'll be sorry to miss your call. She's all right as long as she stays busy. But just sitting around the house is killing her. All she can think about is you-know-who. I think it might help a lot if you can get away and come down here for a few days, take her mind off your brother."

I told him I'd try, knowing I wouldn't. Things were moving too well to give up the momentum at this point. Anyway, the middle of fire season was no time to ask for a week off. We hung up, and I dialed another number, a local one this time.

I loved the sound of Nora's voice on the phone. "Guess what?" I asked her.

"I know, you're going to invite me down to Kelley's to see a fight—one that you're starring in, naturally."

"Please. I've mended my ways, and the Forest Service has recognized this and decided to try me out on a special assignment."

"One that pays more, I hope?"

"Well, not that special, apparently. For the next three days I'll be the new lookout at Coyote Peak."

"Congratulations—I guess. What's it like up there?"

"Oh, the usual . . . terrific view, lots of atmosphere. Why don't you come up and see for yourself?"

"I'll give it some thought, but don't wait supper for me. I'm going to Klamath Falls in the morning and have no idea when I'll get back. Do you like red or white wine?"

"Yes."

"Idiot," she said laughing, and hung up.

Shackle and I got to the base of the lookout at eight, where we saw Diana Fulton beckoning us up. Diana's husband Art stayed below to finish loading their pickup.

Six flights of steel mesh stairs later we were in the cab of the lookout tower admiring an unparalleled view of the countryside for thirty miles or more in every direction.

"Diana's our best lookout," Shackle told me as she stood there blushing. "She can teach you more in five minutes than I could in a week. Don't screw up, now, Harper. Coyote Peak has more first discoveries right now than any other lookout on the forest. Have fun." With that he was gone, his heavy boots clanging down the steps.

I looked around at the strange combination of household items and tools of the lookout trade. "You're a very good housekeeper. I'll try not to mess it up for you."

She poured coffee into a china mug for me. "You just make yourself completely at home, Harper."

Her movements were those of a woman of thirty or so, but the liver spots on her hands and the leathery complexion suggested she was at least twice that age. I spotted a thirty-thirty in a corner and had no doubt she knew how to use it.

"When a storm cell gets to within a half mile," she began, "disconnect the radios and telephone, and stand on this stool."

The legs on the stool were tipped with inverted telephone line insulators.

"Everything in here is grounded—the refrigerator, the bed, the firefinder, the stove, and of course the tower itself. It can get pretty exciting in here when a bolt goes through the tower, but if you stay on the stool and don't touch anything, you'll be all right. You know how to take a reading with the firefinder?"

I shook my head.

"Just like aiming a rifle. Then you read the bearing from true north at this index. Don't worry about the vernier scale, just read it to the nearest half degree for now."

"Why are there two horizontal cross hairs in front?"

"They're for vertical readings. It helps at night, but don't worry about that for now."

"I can see a dozen smokes already. They're okay?"

"There's twenty-seven, all legitimate, and listed right here on this chart."

She went on for fifteen minutes, giving me a rapid-fire course that mainly taught me how little I knew about what went on in these isolated mountaintop pavilions. When she noticed how bewildered I began to look, she smiled mischievously and handed me a folder.

"It's all in here, even about feeding the pets. I found out a long time ago that folks only remember about ten percent of what they see, and almost nothing they hear."

"You discovered the Pegleg fire last year, didn't you?" I recalled that tidbit from the fire report.

"Yes I did." She turned involuntarily to look in that direction.

"Well, I was just curious. Do you remember seeing any dust on the road that leads up there before the fire started?"

"No, not that day. But I did see road dust the day before. That's one of the things you learn to take note of."

"Do you think there was any connection?"

"I just don't know about that. I reported it to Mr. Marklee, but didn't hear any more about it. Well, I've got to get moving before Art starts getting nervous down there. If you run into any problems, give Lois a call in the office. You'll do fine, young man." And then she was gone.

My first day went by in what seemed like five minutes, maximum. There were no fires, but I managed to report the Purple Pond dump and the Green Valley stud mill, both legitimate smokes. Lois told me later that two false reports was about average for the first day, and not to worry about it. The radios drove me crazy, two of them Forest Service sets and one a California Division of Forestry set, and they went on squawking all day. I had to listen for my call sign, and that distracted me from all the other things I was supposed to be doing. Then I had to listen for the Coyote Peak ring, two longs and a short, on the fucking telephone, and it seemed to be burping out Morse code all day.

Then, according to my instruction list, before leaving the tower to go to the head sixty feet below, I had to sign off on the Forest Service radio with a code number, then sign back on when I returned. Damn, I muttered. This had to be the only job in the world where you had to electronically advise two hundred people you were going to take a crap, and then afterward let them know everything came out okay. I vaguely wondered why only the Forest Service and not the California Division of Forestry needed to know about my toilet troubles.

Everyone had to play the game. Should one of the lookouts try to sneak out without signing off and then miss a radio call, the whole forest would soon hear another lookout say, "I think Lola is ten-seven for five minutes." Then after a period of silence, somebody else would come on the radio and say, "Welcome back, Lola."

I could see short portions of the road to the lookout from the tower and about an hour before sunset began watching the fork in the road, the one at which you could turn either toward the lookout or toward Hungry Camp to the north. If Nora were coming to the lookout, she would have to pass that fork. As I watched, a dust plume rose near the fork, so I grabbed the navy surplus 7-by-50 binoculars and caught sight of what well could have been a red Jeep in the fading light. The vehicle stopped at the fork for a few moments, then took the road north toward Hungry Camp.

Why north? I wondered. The directional sign at the fork could not be misunderstood. "Do you like red or white wine?" had sounded like an invitation accepted. Then I saw the second plume of dust, and in moments I could discern the bulk of a dark vehicle, possibly a pickup, arriving at the same fork. It too stopped for a few moments, then turned around and headed back down the mountain toward town. I lost sight of the second vehicle behind some intervening topography but watched for it to reappear a half mile or so below. It did not. Soon it became too dark even to see dust.

Had Nora suspected she was being followed and hence made the unexpected turn? Who drove the second vehicle, and why did he turn back? Why did he stop again? I decided not to succumb to an overactive imagination and forgot about it for the moment.

I put out food below the tower for Diana's deer, coyotes, and birds, filled their water pans from the cistern, then filled a bucket for my own use and attached it to the haul rope. Back inside the lookout cab, I found the gasoline lantern, and after a few minor explosions, got it burning with a bright white glow. But now I could no longer see out the windows due to the reflection of the glowing mantels. Moreover, the device produced an almost deafening roar, so I extinguished it and lit a candle instead. The effect was much more pleasant.

While waiting for my canned beef stew to warm up on the little propane stove, I checked out the thirty-thirty, a model 'ninety-four Winchester, old but in excellent condition. I opened the breech far enough to see a round in the chamber, which meant the weapon probably had a full load of seven rounds. I depressed the loading port on the side and verified that, then stood the rifle back in its corner.

I went outside on the catwalk. The darkness now obscured everything but vague shapes of trees nearby, mountains in the distance, and a few twinkling lights of towns in the valley to the south. The only sounds were those of rustling foliage and a few birdcalls, maybe nighthawks or owls. It was my first experience completely away from all other humans, and it gave me an eerie yet enchanted feeling.

The sound of an engine: a vehicle approaching, a dim shape coming up the hill nearby, but no lights. I felt my scalp tingle, and the sound of that shotgun blast that night on the road back from Purple Pond echoed in my head. Quickly stepping back into the cab, I grabbed the rifle, and went back out onto the catwalk. The vehicle stopped next to the base of the tower and the driver got out. I heard a feminine voice saying, "Is red wine all right?"

"I wanted to study medicine," she began, as we sat opposite one another at the little wooden table. The beef stew in the saucepan was getting cold, but I'd already forgotten about it, and anyway, the wine tasted good.

"I had this dream of going to college, then medical school, and someday being the town doctor in a place like Cedar Valley or Purple Pond. But when I graduated from high school there was no money, so we—my family and I—decided I'd work for a year and save enough to get through at least the first year of college. Great plan, huh? Anyway, it wasn't long before I met Ned. You knew we were married, didn't you?"

"Ned Booth?"

She nodded. "I found him very persuasive, very handsome, and I admired him a lot. He was quite a bit older than I was."

"You weren't really in love with him?"

"No, although at the time I was saying I thought I was. He should have married my mother. She was the one pushing the whole thing the most. If he'd courted me half as much as he did my mother . . . oh, I don't know."

"How long did the marriage last?"

"It never really was a marriage. It's a bad sign when you realize on the way out of the church that you just made a mistake." She poured each of us some more wine.

"But you stayed together."

"Yes. Why, who knows. So it was as much my fault as his, maybe more, when things blew."

"What happened? That is, if I'm not prying."

"It's all right. You're the only person in town who doesn't know about it. Ned was having an affair with the district ranger's wife. When the ranger found out, he confronted Ned and told him he'd bring charges if Ned didn't resign."

"You knew all that was going on?"

"Ned had to tell me. He loved his job and knew he couldn't explain quitting outright."

"Is that when he moved to Winchester?"

"Soon thereafter. I began divorce proceedings right away. Our marriage was such a mess by then it really didn't seem to bother him too much."

She didn't add anything to that, so I asked, "So you got your job in the sawmill office then?"

"No, that came later." She laughed a little. "Are you sure you really want to know what happened next?"

"If you'd like to tell me."

"I moved to Redding because I needed a job and there wasn't anything for me here. Also, they have a college there where I figured I could start taking classes. My dream, remember? I landed a bookkeeping job at the plywood plant in Anderson. It was a very good situation because my aunt, the one who lives in Purple Pond now, let me stay with her at her apartment."

I got up to stir the beef stew and put the coffeepot on one of the burners. I wondered if she'd eventually tell me about her affair with my brother. Glancing at her from a new angle always produced an exciting facet I hadn't yet noticed. It was easy to see why Heath had fallen for her, even without benefit of the candlelight.

"At the plywood plant I met a guy named Bill Jeffers. He seemed to meet all the expectations I'd ever hoped for in a man. You know, thinking back about it, it amazes me I was willing to throw aside all my ambitions just like that, but that's exactly what I did. As soon as my divorce from Ned was final, we got married."

"But you could still go to school, couldn't you?"

"Would you believe he was acquainted with Bob Boardman, and that Bob offered him the saw filer job at his sawmill here in Cedar Valley?"

"And he wanted to come to Cedar Valley to be a saw filer?"

"Of course. The filer is one of the most important men in the whole mill. Anyway, it felt funny to come back so soon, you know, with a new husband and all. I guess the feeling was, if you were smart enough or lucky enough to get out of Cedar Valley, nobody ever expected to see you again."

"And you kept your dream alive?" I tried not to imagine what it would have been like to be married to this woman.

"Yes. Our plan was that in two or three years he'd try to find a situation where he could have a good job *and* there'd be a school I could go to. He dreamed of owning a mill someday."

I knew what had to come next; that was, if she wanted to go on talking. I kept silent, and she blurted it out.

"A month after we moved to Cedar Valley, he got killed at the mill. Maybe you heard the story. He was electrocuted."

She stood up, turned away as if to stare out the window. I knew she was crying. I got up and simply put my arms around her, and we hugged for a few moments.

"How long ago did that happen?"

"It's been almost three years. Bill had no insurance, and the compensation payment didn't amount to very much. Bob Boardman immediately insisted I come to work in the mill office."

"You didn't want to get out of town, away from the mill forever?"

"That was my first impulse. But Sally, Bob's wife, was smarter than I was. We'd gotten to be good friends, and she made me stay. She told me I'd have to face down the situation right there, or I'd be agonizing over it for the rest of my life."

"And you think she was right."

"Absolutely. It was terrible at first, the sight of that ugly mill every morning, remembering how I felt when they told me . . . But do you know what was even worse?"

"Tell me."

"It was how people treated me. I don't mean Bob and Sally, they saved my life. But the others. People I had talked to and joked with on the street and in the store. You know, friends. They would actually cross the street to avoid having to face me. I was never invited anywhere or included in anything. At a time when I desperately needed friends and kind words, hell, even a smile, they avoided me like I had scarlet fever or something."

"I think a lot of people just don't know how to handle something like that. They think they might say the wrong thing, make matters worse. It's not comfortable for them."

"Then came the men I knew through Bill. His friends, married ones, of course. It wasn't a week after the funeral before they started coming at me. You know, like I really needed it, and they were willing to provide it. Bill would have killed them."

"How long did that go on?"

"I guess I became a rather nasty person. I didn't go out with any man for over a year. I threw myself into my job, and I actually began to like it a lot. I can handle anything that comes up in the office. Bob is going to be very unhappy some day when I leave this place."

"Back to your dream?"

"Not necessarily. I'm twenty-eight now, and not sure if I could put up with eight or more years of struggling in school, not to mention supporting myself in the meantime."

"Well, why might you leave, then?"

She laughed, but it sounded a bit hollow. "For almost any reason."

"Then I'll ask it this way: what's keeping you in Cedar Valley?"

"Because I'm not quite finished here."

"Meaning?"

"Nothing." She turned away.

The exchange hit me like a sledgehammer, but I decided against pushing it right then, and clammed up.

"Well," she said, turning back and giving me a devastating smile, "What about the supper you promised me?"

We did supper, such as it was, and when the wine she'd brought petered out, I opened the bottle I'd brought, and we made a party out of it. She worked me for details on my life. I was ready for it, having rehearsed the story mentally several times, and it seemed as if she had a few traps laid in her questions. But then maybe it was only my imagination. When I tried to direct the conversation back toward her life after Bill died, she waved me off or changed the subject.

Two things bothered me: why wasn't she saying anything about her affair with Heath, and what was it she hadn't finished here in Cedar Valley? I thought maybe the second bottle of wine would lead to some revelations along those lines, but she turned out to be tougher than I thought, at least in that respect.

Chapter 7

I learned a lot in three days at Coyote Peak. In reading through Diana's logbook I found she tracked the location of Forest Service units operating in her area, by radio check-ins and dust plumes. She had also noted the sightings of vehicles, dust plumes, or windshield reflections along seldom traveled roads, and unusual sightings such as airplanes at low altitude and blinking lights at night. I thought about two of the suspect fires that fell within Coyote Peak's general area of visibility, but this logbook was fairly new and didn't go back as far as those dates. I couldn't find any older ones in the lookout and supposed Diana had sent them in to the office for storage.

I'd also found out a lot about Nora Jeffers, at least those things she chose to tell me, and I'd been careful not to push too hard to fill in the blank spots. As we grew closer, I thought, she would yield more about sensitive subjects. Or would she? The thought brought up a bothersome point: if she had already figured out my identity and purpose, why didn't she confront me about it? Would this pose a risk to her, cause her to lose some advantage?

There was another possibility. She might have figured me for Heath's brother when we first met, then given up that idea after checking up on me either through somebody in the Forest Service who would have access to my application, or maybe by checking with Becker Industries, as did the caller my father told me about. Heath surely told her his brother was an L.A. cop, and her little investigation might have satisfied her to the contrary.

I had to fight my emotions to keep from going crazy over her, especially while we were together in the lookout that evening. One set of signals told me to plunge ahead, while the other advised me to be cautious, figure things out first. Too, while she seemed warm and sensuous, there had been an aura of reservation on her part. Was she still too much in love with my brother's memory to let herself go, or was she too concerned about my estimate of her readiness to get involved again so soon? I probably came across as an uncertain klutz or an impotent baboon, but I kept thinking about her love affair with Heath, and it robbed me of decisiveness or something. Maybe I felt guilty about using her as a source of information and pretending it was the beginning of a love affair. Or was I falling in love, not wanting to, and looking for a morally proper escape route?

When I'd seen her to her Jeep that evening, I found myself asking if she'd go with me to the Saturday night dance, and she accepted. What was it she'd said? "You're going to be surprised at what happens at a Cedar Valley dance."

"Why not? I've been surprised by everything else that's happened here."

"And a lot more may happen if you don't watch out." She planted a kiss on me that I still remember.

I just stood there for a while, listening to the fading sound of her Jeep going down the mountain. I tried to recall everything she had said as we sat together in the lookout that evening. But most of it was already blurry. Was it the wine, or that I'd been looking and wondering, rather than listening?

Punky Swiftbird gave me a ride back to Cedar Valley on Wednesday night, entertaining me along the way with an account of how Albert Carlisle had got lost in the woods during work and the crew had spent three hours trying to find him.

"Well, it was really only two hours," he said, "Because the first hour was an argument over whether finding him would be worth it or not."

"What happened? Couldn't he find the truck at quitting time?"

"That's what they figured, until they found his pruning saw leaning against a tree. So they decided he'd wandered off somewhere. His foreman came back and got me to bring Donald out to track him down. I grabbed one of Albert's shirts for scent, and we were able to locate him."

"How far away had he gone?"

"Shit, he hadn't gone away at all. There he was, asleep in the crew truck. Been there since lunch time."

"So the crew is down on him again."

"Still. Be glad you weren't there last night. They removed the struts on his bed that keep the legs from folding under. Everybody heard it go down about ten. Then it went down again a few minutes later. That happened about four or five times."

"Did he finally give up and sleep on the floor?"

"Aw shit, I shouldn't have told you."

"Come on, he didn't sleep in my bed, did he?"

"I'm afraid so. But he's a nice guy, what the hell?"

"Yeah? When did he take a shower last?"

"Last? We don't know for sure if he's ever taken one."

"Oh, crap. Drop me off at the motel. I'm off tomorrow anyway."

The next morning I returned to the barracks, replaced Albert's cot with another from the warehouse, laundered both my sheets and his, and made both beds.

I already knew how I was going to spend the rest of the day. A week or so earlier I'd located a copy of the Pegleg fire investigation report in the office and had copied a map showing Heath's movements leading up to his death. With it I figured I could locate the place where he'd died. This was not something I particularly looked forward to doing, but nonetheless, something that had to be done. I think it was my way of spending a last few moments with him, of saying goodbye to my brother forever.

I'd found my way to the edge of the burn before but hadn't

113

gotten much beyond the point of origin, which was near the bottom of the burn. This second trip took me along a road somewhat through the center of the area, and the appearance of the place surprised me. The image that I had created on hearing of Heath's death was that of a blackened moonscape, the charcoal spires of burned-out trees standing their grotesque vigil against the skyline. I did see a few patches like that, but much of the place more resembled a hilly park, one where trees were scorched but not destroyed. Shrubs were sprouting anew, little bunches of grass were poking up, and birds flitted around amongst the foliage. It made me wish Heath were buried there; he would have liked that.

Heath had parked his pickup at a spot where the road widened as it rounded the nose of a hill, a place where he could have looked over the country immediately below. I found it readily, as there was only one such spot. Then I walked down the slope along the course I guessed he must have followed looking for the trapped tractor. In only a few minutes I stumbled onto the fireline the tractor operator had been building when the fire spotted below him.

I walked to the end of the fireline, turned around, then walked slowly back along the tractor's path, studying the ground. Then I saw it—a piece of orange surveyor's tape tied around the top of a wooden stake in the ground. The tractor was of course gone, the shovel was gone, Heath was gone. All that remained was the little depression my brother had dug out in his last desperate attempt to stay alive, and the wooden stake that marked the place where he found it impossible to do so.

It's curious how a damn piece of wood with a ribbon on it can bring you to your knees, make the emotions well up so that the world seems to stop turning, make you wonder whether life is worthwhile, and if so, what it might mean. But it did that to me, and I haven't been able to look unemotionally at a surveyor's stake ever since. It was a hell of a gravestone, and I guess I held my own private memorial services right there and then.

I scooped out the loose soil that had sloughed into the little trench, then lay face down in it as my brother had done a year ago and tried to perceive his emotions and thoughts during those last few moments of life. Having been badly frightened on the fireline myself only a few weeks earlier, it wasn't hard to do. And for a minute I became my brother again, seeing myself at a distance in a policeman's blue uniform, waving goodbye.

The experience almost paralyzed me, almost made me crumble and become a part of the soil, so much was I overwrought by anguish and torment, and it was a struggle to pull myself to my knees. When at last I did, I realized I was whole and somehow, suddenly unburdened of the sorrow and self-pity that had been consuming me.

I guess I just knelt there for a while studying the surroundings, promising Heath I would come back someday, but suspecting that maybe I would not. There was something more important to promise him that day, and I did.

During the trip back to Cedar Valley I felt like a changed person, one who had turned a corner in life. I guess that's what funerals are really good for, but I'd never thought of it that way before. Somehow the "official" funeral at that joint in Sunland hadn't quite done it for me like this one had, a year later. I now felt released and ready to squarely face what I'd come to this place to do.

When Albert got back from work, he sat down on his cot, not noticing that it didn't collapse or that it had clean sheets. I didn't volunteer anything, nor did he ask. He had apparently erased the entire incident from his consciousness, assuming he had any. He got right to work on one of his manuscripts and would have missed supper if I'd not gone back for him. I envied his remarkable ability to concentrate his thinking on a particular subject, vaguely wondering if he'd survive such single-mindedness.

At work Saturday we had a full crew except for Larry Banks and spent the morning on first-aid training and hose-lay drills. The fire danger had climbed to the lower part of the extreme range, and most of the crew hoped for a fire. I paid close attention to their comments and soon found myself figuring out who had which days off. Should a fire break out that day, for example, Larry Banks's whereabouts would become significant. But none of the lookouts called in any smokes, and the workday ended like any other.

Nora had a small apartment on Fir Street, and when she opened the door, I thought at first I had the wrong place. Again, she had achieved a different look, and I wasn't sure whether it was the upswept hairdo or the fact I'd never yet seen her in a dress and high heels.

"Is this one of the surprises?" I asked, nodding my head in approval.

"Only a minor one," she laughed, waving me in. "I don't want to spoil it for you by giving things away."

"Maybe I can handle it."

"Well, don't count on it. You people come up from the big city thinking you've seen it all."

"What haven't I seen, for example?"

"You haven't seen me, for example."

"That's true. How am I going to remember what you look like?"

She laughed, taking a playful swing at me. "It's too early to go to the dance. I should have told you nine. Now we'll have to have a glass of wine or something."

"What does the 'something' include?"

"What would you like it to include?"

When she asked it, the playful glimmer was suddenly gone from her face and voice, replaced at least for the moment by a more somber tone. I thought of our evening together in the lookout and my after-the-fact distress about being so indecisive, a train of thought that momentarily tongue-tied me. She sensed my discomfort.

"You must have thought me a horror, laying all that misery on you that night, all that nonsense about poor me. You should have just pushed me over the rail or something."

"You needed to get it out. Talking about it helps, and I sure didn't mind listening."

She worked a corkscrew into a bottle of wine as we talked. "You didn't seem ready to talk about your life, so you deserved what you got. I won't do that to you again."

116

A lock of hair fell across her face as she struggled to pull out the cork. I couldn't tell if she was on the point of laughing or crying, and I brushed back the lock of hair, bringing my cheek close to hers. Her eyes locked onto mine, and I said, "You can do absolutely anything you want and I'll love it."

She squinted at me. "I want you to do something really important for me, something I'll never forget."

"What?" I asked, marveling at my inability to say it any better than that.

"Pull this damn cork out of the bottle before I go crazy."

When we had each finished a glass of the wine and I was about to pour another, she stopped me with her hand.

"Let's get going. We don't want to miss the opening number. It may be the only one they've practiced. Shall we walk? It's only about a block and a half."

As we turned off Fir onto the main road, we could hear a loud din emanating from Kelley's, and I counted eight cars parked in front of the place.

"Looks like they're getting an early start. I gather there's no drinking in the ladies club hall."

"None permitted," Nora said, "Which didn't used to be the case. One time a couple of years ago everybody got smashed and it turned into a real brawl. Windows broken, furniture destroyed, pies stuck on the wall. Somebody even went to the bathroom right there in the kitchen. I mean serious bathroom."

"Nice group. So that ended things for a while?"

"No more drinking in the club hall. Big deal. Now they stand around outside and do it. The ladies club let it be known that any future incidents of damage or drunkenness inside the hall would mean the end of dances there. This will be the first dance since that incident."

We looked through the window of Mona's Groceries and saw Mona hunched over a ledger, squinting through the smoke of her cigarette and clutching a coffee mug. She looked up and waved. Nora got close to the window and hollered at Mona, asking if she was coming to the dance.

"Nobody invited me," she hollered back. "Anyway, I've got

too much work to do figuring out how much the forestry guys owe me."

"She sure lets us have it. If it weren't for us, she'd probably go broke," I said as we walked across the street toward the ladies club hall.

Nora began laughing. "She was serious. I was in there one day when all the Forest Service people had received their paychecks. Punky Swiftbird came walking in to cash his check and pay his bill. Before he'd even torn open the envelope Mona told him it would be forty-seven dollars and ninety-five cents out of one eighty-one twenty."

"I see. Now I know why he refers to her as Mother CPA."

The ladies club hall sat on a little knoll above an unpaved parking area shaded by tall elm and maple trees. People were standing around by their cars, talking and smoking, waiting for things to begin inside. On the porch we passed Stan Turpin, who glared at us from behind a cigarette as he leaned against the railing. I nodded at him, but, his gaze locked on Nora, he didn't notice. She nodded at him and murmured a hello, but he didn't respond. I idly wondered if it was he who'd followed Nora up the road toward the lookout. He hadn't spoken to me or even looked in my direction since the fire department initiation. I figured he would have been rather pissed, but then he could have at least complimented me on my ingenuity or something.

"Three dollars, please," announced a plump and fortyish man in a Boy Scout uniform, replete with sash and merit badges. Nora introduced him to me as Howard Hickey.

"It's a benefit for Troop Two-ninety-two," he said. "I'm the scoutmaster."

I handed over the money. "Nice jackknife," I said, pointing at the multitool implement dangling from a clip at his waist. "Standard issue?" Nora almost burst out laughing, but I managed to keep a straight face.

Howard forced out a grin. Then he stamped the backs of our hands, assuring us we could get back in without paying again.

"You mean, you won't remember us?"

"Standard procedure. Anyway, I go off duty at ten, and my relief won't know who paid. We're doing this one by the book."

"Uh, right. Attention to detail is important." I gave him a knowing nod, and we walked inside.

"Nora, that guy is too flabby to be a logger and too dumb even to be a ranger. Where did they get him?"

"He drives the school bus. The kids love him. He also plays the organ and does handyman stuff at the church. He's a bit weird, but apparently harmless."

Maybe, I thought, making a mental note to check for his name among the fire time-slip records in the office.

The band began blasting out their first number, and what they lacked in quality they compensated for with volume. I recognized Ray Owens banging away on the drums, and the cowboy Steve Christian twanging an amplified guitar. An attractive elderly lady was belting out questionable chords on an ancient upright, and a giraffesque young man played a quarter-size violin. As he fingered the strings of the tiny instrument with his huge left hand, it looked somewhat like a giant picking his nose with four fingers. The music brought people inside from the parking area, and soon everybody started dancing. Nora seemed to know everyone, and after each greeting identified for me the people I didn't know. I tried hard to couple the names with the faces that whirled by us.

Despite the deplorable music, Nora danced so lightly as to defy the existence of gravity, anticipating my movements precisely. Except for the sensation of touching her hand and waist, I danced with an illusion, a body without substance. But this sensation ended abruptly each time the hulking bodies of loggers and cowboys with their equally hulking partners came crashing into us at what the navy calls "ramming speed." They didn't apologize, just laughing it off as people do in bumper cars at carnivals.

In a half hour I'd had enough, and walked Nora out onto the front porch of the hall. In the shadows I could see a group of men passing a bottle around and discerned among them the silhouettes of Punky Swiftbird, Felton Shackle, and Stan Turpin. Then I noticed the patrol car of deputy J. P. Dhrymes parked beneath a maple tree down by the main road and wondered what he might be waiting for.

A big Oldsmobile pulled up in the parking lot, and a flashy-looking young woman in cowgirl getup emerged and headed into the hall. I took her to be the girl I'd seen with Christian that night in Purple Pond. She passed close by us, and I got a load of her perfume and tight costume. She gave Nora a warm greeting.

"Friend of Steve Christian's," Nora said, smiling at my reaction.

"Not a high school cheerleader, then?"

"Hardly. Abigail's pushing thirty-five."

"I didn't notice, I was distracted by the other stuff."

"So is everybody else. I like her a lot. She's had a tough life, usually falling for guitar-playing cowboy types like Steve Christian, then having things turn out badly."

"How did you get to know her?"

"She was going with a friend of Ned's, and we went out a few times together. She wanted to be a singer in a western band but didn't have the talent. So she settled for trailing along with guys who did and kind of being a colorful personality for whatever band the guy would be with. Once in a while Steve beats up on her, like when he's drunk, or thinks she's been two-timing him, but she seems to think he's curable."

"I know the type. So you still see her once in a while?"

"She usually stays in Purple Pond these days. It's not far from the ranch where Steve works. She calls me now and then, tells me her troubles."

"And you tell her yours?"

"Right now I don't have any," she said, suddenly planting a little kiss on my lips. The way she did it almost made me dizzy. Or maybe I was already a bit dizzy just being around her.

We came back inside and stood there watching. Steve Christian was singing, and his voice sounded terrific. Abigail was already sailing around the dance floor with some logger, the tassels of her white cowboy boots flailing the air, her long blond hair swirling behind her.

We heard a crash and saw Clyde Krafft on the floor, his dancing partner, Vivian Crump, on top of him. She tried to get up, but his hand had somehow got caught in her bodice, and he was unable to let go. Or maybe he was refusing to let go. In the struggle a couple of buttons came off Vivian's blouse and those of us who were close enough could see that Clyde's finger was securely hooked into Vivian's bra between the cups, which were fairly large. She tried to twist his fingers to make him let go, and he simply pulled harder, snapping the connection and allowing Vivian's boobs to pop free to the merriment of all who took it in, including the women.

As the postmistress scurried for cover in the kitchen, two men got Clyde up off the floor, dragged him to a chair at the side of the dance floor and propped him up. Vivian's husband, Chubby, was outside the hall at the time and missed the action.

"That's early for Clyde," Nora said. "He doesn't usually go down until the second set."

"I don't know if the band will manage a second set. They're about half shot right now."

"There's usually three sets, but they might not make it. Looks like Steve has had a few already."

Steve looked okay to me, but then I hadn't seen him in action that much. Maybe Nora had.

The set ended, and Nora excused herself for a minute. I eased over toward the bandstand and got there just in time to see the band passing a bottle of Jim Beam among them. When it got to Christian he tipped it up and sucked in at least a cupful before Ray Owens jerked it away from him. "Jesus Christ," Owens growled. "If I'd known you were thirsty I'd a brought a fucking canteen."

"Well, go get the mother." Christian wiped his mouth on one of his sleeves. "And I don't mean with water in it."

"You'd best hold off on the bottle until we get through here. You're already half in the bag."

"Fuck you and all your dumb-ass ranger friends. If you don't like it I'll pull my fuckin' *gui*tar and go over and play in Kelley's."

I gave Ray a smirk, and Christian whirled around and caught me at it.

"What the fuck are you lookin' at?" he snarled.

Remembering Swiftbird's comments about him and his fighting proclivities, I decided not to escalate things. "Sorry, friend. Just wanted to tell you how much I enjoyed the music, and I hope you don't leave early."

He studied my face to see if I meant it. "Okay. We're just

getting warmed up." He gave Owens a swat across the back, then headed out the door saying something about Kelley's.

"Well, there goes the dance," said Owens with a sigh. "I never should a brought that bottle in here, but he said he wasn't going to drink anything tonight."

"He won't be back?"

"Oh yeah, he'll be back all right. That's what's worrying me. Next time don't do me any favors. And I owe you one for that initiation sucker job you pulled on us."

"What time did you all get back to town that night?"

"That night, shit! It was more like four in the morning. Then the ones with vehicles up there got a compressor rig from Chubby's and went back to pump up their tires. It was daylight by then, of course."

I tried to keep a straight face, knowing what was coming next.

"Well, when they found out their rotors were gone, I guess there was talk of mayhem." Owens started laughing. "Thank God I left my rig in town that night."

"Did Kelley tell them where their rotors were?"

Owens took a swig out of the bottle and offered it to me. I indicated no thanks. "What I heard was that they sent Booth and Turpin in to Winchester that morning to buy new ones. Those two had thought up the stunt, so they got elected. It wasn't till they got back that everybody found out Mona had the rotors."

"Well, did Sid, the preacher, and I pass the initiation?"

"We took a vote on it a few days later, after the guys had cooled off. The consensus seemed to be that if you guys were that much smarter than the rest of us dumb shits, the least we should do is make you members of the department. That wasn't unanimous, I might add, most of the no votes coming from the ones who took their rigs up there."

"Was Turpin's one of them?"

"You better believe it."

I walked outside to join one of the groups near the porch. A guy identified to me earlier by Nora as Codie Foster was offering around his pack of Camels.

"I thought you tough old cowboys rolled your own," said

Swiftbird, pulling one out of the pack. "These tailor-mades must belong to your wife or somebody."

"No," Codie drawled in West Texas tones, "She rolls hers too. I think I found these in a hotel down in Red Bluff. Some pimp or queer left 'em on a table. Thought you forestry guys would like 'em too."

Punky Swiftbird's eyes looked glazed, but he laughed and said, "Why, Codie, is that the kind of place you stay at when you go down there? I didn't know you were that way." Swiftbird then sashayed around, his hands on his hips like an effeminate male. Everybody howled.

"Naw, not me, Codie said. "I was lookin' for one of you rangers and figured there'd be a lot of you in there."

During the conversation, I kept an eye on Dhrymes's patrol car down by the main road. When my eyes became accustomed to the darkness, I could see him standing in the shadows, leaning against a tree, looking in the direction of the club hall. When cars passed along the main road, he paid no attention.

I went back inside and found Nora drinking coffee and talking to the women preparing refreshments to sell at the second break. "What's going on outside?" Nora asked me.

I beckoned her aside and asked, "You sure you want to hang around for the rest of this? The guys are getting pretty loaded out there."

"We can leave if you want, Harper, but you'll be missing all the fun."

"Okay, one more set. How bad can it get?"

"You'll have to stay to find out." She tugged me toward the door.

We took a walk through the parking lot and down the main road past Kelley's, where things were getting even noisier. On the way back we passed the deputy, and he eyeballed us in silence. I gave him a little wave, but he just stared past me.

"Friendly sort, isn't he?"

"I don't think he likes you, Harper. Surprised?"

"Nor you, after that night in the bar. I'll bet he'd like to haul both of us in on a five-oh-two." I bit my tongue the instant I'd said it.

"On a what?"

"A DWI. . . . Drunk driving."

"Oh. Right. This would be the wrong evening to go driving around here. You have a drink with the boys?"

"Yeah, but I held it down to about a pint." She elbowed me, then put her arm around my waist, and we headed back to the club hall. The band was playing again when we got there, much louder now, especially Christian's guitar. Instead of dancing, we stood off to one side and watched the collisions and outright falls, laughing together and enjoying it.

Christian was singing every song now, and each one was louder than the one before. Some of the dancers were holding their ears and yelling for him to turn down his amplifier, but he was too engrossed in his music to perceive it. By this time his body was oscillating so wildly he would have fallen off the bandstand had he not been able to steady himself on the mike stand.

Then suddenly the mike and the amplifier went dead, silencing Christian's voice and his twanging guitar. He realized it in an instant and started looking around to see what might have gotten disconnected. But most of the dancers started applauding, and he went berserk.

"All right, ya dead-head hermaphrodite sonsa bitches and bastards," he screamed. "If you don't like my singin' I don't give a Chinese rat fuck. You can all go listen t' the goddamn juke-fuckin'-box as far as I give a red possum shit."

The rest of the music crashed to a halt, and everybody stopped dancing to stare slack-jawed and horror stricken at the source of this assault on propriety. But Steve Christian was just getting started. Somebody made the mistake of yelling at him to knock it off, and then he really got into it.

As a marine, and later as an LA cop, I'd run into some pretty salty characters and heard some extremely foul language. But that did little to prepare me for the fusillade of obscenities the cowboy spat out while the crowd was still too stunned to stop him. Christian accused everyone present of having been party to every sexual deviation I'd ever heard of, plus several I'd not, and he did so with the most colorful, yet most obnoxious and profane language known within the English speaking world. Terrible as it was, I judged it as world class, and regret not having been able to record it all for future study.

Unbelievably, it went on and on, and with no repetitions I can recall. The kingdom of Cedar Valley stood paralyzed for long moments, not believing what they'd just heard, probably not having much idea what the hell it even meant. Then, slowly, the enormity of the verbal outburst began to sink in, and the men rose up to defend the presumed moral chastity of their womenfolk. In moments, half a dozen men had scooped up the smashed cowboy and rushed him out the front door to pile him and his guitar, amplifier, and hat in a heap next to his purple 1951 Cadillac.

"I wouldn't go back in there, cowboy," one of the loggers told him, "unless you're lookin' to drink outta the toilet after we've all shit in it."

"Yeah, asshole," added another man. "You can clean up your goddamn language or stay the hell outta our motherfuckin' town."

Nora and I, along with others, watched the scene from the front porch. Then we all went back inside, where the band tried to regroup and get another tune going, but the mood had changed, and some people were already leaving. Vivian Crump, her clothing repaired, was in charge of selling the elaborate refreshments at the next break. She apparently sensed impending disaster and began getting the pies, cakes, cookies, and coffee out on the tables at the rear of the room for some quick sales.

The band was playing even louder now, trying to hold the dancers on the floor, but after a few minutes Nora pulled me off to one side and told me to listen, pointing toward the front of the hall. In a moment I heard it: a series of smashing noises and tinkling glass. We hurried to the front porch and got a view of Steve Christian going from car to car with a carpenter's hammer, smashing windshields, headlights, taillights, and bodywork, all in a fairly workmanlike and methodical manner. I shouted at him but he didn't react, continuing his demolition program as if it were his regular job.

As more dancers came out of the hall to be amazed by Christian's mayhem, I caught sight of Abigail running toward her Oldsmobile just as Christian got there with his hammer. She grabbed him and they struggled briefly. He slapped her with an open hand, hard enough to knock her off her feet. Then he began smashing up her Oldsmobile. She got up and ran to his purple Cadillac, jumped in, and zoomed away, rooster tails of dirt and gravel spewing behind her through the parking lot. When she reached the main road, she made a sliding right turn, heading north at full throttle. I caught sight of the deputy taking out after her, perhaps figuring it was the cowboy at the wheel.

When Christian saw his Caddy disappearing into the night, he dropped the hammer, looked around for a moment and spotted a guy getting into a yet undamaged Chevrolet in an attempt to make a hasty exit. Christian pulled the guy out of the Chevy, punched him in the eye, got into the car, and started in pursuit of his Cadillac. But he failed to negotiate the turn onto the main road, smashing broadside into a Buick Century parked in front of Mona's Groceries. Both cars burst into flames on impact.

Everybody was already out in front of the hall by this time, and at the sound of the crash they forgot about their own cars and ran toward the wreck. The impact also brought a crowd out of Kelley's, many of them members of the volunteer fire department, and they also ran toward the flames. Nora and I just sort of stood there in amazement.

Then came male voices shouting to get the fire engine, the station house being just around the corner on Fir Street. I told Nora to stay on the porch and ran toward the wrecked cars to see if anybody might be trapped inside. When I got there, the flames were completely enveloping both cars, the intense heat keeping me back about twenty feet. Some men were shouting to stay back, that the gas tank would explode. I knew from police training that wouldn't happen, but it didn't matter anyway as far as saving anybody was concerned.

In a moment I heard the roar of the American La France fire engine screeching around the corner of Fir Street onto the main road and saw the chief, Clyde Krafft, hunched over the wheel. The way I figured it later, the hand throttle must have been all the way out, because Clyde and the American La France shot by the fire at about thirty-five miles per hour. Also he was quite drunk. He got the rig stopped a couple of blocks up the road and attempted turning it around. I say attempted, because as he was backing up, he ran the truck into a power pole, severing it and knocking out all the lights and telephones in Cedar Valley.

Finally he pulled up opposite the burning vehicles and began maneuvering the truck so as to back toward the fire. As he did so, members of the department began pulling hoses off the rear end and getting the pump primed. But Clyde misjudged the distance and backed solidly into the two cars, the firemen jumping aside at the last moment.

"Go forward! Go forward!" men were yelling. But Clyde was having a bad night, and managed to get the fire engine in the wrong gear. When he gunned the engine, the truck plunged rearward, pushing the two burning cars through the plate glass windows into the front of Mona's Groceries.

I thought of the Forest Service pumper and ran the three blocks to the station to get it. But as I arrived, I saw the pumper already rolling out, with Ned Booth at the wheel, which surprised me, because he didn't even work for the Forest Service anymore. I hopped aboard and, red lights flashing and siren whooping, we sped to the fire.

We pumped our teeny forestry stream on the rear of the American La France, which was now clear of the main blaze, and got the truck fire put out, but the store was now fully involved and there was no way to save it.

"Did Mona get out?" asked Nora, grabbing my arm.

"I don't know. But it looks like nobody was trapped in either of the cars. Shit, we can't even call for any help."

Felton Shackle was standing there directing the Forest Service men who had arrived, and he told me he'd just radioed the Forest Service dispatcher in Winchester, who in turn was alerting all the authorities and other fire departments in the area.

By now most of the town had turned out to watch the fire and look at all the cars with their windshields and headlights smashed out. Word was being passed about that the guitar-twanging cowboy had caused the whole thing, and that so far, nobody could find him.

Soon, people's astonishment turned to rage, and there was talk of a tar-and-feathering, perhaps even a lynching in Cedar Valley.

I saw two groups stalking around with pick handles and shotguns, getting ready to conduct a house-to-house search. I heard several people saying, "We'll find the fucking guitar player if it takes all night."

"Oh, no," people started saying, pointing to the ladies club hall. I could hear glass shattering, boards cracking, giant thumping noises, shouting. It looked like an angry mob was taking revenge for their wrecked cars inside the ladies club hall. I didn't even want to go look at what might be happening in there.

A crowd had gathered around somebody, so Nora and I went over, thinking it might be the cowboy. But standing there in bathrobe and slippers was Mona, clutching an old suitcase, telling and retelling the story of her escape from the store by a back window.

"But you did manage to save some personal things of value, dear," gushed one woman, patting the suitcase as one would pat a puppy.

"Not a damned thing," Mona said. "All I had time to grab was the accounts receivable files."

A poorly muffled groan went up from the group, most of whom undoubtedly owed Mona lots of money.

"Was the place insured?" asked another woman.

"It was. I don't remember for how much, and the policy got burned up in there. But whatever it is, I'm going to rebuild it. Ain't no fucking guitar player running me out of my own town."

In a little while, sheriff's cars began showing up, officers trying to take charge of the situation. Fire departments from distant communities arrived one by one, too late to do anything but pump water onto the charred remains of Mona's Groceries. Winston Burdett, the county sheriff, arrived in blue jeans and cowboy boots, and after a brief perusal of the scene, started talking to witnesses. When he got to me, I told him what I'd seen and described the cowboy's Cadillac for him. He went back to his car to make some radio calls, obviously upset that the whereabouts of his deputy J. P. Dhrymes was unknown.

"I'm worried about Abby," Nora told me. "If they can't find the deputy, it might be bad news."

I glanced at my watch. Over an hour had elapsed since Abigail had roared away in the purple Caddy, the deputy right behind her. "Where do you think she would have headed?"

"She knows the back roads. She and Steve have fished the creeks and nosed all around. I doubt with Dhrymes on her heels she would have stayed on a main highway for long. She's played those games with the police before, with various boyfriends."

"Want to go for a drive?"

She grabbed my arm, and we hurried back to her place and I got my Ford fired up while she ran inside to put on jeans and low-heeled shoes. Then we headed north out of town, speculating on where Abby might have turned off the highway. About four miles from town we came to the turnoff I had taken my first night in the valley, and I braked to a halt. I could see no fresh traces of dirt at the point where the dirt road met the blacktop. That meant to me that one or more cars could have left the highway here, but none had come out recently. So we started up the road.

I drove fast, watching for any headlights coming our way around the curves, and suddenly a huge car loomed in front of us, its headlights extinguished. I stabbed the brakes, as did the other driver, and we halted only about five feet short of colliding. When the dust settled, Nora and I stared in amazement: it was the purple Cadillac, with Abby at the wheel.

All three of us jumped out, and the two women embraced. Abby looked like she'd been in a tussle, her hair messed up, her blouse held together in the front by a single button, her white cowboy vest missing.

"Did that son of a bitch Dhrymes get to you?" Nora asked.

"Almost. Listen, I've got to stash this car in a spot Steve and I know about. Follow me there, will you? It's his only chance to get out of here."

"Where's the deputy?" I asked. "We didn't meet him coming out."

"He's still up there," she said, gesturing over her shoulder with her thumb. "He's not going anywhere tonight. I'll explain later, just help me spot this car and get me out of here, okay?"

Nora gave me a glance that said *just do it,* and so we did.

129

Chapter Eight

A fter hiding the Cadillac at the end of a dead-end logging spur, the three of us drove back through Cedar Valley, taking a back road so as not to be seen passing the scene of the fire. Abby refused to start talking about it until she'd had a drink. We got to Nora's house about two, and over brandy and coffee, Abby finally began to relax.

"I want to tell you about this, in case anything happens to me," she began. "If I'm in trouble . . . well, it won't be the first time. Just promise me you won't say anything about where the car is, okay?"

Nora immediately agreed. I don't like making promises like that and said so, but in the case of J. P. Dhrymes, I told her, no problem.

"I think he thought it was Steve." Abby lit a third cigarette. "He's been laying for him over several things that have happened around here. So when I went by squealing my tires it shouldn't have surprised me that he came after me. I'd only got a half mile past the sawmill when I saw his lights in my rearview, and I was doing about seventy-five by that time. I knew about the Foster Creek road, and fortunately it was just around a turn in the highway. So when I turned off and doused my lights I figured I could lose him.

"He must have seen my dust as he passed the turnoff and then backed up and come after me, 'cause it wasn't very long before I saw his headlights again. Without my lights, I was just barely missing trees and boulders and things, and anyway I was leaving a hell of a dust behind me, so I turned the lights back on and drove as fast as I could, looking for someplace to hide. But shit! I came to the end of the road where it hits a campground, and there was nowhere to run. When he saw he had me, he just parked his car at the campground entrance, blocking the road. There was no place I could go."

"You just stayed in the car?" Nora asked.

Abby nodded. "It wasn't the first time a cop ever ran me down. He gets out of the patrol car, you know, putting on his Smokey Bear hat, and with a long flashlight in his hand. He had his other hand on his gun butt, figuring it was Steve, I suppose. Anyway, he flashes the light on me and says, 'Outta the car.'

"I get out, and now he sees who it is, and he runs the flashlight beam up and down me several times, then says, 'Driver's license and car registration?' I told him I didn't have my purse with me, that I wasn't expecting to drive tonight and all that, you know. Then I looked for the registration and couldn't find it. The glove compartment was full of guitar strings, cigarettes, chewing to-bacco, everything but the registration.

" 'Is this your car?' he wants to know. I tell him it belongs to my boyfriend back at the dance, and he wants to know what I'm doing way out here. I tell him I got scared when I saw his headlights following me. 'Are you scared now?' he asks, his voice starting to sound kind of creepy. I told him no, because he's a police officer. 'Young lady,' he says, 'you're in a lot of trouble. No license, no registration, outdated tags, license-plate lights out, excessive speed in a controlled zone, violation of the basic speed law, failure to signal a turn, reckless driving, driving under the influence . . .' I mean he goes on and on, everything in the book. And meantime he keeps running the flashlight up and down my body.

"Finally he says, 'Get in the front seat of my car, young lady. I'm going to have to write this up.' Well, once we're in the car, he turns the dome light on and flips open his citation book. He writes for a while, then looks over at my legs, and you know, when I sit down like that this little skirt hikes clear up to about here," she said, touching a spot on her thigh about four inches below her groin. " 'No question about it,' he goes on, 'I'm going to have to haul you in to the county jail.' 'You mean for the night?' I ask him. 'Not with all these charges,' he says, kind of tapping his pencil against the little book. 'Best I can do is recommend they expedite a hearing for you for next Thursday. That's when the judge holds bond hearings.' "

"What a lot of bullshit," I said. "You knew what he was after by this time, I guess."

"Oh, yeah, I didn't just fall off a Christmas tree. But this wasn't at the corner of Fifth and Main or someplace like that. This was in the middle of nowhere, and I figured I'd have to outsmart the bastard or who knows what might have happened. Look," she said, touching my arm, "do you mind if I just tell Nora, and she can tell you about it later? It's kind of embarrassing."

"Absolutely not. We're in this together."

She stared at me for a moment. "Okay, here goes. I sort of stuck my chest out like this, and pulled the vest back so he could get a good look, and let the skirt hike up even farther. He wasn't missing anything, and I asked if there wasn't some way we could work it out where I wouldn't have to go to jail."

Abby started to laugh, grabbing Nora's arm for support.

"Did he go for it?" Nora asked, starting to laugh herself.

"He started breathing really heavy then, and it looked like his pants were going to split out in the front. 'Honey,' he says, 'If you was to treat me real good, there ain't nothing we couldn't work out.' So I gave him a big smile and started unbuttoning my blouse. Before I even had my bra off, the big jerk jumps out of the car and starts tearing his clothes off, throwing everything on the front seat. God, I'll never forget how he looked, the rolls of fat bouncing around, the hairy back and arms. . . ."

"I can't believe this," Nora said, shaking her head.

"You'd better believe it. 'Get in the back,' he tells me, and I've got almost all my clothes off at this point, tossing them in the front like he did. The son of a bitch even has his boots off. I get in the back on the right side and he climbs in on the left side and shuts his door. He's just about to go down on me, so I tell him I've got to pee. Well, he gets this disgusted look on his face and tells me to get it over with. So when I got out, I simply slammed my door closed."

"Bingo," I said, knowing police car rear doors usually had their inside handles removed, along with the window handles. Combined with the steel security screen between the front and rear seats, that formed a small jail cell, or "cage," as officers call them.

"That's right, he was locked in. I'd been shut in like that before, but I guess he never had. It makes you remember it better."

"So you just got dressed, got in your car, and left him there." Nora said.

"Not quite. He hasn't got it figured out yet, and sees me starting to get dressed. 'What the hell's goin' on?' he wants to know, yelling at me through the steel screen between the front seat and the back. 'Git yer little ass back in here before I have to give you a spanking.'

"So I get in the front seat and stick my face right up close to the screen and tell him, 'Well, you can kiss my ass, you fat, smelly hunk a shit. You think I'd let a garbage can like you even touch me? You'd gag a fuckin' maggot, you pus-covered leach.' "

By this time I could no longer contain my laughter and almost collapsed on the floor. But Abby was just getting started.

"So he starts lunging first at one door, then the other, his eyes looking like a wild boar's or something. He finally realizes he's been had and tries to calm down. 'Okay, okay,' he's saying, 'let's talk this out. No harm done, open the door. I won't write you up or nothing like that, just let me out of here, for chrissakes.'

" 'In a pig's ass,' I tell him, still getting dressed. 'Listen, young lady,' he says, getting kind of desperate now, 'You leave me locked up out here and I'll have you arrested for every felony charge in the book. You'll do hard time. Don't be stupid. You'd be throwing your life away. It ain't worth it.'

" 'Listen, asshole,' I tell him, 'I've got a fat picture of you describing this to the DA. I can see the headlines now: Naked Sheriff Takes Self Prisoner—Charges Self With Attempted

Rape.' He knew I had him. So he says, 'Okay, I know when I'm beat, I'll pay you two hundred bucks to let me outta here.'

"I say, 'Sure—Monday morning when the bank opens, right?'

" 'I'll write you a check right now,' he says. 'Just hand me my wallet and my pen. Just slip it through under the screen.'

"I find a check in his wallet and hand it through. 'Here, make it out for five hundred, and for cash,' I tell him, and can you believe it, he does it. Then he says, 'Okay, now unlock the door.' "

By this time Abby was laughing too hard to continue and had to take a refill on her brandy and light another cigarette.

" 'You know, you're full of shit like the county dump,' I tell him. 'How the fuck dumb do you think I am? You'd just let me drive away, right? Sorry, buster. If I think of it, I'll call the sheriff and tell him where his ace deputy is.'

"But I wasn't quite done yet. I get into the driver's seat, crank up the car, and drive through the campground straight toward one of those double outhouses at the far end. The deputy's shouting at me, 'What the hell are you doing?' and I tell him it's a sentimental journey—just as we crash into the crapper, knocking it off its footings and sending it toppling away from the pit it's sitting on top of. In fact, I got the car stopped just before it went into the pit itself. I guess I was just flat mad. Because then I gather up all his clothes, boots, gun belt, hat, the works, offa the front seat and throw it all down into that pit full of you know what, and there's this big splash.

"All that was left to do then was to wipe my prints offa the steering wheel, gearshift lever and all that, and then I throw the keys to the car down into the pit too. I take a last look at the deputy before leaving. His face is white, like he's fainting or something. I tell him I hope his gun won't get rusty down there, and that the check had better not bounce. Then I start back down the road and meet you guys."

It took me a few minutes to recover from her story. What was going through my head for some reason was that they'd never believe this if I told it in the squad room back in L.A. It was just too good a story to be true.

Nora thought about it, then looked at me. "What do you

think, Harper? Should we call the sheriff's department and tell them about it? Anonymously, of course."

"Hmm. Wait. I've got a better idea. What's Chubby Crump's telephone number?"

Both women looked at me with blank expressions, but Nora looked up the number and handed me the phone.

The phone rang about ten times before a cranky voice answered.

"This is Sergeant Travis of the sheriff's office in Winchester," I said, rather officiously. "One of our patrol cars has been located at the campground at the end of the Foster Creek road, and we're requesting you tow it in to Cedar Valley right away."

"Well, can't it wait for morning?" Crump asked. "We've had a hell of a night here."

"No, it can't. It's part of the evidence in all that happened there last night, and the sheriff insists on having it brought in right away. And by the way, there is a man locked in the back seat, and our orders are that he be left there until we get the vehicle back into town where the sheriff can meet it."

"Well—what happened? Why is there a guy locked in the back?"

"I'm sorry, sir, we can't disclose that information at this time."

"Okay . . . I guess. Well, where in town do you want it towed?"

"Right there on the street in front of your station would be fine, sir."

I glanced at Nora and Abby. They both had their hands over their mouths and were violently nodding their approval. After I hung up I asked Abby if she still had the check for five hundred dollars. She nodded.

"Don't cash it," I said. "Save it for evidence. You might need it."

"What about Steve?" Nora asked. "What do you think he'll do?"

"He'll find the car," Abby said. "It's where we used to go to have a good time. After that, I don't know. He's lived in a lot of places."

136

"Does he have a record? I mean, do the police have his picture and fingerprints?" I asked.

"He's been arrested several times, but not for anything as serious as what just happened."

"What made him do it?" Nora asked.

"We had a sort of a fight a couple of days ago. I told him if he got drunk again we were all through. Then at the dance, after the first break, I guess it was, I could tell he was tying one on again, and I told him it was all over. He acted like I was just kidding around. But then when I didn't go back into the hall he must have figured I meant it. So, in a way, the things he did were as much my fault as his."

"That's nonsense," Nora said. "It was going to happen sooner or later. What's beginning to bother me is what might happen as soon as Dhrymes reports what you did to him. That'll be in about two hours from now. What do you think, Harper?"

I started to laugh, thinking of the deputy trying to explain how he got into the predicament. "Well," I told the two women, "he's got several options. One, he'll clam up and refuse to explain it. That's what I'd do. Two, he'll invent a cover story, and I'd love to hear whatever that might be. Three, he'll tell the story somewhat like it happened, trying to improve it as much as possible from his perspective, and my guess is, that's what he'll probably do. I mean, he has to explain what happened to his gun, the car, the outhouse, his uniform, being naked . . . Jesus, won't the newspapers have fun with this one?"

"But if he tells the true version," Nora said, "they've got to come after Abby, don't they?"

"I really doubt it. Look at it this way. What would they be charging her with? And would that be productive, knowing the embarrassment it would bring the sheriff? I think they'll think it over, then tell Dhrymes to take his lumps and forget about it. Also, they'd have to be at least a little bit worried you might sue the county for attempted rape by one of their officers, stuff like that. However, to be on the safe side, I would recommend you have an attorney in mind and be ready to call him if and when they land on you. And under no circumstances tell any law enforcement officer or newspaper reporter anything. Anything, understand?"

She nodded solemnly. "Do you think I should leave town, get out of sight for a while?"

"Why should you?" Nora asked. "If it were me, I'd just tell people I took a drive and missed all the excitement."

"What if Steve calls me, wants me to go away with him?"

"I'd tell him to get lost," Nora said.

I grabbed a couple of hours sleep, then headed for the disaster scene, arriving there about seven. Ordinarily, one wouldn't expect much activity at that hour on a Sunday, but now the place crawled with sheriff's officers, onlookers from all over the county, townspeople of course, many of them studying their damaged cars, and even a couple of insurance adjusters just arrived from Winchester, along with two newsmen-photographers for the Winchester paper.

"How did those two cars get in there?" people were asking one another.

"Was Mona selling cars too?" a woman asked.

"They must have been from the valley," an old man said. "We don't drive like that up here."

"It's alcohol, Ethyl," the old man said to his wife, shaking his head in disgust as he looked at the burned-out cars.

"I think you've got that backwards," said a highway patrol officer who had just arrived and was standing nearby.

"What do you mean by that?" asked the old man.

"It's ethyl alcohol, not alcohol Ethyl," he said, chuckling at his ingenuity.

"What's that?" asked the old man, cupping his hand to his ear.

"It's ethyl alcohol," said the officer, speaking much louder.

"What is?"

"That caused the problem."

"What's my wife got to do with it?"

The officer just shook his head and walked away, muttering something about another meaningful dialogue with the informed citizenry.

"Just look at that fire engine," said a woman carrying a baby.

138

"Those firemen must have really been uncomfortable riding back there, burning like that."

"I heard this is the truck that knocked down the power pole," answered a young woman who'd arrived on a bicycle.

"Why did they do that? Was it on fire too?" the woman with the baby asked.

The young woman looked at her for a moment, then pedaled away.

I learned from one of the deputies on the scene that the cowboy hadn't been found yet, but that there was an APB out on the purple Cadillac. He also told me that Deputy J. P. Dhrymes, along with his patrol car, were also still missing, and that the sheriff had ordered an aircraft up to search for it.

The police had put up a couple of tables in the parking area in front of the ladies club hall and were taking statements from witnesses, and I spotted the county sheriff sitting under a tree talking with a highway patrol officer. Two other officers were busy on the main road trying to keep traffic moving, as passersby inched along gawking at the burned store and the wrecked cars. It was beginning to bother me that the patrol car hadn't yet been towed in from the campground. As little as I thought of the deputy, it wasn't really safe to leave him out there in that cage, especially after the sun started beating down on the car. That was why I'd asked for it to be towed in immediately. Maybe Chubby took his sweet time about heading out there.

And then there was a commotion, as Crump's big wrecking truck honked its way through the traffic towing Dhrymes's car. When he clanked to a stop in front of his station, the crowd gathered around to find out what was going on. Soon some of the people spotted Dhrymes in the back seat and began shouting in merriment, swarming around the patrol car in their zeal to get a look. It almost turned into a riot.

"Clear the way, get back everybody," commanded Sheriff Winston Burdett, working his way through the crowd. When he finally got next to the car and looked into the rear window, his face almost turned purple. He looked in the front for a moment, tried the rear door handles, then said, "Get somebody to open this thing up."

Ned Booth was standing near me, and he said he'd do it, heading immediately toward his pickup, which stood nearby. He came back in a minute with a set of picks and had the car open in less than two minutes. A deputy leaned inside and threw a blanket over Dhrymes, and they led him to another patrol car and put him into the back. Burdett climbed in beside him, talked with him for a few minutes, then got back out and walked back over to where most of us were standing.

"Anybody here know where the cowboy's girlfriend is? Believe her name is Abby Munro, or something that sounds like that."

Nobody said anything.

"All right," Burdett said. "She may be in a lot of trouble, and anybody that shelters her will be in a lot of trouble also. Now, I don't want anybody touching this car until we've had a chance to go over it. If you have any information, get it to me or to one of my deputies. All right, all of you who don't own one of these cars here that got damaged last night or have any other official business, I'd appreciate it if you'd go back home so we can get this mess straightened out."

Two officers were now in the front seat of the car they'd put Dhrymes in. The car eased through the crowd on its way out of town, and I got a look at Dhrymes. His eyes locked on mine, and I could plainly read his lips saying, *You son of a bitch, I'm going to kill you*. It took me a while to figure out how he guessed I had been involved.

Chapter 9

L uckily for me we had an easy day on the job, probably because nobody else around the station had gotten much sleep either. Punky Swiftbird showed up at starting time and put us to work washing the fire hoses and cleaning up the truck and equipment from the previous night's fire. Then he took off for the barracks, and we guessed it would be to sack out. So we got the main work done quickly and found places around the warehouse to take some naps ourselves.

By late that afternoon I felt somewhat refreshed, and after supper I decided to do some thinking about what I'd found during my visits to the suspect fire scenes. Albert Carlisle was sitting on his bed working on one of his manuscripts, seeming lost in thought. I got out the photos I'd taken at the points of origin and flipped through them for about the fifteenth time. Then I looked at the map again, trying to find something I might have overlooked.

I kept coming back to the same conclusion: the arsonist had to be using a device that gave him a day or more's getaway time, and one that left no evidence at the scene. How could this be done?

"Albert," I asked casually. He looked up from his papers, his brow wrinkled in concentration. "If you were going to set a fire in the forest and wished to keep it from actually starting for, say, twenty-four hours, how would you go about it?"

He took off his glasses and thought about it for at least a full minute. "I don't know, maybe a long-burning candle, sheltered from the wind, and with some flammable material at its base."

"That might start the fire, all right, but the melted tallow would give you away. I found out on the Rucker's Ridge fire that a fire can spread uphill away from its point of origin, leaving the spot where it started hardly singed."

"You've changed the problem, then. I'm supposed to go undetected in this crime, is it? Well in that case, let me think."

I waited patiently—for four minutes this time, checking his eyeballs occasionally to make sure he hadn't slipped into a trance. Finally he came out of it.

"There are very few possibilities. One would be an incendiary device ignited by a very long fuse. In this case, the fuse and the device itself would have to be completely consumed by combustion, either from the activation of the device itself or from the resulting fire."

I nodded, admiring his logic.

"Another possibility would be ignition by means of a chemical reaction, one in which the residue from the reaction were either absent or would readily be mistaken for ashes from the fire thus started. There is one other possibility, but it lies somewhat outside the parameters you gave me, in that an astute investigation might reveal the device."

"I'd like to hear it."

"If somebody were to use a device that the fire wouldn't obliterate, it would have to remain hidden from view after the fire."

"For example?"

"Something underground, but I have no idea what."

"You suggested a chemical reaction. What kind of chemical could be used?"

"I don't know that much about chemistry. But that kind of information is available in libraries, or from chemists. Why all this interest? What does that have to do with your thesis on fire prevention?"

142

"Oh, I just keep thinking about that fire on Rucker's Ridge. As far as I know, nobody has figured out yet how it started."

"Or why."

"You're right. What do you think about that?"

I was almost sorry I asked, because Carlisle went into another catatonic state, this one lasting about seven minutes. I used the time studying my map and looking at the photos yet once more.

"Well, I can think of eight possibilities," he said, enumerating pretty much the same ones Anselmo Adams had suggested in Nevada City. "It simply comes down to eliminating the ones without merit."

Then he put his glasses back on and returned to his manuscript, leaving the rest to me.

I tried to keep up to date on the aftermath of the "Saturday Night Massacre," as people were calling it. (Most of them pronounced it *"mass*-a-cree.") By Monday noon, word around town had it that neither Steve Christian nor his car had been located, that police had questioned Abby Murrow, and that officers were still trying to find out who had knocked out the windows of the ladies club hall and tipped over the kitchen appliances and done other damage.

That night I ran into Nora in front of the post office. She said she was on her way to her aunt's place in Purple Pond.

"I heard the police questioned Abby," I said. "Did she tell you about it?"

"She called me right afterwards. They wanted her version of what happened from the time she left town with Dhrymes in pursuit. She said she lost him and drove back to town. Then while she was watching the fire, somebody took the car. She said they wrote it all down. But then they told her she would probably be called in for a lie-detector test, and she's quite frightened about it. I think she might decide to take off."

"Does Dhrymes know you and Abby are friends?"

She thought for a moment. "Well, he's seen me with Abby and Steve once or twice. Why? What are you thinking?"

"Oh, just trying to make some connections. What's happening to Dhrymes? Heard anything?"

"According to Vivian, he's been suspended while they investigate the incident. She thinks they'll assign another deputy to Cedar Valley."

"I have a feeling we haven't seen the last of him. He has to be gunning for the prankster who called in the tow truck."

"He's not the only one. Chubby Crump is telling everyone he's out a fifty-dollar towing bill because the sheriff's office won't acknowledge placing the order. He says he told them he acted in good faith, the job needed doing anyway, and if they don't pay him, he'll never take on any more jobs from them."

We laughed again over the incident, then Nora said she had to get going. I asked, "What do you think about dinner together Friday or Saturday?"

"Depends on how my aunt is doing. Give me a ring later in the week. And stay out of trouble for a change, okay?"

Over the next two days I talked to some of the district staff about salvage timber sales, grazing permits, hunting practices, and recreational activities in the forest. I thought at the time I did a good job of feigning general interest in these things and hoped I didn't come across either as trying to ingratiate myself—sucking up—or as someone attempting an informal investigation on my own. But as a result of the conversations, I ruled out half the possible motives for the series of incendiary fires. My list was now down to "pyromania," "glory," "jobs," and "grudge."

Pyromania seemed the most difficult possibility to deal with, because, as in the case of psychotics who feel the need to kill, the tendency among arsonists, I concluded, is often so latent that even close friends and relatives will fail to detect it until it's too late. About all I could do on this one would be to try hard to keep an open mind in thinking about suspects.

The motive of revenge—called "grudge fire" on the report forms—interested me because I had already found people in Cedar Valley whose experience might lead them to set a fire to get even with somebody. Ned Booth, who had been forced out of his job with the Forest Service, belonged in this category. Stan Turpin, passed over for the fire prevention officer job five years ago, could have this motive. Did the deputy sheriff fit in here, I wondered? He certainly didn't think fondly of the Forest Service,

144

and he seemed a little paranoid to me. Then the other, rather dark, possibility: Nora. She was seen exiting the area of the Rucker's Ridge fire and didn't offer any explanation. But what would she stand to gain by starting fires? And if, indeed, she had been in love with Heath . . .

What I had termed the "job" motive might fit with anybody in the Forest Service or the volunteer fire department. While the volunteers normally went to fires in and around town, they were called out occasionally on big wildland fires, and they got paid to fight them. But the remote locations of the fires in question seemed to work against this thesis and fit better with the Forest Service people. While the fire crew guys were already on the payroll, they earned overtime pay beyond their regular tour-of-duty hours.

That last idea intrigued me, because if you went to a fire on your days off, all the work time was overtime, and that could make a huge difference in your paycheck. Theorizing further, I reasoned that a Forest Service arsonist could slip out the night before the first of his two days off, rig a delayed ignition, then be at hand the next day when the fire was reported.

I had seen the work schedules for all eight fire crews on the district and wondered what it would take to narrow the possibilities. But then another glance at my map of fires told me not to waste time beyond the Cedar Valley crew, due to the concentric distribution of incendiary fires around that fire station. In addition, almost all the other district people, the ones not assigned to fire crews or lookouts, headquartered out of Cedar Valley.

One evening's work entering data on a large sheet of accounting paper seemed to result in little I thought might become useful. The data were uncertain due to various changes in tours of duty, emergency hiring on days off due to high fire danger, and so forth. Too, the whole study was premised on my presumption of a device delaying ignition by from eighteen to twenty-four hours which might or might not be accurate. I thought it reasonable inasmuch as the arsonist seemed able to predict burning conditions accurately. Predicting beyond twenty-four hours was pretty unreliable, I knew. But on balance, it didn't look productive, and I decided to drop this approach.

145

★ ★ ★

Marklee, under pressure to make progress on the incendiary fire problem, got approval to conduct a special fire prevention meeting, and, not cognizant it was a day off for me, he arranged through Felton Shackle that I attend. The invitation surprised me because Bill hadn't paid much attention to me around the office, so I suspected Lois Hart of having recommended me.

I got to the little conference room early where I found Bill Marklee taping a map on an easel. He asked me if I'd heard that deputy Dhrymes was already back in town and on the job. I was expressing my surprise when the other guys began coming in. Most of them were fire prevention technicians and fire crew foremen from the outlying portions of the district, guys I had seen either around the station or at the Rucker's Ridge fire. But Stan Turpin also came in, something I hadn't expected, what with the animosity between him and Bill Marklee. Turpin looked surprised to see me there, I suppose because I was only a crewman, and a first-year man at that. After all, how could I contribute in the presence of all this experience and wisdom?

"First of all," Marklee began ominously, "What we say in this room is not to be discussed outside, not even with your crews or anybody else. It's strictly confidential, and any breach of this could compromise what we're trying to do. Okay?"

The men all looked around at one another, wondering what the big deal was.

Marklee glanced around the room, his nose twitching, then continued. "As you all know, we've had a number of sets in the past several years, and so far, nobody has been apprehended."

He unveiled his large district map showing fire locations marked in with heavy black circles. I noticed about twice as many fires there than on my map, and wondered how he'd selected that many from the same data base.

"As you can see, they're pretty well scattered over the whole district, with at least three fires in every initial attack unit, and at least five in each patrol area."

He looked around to make sure we were all listening. "Does that suggest anything to any of you?"

An awkward silence ensued, then one of the men said, "That we've all fucked up about the same amount?"

Everybody laughed except Marklee, who seemed determined to maintain an austere mood.

"That's not exactly what I had in mind," Marklee said, permitting himself a pained smile. "It means that somebody, or some people, are working the whole district, and that none of your units have been exempt. The purpose of this meeting is to talk about what's been going on and why, and what we're going to do about it."

For about the next hour, the men discussed the unsolved fires in their work units and speculated on the reasons for them. They came down the hardest on what I'd termed the "pyromania" and "grudge" motives on my own list, confining proposed suspects to those other than Forest Service people. I was tempted to contest the point but thought it tactically preferable to hold my tongue, at least for now. After an hour there was little agreement.

There was even less accord on how the fires had been ignited. When one man would suggest an object dropped from an aircraft, another would point out that for fires he had investigated, no aircraft had been seen by the lookouts in the vicinity. When another would suggest a particular device that would provide for a delayed ignition, somebody else would remind him that device would have been found or would at least have left evidence at the scene. The discussion went on and on.

"We're not getting anywhere on this," Marklee said. "Supposing we talk about how we're going to prevent it from happening again?"

"Well, if we don't even know what it is, how the hell are we going to invent some way of preventing it?" asked one of the crew foremen.

The question triggered a lively discussion that went nowhere. After another hour one of the fire prevention techs suggested monitoring all vehicular traffic in each patrol unit during periods of very high or extreme fire danger, by taking license plate numbers and vehicle descriptions. But this prompted vociferous arguments as to how this ought to be done, and things started to unravel.

"Well, shit, Bill," said Stan Turpin, who seemed anxious to have the meeting over with. "Whoever is doing this isn't stupid enough to drive through one of our checkpoints and then set the goddamn fire. If he's as smart as I think he is, we'll have the fires anyway, then wonder why we were wasting our time out there. How big a problem is this, anyway? Two, three fires a year, most of them inconsequential? What are we getting so excited about?"

Several of the men, tired of the meeting and unimpressed with Marklee, mumbled their agreement, and I couldn't stand it any longer.

"One of those fires killed a man last year," I said.

Turpin, stung, half turned toward me and snarled, "He was a junior forester. He got himself trapped and shouldn't have let it happen."

"You wouldn't have let that happen to you, would you, Stan," I shot back, "just because one of your men's lives was in danger?"

"Now just a goddamn minute," he said, his face turning dark red in anger and embarrassment. "If I'd been in charge their lives wouldn't have been in danger. Anyway, who in hell you think you are, telling—"

"Hold it down!" rumbled Marklee, surprising me by taking charge of the situation. "We all know what happened on that fire, and there's no point beating a dead horse of a different color. Sandow has a good point. The next fire could be another big one, and we've got to keep it from happening."

Marklee declared the meeting over, stating that he would be developing an action plan based on our input, again asking for our cooperation in keeping the subject confidential. Most of the men tromped out grumbling that once again, not a goddamn thing had been accomplished.

I sat there in my chair thinking about the futility of the plan that Marklee would probably draw up based on the ideas offered in the meeting. How much time and money would be wasted watching roads never to be traveled by the arsonist. And would such an effort ward him off or merely challenge his determination?

"What do you think, Harper?" Marklee asked after the others

had left. "You were pretty quiet, except for that business with Stan."

"Yeah, well, being just a crewman and all, I thought I'd better keep my mouth shut. But I've got a few ideas that might be helpful, and I've done some writing. I wouldn't mind helping you out with your action plan."

"Well, Lois tells me you're pretty good at coding fire report forms, figuring the fire danger and all that. Maybe you could give me a hand looking back through our fire records to get a better handle on any pattern that may be occurring. That has to be our starting point, and I just don't have time to do it alone."

I had to fight off a smile, because things couldn't have been working better. I knew Marklee wasn't good at paperwork and that I could get him to lean on me. Best of all, the analysis was already finished, and all I'd have to do is spruce it up and get Marklee to think it was mostly his doing.

I tried not to appear too eager. "When do you want me to get started?"

"Well, I'll be out of the office the next two days. What say we get together in here Sunday morning and I'll get you started. Meantime, if you have any ideas, plunge in. I'll tell Punky what's going on so he can give you time off from crew work."

Just as Marklee was turning to leave, Don West, the district ranger, walked in to ask Marklee how the meeting had gone, and Marklee gave a much more glowing report than I would have. He also remarked that I would be helping him on the analysis and action plan.

"Good, good," West said, running a hand through his graying hair. "Are you glad you came up here from L.A.?" he asked, grinning at me. Marklee stayed there to listen.

"Yes, sir. This is just what I needed. I love it."

"And you don't miss the excitement of the city?"

"Excitement is where you find it. The city can be very dull at times. In fact, most of the time."

"I wouldn't have thought that to be the case in your line of work down there."

His comment blindsided me. How much did he know? How had he found out? Not knowing, I winged it. "Well, the most thrilling part of L.A. isn't the job, it's getting to and from work through all that traffic. I'll take the mud and the dust here any day, even the logging trucks."

He studied me for long moments. "How long do you figure you'll be here? That is, how long do you think it'll take you to get finished with this part of your life? Or maybe I should ask, what are you really doing here?"

"How do you mean, sir?"

"Well, everybody has a mission, even if they don't understand it themselves. With most people, the mission is fairly obvious, but in your case it isn't. You seem to be a very intelligent, calculating, deliberate person, someone trying to leave no stone unturned. And yet you're impulsive, at times, dangerously so."

"Impulsive?"

"About taking risks. I have the impression you'd put your life on the line for whatever struck you at the moment as being important."

"Yes, I guess I would."

"What's important to you right now?"

"Not having you find out what I'm really doing here."

I thought it was a hilarious comeback, but West merely smiled and nodded.

"Maybe you'll succeed, but I doubt it."

He was right about the impulsive part, anyway; it was a risky comment on my part, but I got the impression he took it lightly. Or did he? As for Marklee, it left him more confused than he already was.

My day off was already half shot, so I decided to get on with the project. Lois Hart set me up with a table and all the fire reports for the past three years, the coding instruction book, and the fire atlas, a large book of maps providing data year by year for all the fires. After lunch I brought my own analysis down from the barracks and started in.

By ten the next morning I had it roughed out, and showed it to Lois, asking for her suggestions. On the title page I had Marklee's name, then hers, then mine. She blinked a couple of times, then flipped to the introduction, a one-page overview.

"All right," she said, squinting through her thick glasses, "This is obviously the Sanskrit version. Where's the English?"

"Okay, so it's a little squiggly."

"A little? What's this first word?"

" 'The.' "

"Okay, yeah, I see it now. What's this second word?"

"Come on, Lois, it's not that bad."

She laughed and began reading rapidly through the report. After a few minutes she asked, "What's all this stuff about tours of duty for our guys?"

"That's to rule out job fires—starting fires to earn overtime pay fighting them."

"Really?" she asked, eyeing me sidewise. "Am I in here too?"

"No, but that's a thought. There is a category covering employees with district-wide mobility."

"You mean for district staff, Marklee, Turpin, and so forth?"

"Yeah. But I haven't figured out how to rule any of them either in or out."

"If you really need to, they all keep official diaries saying where they go and what they do each day on the job."

"Might help. But they could lie about it. Which reminds me, do you keep the lookout logbooks, the ones that are full, here in the office?"

"You are a shifty one, Harper. Cross-check the diaries? Good idea, but it would take you all winter. What else have we got here?"

It took a while, but she got through all fifteen pages of it. Then she said, "I may act a little stupid at times, but you are not, repeat not, going to tell me that you just accomplished two weeks of work in five hours."

"I'm fast. Real fast."

"You're not that fast, Ace. You know, I wondered why you were spending so much time around here. Obviously it wasn't because you enjoyed my company that much. Who are you, anyway? Where did you learn to do work like this? And why are you doing it?"

"Okay, you caught me. I got interested in these incendiary fires and started trying to figure out what's going on. Yeah, I already had a lot of this done."

She eyed me suspiciously. "Are you with the FBI?"

"If I could qualify, maybe I would be."

"With an insurance company, then?"

"Sure, and live all summer in that godforsaken barracks listening to Albert Carlisle shake the walls with his snoring?"

"Good point. But I'll level with you. Right from the start I've had a suspicion you're not who you say you are. Don't ask me why, it's just a feeling. Am I right about that? You can tell me, I'm a good egg."

I had a gut feeling she really was, and I needed an ally like her. "I'd love to tell you, but I can't right now. If even a few people knew I've been working on it all along, the whole thing would be jeopardized. I've already told you too much, more than anybody else in town knows. I know it's asking a lot, but could you find it within yourself to keep it a secret?"

"Who are you doing it for?"

"For myself, and for the Forest Service."

"Why?"

"It's just not right that somebody's running around out there starting fires."

"Does Nora know?"

"I don't think so."

"Okay, you've got twenty-four hours."

"Wha—"

"Just kidding. Sure, Harper, I'll help. For a special reason."

I'd long ago learned not to play dumb with somebody as sharp as this woman. "If I had to guess, I'd say it has something to do with the young man who was killed on the Pegleg fire."

She nodded. "It can't be allowed to happen again."

"If it's up to me, it won't."

I hadn't wanted this to happen, to have to rely on another to keep my secret. But Lois was close to what I was doing, and she was smart. And there was something about the freckled-faced woman that gave me confidence. Anyway, I didn't think she'd yet figured out my real identity.

We talked about the findings section of the analysis, and she made some helpful suggestions on how to strengthen it. Then she wanted to know why I hadn't done the obvious thing and recommended specific action be taken.

"This plan won't go anywhere if Marklee's not behind it. I don't want him to think I'm trying to engineer this whole thing."

"Well, you could list several options, let him decide."

"There's only one option that makes any sense."

"A stakeout on those three dead-end roads during critical fire danger?"

"That's it."

"One question, Harper. It has to do with the delay device theory. How does the arsonist know when the fire danger is going to be either very high or extreme the following day? The fire-danger board out in front only gives today's fire danger."

"That's been bothering me, but I haven't figured out how to deal with it. Any ideas?"

"Let me work on it. You've got my name on the bloody report. I'd like to contribute something to it."

"Believe me, you've already contributed a lot."

Together, we got the paper roughed out, leaving the "Action Plan" section blank, and I went back to the barracks feeling good about what we'd done but wondering how Bill Marklee would react to it on Sunday morning. His ego posed one problem, as nobody appreciates being upstaged in his specialty by someone of lower status. I felt I could handle that with tact and deceit. But the other problem loomed more critical: what if Marklee were the arsonist? Would he react by going underground or by changing his MO, thus undermining the investigation?

I thought again of my conversation with A. A. Adams—known among the old hands, I'd learned, as "the Auto Club". What a perfect setup for an arsonist, the district fire prevention officer assignment! He could start fires, thus making the fire prevention assignment a critical one, but always narrowly failing to catch the arsonist. I tried but could not think of a way to test the idea.

"That's two days you've worked for free," said Swiftbird from his perch on the front porch. "I understand you're working on a plan to catch the arsonist."

153

"Not really. Bill Marklee has me going over some fire reports for him and working on a report, that's all. What have you been up to today?"

"Haircut and laundry. Tomorrow's a no-get-up for me too, so I'm going to do the tour tonight. Why don't you come along with me. Might be educational."

I laughed. "I've heard about your tours. But unfortunately, I'm on duty tomorrow. Got to be in good shape."

"Well, I'll just make it a short tour, then. You might learn something that you can include in your report. How about it?"

"Why not?" I said, knowing without really knowing that Swiftbird had some reason for saying it.

Chapter 10

I ate supper with the fire crew, taking quite a lot of comentary about my "office job." The implication of some of the remarks was that I was trying to make it with Lois, but I put those quickly to rest. Then I rang up Nora, not getting an answer for the second evening in a row. She must be at her aunt's home in Purple Pond, I reasoned.

At about eight, Punky Swiftbird gathered me up and we headed out the back door, where his old Packard, freshly washed, awaited. When I got in, I almost sat on Swiftbird's coonhound, who had already gotten in somehow.

"Get in the back, Donald," said the little Indian. "Hope you don't mind if he goes along. Sometimes he's the only one who remembers the way back."

"How did he know you were going?"

"He watches which shoes I put on. When I put these on, he climbs in the window."

"Pretty smart."

"Not really. He counts days and knew this was Friday, so he was already kind of expecting it."

"You hunt with him?"

"For the things I hunt, he wouldn't be much help. But we do

take him out sometimes when somebody gets lost. He's found three or four people. He gets more Christmas cards than I do, and he can't even read all the words."

We almost veered off the driveway, and I realized Swiftbird had already had a few drinks. But once we'd reached the main road and turned south, he seemed fully in control. Along the way, I asked him how he thought the incendiarist went about picking out places for his fires, and how he started them.

"I thought for a while they were holdover lightning strikes," he said. "Sometimes a white fir snag will hold fire for as long as a couple of weeks. All that time it'll just be smoldering somewhere in the tree, and then cinders will fall out; clinkers, we call them, because they kind of tinkle when they hit rocks. But when I started looking for this, the only big trees where the fires were starting were ponderosas or Jeffreys. They won't ever hold fire like that."

"And I gather nobody has seen any lightning scars nearby."

"That's right. So somebody is trying to give us a hard time, but I don't know how they're doing it."

"And they must know about high fire danger, because according to the fire reports—"

"Well, hold on, Harper. We don't have any record of how many of his attempts have failed during low fire danger."

His point was valid. That idea had never even occurred to me. "You're right. But if this guy is smart enough to escape detection, he must be smart enough to pick the right times to start his fires."

"I don't know. But I'm pretty sure whoever it is knows his way around pretty well and understands what makes fires spread fast."

"You weren't at the meeting yesterday. Did you hear about it?"

Swiftbird chuckled. "Yeah, I heard. Most of the guys figure Marklee will come up with a plan to register all vehicles passing check points, or something along those lines. They think it would be a waste of time."

"What do you think might work better?"

"I talked to a prevention tech from the Angeles forest last year on a fire out there. He said he worked on a task force to catch an arsonist. They had them lying out there in the brush along roads with binoculars. One guy would call out license numbers and the other would write them down. It went on for several weeks."

"Did they catch the guy?"

"The fires suddenly stopped happening, so they ended the task force. Then, of course, the fires started up again. The L.A. sheriff's people caught the guy, kind of accidentally, when he lost control of his car and hit a tree right after starting a string of fires along the road."

"Who was the arsonist?"

"One of the kids from a fire crew, just trying to create some excitement, I guess."

I made a mental note to ask A. A. Adams about that case when the chance came. My bet was that the kid had had more of a motive than that.

We stopped for a drink at every bar along the road, usually one or two in each little town. They were saloons with names like the Rainbow Tavern, and The Antlers or the Wild Goose, and they all smelled of booze and beer and had loud jukeboxes playing western tunes. Everybody seemed to know the Indian, and we got some free drinks.

Then we reached the town of Naco, and went into a bar called *The Staghorn*. This place was just as smelly and smoky as the others, but much quieter, at least at the moment. Four men sat around a table beneath a shaded lamp playing cards. Dusty animal heads leered out from the walls. An inebriated couple leaned on each other in front of the jukebox, deciding which buttons to push.

"Isn't that Ned Booth over at that table?" I asked Swiftbird.

He nodded. "His second home. He says he gets a lot of his customers from down here."

"Punky!" said a male voice from a table nearby. "Get yer ass over here and have one with us."

We joined two men and a woman sitting at a table with an open bottle of Old Crow and several shot glasses in front of them.

"I'm Pete Baldwin," said one of the men, sticking out his hand. "And this here is Art Swinford. And this is Jane," he said, gesturing with his thumb at the brunette sitting between them.

Jane didn't respond, just sat there, staring straight ahead through glassy eyes. She had a cigarette going in each hand.

"Where's Blanche?" Baldwin asked, looking around.

Swinford pointed behind him at a limp body lying on the floor by the wall.

"Oh yeah, I fergot," Baldwin said. "If I told her once, I told her a fer chrissakes dozen times not to put Coke in the goddamn whiskey. Never learns. Punky, what the fuck you doin' down here? Kelley finally run outta booze?"

"No, I heard they had better stuff down here," Swiftbird said.

"You kidding? Why, just look at these dogs," he said, nodding his head in the direction of Jane, who didn't notice the comment. "Two more glasses over here, Bea!" he yelled at a woman behind the bar. "And another jug."

Bea, a mountainous woman, came waddling over with the glasses and bottle, sizing up the newcomer. "Hi, Punky," she said. "You're early tonight. Who's your good-looking friend?"

"This is Harper Sandow, new man on my crew," Swiftbird said.

"No shit?" said Bea. "This the guy that threw Dhrymes outta Kelley's?"

"That's him," said Swiftbird, grinning. "I know he don't look big enough, but he's shifty."

"Looks big enough to me," Bea said, smirking. "Why don't you leave him here with me while you finish your tour?"

"Oh, you horny old bitch," Baldwin said. "Can't you see this guy has class? What would he want with you, anyway?"

"Up your ass, Ding Dong," Bea told him. "And get Blanche the hell offa the floor and outta here. Can't you see it's bad for business? What are the paying customers going to think, fer chrissakes?"

"All right, all right," Baldwin said. "But after she pukes. I don't want her to mess up my car. Last time she barfed in there the goddamn dog wouldn't even get in."

"What happened?" asked Swinford. "You fergit to clean it up?"

"Naw, I usually just let it dry. Easier to brush out the chunks. Speakin' of which, what you got to eat in this slop chute, Bea?"

"Kitchen's closed," she said. "Why don't you try the toilet? Bound to be some chunks left in there for you."

"I already looked," Baldwin said. "Art musta got in there first."

"You people are nasty," Swiftbird said. "I think I'll take this gentleman to some place with higher standards."

"Speakin' of standards," said a cowboy, weaving his way unsteadily toward the table, "who brought this fuckin' Indian in here?" He seemed to be staring straight at me. "I'd say he belongs on a goddamn reservation, and not in here drinking whiskey with white men."

I looked the guy over. He was big and tough-looking, and obviously drunk, but still looking for a fight. He moved toward me and I stood up, kicking my chair backward out of the way.

"Sit down, honey," Bea said, stepping between us. She grabbed the cowboy by the shirtfront with one hand and slapped him across the face with the other hard enough to pop his head clear over against his shoulder. The cowboy, stunned, reeled backward, then regaining his balance, doubled his fists and moved toward her. Bea stepped forward and decked him with a smashing right to the jaw.

"Get up and get outta my place," she said looking down at the limp form of the cowboy. "I don't need your kind in here." Then she turned to Swiftbird and said, "Sorry, Punky, Fred gets like that sometimes, but he don't really mean it. He won't even remember it tomorrow."

Things began calming down, and we finished our drinks and headed for the door, Swiftbird first. As I was about to walk out, I felt a hand on my arm. I turned to look into the eyes of a man I'd never seen, a guy some twenty years older than me.

"I've got a message from somebody for you," he said. "I don't know what it's about, but you better listen."

I looked him in the eye and waited.

"If you're smart, you won't hang around Cedar Valley any longer. That smashed windshield was just a warning."

"According to who?" I asked.

"Just some friendly advice. Take it or leave it."

"What's it about? What's the problem?" I asked.

"Work on it, friend," he said, turning to disappear into the gloom of the barroom.

I grabbed him by the arm, as he'd done to me moments before, and pulled him up close. "I've got a message for your friend."

The man stood there looking at me from under arched eyebrows.

"Tell him his ass sucks wind," I said. It was one of those lines I picked up in the Marines; I never did understand what it meant, but thought it sounded pretty good.

We got Donald into the back seat again and headed out of town. I described the message carrier to Swiftbird and asked if he knew him.

"Yeah, I think I know who you mean. I see him around in different bars in the valley, but I don't know him. Seems to me they call him Jake. Was that him you were talking to on the way out?"

"Yeah. He must have me mixed up with somebody else. Say, Punky, did that bother you, what the cowboy said about being an Indian and all that?"

He smiled. "Where I come from, we're used to it. We let it slide."

"Sure, you're used to it. But how do you feel when you hear it?"

"How would you feel?"

"I'd be mad, probably want to fight."

He pulled the car off the road in a wide spot, reached under the front seat, and pulled out a pint of Jim Beam. He uncapped it and handed it to me. We each took a drink, and then he said, "I might feel that way, just like you said, if I hadn't been born an Indian and grown up where I did and have parents like I had. They made me feel I'm as good as anybody else, and that I didn't have to prove it to people who didn't matter. They also taught me not to hate people ignorant enough to let skin color get in their way, because everybody has their own way of seeing things, their own blind spots. Anyway, a guy as small as me would be crazy to get into a fight in a bar with a white man."

We got out of the car and took a leak. While we were standing there a car I'd seen parked by ours in front of that last bar went by with two guys in it. The one on the right side looked like the man who stopped me in the doorway.

"How were Indians treated where you grew up?" I asked.

"If you mean by white people, like animals most of the time. That is, unless they knew you, figured you weren't a trouble-maker. But like I said, you get used to that. You expect it. You even distrust those who treat you nice; you're expecting a trick all the time."

"That must be a hell of a way to have to grow up, being put down like that."

"That's not exactly how we saw it. We were put down eco-nomically and socially and like that, but we understood why they were doing it, and I guess that gave us some kind of a moral advantage. Trouble is, you can't eat a moral advantage."

"What made you leave Oklahoma? Isn't that where you said you grew up?"

"Yeah. It was right after the war. Everybody thought that things would get better. And for some, I guess they did. But not for my family. My dad died of TB, and my mother had to start taking in wash and do other jobs like that. My brother was trying to look after things and worked part time, but I couldn't find a job. Everybody was saying California was the place to find work. So I thumbed my way out here with less than ten dollars in my pocket. I got a job working in the bean fields near Bakersfield for thirty-five cents an hour, and they fed me.

"Then about the time that work finished, there was a big forest fire in the mountains to the east of there, and a truck came through hiring guys to go and fight it. It paid good, there was lots of food, and I kind of liked it. One thing led to another, and I wound up in Cedar Valley on the fire crew. They promoted me to foreman four years ago."

"And it looks like you have a lot of friends around here."

"It's a good thing, 'cause I sure as shit don't have money."

"You send money to your family?"

"Mom died, and everybody else is making their way. No, I don't know what happens to my money. Just spend it, I guess."

We got back in the car and each of us took another swig of Jim

Beam, and we got underway. After each stop, it seemed Swiftbird drove slower. En route to the town of Grady we probably averaged about thirty. We stopped at a bar called the Mountain Lion.

"Don't get into any fights in this place," Swiftbird said. "There's a guy hangs around here named Charlie. Used to be a circus fighter. Likes to pick fights just for the fun of it. One time some guys brought in a professional boxer to teach him a lesson. Charlie sucker-punched the guy and stomped all over him."

I glanced around at the other cars and recognized the one that had passed us, but when we walked inside, I didn't see Jake among the many people at the bar and the tables. A woman in a tight black skirt moved among the patrons dispensing drinks and collecting money. A guy simultaneously playing a guitar, harmonica, and bass drum was drawing little attention in one corner of the room. We got a guy to move over so we could have seats together at the bar, and it didn't take Charlie long to show up. "Who's your friend, Punky?" he said, leering at me with a grin as wide as his wrestler's neck.

Swiftbird introduced us, looking dubious.

"I hear you're a pretty rough and tough hombre, Harper," Charlie said. "I understand you're the guy who threw that deputy outta the bar in Cedar Valley."

I'd seen a few guys like Charlie before, short guys built like brick shithouses, move like cats with lightning reflexes, iron muscles. And this one had an aura of wildness and dominance about him that could intimidate a charging rhino. It frightened me to even think about having to fight him.

"Buy you a drink?" I asked, not unaware that he was cold sober and that I was not.

"Naw, thanks. I only drink with guys that can whip me."

I looked around and noticed everybody's attention was already focused on us. They obviously knew what Charlie was up to. I also saw Jake looking on from a doorway. The son of a bitch had probably fingered me for this creep.

"Suit yourself, friend," I said, turning back to my drink.

"What is that you're drinking, Harper," Charlie said, "a Shirley Temple? Haw haw haw haw."

162

"That's right. Buy you one?" I asked, trying to tone things down a bit.

"Naw, that's a cunt's drink, and you must be a cunt if you're drinkin' one, right? Haw haw haw haw."

"Let's get outta here," Swiftbird said. "This ain't supposed to be part of the tour."

We got off of our stools, and I was ready to go even if it looked cowardly. Matter of fact, I felt cowardly, and scared. But Charlie wasn't letting me off that easily. He grabbed me by the arm and spun me toward him.

"What kind of a cunt are you, anyway, Harper, and what do you have in mind tonight with this little redskin here?" With that he turned to leer at his audience and let out another haw haw haw haw. "What's the deal? Are redskin braves better than white squaws? Haw haw haw haw."

Nobody in the place was laughing along with Charlie. They were more like a gallery of reporters at an execution, waiting for the first jolt of electricity to ravage my body.

I knew two things for sure: there was no way out of this without a fight, and there would be no winning a fair fight with this animal. If somebody was going to get sucker-punched, it would be Charlie.

He was standing facing me, his weight evenly balanced on both feet, his arms hanging loosely at his sides, his face taking on the morbid hostility of a hardened killer's.

"Let me explain one thing to you, Charlie," I said, trying to look relaxed.

"Yeah?" he replied, moving his hands up to his hips, his chest thrust forward.

In the next quarter-second, I stamped down with my right foot squarely on his left instep hard enough to break his foot—I hoped. His head came down, as I knew it would, and my locked hands came down in a pile driver blow on the back of his neck, sending him to the floor like a sack of sand. Everybody gasped as one, and the place momentarily fell silent.

"Tell Charlie he's over the hill," I said to nobody in particular, making a point of stepping over him as I headed toward the door. Everybody gave us a wide berth on the way out. By the time we reached the Packard, my hands were shaking so bad I could hardly get the door open. I got in, then, on a whim, got back out. There was a brick lying in the gutter, and I picked it up, walked over to the car I'd seen Jake in, and smashed the windshield.

"Now let's get outta here," I told Swiftbird, who already had the car started and in gear. He was driving faster now than he had all evening.

"Why did you do that?" he asked.

"Just sending somebody a message he'll understand. You feel all right, Punky? We damn near missed that last turn."

"Yeah, I feel fine. It's just those last eight drinks—something wrong with the ice."

We drove up a hill and parked in a clearing in front of a green house.

"This what I think it is?" I asked Swiftbird, whose eyes were beginning to get fairly glassy.

"The famous Green House. Come on."

"Okay if I just wait out here?"

"No, this is the highlight of the tour. You don't want to miss it. Just tell them you're window-shopping, or you're my body guard. Hell, they're friendly."

A fiftyish redhead in housecoat and slippers admitted us, saying, "Hello, Punky, you're late. Thought maybe you'd forgot about us. Come on in."

"I would have forgot, Ramona, but my dog reminded me."

She looked out toward the car. "Hell, is that Donald sitting there? Why don't you let him in. I've got a bone he can chew on while he's waiting."

Swiftbird whistled, and Donald jumped out the window and came bounding in wagging his tail.

"Doris isn't here anymore," Ethyl told us. "She moved up to Oregon. Come on in the living room and I'll get you a beer."

This was not your typical American living room, I thought, dominated as it was by the moose head jutting out from the wall over the jukebox. But the linoleum floor looked clean, and the plastic flowers in their ceramic vases added color.

"Here you go, boys," Ramona said, setting down a four-ounce cheese glass of beer in front of each of us. She startled Swiftbird,

164

who was on the verge of passing out. "Two of my girls will be along in a minute. I think they're terrific. You'll see."

"Nice moose head," I said, trying to sound friendly.

"Yeah, ain't it a peach? One of my regulars, a geologist, just flat gave it to us. Said his old lady wouldn't have it in the house. Can you imagine, a gorgeous critter like that? Why, it cost the guy two hundred dollars to mount it."

Swiftbird came back to life. "Yeah, well how come you only charge me five bucks to mount you?"

"Well, they say you get what you pay for. Some guys like women, some like meese."

"Hi, I'm Tammy," announced a skinny six-foot blonde. Her polka-dot sunsuit had an large ungainly bow across the bodice. She looked tired but managed to put a cheerful smile on her pale face.

"And this is Vera," said Ramona, turning to leave the women to us.

Swiftbird's eyes almost popped out as he looked appraisingly at Vera's huge breasts, bulging out of a blouse that was two sizes too small. The woman's thick legs sort of billowed out from inside her pink shorts like balloons being inflated from a helium tank, revealing a network of purple veins. She wore spike heels in patent leather. I sighed, wondering how drunk I'd have to be . . .

It didn't take Swiftbird long to rule out the Eiffel Tower and lead Vera off toward one of the bedrooms. Tammy waited a few moments, then casually sat down in a chair across from me and crossed her long legs.

"Look, uh, Miss . . ."

"Tammy."

"Yeah. Look, Tammy, I don't want to waste your time. I'm just waiting for my friend, and—"

"It's okay. Not everybody likes me, at least not right at first."

"Oh, no, I don't mean that. You're fine. I just don't . . . that is—"

"You want another girl?"

"No, not at all. I just want to wait."

"You don't approve of whores, right? You just want to look at them."

165

"I don't approve or disapprove. I don't judge people. But, yeah, I don't mind looking at a sexy woman, like I'm doing right now. But that's not why I came here."

"You a virgin or a queer?"

When I laughed, she almost smiled. Then she uncrossed and recrossed her legs.

"Well, aren't you going to ask me how I got started in this business?" she asked.

"I'm not that much into personal history. Maybe I should ask how you're planning to get out of it."

"Oh, I see. You're one of those do-gooders from some church. You've come to save me from a life of sin."

The idea struck me funny, and I burst out laughing again. This time she laughed a bit with me. "God no. That's not one of my problems. But it seems to me you're the kind of person who'd be thinking about working your way into a more profitable job."

"But you don't judge people, right?"

"You got me that time."

"Why should you care about that? It's not your problem."

"You're right. Nobody should give a damn about anybody else, right? You do your thing, I do mine, and stay the hell out of the way. Is that how you'd have it?"

She studied me for a few moments. "You from that newspaper in Winchester?"

"What if I said yes?"

"Then I'd tell you some things you'd never have guts enough to print."

"For example?"

"Sorry, I only confide in paying customers. You interested?"

At that moment, a terrifying woman's scream—or maybe it would better be described as a screech—jolted us out of our seats. Tammy, Ramona, and I arrived almost together at the source of the sound, the doorway of the room where Swiftbird and Vera had gone. We were greeted by the rather unusual sight of two people and a large dog fighting on top of a bed. Swiftbird was on the bottom with Vera astride him, and Donald was tugging on one of Vera's ankles, evidently defending his prone master.

"Get this fucking dog the fuck offa my leg!" Vera was screaming.

The three of us managed to pull the snarling Donald away and get him out the front door. Vera was only bruised but vastly enraged.

"Son of a bitch!" she was shouting, "I thought I'd been in every kind of a fucked-up Chinese fire drill that ever happened in a goddamn cathouse, but I'll be damned if that's not the first time I've ever been mauled by a fucking coonhound while I was screwing a drunken Indian."

Swiftbird lay there for a few minutes grinning, then managed to pull his clothes back on and wobble toward the door. When we got outside, I offered to drive and he handed me the keys. I think I was more concerned about being waylaid than I was about his driving.

"You know another way to go back?" I asked, as we headed back down the hill toward Grady. There was no answer. He was out cold.

About two blocks down the hill from the Green House I caught sight of a vehicle coming up. I turned into a side street, where I quickly parked in front of a house and doused the lights. The car had to pass beneath a streetlight at the intersection, and I managed to get a look at it as it went by. It was not the car with the smashed windshield but a pickup truck, moving fast. My guess was the two men in it weren't going to the green house for the usual purpose.

As soon as they had passed, I eased back down the hill, keeping my headlights off until I hit the main road, and then wasted no time returning to Cedar Valley.

Chapter 11

Lois typed up our report the next day, and I redid in finished form the charts that went with it. She had written up a page that summarized who might have consistent access to the daily fire danger prediction, and from this I learned that the figures were called in each day to the lumber company office. This procedure was followed, she explained, because the timber sale contracts required special precautions be taken in the woods when the fire danger reached a certain level. To me, it simply meant that more people could find out about the next day's fire danger forecast than I'd previously thought.

Late in the afternoon I called Nora at her office and asked if she would join me for supper that night, but she said she had been invited to Bob and Sally Boardman's and suggested Monday night instead, at her house. I agreed, stating I'd bring some wine.

The next morning, Bill Marklee was expecting to line me out on screening the fire report forms, and when I handed him the completed analysis and report, neatly typed up and stapled in a folder, he blinked at it in astonishment, his face as blank as a stucco wall.

After he'd leafed through it for a minute, he looked up at me.

"I didn't expect you to do all this. And you weren't even on duty Thursday and Friday. How did you . . . ?"

"Lois and I decided to get as much done on it as possible while you were out, and we can change anything you don't like about it. As you can see, we didn't try to do anything on the action plan until you decide what it ought to be."

"Okay. Give me an hour or so to get through all this, then I'll give you a holler and we'll figure out where to go with it."

By about ten, Marklee had me and Lois back in his office. "I've read through this three times," he told us, "And what I can't figure out is how you did it so fast and, apparently, so thoroughly."

"What do you think of the delay-device theory?" Lois asked.

Marklee's nose began twitching. "You know, that's what I've been thinking myself, it has to be something like that. The only way we're going to catch this guy is by staking out the three roads you've identified. What were they, the Oyster Rock, the Ice Spring, and the Hog Tooth roads?"

"We'd be posting observers who would stay out of sight?" I asked, as if it were the first time the idea had come to me.

Marklee nodded. "For each of those roads we'd need a man spotted where he could get a clear look through binoculars."

"So if a fire were to break out," Lois said, "we'd have a list of vehicles that had passed in and out of the area. What then?" She was playing the game too.

Marklee's face went blank again.

"What about calling in Anselmo Adams?" I asked.

"How did you know about him?" Marklee asked.

"I saw something about him in the file on the Pegleg fire." I could feel Lois fish-eying me at my side. She would probably check it out, but I doubted whether Marklee would.

"Might be a good idea," the fire prevention officer said. "Adams did offer to come back if we stumbled onto anything. Anyway, we don't have to decide on that right now."

We spent the next hour or so discussing the details of handling nighttime operations, overtime authorization, changes in tours of duty, who would be assigned where, and communications needs. We agreed the plan would be drawn up quickly so that Shackle

170

and West could approve it before the next period of extreme fire danger occurred.

Lois and I went to work on it immediately and had it finished up by quitting time. She agreed that a copy of it, once approved, should be sent to Adams for his information.

"One thing I wanted to ask about, Harper," Lois said when we'd finished. "You and Bill were constantly referring to the arsonist as a guy; that is, a male. Isn't it possible it could be a woman?"

"You're a woman. What do you think?"

"My intuition is to doubt it. But I can't back that up with any good argument."

"Would you start fires, provided of course you were mad enough at somebody to use that means of getting even?"

She cocked her head to one side and thought about it. "No," she said, smiling, as she gathered her things and headed for the door. "I think I'd use a knife. By the way," she added, stepping in the doorway, "you get tomorrow off, orders from the district ranger. You can't get overtime for putting in your two days off, but you can at least have comp time. Sorry, one day is all he'd go for."

I knew she'd stuck her neck out to do that for me, but before I could thank her she was gone.

I left the office early enough to beat the crew to the showers. One forty-gallon tank was pitifully inadequate for two crews of dirty men. Anyway, having the next day off was a windfall; I decided to head for Winchester that night, have dinner and spend the night there, and be fresh to get a couple of jobs done the next morning.

I drove the forty-one miles leisurely, savoring the late afternoon light on the distant snow-capped peak of Mount Shasta and marveling at the stately sugar pines and giant white firs along the highway. It all made Los Angeles seem even farther away than it really was, and I asked myself if I'd ever go back there, and if so, why?

Winchester appeared all too soon. I'd been there before but had forgotten how dreary the place looked with its dusty, wind-blown streets and dismal houses and buildings. Main Street—it should have been called Dull Street—seemed devoid of any luster or vitality, the streets inhabited only by errant loggers strolling between bars and a few cowboys standing on corners chewing tobacco and spitting. I saw no women or children walking about.

I spotted a couple of drab restaurants open, and one movie house. *Son of Graveyard Ghoul* was playing, and I wondered if it had been filmed right there in Winchester, starring the city council, if they even had one. Why had I come here instead of to Klamath Falls, or Reno, or even Redding?

I found a no-nonsense motel with small individual cabins, signed in, and after paying the man six dollars, received the key to my cabin. Then I went out and choked down a lousy dinner, walked around for a while, then drove back to the motel, where I spent a mostly sleepless night listening to cars, trucks, and motorcycles coming and going, doors slamming, fights, and the rest of it.

"Nice quiet place you run here," I told the manager the next morning.

"You slept okay, huh?"

"Oh yeah. After about three it was real peaceful."

He laughed. "I've been here so long it doesn't even bother me anymore. Guess I'm used to it."

"I guess I should be—I was in a howitzer battery in Korea. You know where the library is here in town?"

"On Elm Street, just off Main. Say, there was a guy checking on you last night. Wanted to know who was driving the car parked in front of your cabin. I gave him a phony name, like I always do unless it's a cop."

"What did he look like?"

"Guy about your size, maybe a little older than you. Driving a pickup truck, didn't notice what kind."

"He say why he wanted to know?"

"Oh, he had the usual story, thought he might know you. But he wasn't really all that cheerful about it, so I figured there might be a problem."

★   ★   ★

172

I spent the morning in the public library looking at everything they had on flammable and combustible substances, making copious notes on what I thought were the most important items and being mystified by a good deal of it. However, in a handbook published by the National Fire Protection Association in 1954 I found a section on water- and air-reactive chemicals. My eyes jumped ahead to find the words ". . . significant quantities of heat are liberated during these reactions. If the chemical is combustible, it is capable of self-ignition. If it is noncombustible, the heat of reaction might be sufficient to ignite nearby combustible material."

Why not a device, then, containing a chemical that would self-ignite on contact with water or air? But then, how could such a device be arranged to prevent this contact until the desired time, and tougher yet, remain out of sight?

I plowed through a lot of technical information about water- and air-reactive chemicals, making notes about the more promising ones and disregarding the others. My list came down to six substances: charcoal (manufactured by the retort method); sodium or potassium carbide; sodium or lithium hydride; lithium aluminum hydride; calcium oxide (quicklime); white phosphorus; and sodium or sodium hydrosulfite.

Most of these, it said, were water-reactive. An arsonist, then, would have to provide a container of water at the scene and rig a device that would, with a preset delay, bring the chemical into contact with the water while somehow preventing the vapors from being swept away by any little breeze and that would direct the heat or flame directly into burnable vegetation. And would leave no evidence behind. This would be technically insurmountable, I decided, at least in a forest setting, except possibly with charcoal. The library references had said charcoal was air-reactive, meaning that after having been made wet, it could auto-ignite under some circumstances during the drying process. I'd used charcoal before but hadn't yet heard of that possibility. And what was the "retort method" of manufacturing it? I'd been unable to learn anything about that. Anyway, I thought it worthy of an experiment, inasmuch as charcoal ashes at a fire scene would be difficult, if not impossible, to distinguish from the other ashes.

173

White phosphorus, the manual said, was air-reactive. In this case, an arsonist would need a device that kept the chemical in a liquid and released it into the air at the appropriate time. Phosphorous, it said, was discovered in 1669 by a German alchemist who burned evaporated urine with sand in a quest for the philosopher's stone, an imaginary substance thought to be able to turn base metals into gold or silver. Instead, he discovered a substance that glowed in the dark. Fascinating, I thought, but not very helpful to my cause.

I read what else I could find on white phosphorous and charcoal, then headed for the town's chemical supplier, Pete's Pest Control and Chemicals.

"You're Pete, I guess," I said to the man behind the counter who glowered at me over the top of his reading glasses.

"That's right, who are you?" No hint of a smile.

"Phil Smith."

"Well?"

"I want to buy some white phosphorous."

"What the hell you want it for?"

"Indigestion." I didn't smile either.

"That'd cure it, all right. You the new chemistry guy at the high school?"

"No, but my sister's the chem teacher in Grady. She can't get any there, and she thought you might stock it. She only needs about a half pound." It occurred to me that lying was becoming easier each time I did it.

"I don't keep it anymore. No calls for it, and it's a pain in the ass to have around. It's a real fire hazard if the water leaks out of the container."

"Has that ever happened to you?"

"No, and it's not going to. The stuff comes in metal cans, and if it sits around too long it'll eventually rust through. In five years I think I sold phosphorus to only three people, and then only small amounts. So I quit handling it a couple of years ago."

"Where do you think I can get some?"

"Same place I used to get mine, most likely. That would be Corley's Chemical Supply in Reno."

"Do you remember the people who bought it from you?"

"You a cop, or what?"

"No, just curious what kind of people would use it."

"A high school teacher here in town was one of them; another was an army officer from the supply depot in Angel Valley, and, let's see, I think the other was a guy from here in town. I didn't know him, haven't seen him since. Anything else for you today?"

On the way out of town I stopped at Shopper's World One-Stop Groceries and Liquors. They had only one kind of charcoal briquettes.

"Were these manufactured by the retort method?" I asked the clerk.

"Well, what does it say on the package?"

"It doesn't say."

"Then how the hell am I supposed to know?"

"I thought maybe you were knowledgeable, but I guess not."

"You want them or not?"

"Yeah. And these two bottles of wine."

"They probably weren't manufactured by the retort method either."

"It's hard to get good stuff these days."

"Yeah, or vice-versa, my old lady says."

I knocked on the front door of Nora's little house at about six twenty, cradling in one arm the paper sack containing the wine. She appeared at the door in a matching black pullover sweater and skirt, an outfit I guessed she'd worn to the office that day. She looked radiant and expectant.

"You were off today, weren't you?" she asked, planting a little kiss on my cheek.

"You have good spies. Know where I was?"

"Winchester, obviously. Serious affair?"

"A librarian, and very serious. How did you know where I went?"

"Saw you heading north out of town. Tell me more about this librarian."

"Quite different than you. Taller, blondish, slimmer, older—"

"How much older?"

"Oh, I'd say about forty years. But very well preserved."

She'd got one of the bottles of wine opened and poured each of us a glass. "And what was the purpose of this visit to the library?"

I'd already spent a few hours calculating the merits of revealing to Nora what I was up to. My gut feeling was that she had no complicity in the arson fires, and I hoped to God that was true. But her unexplained trip up the Rucker's Ridge road still bothered me, along with her earlier relationships with both Ned Booth and Stan Turpin. Then there were those cryptic remarks she made at Coyote Peak lookout that evening, the ones pertaining to her having unfinished business in Cedar Valley.

On balance, I decided I had more to gain than to lose by giving her some preliminary information, then making a judgment about telling her the rest of it.

I explained the arson problem to her in general terms and told her about my work in the office analyzing fire reports.

She listened attentively, nodding approval all the while. "I think that's wonderful, but what has all this to do with the library in Winchester?"

"My review of the fire reports, and everything else I've found out about these fires makes me think that the incendiarist is using a device with a built-in delay that gives him plenty of time to leave the scene before the fire starts. The fact that no device or other evidence has been found at any of the fire scenes makes me suspect that he's using a chemical agent."

She was hanging on every word. I paused, wondering if she'd ask who I really was, how I knew so much about arson, why the intense interest in the situation. But she did not.

"So you were reading up on chemistry. Is that what the Forest Service wants you to do?"

I laughed, took a sip of the wine. "Hardly. They'd probably be horrified. Anyway, I was on my own time."

"You don't want them to know what you're up to?"

"It could even be somebody from the outfit who's doing it, and I sure wouldn't want to tip him off. Another thing is that I can't risk embarrassing Bill Marklee, because it's his job, not mine."

"So you're taking on the detective work yourself. Isn't that a bit risky?"

"How do you mean?"

"Well, Harper, after all. If the arsonist finds out what you're doing, it could be dangerous for you. I wouldn't like that."

I hoped she meant it, and it gave me a little thrill to hear her say it. "I take precautions," I told her.

"Sure, like staying out of fights in bars, right?"

"You mean Kelley's? That was one of those freakish things—"

"I mean the place in Grady, and just Friday night."

"Who told you about that one?"

She gave me an almost disgusted smirk. "It's all over town. You're practically a celebrity, at least to those who like bar fights."

"Somebody obviously set me up for that one."

"Exactly what I'm getting at. Somebody will set you up for something even worse, and you'll walk right into it. That's what you're like."

I knew she was right, thinking back about the guy with the shotgun, who blew my windshield out. On a whim I said, "Do you have any boyfriends that might be upset about our . . . friendship?"

"You mean somebody who also has a shotgun?"

Shocked, I said, "Where did you hear about that?"

"Somebody in the office said they heard about it at Kelley's. Is it true?"

"It's true, all right. Happened that Sunday night, just after the Rucker's Ridge fire, the night I saw you in Purple Pond. Listen, Nora, this is important. Can you find out who brought it up? That is, without making a big point of it?"

"I'll give it a try. But to answer your question, yeah, I've had a few boyfriends around here, but I doubt if any of them would try anything like that. At least, not because of me."

Her face darkened, and she seemed to be deep in thought. Then she brightened a bit and said, "What did you find out at the library? Was it worth the trip?"

"I got some good ideas to chase down, but I doubt if you want

177

to hear about all the chemicals that can cause fires. There are dozens of them."

"Not really. But after what you read, what do you think?"

I told her what I'd found out at the chemical supply store. She listened, fascinated. Again, I expected her to pin me down about my level of interest, and her failure to do so gave me an uneasy feeling, and I wasn't sure just why.

"Then the analysis you've been working on for the Forest Service is really more than just an analysis, isn't it? I mean, part of what you're doing is tying down the probable cause and then making recommendations about what do about it."

"You could say that."

"Seems like you're the brains on this job. What are you planning to do about it?"

I drained my wineglass and held it out for more. "If I were the district ranger, I know what I'd do. But remember, I'm just a crewman."

"But from what I've learned about you, I'd guess your analysis would leave them little leeway."

"I hope it doesn't leave them any, but we'll soon know the answer to that."

"Can I help, be part of it?"

"Can't chance it. You may be the arsonist."

She laughed so spontaneously and merrily that I began to question my sanity in still harboring any suspicions at all about her.

"That did, in fact, occur to you, didn't it?" she said, jabbing me in the ribs with an elbow. Should I tell her who I am, I wondered then, get it all out in the open, make it possible for her to share more with me about my brother? In fact, but why had she not yet shared with me her relationship with Heath? I went into a trance-like state for a few moments pondering the questions before she brought me out of it.

"What about the charcoal? You can buy that anywhere."

"I bought a sack, but I'm not sure it's the right kind."

"Maybe I can help. I'm really very good at experiments."

We talked about it, and she insisted on taking the sack of charcoal and running a set of trials in her back yard. We talked

178

about the need for secrecy, and she promised not to reveal to anybody what we were up to. Talking about our project, the secrecy and all, seemed to have the effect of energizing her. Suddenly, she seemed more alive, attentive, full of purpose.

"This outfit is too warm. Don't drink too much while I'm changing. That other glass is mine, you know."

She went into an adjoining room and closed the door between us. I took a sip of my wine. It probably wasn't very good, but I knew little about wine in those days and likely thought it was fantastic. Now I know the difference, the problem being I can't afford what I really like.

As I sat there looking around the little living room, the simplicity of the decor amazed me. For the lack of things like photos, reading materials, and other personal touches, it could well have been a room in the YMCA. Little money had been wasted on fancy furnishings by the owner, but beyond that, little had been added by the tenant. I wondered what this said about Nora, about her life. What did this place really mean to her? Was it just a hotel room to her, a place to stay until something happened that would enable her to get out of Cedar Valley?

"Harper!" Nora called from behind the door. "Will you come help me decide what to wear?"

Carrying the two wineglasses, I worked my way into the dimly lit bedroom. Nora was standing by a vanity mirror holding up two dresses. She was clad in a brown bathrobe.

"Some people are sure slow getting dressed," was all I could think of to say.

"But the end result will be worth it. You have three choices. There's this black job that's pretty tight on me, but devastating in dim light. Then there's this sort of western denim dress the cowboys think is great. What do you think?"

"You said three choices. What's the other one?"

"Just plain me."

"What's that like?" I asked lamely.

"Find out."

I shakily set the wineglasses on the vanity, turned toward her, and pulled loose the tie at her waist. The bathrobe swung open. She had nothing on beneath. As I stood there transfixed, she wriggled a little so that the robe slipped off her shoulders. My eyes never left her as my clothes somehow—magically?—fell away and we were suddenly entwined, still more or less on foot, doing a sort of slow, writhing dance among the discarded clothing.

And then we were on the bed, our hands and mouths discovering each other, both of us free for at least those precious minutes to unleash without restraint the pent-up passions and frustrations we harbored. Her strength was that of an enraged panther, and I thought for some moments I was in a fight for my life, so violently did she attack and twist and grasp and bite and claw and squeeze. And then, as quickly, she would relent, leaving the aggression to me, pulling me to her, asking for more than I could give, inviting me into positions I thought physically impossible, making me wonder where this devil lady ever learned to fuck like that. Or was she simply making it up as she went along?

Finally, we lay there deflated, her lithe body still astraddle mine. "What hit me?" I asked in bewilderment.

She lowered her torso, dangling her breasts about my face. "Now do you think you'll be able to remember what I look like?"

I grabbed her again and rolled her over. But the bed was narrow and we went off the side, crashing to the floor, me on the top. I tried to take her again but it was too soon—maybe by about three hours. Anyway, it didn't work and she wound up getting a good laugh out of it. It wasn't a derisive laugh; she knew what was going on and laughed out of good spirits, and I laughed too. Now it was time to finish the wine, as good or as bad as it might be. Anyway, who would notice?

For all the earlier restraint imposed on each of us by my dead brother's memory, what happened between Nora and me brought us a lot closer together both emotionally and physically. Gone now was my fear that Nora would be repelled by my natural affection for her—my lust, I guess, to be more specific. And for her to have unleashed such passions, fleeting though they may have been, told me that the memory of Heath would not forever thwart her sensuality.

The rest of the evening was suddenly devoid of the unspoken

tension that earlier had commanded our behavior, and now I revelled in the touch of her arm against me, heard new tones in her voice, and recognized a gracefulness in her movements I hadn't seen before. I felt less guarded about what I could say to her and was almost tempted to ask if she felt the same. It was a delicious magic that seemed to be enveloping me, but one that my instincts told me to be wary about. The thought was discomfiting. But at least for now, I felt terrific.

My watch said one ten when I got back in my car and started down Fir Street toward the main road, where I noted a pickup truck parked under a tree. This was not an unusual sight, there being about fifty pickups in and around the town, but something about it bothered me, and I kept it in sight in my mirror as I drove back through town toward the turnoff to the barracks.

The vehicle didn't appear in my mirror during the short drive to the turnoff, and I started up the little hill toward the barracks. I guess I had pickup fever, owing to the incidents I'd been involved in lately, but I decided not to ignore my present suspicions. Stopping halfway up the hill, I turned off the lights and let my Ford roll backward down to the main road, using the hand brake to control its descent in so as not to show a brake light. I stopped my car before it entered the main road, looked back the way I'd come, and there it was: a pickup truck, moving toward me with no lights.

When the vehicle came to a point about a hundred yards from me, it braked to a stop, the driver obviously having spotted me. I quickly backed onto the main road and turned to go toward him. He remained motionless a few seconds, then, tires squealing, heeled about to head back the way he'd come.

"All right, you son of a bitch," I found myself saying aloud. "Let's see how *you* like being followed."

The pickup, now only about a block ahead of me, turned right on Pine Street. My instinct was that he'd make a right on Chestnut, then come back to the main road on either Fir or Cedar. As a cop, I'd played similar games numerous times and had a feeling for what my quarry would do. I stopped in a shadowy spot beneath a tree. In moments I caught sight of him zooming across the main road on Cedar, which became Juniper on the south side. From Juniper he'd have to exit either on Oak or Elm, so again I waited.

Nothing happened. The town was as dead as a broken promise, so, going in the opposite direction, down Elm, I decided to dig him out. With my lights still out, I eased the Ford down Elm, watching for pickups, and now I was looking for one with a large jockey box mounted behind the cab. I found nothing on either Elm or Ash, which led me to the intersection of Oak and Dogwood.

There I spotted several pickups in a half-block area that met the general description of the one I sought. I figured the best thing to do would be to park and wait, which I did. It was a cold evening, and I knew the windows in an occupied vehicle would probably fog up. But after a ten-minute surveillance, nothing showed. It was time to feel radiators.

I dug out my .38 from beneath the dash and planned my visits to the three vehicles I had singled out—a Dodge, an International, and a Chevy. The dim glare of the streetlight at the corner wasn't enough to reveal any silhouettes in any of the pickups and in fact made it harder to tell if there was someone inside. My quarry, I thought, either was crouched down in the seat or had gone into a house.

Here I was again, doing exactly what Nora said I'd do, risking my butt to carry on the investigation. And who the hell was I investigating this time? An unhappy boyfriend? An arsonist? Jake, whoever the hell he was?

I gingerly climbed out of my Ford, the revolver stuck in my waistband, leaving the door open and the keys in the ignition. Moving slowly, I went to the Chevy pickup, felt its radiator, and found it cold as an ice axe. I looked at the houses nearby and saw no curtains being pulled aside or other signs of life. The Dodge was in the driveway of a house on Dogwood, and I slowly approached it.

Bam! As I instinctively dived to my right into some skimpy bushes I heard the ricochet of the shot that had whizzed past my face. The shot sounded like it came from a high-powered rifle. I suddenly felt quite vulnerable lying there clutching my snub-nose revolver.

Bam! One zipped over my head this time, but I saw the muzzle flash in a field between two houses on the other side of the street. I fired two fast shots in the general direction, not really hoping to do anything but create some diversion so I could get the hell out of there. Half a dozen dogs now barked angrily, and the first lights began flicking on in bedrooms as sleepy residents tried to figure out what the commotion was. I sprinted for my car, got it started on the first try, and zoomed away, before anybody could get a description of it, I hoped.

In less than two minutes I had the car parked behind the barracks, but instead of going inside, I walked back down the drive to the main road and lay down in some shrubbery, whence I could see back toward the middle of town. But there was nothing to see except the row of streetlights and the silhouettes of houses.

A rustling in the bushes just behind me caused me to whirl around and point my revolver. A shape appeared suddenly, one with long ears and a wagging tail.

"Good morning, Donald. What do you think?"

"Uff."

If asked to summarize what had just happened to me, I'd have said about the same thing.

Chapter 12

At breakfast the next morning Vaughan Day reported that there'd been a gunfight in town the night before, but the rest of the crew, sleepy-eyed, wasn't giving it any credibility.

"Where'd you hear that, V.D.?" Jurgenson asked, always anxious to toss out the nickname he'd earlier planted on Vaughan Day. "You been having dreams again?"

"No, they're all talking about it down at Chubby's. I was there gassing up this morning. Chubby said it was like a war, right there about a block from his station. And a guy who lives on Oak Street said people were running around, cars squealing their tires and all kinds of shit."

"Did he say if anybody got shot?" Swiftbird asked.

"No. Nobody knows about it if they did."

"Did they say if there was a 'fifty-one Ford involved?" Jurgenson asked, giving me a mirthful sidewise glance.

"Yeah, you were out till late last night, Harper," said Larry Banks. "I heard you come in about one thirty."

Everybody stopped eating and looked at me. I shrugged my shoulders and kept on eating.

"Well, where were you last night?" asked Jurgenson. "Just for the record, as you say."

"Out of town on a late date," I said, laughing it up. "Go ahead. Check out my car for bullet holes. If you find any, they're from another time. You can tell from the rust."

"I already looked," said Day, making me wonder if he really had. "Dhrymes told Chubby he thinks you were involved in it. He's telling people that ever since you came to town there's been trouble here."

"Yeah, trouble for him," Fred Sweeney said, and everybody laughed.

At nine Swiftbird put us to work digging a drainage ditch behind the ranger station, but he came to get me a short time later.

"Mr. West wants you to come to his office at ten, Harper," he said, kind of smiling. "He didn't say what it's about."

I said okay and kept digging. If it was about the gunfight, I hadn't yet decided how much to say. If my car had been identified I'd have to admit what had happened, but if not, I felt it more prudent to deny it, especially if I expected to keep my job with the Forest Service.

Shortly before ten, I saw Boyd Robbins and Bud Griffin, two of the fire prevention technicians, drive into the station, park their pickups, and wander into the office by the back door. When I got to the district ranger's office they were already in there, along with Felton Shackle, Ray Owens, and Bill Marklee. In a few minutes Don West and Lois Hart came in, and West got the meeting started.

"This is about the incendiary fire problem," he began, not bothering with preliminaries, "and what we're going to do about it."

Robbins, Griffin, and Owens looked at me, wondering what the hell I was doing in there. Robbins, neatly outfitted in clean and pressed shirt and trousers, stared grimly at my muddy boots and wrinkled jeans, his disdain obvious. I noted that neither Robbins nor Griffin had prevention responsibility in any of the three units to be staked out, exactly as I'd recommended.

"Bill Marklee turned in an analysis and some recommendations," West went on, "that Felton and I think are right on the money. I understand that Harper here and Lois did a lot of the work on it, and they, along with Bill, are to be complimented for an excellent job."

Marklee was looking down, his face reddening slightly. Robbins had quit looking at my muddy clothes and now, stern-faced, appraising, he shifted his attention to the rest of me.

West summarized the analysis, referring from time to time to a district map on the wall. Then he went over the recommendation to stake out each of the three identified roads beginning the day before extreme fire danger was expected.

"Why is it," Robbins wanted to know, "that the FPT's from those three units aren't here, aren't going to be involved in the stakeouts? What's Johnson going to think, for example, when he finds out one of us is working his unit?" He was coming across as if he felt the honor of his fellow prevention techs had been besmirched.

"Bill?" West said to Marklee.

Marklee looked distressed. "Well, that wasn't my idea. Why don't you explain it, Harper?"

West looked amused at the baton passing. Robbins was almost slack-jawed that a crewman like me was in on an important matter like this. I rather enjoyed it and looked forward to deflating this man's imperious ego.

"My impression is that within an FPT's own unit, he tends to go blind to things he's been looking at for a few years. He might not be paying attention to people he regularly sees coming and going. He might just assume everything is okay. If another FPT comes in, the new man is more likely to question anything he sees. It's human nature."

"What a pile of crap," said Robbins, fuming. "Who the hell are you to make a judgment like that?"

I was ready for the challenge, having looked at the fire reports over and over. "Well, if you put it that way, the Yellow Springs fire was in your unit, the Salt Log fire was in your unit, and as we all know, the Pegleg fire was in your unit. I'm not suggesting you weren't doing your job, just that somebody else, if they'd been watching those roads, might have seen something that could have helped, that's all. And I'm saying that you could do that in somebody else's unit."

187

If Robbins had been holding a railroad spike between his teeth he would have snapped it off cleanly. I could almost see the smoke coming out of his ears as he fought for control of his temper. I gave him the cold stare I used on guys I'd collared who were giving me a ration of shit.

"I agree with that," West said, precluding any possible rejoinder by Robbins. "Let's get on with it." He turned control of the meeting over to Shackle, who went into the details of managing the stakeouts, ending with a reminder about the need for secrecy throughout.

West said finally, "This is not a game we're playing here. When Special Agent Adams was here last fall investigating the Pegleg fire, he told me he was involved in a serious confrontation with an unknown assailant. Then last night, as many of you already know, there was some shooting right here in town. I'm not convinced that in both cases it doesn't have something to do with all this. So I'll tell you again, avoid confrontations. When we find out what we're dealing with, we can call for the kind of help we need."

I suspected that as the meeting broke up, ranger West would call me aside to ask if I'd been involved in last night's ruckus, so I lagged behind the others to make it easier for him.

"Anything you need to tell me about?" he asked, his eyebrows arching high toward a receding hairline. His meaning, though not specified, was clear. I'd already made the calculation; there was no way I could tell him what happened without forcing him to take some kind of action that would compromise my whole reason for being there.

"Absolutely not," I said. "And I want to say how much I appreciate your willingness to go along with our plan. I'm confident we can get some results."

He seemed willing to be given a pretext for not following up on his question but still regarded me coolly, an indication, perhaps, that he was knowingly letting me off the hook—this time.

"I'm giving it a try, Harper, but only with some reservations I didn't want to make known in the meeting. There's something going on here that bothers me, and when I find out what it is, everybody involved in it will hear from me. Just in case you're not aware of it, I have a boss who expects, among other things, that we maintain a good reputation in our community. I expect that too—in fact, insist on it. I haven't yet figured out who you are, or why you're here, but from what's happened so far, you've definitely aroused my concerns. You're already on the edge; don't push it." With that, he flagged me out of his office, leaving me wondering exactly how much he did know.

Lois was at her desk, talking on the telephone. She stopped me and handed me the phone.

"Harper," Nora said, the tension in her voice unmistakable. "I know you can't talk freely there in the office, so just answer questions, okay?"

"Sure."

"I heard all that gunfire last night right after you left. I was scared to death. Was somebody shooting at you?"

"It sure seemed like that at the time. In fact, I would say definitely, yes."

"My God! Do you know who it was?"

"I tried to find out. Maybe that was part of the problem. But to answer your question, no."

"What happened? Were you followed from my house?"

Bud Griffen was standing there, clearly waiting to use the phone, and I held up one finger to indicate I was almost finished.

"Yes, I was, and I want to thank you for getting me the spare parts. They turned out to be exactly what I needed."

I glanced at Lois, who had been following my end of the conversation, and she gave me one of those rolling-eyes expressions that almost made me burst out laughing.

"Okay, I understand," Nora was saying. "Can you meet me at the cafe in Purple Pond at about eight?"

"You've got a deal," I said, and hung up.

After work, I got to the shower before V.D., who generally drained the tank, despite the sulphurous odor of the water. While getting dressed, something I tried to accomplish before Albert Carlisle returned from the woods to stink up our little room, I thought about the stakeout plan and wondered if there were any serious holes in it. I had a vague feeling I'd rushed through the analysis so fast that one or more roads might have been overlooked, so I decided to take one more look at my original map, one of the items I had earlier secreted away in my suitcase beneath my bed.

But when I opened the large manila folder containing my incendiary fire materials, I was surprised to find the map folded up in a way in which I never would have done it. The thought blazed through me like an electrical current that somebody had gone through the envelope, figured out what I was up to, and tried to scare me away—or maybe worse—last night.

When could this have happened? The last time I had unfolded the map had been just before the first fire prevention meeting, five days ago. Since then, I'd been away from the station only once, from Sunday evening through Monday afternoon. Pondering it, I looked in the folder for my photos. Another shot of adrenaline made my skin tingle. The photos were gone! But I had stored the negatives separately, placing them in an envelope beneath some underclothing in one of my dresser drawers. I found the envelope where I expected to, but I also found that it contained not only the negatives but also the prints.

Was my imagination playing tricks? No, I distinctly remembered deciding to keep them separate. Whoever had shaken the room down had been a little careless in replacing what he'd looked at. But who was it? My roommate, Albert, didn't know what was in his own drawers, let alone mine. I dismissed all the other guys with routine access to the barracks as suspects except for Turpin, and he only came there for supper. Indeed, two silver dollars in plain sight in the drawer remained undisturbed. Information about my investigation and my activities was clearly the target.

Then I remembered the shotgun shell, and rummaged around in the drawer. It was gone.

I knew that from the office, just across the main road from the barracks, Lois would have a clear view of the approach to the barracks, and thus knowledge of the comings and goings of people other than the regular residents. I would ask her about it tomorrow. She was the only person I could ask about this without having to answer a lot of questions myself about my interest.

★　★　★

At eight I waited for Nora in the same restaurant booth where she'd found me almost a month before. She didn't arrive until twenty after, surprising me with a kiss on the ear.

"Any problems?" I asked, noting her rather harried appearance.

"I'm not sure. In view of what's been happening, I headed north when I first left the house, then swung back to see if anybody was following. Just after turning back, a greenish pickup passed going fast the other way. I didn't get a clear look at the driver."

"Then what?"

"Well, going through town, I saw a beer truck parked in front of Kelley's, so I pulled in just in front of it, out of sight of southbound traffic, and just waited. The pickup didn't come back through town, so I came directly here. What do you think?"

"That you did it just right. And that both of us are going to have to be very careful."

The waitress came and took our order. Then Nora said, "Okay, tell me all about last night." Everything about her, her attitude, her manner, was completely different from the night before. I noticed the wrinkles in her forehead, and a jerkiness about her motions that was new to me. I began telling her precisely what had happened from the time I left her house. When I got to the part about getting the revolver out from under the dash, she stopped me.

"Harper! You had a gun with you in your car?"

"Of course. Doesn't everybody?"

She didn't think it funny. "Then some of those shots were yours?" she asked.

"Only half of them. I didn't want to run out of ammunition, and it takes a long time to reload a revolver."

"Will you be serious? I don't believe this."

I put my finger to her lips, telling her to let me finish the story, which I did, concluding it with my encounter with Donald.

"You could have been killed," she said, frowning.

We waited while the waitress poured our coffee.

"Any idea who the hell it could have been?" I asked.

She stared into her coffee cup, cradling it with both hands. "I wish I knew."

"What kind of rig does Ned drive around in?"

She looked up, startled. "Ned? I doubt it. He can be vindictive, but he's not homicidal. At least I have no reason to believe so."

"A pickup, or a car?"

"A pickup. A Dodge, I think. Dark green, about a 'fifty-one or 'fifty-two."

"Anything else, like a winch, trailer hitch, gun rack?" I asked, deliberately leaving out the jockey box.

"Yeah, all that stuff. Plus one of those toolboxes behind the cab. He leaves it parked behind his shop, and you could get a look at it there."

"What about Stan Turpin?"

"I knew you were going to ask about him next. Whatever is between us is nothing serious, at least with me. He'd come on strong if I let him, I suppose."

"Why don't you, if you don't mind my asking?"

"It's okay. Main reason is, I think, just no chemistry there for me. Then, he's a control sort of a guy. I'd never be able to even talk to another man, ever go off by myself."

"Why do you think that?"

"He criticizes where I go, who I see. And we've never even . . . been together, made any kind of commitment."

"You were about to add something to that."

"He's been in a scuffle or two with other guys over me. You know, if I'd made a play for him, or even just let him think we had something going, I could understand it. But can you imagine how he'd be if we were married or something?"

"Who were the other guys? It could be helpful to me."

She smiled and cocked her head to one side. "Now you're being like him."

"Seriously."

"Nobody you know of, or who could figure in this thing. Just guys around. Oh! You asked me to find out who was passing that story around about the shotgun incident. About all I could find out was that Kelley was discussing it with a couple of guys across the bar. Stan was one of them, but he may just have been on the receiving end."

"The other?"

"Somebody, apparently, from out of town."

"Who was able to get you this information?"

"Bill Devlin, the man you talked to in the mill office the first day you were here."

I shook my head and took a drink of coffee. "Is there anybody else who might have reason to watch your house, keep track of your visitors?"

"It just doesn't make any sense, Harper. But what about you? Maybe it doesn't have anything to do with me. Might somebody have a reason to find out what you're up to?"

"Well, how do you mean? Who, for example?"

The way she studied me after I said that caused me to wonder if she knew I was playing games with her, but if so, she didn't reveal it.

"Dhrymes, for example. He's got a couple of pretty good reasons to be on your case, I'd say. Word around town is that he's saying he slept through the whole thing last night. What an alibi, right?"

I laughed. "Believable, coming from him. Does he have a pickup?"

"Not that I know of. Then what about what you're working on for the Forest Service? Maybe somebody thinks you've got more of an interest there than you're letting on . . . even to me."

Her last phrase was delivered dramatically, I thought. "How much do you think Vivian Crump knows about me?"

"Probably more than you think she does."

"How much do *you* know about me?"

She smiled, then asked, "How much am I supposed to know? Do you realize ninety-nine percent of your conversation with me has to do with your work? Look, I'm the kind of a person men pour out their souls to in infinite detail, I mean endlessly. But you? No." She dragged out the word to make it sound derisive. I get to learn all about sharpening Pulaskis and priming pumps and cutting fireline. What have I learned about your life, your loves, your boyhood, your successes and failures? Not a lot, mister."

"I've shut out a lot of the past," I said meekly. "I'm sorry if that comes across as secretive, or boring. Anyway, for what it's worth, you're the first woman who's told me she wants me to torture her with my life story."

"I told you mine, remember? Were you tortured by it?"

"Not in the least. But you left out some things."

She took it in stride. "Well, you can't expect a lady to tell everything. Was it something in particular?"

The waitress appeared with our food, and then two men sat down in the booth next to ours. Further private conversation became impossible, and so we talked of other things until leaving. Outside the restaurant, she suggested I call her the next evening. I said I might be in the field until late, but she said it didn't matter, she planned on being home all evening.

After saying good night, we got into our cars and drove back to Cedar Valley. I drove behind at a distance of about a half mile and kept a watchful eye on the mirror, but nothing happened.

When I took the fire weather observations the next morning at ten, the relative humidity was only fourteen percent, a very low reading for that time of day, with an air temperature of seventy-five. If the forecast for one o'clock that day of ninety-five degrees came true, that meant the humidity would drop to about seven percent, critically low. The fuel moistuer measurement showed only five percent, an indicator of intense burning conditions.

When I showed the figures to Lois, she whistled softly and said, "I'd better alert Bill. We'll probably be in extreme by this afternoon."

"Plan Harpoon?"

"Plan Harpoon?"

"Combination of Harper and lampoon. What do you think?"

"Lousy," she said, wrinkling her nose. She ran the numbers through a chart and told me the situation met the criteria for our stakeout operation. Marklee sensed what was going on and emerged from his office, his nose twitching, as it always did when he got curious about something. He looked at the figures.

"Let's do it," he said. "Harper, get your stuff together. You'll be on the Hog Tooth road as we planned. Stan Turpin will drop you off there."

"Stan?" I asked, shocked. He hadn't been at the second meeting, when the plan had been unveiled, and I thought nobody else was even supposed to know about it. Lois and I glanced at each other, and she looked as surprised as I'm sure I did.

"Felton insisted on it," Marklee said, looking a bit apologetic. "We just didn't have enough people to deal with the transportation end of it. Anyway, he's been told this is a confidential operation, and there won't be any problem."

This put a whole new slant on the operation, Stan being one of my prime suspects, at least until I could rule him out. Therefore, his being party to it stood to compromise the whole plan, and conceivably, my investigation. As I threw my things into a knapsack, I struggled to think of a way to turn this development to my advantage. No good ideas came to me.

At ten thirty I climbed into Stan's government pickup, and we left town on the main highway headed toward Winchester, turning off to the west on the Carlson Grade road, an old logging railroad grade. Thence we bounced along the washboard surface for about eight miles, finally turning off on the Hog Tooth road.

During the trip, Turpin remained sullen, as if waiting for me to open a conversation with him, but I decided to hell with him. At least he had nothing to say about the fire department initiation incident, or the tiff we'd had in the first fire prevention meeting.

Meantime, as the road meandered among second growth stands of fir and cedar left over from the heavy pine-logging shows of years past, Stan, out of habit, inspected the telephone line that paralleled the road. He would occasionally grunt, muttering things like "Too much slack," or "Broken insulator," or "That one needs trimming." His behavior, to me, wasn't characteristic of somebody toying with people trying to catch him at arson. Or else he was a pretty good actor.

He suddenly braked to a halt, backed up about fifty yards, and stopped. I looked on with no small concern as he reached between his legs and extracted a revolver from beneath the seat, one that looked like a .22. He glanced at my shocked expression and gave me a kind of twisted grin.

"Porky," he said, climbing out of the truck. I got out on my side and watched him bring the animal down from its high perch in a pine tree with a single shot to the beast's tiny head. His smile of satisfaction at killing the little animal gave me the creeps.

"Good shooting," I said. "But wouldn't a shotgun be easier?"

"Yeah, but shotgun shells cost more. Last year on the district we killed over a thousand porcupines with twenty-two's, all of the ammo bought by Uncle. This one's a bull," he said, turning the animal over with his boot. "Hung like a stud goose."

"Look at all those ticks on his belly," I said. "And people really eat these things?"

"You have to be real hungry. Want to see the worms inside?" he asked, offering me his pocket knife.

"No thanks, I had a late breakfast."

"Too bad. Last guy I talked into cutting one open stuck the knife in too far and the juice squirted him right in the eye. Stink? My God, I damn near puked."

"You own a shotgun?" I asked him point blank.

The question seemed to startle him, but then his angular face took on that grin. "Sure. Why?"

"I was thinking of getting one myself. What kind do you have, and what do you use it for?"

"Oh," he said, chuckling. "I thought you were sizing me up as the guy that blew out your windshield."

"Why would I blame that on you, Stan?"

"I don't know. Looks like you ought to be blaming somebody, I guess."

"How much did you hear about that incident?"

"Not too much," he said as we got back into the pickup. He put the revolver back under the seat. "But it's around town that somebody wants you out of here real bad."

"I've been getting that message. But whoever it is doesn't have the guts to tell me face to face. You get around. If you've been hearing it, you must know who it is, and why they want me out. Don't tell me I'm wrong about that, or I'll figure you're lying to me."

His jaw clenched and he swallowed hard. "Don't get your balls in an uproar, Murphy—er, Sandow. You know as much as I do about it."

"You started to call me Murphy. Who's Murphy?"

"Yeah. You remind me of a guy by that name. He's the one got himself killed on the Pegleg fire last year."

196

"What was this Murphy like?"

"Like?" He shrugged. "Just another college boy, as far as I was concerned. Who's going to be up on the Oyster Rock road?"

"Bud Griffen," I said, having the strong feeling he already knew. "I hope all this isn't going to be a waste of everybody's time."

"You pick your spot," he said, cutting off the opportunity to pursue things further.

I selected a place that suited me, got out, retrieved my pack from the bed of the pickup and stepped back. Turpin drove away without so much as a wave. By the time he'd found a place to turn around and come back past me, I was already out of sight in the brush looking for the best spot. I soon found one that offered a view both up the hill and down and that was shaded by the canopy of a young stand of ponderosa pine. I positioned myself about thirty feet from the road, on a knoll right by a turn, where any vehicles coming by would have to slow down. From this vantage point, using binoculars, I felt I could definitely identify the driver of any vehicle proceeding down the hill, and possibly of one coming up, when the driver would be on the far side of the road from me.

Not many vehicles came up the hill, so when one did I scrutinized it carefully, noting the vehicle description, license number, occupants, and anything else of interest on a page on my clipboard. For each vehicle, I tried to figure out the purpose of the trip. The first one was a woodcutter, his pickup bed empty except for a dog, a chain saw, and a gas can. The next one was a white Buick with a man driving and woman sitting close beside him. I thought the guy looked like Acton Price, the Baptist minister and my fellow volunteer fire department initiate, which raised an interesting question about the purpose of his trip. Then the local U.S. Fish and Wildlife Service guy drove by, probably to check his coyote traps.

Next I saw a green Chevy sedan coming down the hill, one that hadn't passed me going up. It meant the driver had to have been up there for at least two hours. To do what? I couldn't figure that one out.

Another vehicle from below: a black Dodge pickup with a man and a woman in cowboy hats. Couldn't figure this one out.

At about five, the uphill procession had long since ended and the vehicles, one by one, came back down the hill, and I checked each one off my list. Pretty soon there came the last one, the black Dodge pickup, but the man wasn't in it. I entertained myself for the next hour guessing what had happened to him, when here came a green Jeep with him driving. If the Jeep had broken down and he'd brought the tools and parts to fix it, why hadn't the woman waited to be sure he was successful?

There were no other vehicles until Bill Marklee came driving slowly up the hill just before dark, stopping when he heard my yell.

"Any fires today?" I asked him.

"Just a small grass fire down by Scarface Junction."

"Think we scared the arsonist off?"

"Too soon to say. Fire danger was at the low end of extreme today, and it looks like it'll be at least that high tomorrow. You have much traffic up here?"

"Six is all. By the way, how did Turpin know about the Oyster Rock road?"

"Beats me. Maybe Shackle mentioned it to him. We'll probably need you up here again tomorrow. Okay by you?"

"Absolutely." I had one of those strong premonitions that the next day would produce some surprises, but as it turned out, they weren't the kind I was expecting.

Chapter 13

On returning to the station at about eight thirty, I gave Nora a call, more to hear her voice than to tell her how I'd spent the day. As a precaution, I'd avoided mentioning the stakeout to her at supper the night before, and had an evasive answer ready in case she asked. But when I called there was no answer, and this worried me. She had been quite definite when she suggested I call her. Maybe her phone was simply out of order, and ten minutes later I found myself knocking at her door.

The gauzy curtain permitted me to see hazily into her little house. The lamp on the kitchen table was lit, as she usually left it when away, but there were no other signs of life. I gently tried the doorknob, but it was locked.

Probably at her friend Sally Boardman's, or maybe an emergency call from her aunt in Purple Pond, I thought, turning to leave. It was then that I spotted a man sitting in the car parked near her house. I didn't recognize the car, but as I approached it a smile slowly spread across the man's face. It was Steve Christian.

"Say, you're Harper Sandow, aren't you?"

"That's right. And you're taking a bit of a chance being here, aren't you?"

"Get in." He gestured at the passenger-side door.

I climbed in and got a strong whiff of bourbon. He got the car in motion, then reached under the seat and pulled out a bottle, which he handed me. I took a drink out of it.

"Yeah, I suppose so, but what the hell. The bastards'll probably catch up to me sooner or later anyway. Abby's sick. She sent me over here to pick up some things Nora has for her. Nora musta gone out."

"I don't know, but it worries me. She was supposed to be here this evening."

We drove up the little hill behind town, and he parked in a spot where people went to watch the sawmill burner after dark. The shower of sparks flowing out of the screened top looked vaguely like an inverted fiery waterfall. I remembered Swiftbird's warning about how Christian got nasty when he drank, but so far he was acting quite friendly.

Christian passed me the bottle again. "I won't ask where you're staying," I said. "But how are you getting along?"

"I always get along, one way or another. But this is gettin' old, just coming around at night. I feel like a damn polecat. How's your project coming?"

"Which one?"

"Shit, don't which one me, man. I'm not the only one around here who knows what you're up to."

"Not making much progress," I said. "I sure could use some help."

Christian laughed and took a drink. "You forestry guys are a panic. Last ones to know what the hell is going on, and it's always been that way. Know what's wrong? They sit in their little offices, or big offices, or whatever, and fill out forms and write reports. Then they collect their paychecks every month and expect everything to be wonderful."

"Wrong. We get paid every two weeks."

"Whatever. Anyway, I owe you some thanks for helpin' us out that night, an'—"

"Forget it."

"Fuck you. And I plan on payin' you back for it. You know what I think?" he asked. His speech slurring. "I think you guys are gonna have one hell of a big fire one of these days when the wind's up and it's dry like it is, and there ain't nothin' any of you will be able to do about it."

"Maybe so." I hoped he'd keep on talking.

"An' it don't really make a rat's ass if he keeps settin' 'em or not. Could be lightning, could be simultaneous combustion, a bullet richocheting off a rock, or any other damn thing. Point is, you got too much underbrush stacked up out there that needs to be burned once in a while."

"Do you think he'll keep on setting them?"

"Shit, I don't know. Probably so, long as you guys can't figure out how he's doin' it."

It sounded to me like he knew something, but I doubted if a guy like him would intentionally betray a confidence. That would be breaking an unwritten code. "How do you think he does it?" I asked.

"Everybody wants to know the answer to that one."

"Does everybody know who it is except me?"

He was silent for long moments, then said, "Sandow, when you owe somebody, you don't rat out on them. I owe you, so that's the only reason I'm talkin' to you at all. Now get offa my back, okay?"

"Yeah, sure, Steve. So what if a guy gets killed now and then fighting the fires."

"Yeah, that was too bad. But what the fuck does that have to do with it? He could just as easily have got killed on any fire. Anyway, I don't know who might have set that one."

"I thought maybe you heard something, that's all. It's like you just got through saying, the forestry guys are the last ones to find out anything like that."

"Why're you so interested in it? You some kind of investigator or something?"

"No, I'm nobody. I just got to wondering why it is somebody wants to burn the forest. I mean, if I get pissed off at somebody I don't go burn down their fucking house. Know what I mean?"

"Yeah, good point. That's not my style either. But who the fuck am I to try to tell everybody else how to run their business?"

I hoped if we kept talking about it, he'd loosen up and maybe even level with me. But every time I'd inch too close, he'd begin to get angry. I gave up on it finally but made a mental note to try to get Nora to pry it out of Abby—that was, if she hadn't already done exactly that.

We sat there talking about other things until the whiskey was gone, then he drove me back to Nora's at about eleven, where I was distressed to find her still gone. I drove back to the barracks, and while going up the gravel drive I saw a pickup truck heading west through town. It looked like Stan Turpin's rig, but I wasn't positive.

Entering our room, I managed to wake Albert Carlisle, who rolled over, looked at his wristwatch, grunted at me, then fell back into his usual comatose slumber. Soon he was snoring, and as I lay there, restless, I had a foreboding that something terrible had happened to Nora. It was one of those feelings that seems unshakable, even though one can find no logic for it. It so disturbed me that I got up, dug out a bottle of bourbon, and lugged it out into the cool night air on the back porch, where I had two more drinks I surely didn't need.

But once again in bed, the foreboding got even worse. I guess I attributed it at the time to some of the grisly crime scenes I'd witnessed as a policeman, some of the worst of which I relived before finally succumbing to fatigue and alcohol.

Only a short time later I was awakened by a horrible nightmare—one about Nora being pursued and maimed in the forest by an assailant with no face. The images had been so powerful and graphic I found myself shaking in fright and perspiring profusely. Thank God it was only a dream, I told myself, being almost ironically reassured by the vibrations of Carlisle's snoring.

But yet, where was Nora, in fact? I looked at my watch: only one twenty. I spent the rest of the night thrashing about in the bed, only dozing fitfully.

The next day was pretty much a copy of the day before, except this time there were only four vehicles to glare at on the Hog Tooth road, none of them suspicious in the least, I thought.

When Marklee dropped me off in front of the office a little before ten that night, I went inside to leave my data sheet on his desk and pick up new batteries for my flashlight. I gave Nora a call, but once again, there was no answer. After having spent a good part of the day brooding over the situation and half convincing myself there was no cause for alarm, the endless ringing at her end of the line did nothing to calm my nerves. I headed for the barracks, trying to remember if there was any whiskey left from the night before.

When I pushed open the front door, the acrid fumes of a cheap cigar assaulted me, and when I flipped on the lights of the front room, the disgusting figure of J. P. Dhrymes appeared before me like a hideous character from another bad dream. The man had been sitting there in the dark astride a wooden chair, evidently doing nothing more or less than awaiting my arrival.

"What do you want?" I asked, eyeing him coldly.

He glowered at me for about ten seconds. "Where have you been all day? And don't give me any bullshit. Then when you finish with that, you can fill me in on where you were yesterday as well."

I studied the man for long moments, noting he was sober, serious, and intent. What did he want with me, other than to harass somebody he'd come to hate? My police background told me he didn't have enough of anything to arrest me or he wouldn't be screwing around like this, asking questions about where I'd been.

"Who invited you in here, Dhrymes? This is federal property. You got a warrant?" I talked extra loud, hoping to wake up the guys in the barracks, because instinct told me I might be needing witnesses.

"I was invited in here, smart-ass, and you'd better answer up as to your whereabouts or you're under arrest."

The big turd reminded me of a drill sergeant I'd had in the marines, except this guy was obnoxious by nature, rather than by design. The other big difference was that the marine sergeant had the authority of God and knew it, while this prick-with-ears obviously didn't know which side of his shirt to pin his badge on.

"Fuck you, you overstuffed scumbag," I said, noting two or three heads peering out of bedroom doors down the hall. "You think you're a cop? Then get off your slimy butt and figure out where I've been, because I don't have to tell you a fucking thing, except get offa my ass or the sheriff will get a full report on how you're harassing me, with a copy to the newspaper, the county supervisor, and my congressman. They already know what an asshole you are, because you've proved it to them. Want to finish the job? If not, get the fuck outta here."

As I laid it on, he rose and put his beefy hand on the stock of his side arm, a .45 revolver with an extra-long barrel.

"Go ahead, pull it out," I told him, "And I'll add that to the charges."

Dhrymes, his face purple in frustration and anger glanced around and noted his growing audience, naked bodies except underpants or pajama bottoms. He gave me what he must have thought was his most intimidating scowl, stuck a fat index finger against my chest, and said, "I'm checking up on you, buster. And if you're involved in this, your ass is in deep trouble."

With that, he stormed out, slamming the door hard enough to shake the entire barracks. Our audience greeted his departure with cheers and some hand-clapping that made me feel a lot better, but only until I started wondering if the deputy had been here in connection with Nora's disappearance. I went through another long night with little sleep.

First thing in the morning I went straight to Bill Marklee's desk to check the log sheets from the other two stakeouts. I looked first at the ones in the envelope marked ICE SPRINGS, and found nothing of interest among the seven vehicles catalogued. Then I grabbed the Oyster Rock envelope, concentrating on the sheet the previous day's stakeout. My heart jumped into my throat when I looked at the fourth entry; it was a description of Nora's Jeep. The vehicle had been logged going up the road at ten fifteen that morning. When did she come back out? That line was left blank on the form.

My head began reeling, and I slumped into Marklee's chair trying hard to fight off the effects of the adrenalin that was taking control of my emotions, making it almost impossible for me to examine the possible explanations for what I saw on the paper.

I grabbed the phone and dialed Nora's number, guessing she would not yet have left her house for the office. No answer, not even after twelve rings. So I rang up her office, where a man answered. I asked to speak to Nora.

"Who's calling?" the man wanted to know.

"I'm calling from the Forest Service. Nora gives us the log scale from the gyppos, and we just wanted to check some figures."

"Oh, well, she doesn't come in until nine. Can I have her call you?"

"Fine. Uh, was she in the office yesterday, or was it somebody else who called in the figures?"

"Matter of fact she wasn't. Probably sick or something."

I thanked him and hung up, feeling substantially more apprehensive. Nora's unexplained absence from home and from the office and her Jeep having been seen on the Oyster Rock road the day before meant nothing but trouble. And then the bad dream of two nights before shot across my dizzying brain. What did it all mean?

I hurried across the road to the barracks, got my car keys, and got rolling southward out of town. Logic told me to wait, find out more before plunging in, but there was no abiding the fear and apprehension that were beginning to overcome my thinking.

The miles rolled by as if in a dream. I'm sure I was exceeding the speed limit, and almost overshot my turnoff from the main highway. A few minutes more, as dust filtered up through the floorboards and farmhouses whizzed by, and I was on the Oyster Rock road. I drove clear to the end of the road without seeing another vehicle, without noting anything unusual. I turned around and started back, this time turning off on each logging spur and following it to its end.

Nothing. Nothing but mile after mile of dusty logging roads, abandoned log landings, piles of rotting slash and cull logs.

I managed to get back to the station only an hour late for work but in time to take the ten o'clock weather observations. Lois told me Operation Harpoon was off for the day, and I wouldn't be needed for duty, it being, after all, one of my regular days off.

"You're covered with dust, Harper," Lois observed. "Where did you go this morning?"

"Doing some checking. Say, do you think I could reach Bud

Griffen by phone? I really need to ask him about one of the entries on his stakeout sheet."

"About Nora's Jeep?"

"Oh, you already saw that."

"I sure did, and now I'm *really* worried. Is that where you went, to look for her?"

"Yeah, nothing. You know anything?"

"I tried to call her yesterday about the log scale, and couldn't reach her at the mill office or at her place. Then I saw her Jeep on that stakeout report. . . ."

"I know, I called too. It looks bad to me. Dhrymes was waiting for me when I got back to the barracks last night, wanted to know where'd I'd been. I told him to buzz off."

"I tried to reach Griffen about his fire time slips, but he's off the air somewhere right now. You be where I can grab you if he calls in?"

"I'm staying on the station. I have that funny feeling that something's going to happen today, and it has something to do with the Oyster Rock area. Will you let me know if you find out anything about Nora?"

Lois gave me a gentle little punch on the shoulder to let me know she understood how I was coming to feel about the mysterious lady of the red Jeep. But I don't think she understood exactly how tormented I felt at that moment about what Nora might be up to or might have stumbled into. The stark images of my dream were beginning to blend with the very real situations I was encountering hour by hour, and I was having difficulty keeping them separated in my mind.

A few minutes before noon the klaxon sounded, the signal for our crew to head for the truck. By the time I got to the garage, Fred Sweeney was rolling the old Marmon-Harrington out, and we all clambered aboard except for Larry Banks, who was off that day, and waited for Punky Swiftbird, who was in the office getting the fire location from Lois. In moments we were heading south down the main highway.

"Where do you think it is?" Vaughan Day asked me, fastening the chin strap of his hard hat.

I shrugged mechanically, knowing full well it had to be Oyster

Rock. It was another piece of the jigsaw puzzle finding its place in the panorama of scenes that were comprising this story. Now I had the four edges of the puzzle done and was working on the center. But there were several pieces I couldn't make fit, and they all looked remarkably alike. I knew I would fit another piece in before the day was finished.

We made the same turns I'd made that morning, and coming around a turn we could discern a column of bluish smoke several miles up the hill. But just as quickly the smoke was out of sight, obscured by topography as we made our approach.

We stopped at a point Swiftbird believed to be directly down-slope from the fire. Jurgenson and I jumped off to place chock blocks behind the rear wheels, and the other men began unloading tools from the side compartments.

The six of us hiked to the base of the fire, and I noted that this one too was on a southwest-facing slope. The wind was almost calm, and the fire hadn't really started to roll yet and remained confined to the forest floor. As I stood there gaping at it, Felton Shackle and Bill Marklee appeared, having come down from a logging spur above the fire.

"Where did it start?" asked Marklee.

"Looks like right about here," said Swiftbird. "We stayed away from it, but it looks about like the others, doesn't it?"

"Sure does," said Marklee, crouching down on one knee for a closer look. "Any of you see anybody coming out of the area?"

"Nobody," Swiftbird said.

"Have your crew put a line around this and mop it up," Shackle told him. "Bill and I are going to shake down the point of origin."

Marklee steered me over to one side, away from the others. "You look at the stakeout sheet for this road, Harper?"

I was pretty sure he already knew that I had. "Yeah. There was one curious item, a red Jeep that entered at ten something but wasn't logged coming out."

"I saw that too," Marklee said, his nose twitching more than usual. "Maybe there's another way out, something that's not on the maps. Or could be it just went cross-country."

His remark gave me some breathing room, but not a whole lot, and I fell in with the rest of the crew cutting line up the flank of the little fire. By about four fifteen we had it in good enough shape to leave unattended; we'd check on it the next day. We packed our tools back down to the truck.

I took advantage of the opportunity to check out the steep downslope side of the road as we moved slowly out of the area. On one of the curves, where the downhill side was to the right, the truck lurched to a halt, and I could see Swiftbird's arm out the right window of the cab, his finger pointing to the berm of the road. Then the truck backed up for about fifteen or twenty feet, and again halted, the Swiftbird studying the ground along the edge of the road. I could then see where the berm had been mashed down by the wheels of a vehicle, as if it might have gone off the road and down the steep hillside.

I vaulted over the side, disregarding standing orders to dismount only by the ladder, and landed on the cut slope a few feet below the edge of the road. It was then that I saw the red Jeep, partially obscured by foliage, its front end smashed squarely into a large cedar tree. I was there in seconds, my heart pounding, my chest tight, expecting the worst, but finding nothing except the Jeep itself. Nobody inside.

The rest of the crew clambered down the slope, looking at the Jeep, and all around it, for signs of life.

"Don't touch the steering wheel or gearshift knob!" I advised them, almost without thinking.

"Looks like it was in neutral," Swiftbird said, craning his neck into the canvas-topped vehicle. "Maybe that's why the driver lost control."

"Impossible," I said. "Did you see the angle of those tracks on the berm? Looks like it was *aimed* to go off the road."

It struck me as peculiar that the side curtains, canvas flaps with small plastic window panels for the front seat occupants, were snapped in the up position, rather than folded down and secured at the bottoms as Nora would usually have kept them during fair weather. I got down and crawled beneath the vehicle far enough to check out the tie-rods and the rest of the steering linkage, finding nothing obviously defective. Next I depressed the brake pedal, and it stopped halfway down, as normal.

"Punky," I said, "if the driver of this Jeep knew the country as well as you do, how would he or she walk out of here without coming down the road itself?"

"I'd take the road," he said. "There's no shortcut, not when you have to fight through all this brush."

Bill Marklee stopped his pickup when he saw the halted fire engine, and then he too worked his way down the slope to the Jeep. Without asking questions of us, he looked at all the same things we had, then got out his camera and took pictures of it from several angles. As we struggled back up the steep slope, he invited me to ride back to the station with him, and Swiftbird okayed it.

"Dhrymes called me at home last night," Marklee said as we started down the hill in his pickup. "Wanted to know where you were yesterday and the night before. Wouldn't say what it was about."

"What did you tell him?"

"I told him I had you on a special assignment and could vouch for your whereabouts, but he acted like I was just covering for you. What's he after?"

"He was waiting for me in the barracks when I got back last night. Asked me the same questions. I didn't know then what he was after, but finding this Jeep up here makes it look like Nora Jeffers has disappeared, and for some reason, he's tying me to it."

"That's her Jeep?"

"Definitely, and it looked to me like it was intentionally run off the road."

"By Nora?"

"Hell no. Why would she do that? I don't think she was even here. That's why I need to talk to Bud Griffen. He logged the Jeep. Another thing, Bill. This fire doesn't fit the pattern we've had so far. The fire danger today was only in the medium range, while all the others have been on days the fire danger was very high or extreme."

"Hmm. Could be this was intended to break out yesterday, when the fire danger was extreme." Then he laughed, the first time I'd heard him do so. "That's good; a holdover arson fire for a change instead of the usual holdover lightning fires."

It didn't strike me funny, and I mulled it over. Either the arsonist's device delayed longer than intended this time, I thought, or his hand had been forced somehow, requiring a quicker move than he might have wished. Again, the thought introduced unpleasant images.

Marklee passed the turnoff to the station, stopping instead at the post office to check his box. I went in to do likewise, not really caring if I had any mail or not. But there was indeed a letter for me, postmarked, curiously, Cedar Valley. I ripped it open and got an immediate shock:

Dear Harper,

I asked Sally Boardman to mail this note in case I had to leave suddenly, or in case anything happened to me. (Hope you never get it.)

About the arson problem you're working on—to add to your collection of clues—Ned Booth swore revenge against the FS for making him resign, for whatever that's worth, maybe nothing. But the fires started soon after his return from Winchester. I don't mean him any harm, but if it's Ned setting these fires, he must be stopped before somebody else gets killed.

I started watching his pickup, trying to match his absences from town with the occurrence of fires, in fact, I've been writing down his odometer readings and found that the day before the Rucker's Ridge fire he drove approximately the round trip distance to the fire! (I drove up there three days after the fire to check that out. But maybe the mileage was a coincidence.)

One other tidbit: I checked in his cargo box and saw a bunch of climbing gear in it, the kind telephone line workers use. I don't know of his climbing anything since he worked for the F.S. (?)

Trouble: this afternoon he saw me drive away from behind his shop where he parks, so I'll have to be careful. (Maybe a neighbor reported me.)

Harper, I'm sorry to be such a mystery woman, but there are

reasons for it I hope to explain to you sometime. Meanwhile,
good hunting!

Love,
Nora.

Chapter 14

T he minute we got back to the station I went into the office and called Bud Griffen. This time he answered.

"Bud, we were looking through the forms you filled out yesterday on the Oyster Rock road, and—"

"Right!" he burst in. "There was a fire there today, wasn't there?"

"Correct. Get to that in a minute. First, you remember the red Jeep?"

"Sure. That's the only rig that didn't come back out."

"Do you remember what the driver looked like?"

"It was a woman. Fairly good-size one, but I couldn't see her face."

"Anything about her? Her hair, how old . . ."

"The Jeep had those side curtains on, you know, the ones with those little plastic windows. It was hard to get a good look."

"What made you think it was a woman?"

"She had a bandanna tied over her head. I remember the bow on top."

"Where exactly were you?"

"You know where the first logging spur takes off to the east? Well I was about a quarter mile below that fork, on the uphill side of the road."

213

"Was she driving fast or slow?"

"Fast, like she wanted to get somewhere. Not just looking around or anything like that."

"And she was alone?"

"That's what it looked like. Why? What's going on? Did somebody find the Jeep?"

"Yeah, we did. Wrecked, but no driver. Bud, you didn't see anybody come walking down the road, or any extra occupants of the other vehicles coming out, did you?"

"No, no, I don't remember any. What about the fire? Start like the others?"

"Exactly. You say you were on the uphill side. Was that pretty high above the road where you were?"

"Yeah. I know what you're getting at: no, I couldn't see the drivers when they were passing by me on the way up, but I got a good look at every one of them through the windshields before they got to me. You think it might have been a man driving, or what?"

"I don't know, Bud. But if anything occurs to you, please let me know as soon as you can."

I passed the information on to Bill Marklee, who sat at his desk writing up a report on the fire investigation. He listened, then said, "Harper, what do you think of finding out who these other vehicles belong to, the ones that were up there about the same time, and seeing if the owners noticed anything unusual?"

"I'll see what I can do. Do you think it would be a good idea to call Anselmo Adams? We might be getting in over our heads before too long."

"Felton called him when he got back from the fire, says Adams will try to get here as soon as he can."

"What about the Jeep? Will it just sit out there or what?"

"I had Lois call it in to the sheriff's office in Winchester. They said it was our responsibility unless it was on a county or state road. I suppose we'll wind up towing it in as soon as the investigation is finished."

"They know it might be related to Nora's disappearance?"

Marklee shook his head, looking tired and defeated. "Well,

they either haven't made that connection or maybe nobody's even reported her missing yet."

I growled a bit, then grabbed the phone and dialed Nora's number: no answer. I then thought about Nora's letter, and called the Boardman residence. No answer there either. I told Marklee I was going to take a shower and would come back to the office later.

The rest of the crew had used up all the hot water, but a cold shower beat living with the second skin of soot, grime, and sweat that I'd brought back from the mountain with me. Then I decided to have another look at my pictures of the various points of origins, Nora's letter and her remark about the climbing gear foremost in mind.

I spread the photos out on my bed and got an instant revelation: In each scene, within fifteen or twenty feet of the point of fire origin, stood a large ponderosa pine, the smallest of them appearing to be about three feet in diameter. Only a coincidence?

Three things bounced around inside my smallish skull: Carlisle's remark that a device would have to escape detection, Nora's discovery of the climbing gear in Booth's pickup, and the presence of a large tree near each point of fire origin. There had to be a connection.

I quickly dressed and returned to the office, where I grabbed the Oyster Rock folder off Marklee's desk and scanned the vehicle list. Booth's pickup wasn't on it, which didn't especially surprise me.

When I headed out of Marklee's office, I saw that Lois had come in to finish up some work that had piled up on her desk. She asked what else we'd found out and said she'd been unable to learn anything about Nora either.

"Think real hard," I told her. "You've got a view of the barracks road from here. Do you remember seeing any unusual comings and goings last Sunday afternoon or Monday?"

"Well, I wasn't here Sunday after six. On Monday, let's see, just a normal day, I think. Except, yeah, I believe that's the day Ned Booth checked the refrigerator. He has a contract to maintain all of the fridges on the station and he checks them once in a while."

"Were you expecting him that day?"

"Not really, but then he doesn't have a fixed schedule. Only thing, it seemed funny that was the only one he said he looked at that day."

Monday, I said to myself. The day I was in Winchester, and the evening I had supper at Nora's, which ended in the gunfight. It added up.

I went back to the barracks, picked up some navy surplus 7-by-50 binoculars and a flashlight, then got into my car and had it gassed up at Chubby's. Coming back through town, I noticed Booth's repair shop had closed for the day and got a glimpse of his pickup parked behind the shop in its usual spot. Concerned about fading daylight, I wasted no time en route to Oyster Rock.

I parked exactly where we'd parked the fire engine earlier that day and hurried up the mountainside to the base of the fire. I looked closely around the base of the large pine tree near the point of origin, and about two feet above the ground found what I was looking for: a spur hole. Two feet higher up, and offset from the first, another. Fresh sap was only now beginning to ooze from the holes, telling me the tree had been very recently climbed with spurs, or tree hooks, as we called them.

I looked straight up into the tree's canopy but could see nothing but the first whorl of branches about forty feet up. So mindful of the fading light, I hurried upslope to a point from which I could look horizontally across at those branches. With my binoculars I scanned along the branches slowly until I saw it: a small, light-colored object hanging from a string or wire about eight inches below a branch. It was by now too dark to identify the object, but it definitely was not a natural part of the tree.

The discovery thrilled me, because it meant I'd finally found a way to begin unraveling this mystery. But at the same time it unnerved me, because it also meant I'd found a trail that might lead me to discovering something terrible that might have happened to Nora.

There was no way for me to climb the tree, no way right now to find out more about the object hanging up there almost forty feet above the ground, and it was getting dark fast. I drove back down the hill trying to get inside the arsonist's mind. It was

216

looking like he'd set Nora up for the arson, but if so, where was she? And then, after he'd ditched her Jeep, how did he get back unseen to Cedar Valley? I knew I was again being impulsive, but I had an almost uncontrollable urge to find Booth and squeeze the truth out of him.

By the time I got back to Cedar Valley, the crew had finished supper, and tired from the fire, most of them had gone to bed. I grabbed a bite at the cafe just before it closed, then walked back toward the barracks. I knew Booth was an experienced climber, and Nora's letter said she'd found climbing gear in the cargo box on his pickup. If he kept the climbing gear in there, maybe there was something else of interest.

I rested about two hours in an armchair in the front room of the barracks. At about midnight, I rose and walked down to Booth's shop. His pickup was in back, and I approached it cautiously. The cargo box was locked, an unpleasant discovery, and I was pondering what to do about it when my eye fell on a dark shape next to the box. It was a knapsack similar to the one I remembered seeing Stan Turpin use for his own climbing gear.

I undid the straps that held the flap closed and felt around inside, recognizing the lineman's belt, come-alongs, hardware items, tools, and in the bottom, the climbing spurs. What was Booth doing with all this stuff if it didn't have to do with the arson?

Thinking it might be possible to determine if the spurs had been sunk into a tree recently, I pulled one of them out and ran my thumb along one of the spur blades. It was quite smooth and dry, not sticky with pitch, as one might expect. But then Booth was a journeyman, a stickler for caring for his equipment; he probably cleaned the spurs and maybe even sharpened them after each use.

But there was something else about the blade. Like the ones I had seen before, it was shaped somewhat like the point of a bayonet. But this blade was perhaps an inch and a half shorter. Or was my memory of the others defective?

My hands felt over everything in the pack, and I was disappointed not to stumble onto any strange objects or materials. It was just the regular side-cutters, crimpers, hand axe; stuff any climber would take along. I folded the pack up and put it back where I'd found it and walked back toward the ranger station.

Still curious about the climbing-spur discrepancy, I went to the warehouse behind the station and, using my standard key, the one that fit all Forest Service standard locks, entered by the side door. I knew telephone-line-maintenance gear was stored in the "rat room," so called because it was specially constructed to prevent entry by gnawing rodents. Unfortunately, I didn't have a key to the rat room, and at this time of night one would be nearly impossible to come by. So I started looking around the main room, using my flashlight instead of flipping on the overhead lights.

Along the back wall of the warehouse was a row of large bins, each identified with the abbreviated title of the person who kept his tools there for quick loading. The third one from the end was marked IMP FMN. That would be Turpin's, and I flashed my light into it. I got a shot of adrenaline when I spotted the big knapsack labeled TELEPHONE GEAR. It was the same one I'd carried when working that day with Turpin on the ground line near Coyote Peak.

I felt no need to be quiet about it—who else would be here at this hour?—so I simply dumped the contents onto the concrete floor. No immediate surprises: lineman's belt, climbing spurs, climbing rope, hand axe, side-cutters, and a few large staples. I grabbed one of the spurs. The blade on this one was definitely longer than the one I had seen in Booth's pickup.

Did Stan also keep the shorter ones on hand? I checked his bin and found no other climbing gear, so I decided to check out his Forest Service pickup, parked outside in a row with several others. His was easy to spot, one of the last of the dark green ones, which were being replaced by trucks with the new gray and green two-tone paint job.

His jockey box was locked, as were most of them, with a standard lock, and I opened it and looked inside. There was a sleeping bag, emergency rations, a large toolbox, and a cardboard box containing an assortment of hardware. Among these I recognized telephone splicing sleeves and nuts, different-size staples, split insulators and tie wires and other odds and ends. Aside from this box, there were various hand tools, a coffee pot, a propane soldering outfit, and a set of come-alongs that looked like those Stan had used on the Coyote Peak job. But there were no other climbing spurs.

Satisfied, although still a bit curious, I relocked the box and went back to the barracks. I didn't realize how tired I was until my head hit the pillow, because that's the last I would recall until morning.

Before breakfast I went to the office, knowing no one would be in yet. I called Nora, again not getting an answer. I kept telling myself she'd left town as she'd said in her letter and then asking myself how could she have done that without her Jeep? Somebody had to know something. Abby seemed to be a good friend to her, but she didn't have a phone, and I didn't even know where she lived. I thought again of Sally Boardman and decided to risk awakening her with a phone call. She answered immediately, sounding wide awake. I started to tell her who I was, and she interrupted me.

"Yes, of course I know who you are. Do you know where Nora is?"

"No, Mrs. Boardman. That's why I called you. We found her Jeep wrecked off the road near a fire we went to yesterday at Oyster Rock, but there was no sign of her."

"Oh, God, you found her Jeep. We haven't seen or heard from her since Tuesday. I was afraid of something like this."

"She didn't say anything to you about going away for a few days?"

"No, just that she thought there was a possibility of trouble. I asked whether it had anything to do with her aunt in Purple Pond but she said no."

"Well, how did she seem? Was she upset?"

"I would say not. If anything, she was acting excited, but seemed to be concerned about something. She didn't really give me time to ask her anything more. Why do you think she would have gone up that road into the mountains?"

"Well, Mrs. Boardman, I'm not at all sure she did. It's beginning to look like somebody else took her Jeep up there to make it look like she went there."

"I see. So that's not necessarily good news either, then."

"In view of her absence, not at all. I'm sorry to have to cause you any further distress, but I felt you would wish to know."

"I do indeed, Mr. Sandow. Please call me immediately if you learn anything else, will you?"

That call didn't do anything for my morale either, and after brooding about it for a while I tried to figure out what to do next. The only thing that made any sense to me was to return yet again to the Oyster Rock fire scene, this time in full daylight, to figure out exactly what the incendiary device high up in the pine tree was. To do that I'd have to climb the tree, and the closest I'd ever come to doing that was watching Turpin. After thinking over the hazards involved and my total lack of experience, I gave up the idea.

While debating the prospect of facing the usual breakfast fare at the barracks, I saw a Forest Service sedan pull up in front of the station. An older, gray-haired man climbed out clutching a brief-case, and I recognized Anselmo A. Adams. It was a joy to see him, and I sensed somehow things might begin turning around now that he had arrived. I opened the office door for him.

"I thought you'd never get here," I said.

He stopped on the threshold to look at me. "Well, Jesus Christ."

"No, but that's close."

"I doubt it. Let's try Gene Murphy, then."

I put an index finger to my lips. "Harper Sandow."

He patted me on the shoulder. "I'm not really surprised, young man. You probably lied about your age too."

"No, sir. But I gave an entirely fictitious background, references, the works." Somehow, I felt comfortable admitting these things to the old man.

"Shit. Just shows you how efficient the government is. It's a wonder the paychecks are only two weeks late."

I led the investigator into Bill Marklee's office and got him

220

seated, then put the coffee pot on. Adams used the time to scrape out his pipe, fill it from a sack, and get it lit.

"What have they got you doing here, Harper?"

"Fire crew. They let me analyze the fire reports and help develop a stakeout plan."

"Meanwhile conducting your own unofficial investigation, I would suppose?"

I nodded. "How much did Felton tell you when he called?"

"Only that there'd been another set with the same circumstances, and that this time there was a wrecked vehicle possibly involved. You know anything the rest of them don't?"

It was a quarter to eight, meaning the office would be humming in a few minutes, so I talked fast. I gave him Nora's letter and told him what I'd seen at Oyster Rock the night before and also detailed the results of my search of Booth's gear and my examination of Turpin's climbing spurs.

"This vehicle that was off the road up there, know whose it was?"

I tapped my finger on Nora's letter, lying before him. "Hers."

He pursed his lips and whistled softly.

I explained her being missing, and why I thought it was somebody else who had driven the vehicle up there.

"Any idea where she might be?"

I shook my head.

"What else? Any idea how he's doing it?"

I poured him a cup of coffee. He waved off the sugar and cream. "I'm guessing white phosphorous," I told him. I didn't need to elaborate. I could almost see the wheels spinning behind his wide-set gray eyes.

"Son of a bitch," he said. "Yeah, that'd work, all right. I don't know exactly how it'd be rigged, but I can sure as shit find out."

I heard the back door open and people coming in, so I left immediately to take the morning weather observations. When I returned from that chore West's door was closed, and Lois told me that he, Adams, Shackle, and Marklee were all gathered in there and didn't wish to be disturbed. I spent a few minutes tidying up the weather observation sheets, then reported out back

221

to Punky Swiftbird. He set us all to work cleaning up the truck and the tools we'd used on the fire the day before.

About ten, Ardis Corbin went back to the barracks to get a pack of cigarettes, and when he returned he had some bad news.

"Hey, Harper," he yelled, from at least twenty-five yards away, "the police are up there searching your car!"

Everybody stopped working and gaped.

"Who is it, that jerk Dhrymes?" I asked.

"Yeah, him and two others. And they asked where you were."

"And you told them San Francisco, right?" I tried to put up a humorous if not intrepid front. But I didn't think it was at all funny. In fact, I suddenly felt naked, vulnerable, and almost helpless—just like, I suppose, many of the people I pursued when doing my police officer routine in L.A.

In a matter of a few minutes, two sheriff's cars rolled down the driveway past the office into the yard in front of the warehouse where we were working. The ugly figure of J. P. Dhrymes hauled himself out of the first one, and two other deputies came right along behind him. One of them carried a shotgun.

"You! Dhrymes said, pointing a meaty finger at my face. "You, turd head! Up against the wall, now!"

While the officer with the shotgun stood guard, probably hoping I'd resist the collar, the other two patted me down, cuffed me, and pushed me into the back seat of one of the cars. I have a vague recollection of the rest of the crew standing there, their faces blank, arms hanging at their sides, wondering, undoubtedly, what it was all about.

By the time the two sheriff's cars had turned around and headed back out the driveway, everybody from the office had come out the back door to see what was going on. Don West tried to flag down the car I was in to talk to Dhrymes, but the deputy merely turned to the driver and said, "Fuck 'em."

We hit the main road, turned north, and zoomed out of town, bound, undoubtedly, for Winchester, the county seat. While being cuffed I had heard one of the officers tell me I was being charged with murder.

Chapter 15

M urder? The ugly word rolled around inside my skull like a loose cannonball in a storm-rocked ship. *Nora?* The very thought made me nauseous.

"Who am I supposed to have murdered?" I asked through the security screen separating me from Dhrymes and the other officer. He glanced back at me but didn't answer.

We passed the sawmill, then made the turn heading out of town. Dhrymes lit a huge cigar, then turned in his seat so that his broad back was against the door and he could leer at me through the wire mesh.

"Well, how does it feel now, asshole?" he said, blowing a puff of acrid smoke at me. "Things look a little different from the back seat, don't they?"

I was tempted to remark that he ought to know, but I knew better than to talk back to him. As a young cop in L.A. I had seen my sergeant use the same tactics on pimps he wanted to beat up. Dhrymes would jump at the chance to belt me around.

I kept silent and tried to figure out what was going on, hoping it didn't involve Nora. Booth, her ex-husband, was a bad egg, a bitter man who could cause trouble. It again flashed through my mind that he could easily conceive of killing her and framing me.

I shuddered and tried to push the idea away. But after what I'd done to Deputy Dhrymes, he would be quick to pick up on anything remotely resembling evidence against me.

"Pull off the road right here," Dhrymes said, taking off his trooper's hat and placing the cigar in the ashtray. The other deputy, a young, angular man whose uniform was too big, obeyed. Dhrymes was out quickly, jerking open the rear door.

"Get out, asshole."

"What for?"

"I'm gonna search you."

"You already did."

He reached in and dragged me out, my head and elbows banging the doorframe. He pushed me up against the car and made a pretense of patting me down. Suddenly, his knee came up toward my crotch in a vicious thrust. I expected it and was able to turn enough to deflect the blow off my thigh. He followed with a right to my belly, and then, as I recall it, a left to the side of my face that flattened me against the car and opened a cut on my cheek. It's funny now, thinking back about it and not being able to remember the pain he inflicted. What I remember is his onion breath.

"Easy, J.P.," I recall the younger deputy saying. "Don't mark him up too much. The sheriff don't like that."

"Fuck the sheriff," Dhrymes said, wiping saliva from the corner of his mouth with the back of his hand. "This turd was taking a poke at me. You want a piece of him, Arny?"

"Let's just go, J.P."

"Get back in the car, asshole, before I stomp the shit out of you. Maybe you'll think twice about trying to fuck me around next time."

We drove in silence the rest of the way to Winchester, and I spent most of the time planning eighteen ways to take J.P. Dhrymes apart at the seams when I got the chance.

We came down the hill into dismal Winchester, turning off onto a side street, where we pulled up in front of the sheriff's office,—the SO, as Dhrymes and the younger deputy called it.

There, I was unloaded and dragged into the front office to be stared at by the half dozen officers and dispatchers present.

"I got him," Dhrymes announced, pointing his right thumb at his own chest. "Been layin' for this sucker for weeks, and I finally nailed him." He was coming on as if I was a long-time fugitive from the law or something.

"You got who?" asked a deputy wearing sergeant's stripes. It was obvious from the way he glared at Dhrymes that he wasn't the hammy deputy's most ardent admirer. "Is this the one-eight-seven suspect out of Cedar Valley?"

"That's him," said Dhrymes. "I'm booking him on a murder one."

"What the hell did you do to him?" asked the sergeant, eyeing my bloody face and shirt.

"He tried to rough me up, so I showed him a few tricks," Dhrymes said, winking cutely at his partner.

"You adding that to the charges?"

"Damn right. Resisting arrest, assaulting an officer—"

"Forget it, Dhrymes," said Arny, shaking his head.

The sergeant looked back and forth between the two officers, then said, "Just get him out back and book him, okay?"

I was booked, photographed, and fingerprinted while Dhrymes looked on, proudly soaking up the credit for the arrest. Then they recuffed me, with my hands in front this time. This turned out to be a lot more comfortable, as well as convenient. One of the deputies escorted me to a small room and told me to sit down on a wooden chair. Over an hour passed before anything happened.

Then two plainclothes officers came in, guys I'd seen in the front office. One was a smallish, hawk-faced man with a sallow complexion and receding hairline. He was carrying a notebook and pencil. The other was a stocky man of about forty-five whose neck was too big for his shirt. Hawk Face took charge.

"You're in here on a murder charge, understand?"

I nodded.

"You want to tell us about it?"

"Who is it I'm supposed to have murdered?"

225

"We'll ask the questions. Would you like to make a statement?"

"I haven't murdered anybody. I don't even know what you're talking about."

"What's your name?"

It was a strange question to ask someone who'd just been booked. They didn't have my real name, of course, but at this point they probably had no way of knowing that. "Harper Sandow."

"Your driver's license is a fake. Want to tell us about that?"

"It's real. Check with the DMV."

"We did. They've got no record of it."

"That's not my fault."

"Then what about your license plates? Where did they come from? There's no record of them either."

"Then they must have lost my records." I breathed a small sigh of relief; my homicide detective buddy in LA had done a good job for me.

The two men glanced at one another. "Who are you, anyway?" Thick Neck asked. "You might as well tell us."

I probably winced when I thought about mentioning my Marine Corps tour on my application for employment. Whether they'd seen that yet or not I didn't know, but I was pretty sure when they did, they'd think of checking my fingerprints against the military record. I decided against making this one any easier for them and said, "I already did. Check it out."

Hawk Face resumed his questioning. "Where were you on Wednesday?"

I told them what I'd been doing, and that Bill Marklee could verify it.

"What about that night, after you got back to town?"

I gave them a summary of my attempt to visit Nora and said I'd had some drinks with a cowboy, returning to the barracks at about eleven.

"Who is this cowboy?"

"A guy I see around town once in a while. I don't know his name, or even where he lives."

"Sure," Hawk Face said. "But you do admit to knowing this girl Nora?"

"Yes. Does this have anything to do with her?"

"You ever been in trouble before?"

The questioning went on and on. I answered truthfully except when it concerned my identity and my knowledge of who the cowboy was. They didn't give Miranda warnings in those days but I certainly knew better than to blab off to detectives. But I was innocent of any murder and didn't mind having my statements checked on. What I wanted was to get out of there and back on the case, and I thought giving true answers would speed that up. It didn't.

I tried several times to find out who had been murdered and why I was being interrogated concerning it, but they were answering no questions. Finally I told them they had all my information and I was through talking to them without a lawyer.

"All right, young man," Thick Neck said. "We're about to lock you up for the weekend. Anything at all you want to say?"

"Why don't you say who was murdered?"

The detectives glanced at each other. "We don't have a positive ID," Hawk Face said. "Why don't you help us out?"

"Was it a man or a woman?"

"He's playin' games with us," Thick Neck said. "Let's lock the son of a bitch up."

A uniformed deputy took charge of me, leading me down a corridor and through a steel door. We stopped in front of a cell and he took off the handcuffs, removed my belt, and pushed me inside. The clang of the cell door closing was a familiar one, but I'd never before heard it from the inside.

I plunked down on the steel cot and tried to make sense out of the whole thing, but nothing added up except how Booth had been able to start the fires and avoid discovery—until now, thanks to Nora's finding the climbing gear in his pickup. But then I would repeatedly get lost trying to come up with a scenario that would have allowed him to bring about her disappearance, fake her presence on the Oyster Rock road, and not be seen exiting the area. Not to mention setting me up for a murder charge in the process.

The cellblock, quiet at first, gave way to the usual late night noises of any city or county jail, and I spent most of the night brooding about Nora, Booth, and that loathsome Dhrymes.

By Sunday morning I expected the sheriff's office to have discovered my true identity via my fingerprints, but if so, nobody told me. Obviously, things didn't move as fast up here in these mountain communities as they did in Los Angeles. They probably figured Monday would be soon enough to start on it. It wasn't until about four that afternoon that I got a visitor: Anselmo Adams. He stared at me through the steel bars, with a deputy standing nearby.

"How are you doing, Harper? Looks like they roughed you up a bit."

I was relieved that he'd remembered to call me Harper. "I'm all right," I told him. "Who got murdered?"

"A woman." His face looked gray and tired.

"Was it Nora?" I didn't want to hear the answer.

"I'm sorry to have to say it was, Harper, at least according to preliminary indications."

It felt like a battering ram in the gut, even though I'd allowed that possibility in my thinking.

"Where?"

"Place called Champion Springs campground, east of Purple Pond, in the mountains."

"How was she killed?" I managed to get out before choking up entirely.

He shook his head. "You don't want to hear."

"Tell me," I said through clenched teeth, my mouth dry.

"Struck in the forehead, maybe an axe. Dumped in a garbage vault right there in the campground."

I turned, retching, and vomited profoundly into the little porcelain toilet bowl, my psyche telling me it was the nightmare continuing, and not something real, a horrible set of images that would remain etched in my memory forever.

The old man waited patiently while I fought to regain control.

"Why did they arrest me?"

"The Boardmans reported her missing on Thursday. Evidently, Dhrymes entered her house the next day and found a

228

note, supposedly from you, on the floor, asking her to meet you at Champion Springs the night before. That would have been Wednesday."

"But it couldn't have been in my handwriting."

"It was typed. Problem is, the detectives were able to tie it right away to one of the typewriters in the ranger station office. Bill Marklee got real upset when he found out it was the one on his desk. And that's not all, Harper."

"Wonderful. What else?"

"They say they've got the murder weapon, and it was in your car."

I guess I just shook my head. "That son of a bitch has really laid a number on me."

"I've got some miles to cover yet today, Harper. The letter from Nora helped. You know anything else I might not know?"

"In my room in the barracks. In my suitcase is a folder with my notes and photos. Also, talk to Sally Boardman. I think Nora may have told her some things I don't know about."

"Harper, they'll probably bring you before a judge tomorrow or the next day and charge you. Otherwise, they'll have to turn you loose, and it doesn't look good for that right now. You'll need a lawyer. I made a few calls. You got five hundred for a retainer?"

I shook my head. "They have a public defender?"

"I'll tell them. Meantime, don't talk to anybody else about anything."

With that, Adams simply nodded and ambled away down the corridor, and I heard the steel door slam shut after he left. I lay back down on the cot and tried to shut out the world, but the next sixteen hours were probably the toughest I'd ever spent. I didn't give a damn about facing a murder charge or anything else that had happened to me. The whole thing had come down to Nora's hideous murder at an isolated campground. I don't remember how many times I had the nightmare that night, and woke to ask myself how I had perceived something so similar to that awful event. The worst questions had to do with the suffering she knew before the end came, with what her thoughts must have been.

If I hadn't come here with this lust for revenge for my brother's death, none of this would have happened, I reasoned. Her death had to be linked to my investigation of the arson, it seemed to me, and with my relationship with Nora. How could I have thought she might be involved in the arson? The questions, the torment, the self-recriminations were unending.

Sunday finally ended, and I managed to get a few hours sleep, and then at about ten in the morning an officer unlocked my cell door and admitted a man of not more than twenty-five. I thought at first he would be a cellmate, but he introduced himself as Frank Pierce and said he had been appointed as my defense counsel. He kind of looked at me in awe, as if he'd expected a monster to confront him.

"Sit down," I said, pointing to the other cot. Could this unwhiskered, pimply kid with a butch haircut, khaki pants, and white socks actually be a real lawyer, I wondered? He must have read my thoughts.

"Sorry, I guess you were expecting someone older, and maybe in a three-piece suit. But if it will make you feel any better, you're my first client."

I couldn't tell if he was trying to be funny, but it made me smile. Then I wondered if the funny part was my realization of how bad things were getting.

"The three-piece suit wouldn't help anyway. What I need to do is get out of this place. Can you help me do that?"

He squinted at me as if to figure out whether I was kidding. "They've got you in here on a first degree murder charge, and the population of the county is outraged. Forget it."

"Now tell me the DA is running for reelection."

"Yeah, well he might as well be. This is the biggest case they've had in years, to hear them talk."

"What are they saying, open-and-shut case?"

"I got that feeling," he said, laughing nervously. "But then, all I know so far is what they had in the paper and on the radio. In fact, I didn't find out I'd be representing you until this morning. You want to tell me how you got yourself into this mess?"

The way he asked it, he could have been referring to mud on

230

my trousers or something. But his question was right on the mark, and it was one I'd been asking myself for the last two days. I gave him a full, but unembellished recitation of events, and he listened intently, making several pages of notes in a spiral notebook.

"That's a hell of a story," he said when I'd finished. "You have people who can vouch for your whereabouts during the critical time?"

"When are they saying it happened?"

"I don't know yet. But from what you've told me, it sounds like it must have been Wednesday night or thereabouts. That sound right?"

"Yeah, it does. I'm covered all day Wednesday until eight thirty that evening."

"You were alone after that?"

"No, from about nine until eleven I was with a guy—you're going to love this—who is a fugitive from justice." I explained the circumstances.

"Not so good, and in more ways than one. So, what they have on you so far is the typewritten note, the murder weapon from your car, and uh, would that have your fingerprints on it?"

"I don't even know for sure what it is, for God's sakes."

"What else have they got?"

"Nothing I know of."

"Yeah. Well, what about motive?"

"Me? I don't have any. I was in love with her."

"Yeah, but if you thought it was she who'd killed your brother by starting that fire, or if she was dumping you for some other guy, or if you decided to kill her during an act of rape, or if she found out something about you that you didn't want known, or if—"

"All right, all right. So who the hell are you working for?"

"Take it easy. I'm just trying to get a feel for this thing, and frankly, it doesn't look too good. Uh, you didn't kill her, did you?"

"No, I did not kill her."

"Okay, then. You are to be brought before Judge Peter David-son tomorrow morning at ten, where the charges against you will be read. We'll plead you guilty, then see where we can go from there."

"Guilty?"

"Oh, sorry, I meant *not* guilty. Did I say guilty?"

I watched Frank Pierce leave the cell, and it reminded me of a high school boy leaving a classroom, his cares behind him. I tried to conjure up an image of a Pronghorn County jury taking this young man even halfway seriously at the outset of a murder trial. It wasn't easy.

The next morning I appeared before the judge with my boyish attorney, had the charges read to me and then was returned unceremoniously to my cell.

They were still calling me by my assumed name, and that was still fine with me. Adams had promised not to give it away, as had Frank Pierce, however reluctantly. I couldn't understand why I hadn't been identified by my prints. Maybe somebody in the LAPD was working extra hard for me. Fine, I'd let it ride.

The next week was uneventful but for a few visits from Frank Pierce. Pierce told me the coroner had established the time of death at between noon and midnight on Wednesday. Pierce had driven from Cedar Valley to Champion Springs and back, and it had taken just over an hour. The two-hour gap in my alibi was thus a big problem. He'd managed to find Abby Murrow, but she'd told him she had no idea how to contact Steve Christian. That didn't surprise me in the least.

The murder weapon was a Forest Service hand axe, he said, and bloodstains found on the blade matched Nora's blood type. He didn't know if they'd found prints on the handle. Inasmuch as I'd never carried such a tool in my car, it was an obvious plant.

We discussed the typewritten note. I had remarked to him that a jury might think it strange I would type a short note like that to someone I was in love with, not to mention that I would type my name on it rather than signing it. But he said in his view it wouldn't be at all helpful to make that point. If I had planned to murder Nora, this would be a simple ruse to try to deflect blame from myself.

What else did they have on me? According to Pierce, nothing.

Just opportunity, a questionable note, a murder weapon possibly without prints on it, let alone mine, and a possible but unproved motive.

"And they're willing to take me to trial on just that?"

"I doubt it, but they'd like to have us think so. The DA asked me yesterday if we'd go for a reduction to second degree. If he was really offering it, that would mean they can't prove premeditation. But he might just have been fishing."

"Wait a minute. I haven't even been indicted yet. How can we even be talking about a trial?"

Pierce looked sheepish. "They got you indicted last night in a special session of the grand jury. I was going to mention that."

"Thanks a lot, Frank. What did you tell him about the deal he offered?"

"I told him he had the wrong guy locked up, and we weren't about to plead guilty to any charge whatever."

"How did he take it?"

"He wasn't pleased."

"So where does this all leave me?"

"I'll be blunt: we don't have a defense. All we have is a story, one we could support with testimony of course, about who you are, what you came here for, how you've been assisting the Forest Service in getting to the bottom of the arson problem, and how you and Miss Jeffers got too close and somebody set you up. It will eventually come down to what the jury believes."

And how persuasive the trial lawyers were, I knew, shuddering not a little at that idea. "Frank, can you give me a feel for the jury we might wind up with, what they might think now about my guilt or innocence?"

"Oh, I hear chatter about it around town. Most people assume that since you've been charged you're probably guilty. But the DA's done a good job of keeping the details of the case away from the press. All people really know is that they found a hacked-up body in the campground garbage vault, and that you've been arrested for it. If I can offer any encouragement at all, I heard the DA isn't going to personally prosecute the case, that he's leaving it to an assistant while he goes elk hunting in Idaho."

"That's supposed to be encouraging? He's confident an assistant can handle it with no problem?"

"I was going to say it meant he didn't want to suffer the embarrassment of losing it, that he thought it was a weak case. But maybe you're right. Anyway, he already had his elk tag and probably would have gone in any case."

"You're a real jewel, Frank, you know that?"

Frank left me to ponder the situation. An inner voice was telling me to get in contact with my father and arrange for an experienced defense counsel before things went any further. Pierce was a sharp young man, but up against a seasoned prosecutor, he would be outgunned from the beginning.

But on the other hand, with all their other troubles, handing my mom and dad news of all this and asking for their help was about the last thing I wanted to do. I decided to wait a few more days, hoping things would change.

I lay back on my cot, and tried once again to imagine what, in fact, had really happened that Wednesday night. The typed note had obviously lured Nora to the campground, and she would have gone there in her Jeep. But that was at least five miles, cross-country, from where her Jeep was seen on the Oyster Rock road the next day. Therefore, the murderer had to return the next day in his own vehicle, drive the Jeep up the Oyster Rock road, set the ignition device, then run the Jeep off the road. He then would have had to hike back through the brush to retrieve his own rig, then return to Cedar Valley, or go about his business elsewhere.

Every time I ran through this drill it came out the same, but I still couldn't tie it to an individual. Booth was high on my list, but I couldn't rule out others, like Turpin and Marklee, who also had motive and opportunity. And was I leaving out anybody who should be included? Dhrymes came to mind, but since I'd discovered the probable device high in the pine tree, he seemed unlikely, as he probably lacked the agility to do that kind of climbing.

I spent another restless night, having fragmentary dreams about climbing trees, sorting through climbing gear, driving endlessly up and down the Oyster Rock road, the horrible scene in the campground, and then, strangely, Anselmo Adams behind the window at the post office. That image awakened me or at least was on my mind when I awoke, and it gave me an idea I hoped I'd be able to use later on.

On Wednesday, August 20, Don West paid me a call. He said my mother had called asking for me.

"She seemed quite concerned about getting in touch with you, and I told her you were temporarily unable to reach a phone and asked if I could take a message."

"You didn't tell her I was in jail, I hope."

"No. I didn't know if you'd told her about it yet. . . . Harper, she said your dad is in the hospital, and she thought you ought to come home. She said they think it's a stroke, and they don't know how serious it is yet."

"When did it happen?"

"Didn't say, but it sounded like it just happened. She called this morning."

"How did she sound?"

"I'd say upset, worried, anxious to have you there."

"Uh, I mean, did she sound pretty much in control, voice strong?"

"Hard for me to say, not knowing her. Does she have a health problem?"

"Nothing special, but she is subject to spells of depression. Can you do me a favor?"

"Sure, name it."

"I've already asked if I can make a collect call to my parents, and they've said it's not permitted. Will you do it for me, and tell my mom I'm involved in a trial and will break away just as soon as possible?"

"Of course. First thing when I get back to Cedar Valley. We were really surprised to hear they were going ahead with it next week."

"With what?"

"The trial."

"What?" I was shocked. Nobody had even told me yet there

was definitely going to *be* a trial, let alone so soon. How can they even get a jury together that quickly?"

"I heard on the news they were going to do it today or tomorrow. Impaneling a jury in this county, from what I've heard, doesn't take long. You mean your attorney didn't say anything to you about it?"

"I haven't even seen him since day before yesterday. You're sure the trial's to be next week?"

"Yes. Several of us have already been told to be available as witnesses starting Monday."

"For the prosecution?"

West nodded, looking apologetic. "I think in my case it's mainly to establish the facts about your employment, residence, and all that. Your attorney will also call on some of us to testify regarding where you were on that Wednesday and Thursday and how you were helping with the investigation, and about your reputation and so forth."

"Have you heard who else the prosecution has lined up to testify against me?"

"Vivian seems to have some information on that. Maybe it's just speculation on her part, but she says Ned Booth, J. P. Dhrymes, and Kelly Puckett have all been told they'll testify."

"Booth? Why Booth?"

West shrugged. "Don't know. The detectives were out to see him a couple of times, but I have no idea what it involves."

"What's Adams been doing?"

"He and Marklee got the incendiary device figured out, but not who the arsonist is. He's been gone for several days now, off on another case. Says he'll get back as soon as he can."

We talked a little longer, then West left. If I'd had any question in my mind about having my family get me a better lawyer, the district ranger's message from my mom eliminated it. It looked like I was now stuck with this refugee from Boys' Town and would have to hope for the best. But there was a bit of consolation, if only a tiny one: West would not have to lie to my mother about my being involved in a trial.

Chapter 16

M y trial began in Superior Court of California on Monday, August 25, 1958, and was entitled *The People of the State of California, Plaintiff, vs. Harper Sandow, Defendant.*

During his last visit to my county jail cell, Frank Pierce had briefed me, advising me not to worry, the state's case being a weak one. I was not reassured when I heard the judge advise the jury I was being tried for violation of the California Penal Code, section 187, murder in the first degree.

The Superior Court judge hearing the case was Brisbane Apperson, a lawyer who, according to Pierce, spent most of his time running the family cattle ranch and was a long-time enemy of the Forest Service. The district attorney, who had the reputation of not losing cases in front of a jury, had turned the case over to Arnold Miller. Pierce's analysis was that the Pronghorn county jurors would dislike Miller, a slightly built man with a strong New York accent. Miller had come to California on his doctor's advice to cure his asthma, Pierce told me, but it turned out that the juniper pollen in Pronghorn County was making it worse.

The jury, nine men and three women, were of all ages and their clothing and general appearance varied greatly. They regarded me with what seemed a blend of curiosity and foreboding, and I made it a point to look each of them in the eye.

At the outset of the trial, Frank Pierce seemed amazingly calm and even a bit cocky. I know in his place I would have been petrified with fear and concern. It was almost as if he had some aces up his sleeve he wasn't telling me about.

Miller's opening statement was straightforward: the defendant had invited his girlfriend to the campground, where he hoped to have sex with her. When she refused, he attempted to rape her and was then forced to kill her to eliminate her as a witness to the crime. Miller promised to introduce evidence that would prove the defendant committed the crime.

The rape attempt allegation appalled me. First, if there was anything to it, my heart went out to Nora for what she might have had to suffer before being killed. Second, what led the prosecutor to believe there was a rape attempt anyway? There must have been something, but apparently not enough to have me charged with that offense.

During Miller's presentation, the jury looked at me as if I were a wild beast hell-bent on ravaging their children or something. Despite his big-city looks and New York accent, out of place in rural Pronghorn County, the assistant DA had made a powerful first impression on the jury.

Pierce's opening statement was more complex. He described the arson problem and the investigation of it by myself and Nora Jeffers. When we got too close to the arsonist, Pierce told them, the murderer lured her to the campground, killed her, then rigged the evidence to implicate her for the arson, and me for her murder. Why should I have led her to the campground for sex anyway, he asked them, inasmuch as Nora lived alone right there in town. He said the prosecution could not prove their stated motive and would be unable to tie me to the murder weapon or place me at the murder scene. The jury had regarded Pierce skeptically to begin with, I thought, but now seemed more interested in what he was saying.

Miller wasted no time presenting the meager evidence against me. He introduced deputy J. P. Dhrymes to testify that he had found the note I had supposedly written to Nora, and about how he and another officer had traced it to one of the Forest Service office typewriters.

On cross-examination, Pierce asked whose fingerprints had been found on the note and got Dhrymes to admit that no attempt had been made to get fingerprints from it.

Miller then called the coroner and had him describe the condition of the body, something I was unprepared for. While I had a general idea about what the murderer had done to Nora from Adams's comments, he had spared me the nitty-gritty, which the coroner now gave the jury in every grisly detail. To this day my memory has blocked out the coroner's words, so detestable were the images and so crushing were they to my recollection of her beautiful face and body. I remember it only as a few minutes during which my whole consciousness was consumed with despair, remorse, and hatred.

I was told later that the jury was truly shocked by the coroner's account too, but I was in no state at the time to be aware of that.

The coroner said the time of death had been between noon and midnight on Wednesday, August 6. On cross, Pierce challenged him on the exactitude of the time of death and allowed him to substantiate it with medical criteria that sounded quite persuasive. I wondered at Pierce's sanity in doing this, knowing that the coroner would stoutly defend his determinations, which he did. But on returning to our table, Pierce winked at me. Had it not been for his boyish looks, I would have felt reassured.

The murder weapon was the prosecution's only tangible evidence. A Forest Service hand axe was introduced, and Miller put one of the sheriff's men on the stand to state that he'd found the axe beneath the front seat of my car. Then Miller called up a state crime lab technician from Sacramento to testify that the bloodstains on the axe matched Nora's blood type.

"Did you examine the handle of the axe for fingerprints?" Miller asked.

"We did. That evidence pointed to the accused."

On cross-examination Pierce asked, "What evidence, specifically, were you referring to when you said you examined the axe handle, and how, exactly, did it point to the accused?"

"Fingerprint evidence, possibly prints of the accused."

"What the hell, if anything, does that mean?" roared Judge Apperson.

The crime lab witness, somewhat shaken, replied that the fingerprint matching produced insufficient points in common, at least according to the state's rigid criteria, to positively identify the subject.

"Can you save us all some time and say in plain language what that means?" Apperson again demanded, his face growing scarlet.

"It means, sir, that we cannot positively say whose prints those are on the axe handle."

I glanced at Miller, enjoying his scowl. He then called Stan Turpin to the stand and asked him if he'd seen anything unusual Wednesday night in Cedar Valley.

"Yes, sir. I was driving home from Kelley's bar about eleven that evening, and saw Sandow driving up the road to the barracks."

It was a shocking bit of testimony, and probably true. It established that I had been out and had not arrived back at the barracks until late. I glanced at Pierce, whose face showed no change of expression.

By noon, the prosecution had already rested its case, and Pierce moved for a dismissal. The judge denied it.

In the afternoon session, Pierce documented the arson investigation and how I had been involved in it as a Forest Service employee, calling Bill Marklee and Felton Shackle to testify. Then he got down to the day of the murder and had Turpin testify that he had dropped me off on the Hog Tooth road early in the day. He then called Punky Swiftbird, who related how he had picked me up that night and dropped me off in Cedar Valley at about eight thirty.

Where is he going with this? I asked myself, appalled. He next called Bill Marklee and had him testify as to how long it would take someone to drive from town to the Champion Springs campground and return. Marklee said it would take approximately one hour and twenty minutes.

Then Pierce called Albert Carlisle, who testified that I had been out all evening, returning to our little room at about eleven. Things didn't seem any better, there being a two-and-a-half-hour gap in my alibi.

Judge Apperson seemed on the verge of breaking for the day and tapped his pencil nervously on the bench waiting for Pierce to reveal what it was he was trying to accomplish.

At that moment a bailiff stuck his head in the door at the back and nodded toward Pierce, who beckoned his next witness.

"The defense calls Steven R. Christian," he said, and I looked on in amazement as the guitar-playing cowboy sauntered down the aisle.

Miller, surprised, tried to protest it, but Apperson let him come to the stand and be sworn.

"Where were you at approximately nine on the evening of Wednesday, August sixth?"

"I and a girlfriend were shacked up out on a ranch near Cedar Valley. She's a friend of Nora's, Miss Jeffers. That is, she *was* a friend of hers until Nora got killed. Anyway, she got sick and asked me to pick up some things Nora had bought for her in town. When I got to Nora's house she wasn't there, but a light was on, and I hoped she'd be back in a little while, so I waited in the car. About nine I see this fellow Sandow drive up and knock on her door. I called him over and we got to talking, and I invited him to go for a drive and have a couple of drinks. Then afterwards I dropped him off at his car back at Nora's house. That was at around eleven."

"You're sure it was Wednesday, August sixth?" Pierce asked.

"Damn sure. That's my birthday."

"What about the time? How are you sure of that?"

"My girlfriend tried to call Nora before I left the ranch. I remember her saying that Nora should be home by then, it was already eight thirty. I figure it took me about a half hour to get to her house. Doesn't take that long to drive in, but I had to jump-start the car before I could leave."

"What about when you dropped Sandow off?"

"Well, when we got back to Nora's house and saw she wasn't home yet, he looks at his watch and says he's really beginning to get worried about her. I remember it was close to eleven."

Miller, outraged, couldn't wait for cross-examination.

"Are you the Steve Christian who is wanted on a number of charges including disturbing the peace, malicious mischief and vandalism, flight to avoid prosecution stemming from an incident in Cedar Valley the night of Saturday, July twenty-sixth this year? And in fact are you not now a fugitive from justice?"

"I was until a few hours ago."

"And who persuaded you to come here to give this amazing testimony?"

"My girlfriend. She knew what was going on and told me they had the wrong guy on trial, and I was the only one who could say where Sandow was that night."

"I see. Who is this young lady friend of yours, and why isn't she here in court to verify what you're telling us?"

I glanced at Pierce, expecting him to object to the question, but he just sat there looking amused.

"Look, uh, Mr. . . . what did you say your name is?"

"Miller," the prosecutor said. A few of the jurors tittered.

"Well, didn't you just tell everybody here I was a fugitive from justice? And don't you know that for me to identify her could get her into trouble too?"

Now most of the jurors were smiling, enjoying the show. Miller was not amused.

"And what promise have you received for giving this remarkable testimony at this time?" His voice dripped with sarcasm.

"No promise at all. I came here to tell the truth."

"Yes, of course you did," he said, sneering. "To rephrase my question, what are you getting out of it?"

"Probably about a year in jail."

Pierce and I exchanged small smiles. Christian had turned himself over to the law in order to testify on my behalf, thus gutting the prosecution's already flimsy case.

There was a rumble in the courtroom, and I saw some members of the jury nodding to one another and talking amongst themselves. Judge Apperson called counsel to the bench. There was some talk, some nodding of heads, and the trial was over even more suddenly than it had begun, charges dismissed.

"How did you do it?" I asked Pierce.

"Abby Murrow told me the cowboy was about to turn himself in last week anyway, and I suggested he wait until today. It did work out better this way, didn't it?"

Six days later I was back in Cedar Valley. I'd planned on spending at least a full week with my dad and mom in Sunland, but after finding my father recovering well and my mom coping with his needs, I was out of there after spending only two full days. I doubt if they even missed me. It seemed that my father's stroke had supplanted Heath's death as the main item of concern in their lives. They didn't even mention my brother's name while I was there.

It was Sunday afternoon when I got back to Cedar Valley; I drove past the ranger station and into town to get my mail from the post office box. The town looked normal, except for some new construction where Mona's Groceries was being rebuilt.

There were four letters for me. I first opened the one from A. A. Adams, postmarked Nevada City three days earlier. He'd heard about the trial and said there'd been no doubt in his mind of the outcome. Easy for him to say now, I reflected. He said he'd be back in Cedar Valley on Monday, looked forward to seeing me, and that he believed he could still get to the bottom of things with my help.

Next I opened a letter, a note, really, from Sally Boardman, Nora's good friend, in which she expressed her relief at the outcome of the trial and asked me to call her when I returned to Cedar Valley.

The third letter was from my mother, postmarked over a week earlier, rebuking me for not coming home in response to my dad's stroke. She hadn't mentioned it when I'd been home.

The last letter, postmarked August 26 in Cedar Valley, was addressed by typewriter. The message was also typewritten, and it said simply YOU'VE BEEN LUCKY UP UNTIL NOW. The menacing note actually pleased me; it meant my quarry was still out there, still playing the deadly game.

I went to a pay phone at the gas station and called Sally Boardman. She invited me to her home for supper that very evening, "if you can make it," and I assured her I could.

I showered, changed clothes, and got to the Boardmans' at five. When their door swung open, I handed a pathetic bouquet of wildflowers to a slender woman of about fifty. She had long blond

243

hair and green eyes, and I then remembered having seen her in town but had never known who she was.

"Come in, Mr. Murphy," she said, beckoning me into what had to be the most spacious living room in Cedar Valley.

"Ask the man what he'll have to drink, will you?" said a booming male voice from another room."

"Yes, if you please," she said. "What can I offer you?"

"A beer would be fine. But Mrs. Boardman—"

"Sally."

"All right, Sally. You called me Murphy. You're a jump ahead of me already."

She merely smiled and motioned me to be seated, and we waited for her husband to bring in the drinks. He did so shortly, turning out to be a bear of a man, one whom I'd also seen in town a time or two.

"We were worried, if you want to know the truth," he said. "We knew they had the wrong guy, but in a county like this one, you never know what'll happen."

"I'm glad I had a few friends. When I got back here last Monday night, folks were looking at me like I had a contagious disease or something."

"Well I think that's pretty much changed," Sally said. "Most people are saying that with the case they had against you, they had no business taking you to trial."

"But some of them still think I'm the one, I suppose?"

Bob Boardman snorted. "A few of them anyway, and they'll go on thinking it until the real murderer is found. And that's probably the only reason you came back here, we're guessing."

"Maybe. But even if I thought that impossible, I'd still have come here to meet you and try to convey to you my thanks for what you did for Nora . . . for what you meant to her. You were her very best friends in this world."

Neither said anything, Sally clasping her hands in her lap, her eyes looking a bit reddish, and Bob staring out the window.

"Um, I don't know how to say this," I went on hesitantly, "but I can imagine your shock and outrage on hearing what happened. During my days in jail one of the things that bothered me most, of course, was the part I played in triggering what finally happened to Nora. I should have weighed that possibility more carefully, and—"

"Stop it!" Sally said. "What kind of people do you think we are? We knew what was going on, and the three of us discussed the fact that she might be putting herself in danger."

"Easy, Sal," said Bob Boardman. "He doesn't know how we feel. Hell, he doesn't yet have any idea how much we know about him. Let's just relax a bit, can't we?"

"I'm sorry, Gene," Sally said. "I know you're trying to be gentle with us. Maybe I should explain a few things. Nora knew or at least strongly suspected who you were the very day you came to town, and within a few days she was certain of it. Does that surprise you?"

"Not now, I guess. It was pretty dumb on my part to try to pull it off. Did she confide in you right at the start?"

"Of course. She had been so involved with Heath, and you were practically a mirror image of him, at least to her. To me, you look little like your brother, but she said she would have recognized you a mile away."

"You know, apparently, that Nora and I became quite close ourselves. Why couldn't she tell me that she knew who I was? She let me be a liar and an imposter the whole time we knew each other."

"I knew you would ask that. It was because of Alice, Heath's fiancée, and your mom and dad, and of course, yourself. In the wake of Heath's tragic death, the last thing Nora wanted to do was to let your whole family find out his last act on earth was to have a flaming affair behind the back of his betrothed, with an older, twice-married woman from a lousy little sawmill town. She didn't think any of you needed or deserved that."

"She never mentioned Heath to me. Was it possible she thought I wouldn't find out?"

Sally nodded. "If you'd come right out and asked her, I think she would have told you. But until then, she felt she couldn't be sure."

"During our time together, I had the feeling she was still in love with Heath. They must have meant a whole lot to each other."

"Of course." Sally said. "That doesn't make you feel wonderful, I know, but if it's any consolation, my feeling is that she might never have fully gotten over Heath. He would always have been there in the background, and she was smart enough to know that." She looked at me hesitantly.

"I think that only makes me love her more, somehow," I told her. "Did you ever meet my brother?"

"We never saw them together," Sally said, glancing at her husband for confirmation. "I think they were trying to keep their affair secret from the community, not a realistic goal in a town like Cedar Valley. But I came to know Heath quite well, I think, if only from what Nora told me."

"You may think this really absurd, but when I was first getting to know Nora, I had her on my list of suspects."

Both Boardmans smiled for the first time. "She told Sally she thought so," Bob Boardman said. "Something about her Jeep being seen coming out of a road that was being watched."

"She really didn't know if you were bluffing about that or not," Sally said, "but we had a good laugh about her being a suspect in a case she was trying hard to solve herself."

"Is there anything at all about this you don't already know?" I asked looking back and forth between them.

"Probably not very much, at least from Nora's perspective. But she made us swear not to upset your scheme by divulging a thing," Boardman said.

"And we didn't," Sally added. "We had our own list of suspects and theories on what was going on. Did you get the letter Nora had me mail to you?"

"Yes, the night I got back from the fire in the Oyster Rock area. Until then I didn't realize she was doing her own investigation. Her work enabled us to discover the incendiary device used to start that fire."

"But apparently not the culprit, I take it?" Boardman asked.

"That's right. But it sure narrows things down. You know, this fellow Steve Christian sure saved my bacon. It was lucky for me we ran into each other in front of Nora's house that night, because I really needed someone to give me an alibi."

"We heard about his testimony," Sally said. "How in the

world did you manage to spend two hours with that man? What did you find to talk about?"

"Oh, one thing and another. You know how it is when you start drinking and talking. We had a good laugh about when the deputy tried to seduce Abby in his patrol car, and he seemed grateful for the help Nora and I gave her that night. Nora told you about that too, I guess."

"A memorable night if we ever had one here," Bob said.

"Your name came up with Steve the other night, Bob," I said. "He thinks pretty highly of you. Said something about your hiring him after he'd gotten fired for drinking on the job at some ranch."

"Oh yeah, that's right. Stan Turpin talked me into it. But come to think of it, I had to fire him a couple of weeks later for the same reason. Steve is one of those guys who can't drink. Maybe some time in jail will convince him of that."

"I missed it, being gone this last week. Did he plead guilty to all those charges?"

"Way I heard it—or I should say, the way Vivian heard it—they dropped everything except the vandalism charges. But still, he wound up with three months in the county jail."

While Sally prepared dinner, we suspended talk of murder and arson, and I had a chance to ask Bob Boardman how he'd become owner of the sawmill. He said it all started after the war when he went to work on a logging crew. After two years of working his way up through the different jobs he signed on at a mill, determined to learn those jobs too. Later, he and two friends built and operated their own small sawmill until he bought his friends out. Boardman said his big break came when he found out the Cedar Valley mill was failing and he was able, with the help of some loans, to buy it out and change its name to his own.

Sally, who had been kibitzing from the kitchen, called us to supper. I judged the dining room elegant by local standards, and the meal sumptuous. While enjoying the food and wine, I learned the Boardmans had met in Chester where Bob had owned the small mill. Sally had been the dancing teacher there, where she'd come from San Francisco to realize an ambition of owning and operating her own dance studio in a small town. Her tap dancing classes became popular with adults, and Bob had been one of her first pupils. When she said that, they exchanged glances and I got the impression there had been more than just dancing lessons.

Over coffee in the living room, Bob asked if I planned on going back to Los Angeles eventually.

"My dad asks that too. I don't know. This place grows on you, or at least did on me. I was happy here until . . . now I don't know."

"If you decide to stay, will you still work for the Forest Service?" Sally asked.

"Eventually they'll find out I lied on my application. Then there was the gunfight, and Don West thinks I was involved in that. Too, I guess a lot of people will blame Nora's death on my intervention in the arson thing. Anyway, I'm only a seasonal employee, and there wouldn't be work for me this winter."

"Sounds like the lumber business. When the snow flies we lay off a lot of our men. Anyway, don't leave town for lack of a job without checking with me, you hear? I have some connections in this county."

"Thank you," I said. "I should know more in a day or two."

"Keep us up to date, won't you?" Boardman said. "We lost someone we considered a daughter, and I'd be pretty disappointed if her murderer gets away without justice being served."

"He won't, sir. But nobody can promise legal justice."

They both looked at me with shocked expressions, and I immediately added, "Living with the fear of final justice can be worse than life in any jail."

"You mean the fear of going to hell?" Sally asked.

"There's more than one kind of hell. I think he's going to find his."

Chapter 17

The post office opened at eight the next morning, and I was there a few minutes later to mail the notes that I'd scribbled off the night before. Vivian Crump, looking radiant and mischievous as usual, greeted me.

"Hello, stranger. I'm surprised to see you. After the way you got treated around here, not many of us expected to ever see you again."

"Yeah, well here I am. You're stuck with me for a while longer, it looks like."

"Harper, I didn't get to tell you this, but I and a lot of other people around here are real sorry about what happened to Nora. I know you two were, well, close."

"Thanks, Vivian. Nobody is more sorry about it than I am. She was one of the finest people I've ever met, and someone I hoped to know a lot better someday. But now . . ."

Vivian reached across the counter and put her hand on mine. "It'll take time, dear. It always does. And in the meantime, let me know how I can help out. The post office can do more than just sell stamps and deliver packages, you know."

I walked out of there wondering what exactly she might mean by that, and it conjured up an image from the dream I'd had in jail, the one in which A. A. Adams was standing behind the post office window waiting on people. Or was Vivian talking about a sexual encounter? Could the queen of local inside knowledge and gossip be pondering an involvement of her own? As usual in a potentially embarrassing situation, I'd failed to find out what she meant before terminating the conversation.

I hadn't been in the ranger station office since being arrested, and when I walked in the back door I ran smack into Lois and she gave me a big hug. More than anyone other than the Boardmans, she knew how much Nora meant to me. She stepped back, seemed about to say something but turned away, choked up.

"Am I still on the payroll?"

She nodded. "Don and Felton are at the forest supervisor's office today in Winchester. When they left, Don wasn't sure what would be decided about your status, so I'm keeping my fingers crossed. Mr. Adams is in Bill's office. He wants to see you the minute you come in."

I turned toward Bill's office, but Lois put her hand on my arm. "I'm glad you're back, Harper," she said.

Adams was hunched over a notebook scribbling away when I walked in. He looked up at me over the top of his glasses.

"Well, shall I call you Harper or Gene?" he said when I'd closed the door.

I laughed. "Gene is fine. But I'm still wondering why the sheriff's people didn't find out who I really am. Didn't they check me out through the FBI or the marines?"

He shook his head and smiled. "Who knows what might have gone wrong. Files misplaced, unclear prints submitted, incompetent records clerk, I've seen it before. Anyway, I supposed you'd like to know how the hell I was spending my time while you were in the clink."

I sat down and waited while he went through all the business of getting his pipe going. The big map showing fire locations was hanging on a wall, and Adams hobbled over to it and started pointing at spots with his stubby index finger.

"This one, this one, this one, and this one. We found the same device at each one of them. We started with the one you saw in the pine tree at Oyster Rock."

"We?"

"Bill Marklee and I. We took climbing gear, and Bill went up the tree. Know what it was?"

I waited.

"It was a paper cup, suspended, originally, like a tiny flower pot, by three very fine wires. It was rigged in such a way that if any one of the three wires broke, the cup would turn over and release its contents."

"White phosphorous in a paper cup of water?"

"Correct. Way I figure it, two of the wires were treated with a strong acid, sulfuric, most likely. I found pieces of tape around two wires in each setup, and my guess is that the tape had been soaked in the acid. When either one of those wires broke, down goes the phosphorous."

"And the third wire keeps the cup up in the tree and out of sight of investigators."

"Yup."

"Hmm. No telling how many devices may have been set that didn't work."

"That's right. In some cases the phosphorous might have been released but failed to kindle a fire on the ground. Other times, say if the acid failed to sever the wires, the water would have evaporated in a couple of days allowing the phosphorous to start the cup itself on fire. In those cases the burning phosphorous would either fall to the ground or get hung up in the branches."

"Well, in either case, then, there's no danger of a device set more than a few days ago still starting a fire."

Adams puffed on his pipe. "Highly unlikely as far as I'm concerned. The guy had things pretty well thought out."

"Did you look at any of the other suspicious fire sites?"

"Well, Marklee doubted how easy it'd be to find them readily, or whether this old man with a game leg could get that far up the hill and back in a day."

"What about the Pegleg fire?"

"I knew you'd be interested in that one, and why, of course. But maybe Marklee didn't. He said he'd seen that tree when he

251

initially investigated the fire. He described it as about a sixty-incher with no branches below about sixty feet. Said if I wanted that one climbed to get somebody else."

"Yeah?"

"So I did. I got Stan Turpin. We went out in his pickup and hiked up to the point of origin. Marklee had told him exactly how to find it. I got up the hill a ways where I could look horizontally across at the first couple of whorls of branches. I couldn't see a cup, but could see what looked like some wires dangling. To be sure, I sent Stan up the tree and watched as he pulled them loose where they'd been stapled to the branch. They were just like the ones from the Oyster Rock fire, pieces of tape and all.

"What gear did Stan take with him from the pickup?"

"About what you'd expect, I guess. Belt, spurs, climbing rope, a pair of pliers or wire cutters. I guess that's all."

"Same as Marklee took for the trees he climbed."

"Yeah, but Marklee took a hand axe with him. I don't believe Stan did."

"And probably no sign of the paper cup near the tree, I suppose?"

"It probably blew away when it finally became detached from the third wire. We looked around for a while, but couldn't find it. Stan wondered what we were looking for, but we didn't say.

"What about Ned Booth? Did he have any idea what was going on?"

"We weren't broadcasting it," Adams said. "If Booth knew what we were up to, it would almost have had to come from either Marklee or Turpin. I did talk to him. Went to his shop right after they took you in. What I had in mind was the climbing gear Nora saw in his pickup. I told him we were looking for somebody with climbing experience to do some contract work for us on an investigation."

"How did he react?"

"No special reaction. He said if the price was right, he'd be interested. So I asked him if he had his own gear or would need us to furnish it. He said he had his own, that he had a contract with the Rural Electrification Corporation to troubleshoot lines weekends and nights in the area near Cedar Valley. He explained that that saved the corporation sending a crew clear out from Winchester."

Things started clicking in my smallish brain canister. "Well, I've got a strong hunch," I said, a wave of hatred welling up inside me.

"You got it figured out?"

"Maybe," I said, and explained why I thought so. "But there's no proof. Everything is very circumstantial at best."

The old man tapped out his pipe into a wastebasket, peered inside the bowl, then set the pipe down on the table. "That's a fair analysis, Gene. But as you say, there's no proof. It's all based on observations. I doubt if the sheriff's detectives would even be interested in it, other than to satisfy their curiosity."

"Where can we go from here, then?"

"I won't be able to spend much more time here. It would be nice to sit and wait and watch, but that's impossible. We've got to make a fast move."

"Set a trap?"

He nodded. "Can you provide some bait?"

I'd already thought about it. "Way I see it, the only thing that would bring him out would be to get his hands on what he thought was strong evidence against him. What about Nora's letter?"

"That's exactly what I had in mind. She copied down some odometer readings. Maybe we can elaborate on that."

I started writing on a note pad, and soon handed Adams two proposed messages:

Sep. 3

> *Harper: I just remembered this envelope (enclosed) that Nora gave me the day before it happened. As you will see, it was intended for you. I hope it will help. Thanks once again for your condolences; we loved her very much.*
>
> *Good luck and God speed.*

Sally

Aug. 6

Harper: In case I have to leave or something happens to me, I wanted you to know where the materials are. His odometer readings for the days in question are in a brown envelope taped under the driver's seat in my Jeep. There are also instructions on how to locate the other evidence I mentioned to you. Sorry I couldn't tell you why I was doing all this, but if you should receive this note, you'll by now probably know why.

I'm not sentimental about last requests and all that, but if I had to make one, it would be . . . Don't let me down.

Love,
Nora.

The old man studied the two notes, looked up and said, "They're perfect. Can you get Mrs. Boardman to write the first one?"

"No problem, believe me."

"How about the other?"

"The post office lady tells me they can do more for me than just sell stamps and deliver packages."

"Vivian Crump? The town gossip?"

"I think she'd rather enjoy getting involved secretly in this thing."

Adams snorted, stuck his empty pipe in his mouth. "Gene, we don't know where this might take us. I think we ought to keep it just between the two of us, same as for your identity. I'll write the note to you from Nora, using her letter to you as a model of her handwriting. I'm pretty good at that. And I wouldn't advise telling Mrs. Boardman why she's writing the other note for you, or who it's going to be delivered to, either."

"But she—"

"I know she loved Nora and all that, but you don't know her that well. Anyway, we might be putting her in a bad spot, depending on how this comes out."

I finally agreed with him. " 'Selmo, I don't know how you'd

254

handle this, but as far as I'm concerned, it's got to be me up at the Jeep to identify him when he comes up there."

"Not a good idea, Gene. First of all, I'm afraid of how you might react, and we can't have an incident. Second, you and I are the ones the guy will most suspect of running a scam on him. We've both got to be accounted for whenever he decides to go up there."

"Well, if not you or I, who? Has to be someone who will be able to identify him, even in the dark. That rules out outsiders. If we get somebody from the outfit, we'll compromise the whole thing."

"Let me work on it while you go ahead and get these notes prepared for mailing. You're sure he has a post office box?"

"I've heard him say he gets his check sent there. I'll find out the number from his payroll address in the files. We can make it look like a mistake: my name with his box number. Shall we set it up for delivery of the letter tomorrow?"

"Too soon. We need some elbow room. Make it for Thursday afternoon."

Adams wrote the note supposedly from Nora to me, I checked in the files for the box number, then left for the Boardmans'. When I explained without mentioning names what we were up to, Sally's face lit up radiantly, and she immediately sat down at her desk and wrote out the note to Nora. I also had her address an envelope to me using the incorrect box number, then placed "Nora's" sealed note to me inside.

"I hope all this will indeed help, Gene. Can I ask what Nora's letter to you says?"

"Sally, I would dearly love to tell you, because you would approve heartily. But for reasons I can't explain, it might be unfair to do so. Let's just say I have a strong feeling we're both eventually going to be happy with the results."

An hour later, I was parked near the post office, waiting for it to be free of customers. Then I went in.

Vivian eyed me suspiciously. "Been thinking of my offer?" The way she said it, she could have meant almost anything.

"As a matter of fact, yes, Vivian. Would you be interested in

255

helping the federal government get to the bottom of something very important?"

"Oh," she said, sounding almost dejected. Part of her continuing playfulness, I judged.

I handed her the letter addressed to me from Sally Boardman and asked if she would see that it was posted on Thursday. She gave me a real fish eye.

"Mailing yourself a love letter, and to the wrong box number?"

"Can you do it for me? It's for a good cause, believe me."

She squinted at me. "Sure Ace, but remember, you owe me one now."

"You are a doll. Next time I catch you out from behind that window I'm giving you a big hug and a kiss."

"I'll need three cents for the stamp, don't forget that. And I won't forget the other. Oh, one other thing. What if he turns it in to me?"

"Then put it in my box where it belongs."

Back at the station I let Adams know things had been set in motion.

"Okay, Gene. I want you to go back to work just like everything was normal and wait for things to start developing. Under no circumstances should you divulge anything about what we're doing. Don't even hint around about it. As far as you're concerned, it's all over, you don't want to even talk about it. Okay?"

"All right. What about the stakeout?"

"I guess it's going to be you, much as I don't like it. Just remember this. Whatever happens between now and then, be ready to be up there by the time that mail is delivered, and be prepared to spend at least three days and nights. And I want your solemn promise there will not be a confrontation, under any circumstances whatever."

I nodded, somewhat perplexed, as he repeated the statement word for word.

"One other thing, Gene. Be best if we aren't seen talking together from here on out."

"All right. But can you give me an idea where we're going with this when we find out if we're on the right track?"

"That's something I'll be working on during the next few days. I think you'll like what I have in mind. Meanwhile, it's going to look like I'm out of here, finished with the investigation. Don't let that worry you. If you feel you have to contact me, call my office in Nevada City, ask for my secretary, Millie, and give her your real name."

A few minutes later I reported to Punky Swiftbird in the fire warehouse. He offered me his condolences on the Nora's death and said he was glad to have me back on his crew.

"I don't know for how long, Punky. Don West has probably had about enough of me by this time."

"I didn't really look for you again, Harper, once I heard you took off for Southern California after the trial. Figured you'd had enough of this whole thing up here. You honest to God gonna be working for me again, or are you still involved in that investigation?"

I laughed. "No, I doubt if I'll be involved anymore. I just hope I get to keep my job as long as fire season holds out."

"So nobody knows yet who it is that's been starting the fires, or, for that matter, who . . ."

"Who butchered Nora. That's right, Punky. I don't think the detectives are still even working on it, what I hear."

"What about the Auto Club?"

"Adams? Said he's leaving. Has other work to do. Nothing further to follow up on around here."

Swiftbird started to wander away shaking his head, Donald trailing along behind.

"What do you want me to work on?" I asked after him.

He turned back. "If you want to, you can pull an eight-oh-eight on the Marmon-Harrington. It's a few days early, but I don't expect you want to spend all day with the rest of the crew. They're out back rebuilding the paint house. Fact, I'll tell them to stay the hell away from you for a while."

The next morning Swiftbird told me I was wanted in Don West's office at nine, and when I got there I found Felton Shackle, Ray Owens, Bill Marklee and Lois Hart seated around a large table. Don, it appeared, had been going over with them some things he had learned the day before at the supervisor's office. Don waved me to a chair while he finished his briefing. Then he turned to me.

"We're happy the way things turned out, as far as the trial is concerned," West said, looking somber. "Some of us were prepared to testify further on your behalf, but it ended so suddenly we didn't have the chance."

I nodded, and the room grew quiet. West seemed to be getting ready to say something difficult for him. He fiddled with things in front of him, and finally began.

"Harper, you're being terminated, effective tonight at quitting time."

As his statement began to sink in, I glanced around at the others. Nobody looked surprised; they obviously already knew it. I waited for him to elaborate.

"Inasmuch as you're only a seasonal, I don't have to have any particular reason to end your employment here, but I will explain why I'm taking this action. This is something that's been brewing since the time you arrived here. You are obviously a person who, once launched on a cause, can't let it go. That part is okay—in fact I wish I had more people with that quality. But in your case, the intensity with which you've gone about it has been such that I can no longer deal with the disruption you cause.

"Part of it is my fault, that is, for letting you be a part of this fire investigation, and then not keeping a tighter rein on you. Indirectly, and not entirely your fault, this has led to a murder, scandalous notoriety for the organization, and general disruption in what we're trying to do here. If the arsonist had been caught, the murderer been found out and brought to justice, maybe we could try to go on as normal. But basically, the situation is back where it was two months ago. Frankly, I cannot go through another two months, two weeks, or even two more days like you've brought us.

"You may not agree with my position on this, and I'm sure there may be others who don't either. But I hope you can at least understand it."

I saw his chest heave, and knew he was glad to have unburdened himself. He stared at me almost defiantly, expecting, I suppose, a rebuttal, but I decided to remain silent.

"Is there anything you'd like to say?" he asked.

"If I can stay on until the end of the pay period, I believe I can be helpful in getting to the bottom of the arson situation."

Before I finished the sentence he was already shaking his head. "Tonight," he said with finality. "And I'd appreciate your being out of the barracks by tomorrow morning. Obviously, I don't have the authority to make you leave town, but for the good of the organization, that is my preference, and I hope you'll respect that."

"Okay," I said. "I'd like you to know that everything I've done has been with the best interests of the Forest Service in mind, and I'm truly sorry for any damage I might have done to the image of the outfit, or to your career."

That one kind of stung him, being delivered in front of some of his subordinates. I thought he had it coming.

"This isn't about image, or my career," he said, sitting up ramrod straight in his chair. "This is about getting your job done in a competent manner, without starting World War Three in the process."

"Sorry. I didn't mean to come across as sarcastic. It's just that I've learned what's important to you, and I think my clumsiness is a problem from that standpoint. I bear you no ill will over it, Don."

He was clearly pissed by now. "You don't know what's important to me at all. My mission here is the administration of this ranger district to the end that the public realizes an optimum of goods and services from the land. I'm here to see to the management of timber, water, recreational opportunity, forage, and minerals. That's what's important to me, and not image and career."

He went on like that for a few minutes, kind of lapsing into a small-town Rotary Club speech. It would only have surprised me a little if at the end he had stood and sung "America the Beautiful." I thought of some choice remarks, but some instinct told me to keep my big mouth shut, and later I was glad I did.

During the exchange, the others had mostly looked down at

their tablets, only glancing at me furtively now and then. Lois looked upset and dejected.

"Lois will have your termination papers ready to sign shortly, and I'd appreciate it if you'd turn in your standard key, hard hat, and any other property you have checked out. We all appreciate your efforts here and only hope you can understand our position."

With that, apparently, I was all through, at least as a Forest Service employee. Adams, I'd learned, had left early that morning, so I guessed he knew nothing of my termination. Where did that leave our stakeout plans? With no hope of getting in contact with Adams for the next several days, I had no choice but to carry out my agreed-upon part of the plan. Unfortunately, he had not yet told me about his part.

Rather than spend another night in the godforsaken barracks, I packed my things, loaded the car, said my good-byes around the office and to the crew, and headed south out of town. I stopped, made a U-turn, and headed back to the post office.

"I want to close out my post office box," I told a surprised Vivian.

"But I thought—"

"I've been terminated. The Forest Service thinks I'm giving them a bad image, I guess."

"I'm really sorry, Harper. Where will you be going, then?"

"To look for a job somewhere, I suppose."

"What about that letter? Is that off now?"

"No, it's very important that it be delivered Thursday. Otherwise, all Mr. Adams's work here will probably be useless, and I would be very disappointed about that."

She had me sign a form to close out the box, and I left, telling Vivian I hoped to see her again before too long. Just outside the post office I ran into Mona, who had come across the street from the grocery store reconstruction job to mail some letters.

"Glad to see you back, Harper. Good to get back on the job again?"

"I told them to stick the job," I said, making it sound abrupt, then climbed into my car and accelerated through a U-turn, heading south.

There was a job yet to be done at Oyster Rock before the stakeout could begin, and so once more I headed up the dusty mountainside. Seeing the red Jeep brought back a flood of memories, and it still seemed impossible Nora was dead. I guess I talked aloud to her as I stuck the pieces of tape up under the seat, making it look as if an envelope had already been removed.

Next I reconnoitered the area for an observation post. I decided on a place in the rocks on the uphill side of the road, above the spot where the Jeep had been pushed off. While that site denied me a direct view of the Jeep, it did provide a view of anyone coming or leaving and was just downhill from a place in the underbrush where I could camp.

Then I had to figure out where to leave my car. Certainly the murderer would check out the road and logging spurs above the Jeep before stopping there, so it had to be well concealed. I could leave the car and hike the five or six miles up there. It would be difficult with camping gear and would still leave me with the need for a place down near the main highway to stash my car. Adams could have dropped me off, but he was long gone. How did the old investigator figure I'd work this out?

It took me a couple of hours of looking, and some hard work dragging and wedging rotting chunks of cull logs around, but I finally carved out a place for the car in an abandoned log landing just off the main road. I figured that once I'd thrown some cut branches over the top, it would be hard to spot from the main road.

To be on the safe side, I waited until dark to descend the mountainside, fearful of meeting somebody coming up who would mention my presence around town. Then, having achieved the main highway unseen, I drove all the way to Redding and checked in at a good motel.

On Wednesday morning I called for Anselmo Adams at his Nevada City office, giving my real name to the secretary. She asked me what the call concerned, and I told her the Cedar Valley investigation. She said that to the best of her knowledge, Mr. Adams was still in the Cedar Valley area and wasn't expected back right away.

Her answer gave me some hope, and I told myself it added up with the other mysterious things that were happening. On the other hand, maybe he was just lousy at communicating with his office. Anyway, at this point I had no option but to go on with my part of the plan.

It would just not do to be seen going up the Oyster Rock road Thursday afternoon, the day the mail would be delivered, so I had to do it Wednesday night. I hadn't done a good job of preparing a campsite, so I slept in the car for the first time since the night I'd arrived in Cedar Valley. Then at first light I camouflaged the car with branches, one of which I first used to erase my tire tracks between the main road and the log landing. Finally I rolled a huge chunk of rotten log across the approach to the landing.

By about eight that morning, I was settled in my campsite among the fir samplings about fifty yards above my observation post in the rock outcropping. After a simple meal of fruit, cheese, and crackers, tired from the long drive and hard work, I lay on top of my blankets and slept for several hours.

During the long afternoon, several vehicles came up the hill and later went back down. My car was hidden about a quarter of a mile up the road from the Jeep, but I heard none of the vehicles stop in that vicinity.

I figured the mail would be delivered at about three. I must have looked at my watch fifty times that afternoon, asking myself why I worried about it; my suspect wouldn't go to his post office box until after work anyway, and maybe not even until the next day. So I finally began to relax, and spent my time trying to figure out what kind of a plan Adams was developing to carry out the next steps of our investigation.

As evening slowly gave way to night, the breezes subsided and it grew immensely quiet on the mountain. I could actually hear trucks on the highway in the valley, at least five miles away. Imagining vehicle sounds coming up the road kept me awake and intent, but nothing happened; nobody came, and the night became morning. I had dozed off and on but was sure that my anxiety would have instantly awakened me had a vehicle ascended the road just below me.

It was Friday. By now, everybody in town had to know I'd

262

been dismissed last Tuesday and had left the valley. They also had to know that Adams had apparently ended his investigation and left also. What I didn't know, of course, was whether I was wrong about my suspect. If so, he would probably turn in the envelope to Vivian, and I'd be stuck up here indefinitely, not knowing it.

That Friday must have been the longest day of my life, because nothing happened all day, into the evening, the night. It gave me all those hours to dwell on Nora's hideous death, my part in leading her to it, my failure to prevent it or make substantial progress in gaining the revenge I lusted after.

To make matters worse, the ants had discovered me, and I had to move my camp back farther into the woods to a less desirable spot. And I had been stupid enough not to bring along a book or any other reading material to help get my mind off everything that had gone amiss in this horrid place.

By Saturday afternoon, I concluded something must have gone wrong, but I sat out yet another night on the mountain. At dawn Sunday I decided to leave, to drive to Purple Pond and make a phone call, running the risk of meeting my quarry along the way. I also wanted some fresh food but doubted whether I'd be able to find a store open early on a Sunday morning. I still had a pretty good supply of canned stuff, but I'd gotten good and sick of it.

At seven I called Lois at her home, a small government residence on the compound of the ranger station.

"Harper! Where are you calling from?"

"Bakersfield. Sorry to call so early on a Sunday. Has Adams come back yet, or do you know how I can contact him?"

"Uh, you didn't hear? No, of course not. You had no way of knowing."

"Knowing what?"

"He's dead, Harper. It's just awful."

"Dead? How?"

"Heart attack. It happened Wednesday night, I guess the day after you left. He was in a motel in Winchester."

"Oh my God, I don't want to believe it. So he was still working on the arson case, he wasn't really leaving the area as he indicated?"

"We don't know. The sheriff's office says they don't know either. What are you doing in Bakersfield?"

"Visiting old friends. Well, damn. I really liked that old man. You know, he was working on a plan to catch up with the arsonist, but I guess that's out the window now. Know anything about the funeral?"

"They shipped his body to someplace in Southern California. We don't have any details. Don wanted to send condolences to Adams's wife, but evidently he was a widower. Really a shame. What are you going to do now?"

"Lois, I have absolutely no idea. What you just told me makes me feel like my guts have been ripped out again. I don't know. Maybe look for a job somewhere, I suppose. Uh, anything else happen around there since I left?"

"No, just people around town saying they're sorry to see you leave, mad at the Forest Service for firing you. Will you let me know when you have an address? I've had several people already ask me where they could write you."

After that call I felt like I was in a daze. I sat in my car for a while just wondering what the hell was the use of even trying. So what if I found out for sure who killed Nora? The police wouldn't be interested in the case with what little I had to offer, and some of them probably still thought I was the guilty one anyway. Add to that their demonstrated lack of investigative skills and the whole thing spelled futility. Then on top of everything, Adams was dead, along with whatever plans he might have had.

Pretty soon the anger began to mount up. I got the car gassed up, filled my canteens with water, and headed back toward the Oyster Rock road. And this time it wasn't only for Heath and for Nora, it was also for Anselmo Adams. Or was it mainly for me? That was a question I didn't want to try to answer, at least not yet.

Chapter 18

While making the long drive back up the mountainside I pondered the apparent meaninglessness of everything I'd tried to accomplish during my stay in Cedar Valley, arriving at my observation post in an almost desperately black mood. Our plan to force the killer into some misstep now had little purpose. All I could accomplish at this point would be to identify whoever came to retrieve whatever he thought was taped up under the seat in the Jeep. Then I would know whom to focus my rage on for years to come.

I decided to change things a little, at least give the son of a bitch something to think about. I clambered down through the brush to the Jeep and taped an envelope where I'd left the pieces of tape. Inside the envelope was a simple message:

you are a dead man

I was careful to use gloves to keep my fingerprints off the jeep as well as off the note, envelope, and tape.

By midafternoon the cumulus clouds were growing as large as

mountain ranges in the sky, and I began to hear thunder in the distance. I hadn't thought of rain when I got my gear together and had to make a quick trip to my car to get my heavy wool jacket and stocking cap. Soon the drops began falling, and in minutes it was coming down heavily. I got soaked.

The rain kept coming, and I could do nothing but sit there in the foliage and take it. There was the option of getting in my car, but at this point I was unwilling to risk missing my visitor, when and if he should come. Too, it would mean crossing the road in the mud and leaving obvious tracks.

Then it occurred to me that the muddy road would be an advantage. My quarry would find no fresh tracks to advise him of a stakeout.

My shelter in the brush was really no shelter at all, at least from the rain, so I moved down into the rocks, whence at least I had a good view of the road below. I lay there all afternoon, shivering and questioning my sanity, kept immobile only by the hope of hearing an engine and of seeing the shape of a pickup truck or car coming up the hill. I didn't care if I caught pneumonia or died of exposure or anything else that might happen to me; everything was coming to be focused on the goal that overrode every other consideration. Everything would be worth one chance to set things straight.

With the heavy clouds overhead, darkness came at about seven, and the rain continued. It was beginning to look like another long night ahead.

But finally I got my reward: the sound of a vehicle coming up the road. I could tell the road was slippery; the engine would suddenly roar momentarily and then, as the knobby tires took hold once again, would settle back into a steady grinding. Soon the engine noise grew louder, but still I could see no headlights illuminating the trees. The idea that he would approach without lights on such a dark night thrilled me; it could only mean what I hoped it did.

When the vehicle was almost directly below my vantage point I stuck my head up and saw a pickup truck halting at the place where the Jeep had gone off the road. I was astounded to discern the shape of a decal on the door and realized it was a Forest Service pickup.

The driver played a powerful light from his window down the side of the hill toward the Jeep. Then the light snapped off and the vehicle moved ahead up the rain-soaked road. It wasn't lost on me that the driver of the pickup that had forced me off the road the night my windshield was blasted out had also had a powerful spotlight. I silently cursed myself for not doing a more thorough job of placing branches over the reflective portions of my car.

But as I held my breath, the pickup went past where my car was hidden without stopping and was soon out of earshot. Soon he would be back, I knew, after checking around for vehicles, and it would by then be almost too dark to make a positive identification of the man himself, an essential piece of business now that he'd arrived in a government rig rather than his own. I thought it almost impossible anybody except the murderer would come up here on a night like this, but I had to be sure.

He would have to get out on my side of the pickup truck when he returned, but where would he stop, exactly, and what cover was I offered that would be closer than these rocks? I stood up and checked around—nothing to hide behind. And getting closer would be dangerous. I had my revolver with me, but this guy probably had his shotgun, and I have great respect for shotguns, especially when it's the other guy who has one.

The other thing that bothered me was my promise to Adams not to have a confrontation. It was the one thing he had absolutely insisted on, and at this moment, I had little argument with his philosophy on that one, even if the old man was now dead.

But I have always been an impulsive sort, one given to changing the plan at the last moment and going by instinct, and the trait had not proved fatal yet. Maybe I could count on it one more time.

As these thoughts rattled around, I heard the vehicle coming back down the hill, and when I saw it, it seemed the silhouette of a demon monster, looming up as it did through the gloom. It was now dark enough that I had no fear of being seen, remaining motionless, with my head sticking up above the rocks, and I could watch what was happening below. The vehicle stopped in the middle of the road above the Jeep, and I could hear the driver pulling hard on the ratcheted hand brake. I hoped he would leave the engine running to cover any sounds I might make clambering down the cut slope to get a better look, but he shut it off, leaving the pickup in gear, I was sure, as most anybody familiar with mountain driving would do.

Then the driver got out, and I could see he was carrying either a rifle or a shotgun in his left hand, and a long flashlight in his right. But it was too dark to recognize the man, and as he moved around the pickup I felt a deep hatred, because this had to be the animal who had hideously destroyed Nora only a few miles from this very spot. At that moment I knew I was capable of killing him, and somehow the thought no longer seemed immoral to me.

I think it was when he went out of sight down the slope that I realized what I would do. He would be gone only two minutes at most, I estimated, so I allowed about a minute to tick by to be sure he found the note beneath the front seat. I pulled my wet gloves on, moving fast to carry out my spur-of-the-moment tactics. I let myself slide crudely down the muddy cut slope and went directly to the left side of the pickup. He had left the driver's door open, and I simply climbed in, eased it out of gear into neutral, and gently released the hand brake. I was certain his first reaction as soon as he heard it start rolling would be to chase after it.

The vehicle picked up speed quickly on the hill. I had to slow it down and did so using the hand brake so as not to show the brake light. The road ran straight for about an eighth of a mile, then curved sharply to the right. Just before reaching the curve, I slowed it enough to be able to jump out safely, rolled out, and watched with huge satisfaction as it plunged off the side of the road. I heard it bounce at least three times and come to rest with a reverberating crash against what had to be an immovable object.

I moved back up the road a short way and found a hiding place behind a rock just above the road. The rain had let up and the clouds had lifted somewhat, and I now judged the visibility good enough to permit me to get a good look at my quarry when he passed me going down the road to locate what was left of his vehicle.

But he did not, not even after I'd waited a half hour. Maybe he'd seen my footprints in the mud on the bank, or near where his rig had been parked, I thought, and was being smart enough not to blunder into my ambush. If he'd read the note I'd left for him he'd be on edge and looking for trouble. He was smart enough to consider me armed, and to know I'd have the advantage of surprise. What would he decide to do? My guess was he'd do exactly what he'd done before, take the shortcut back to the campground, then hike from there into town, arriving much more quickly plus avoiding an ambush.

Adams and I had discussed the killer's probable movements the night of the murder and the next morning when he'd driven her Jeep up this road and pushed it off the edge. I figured that for a crude attempt on his part to credit Nora with igniting the Oyster Rock fire. Then after ditching the Jeep he had hiked to Champion Springs campground, we'd theorized, where he retrieved his own rig and drove back to town. I remembered tracing out on a map his probable route from the Jeep to the campground, figuring he had simply gone downhill to Rucker's Creek, followed it to its intersection with the Westside Trail, then followed the trail to Champion Springs campground, where the trail ended. Now that he was familiar with the route, he could easily do it at night. By day that route, I had calculated, would take him about two hours. At night that would translate to about two and a half, I guessed.

I started walking back up the road, watching for his footprints coming down, but there were none. The conclusion seemed clear: he was heading cross-country on foot as he had before, destination Champion Springs. Because of my stupidity in putting the note under the seat, he had to believe now that I was on his trail, that I had lured him there for the purpose of identifying and then killing him.

He could reach the campground by about eleven, I figured. From there it would be another hour's hike to the highway, then about three hours more into Cedar Valley. Once safely back in town, he could either slip away forever in his own pickup, or stay right there and play dumb about who went out for an evening spin in one of the government trucks.

It was clear, therefore, that I had to go to the campground to identify the killer of my brother and of Nora. Not to do so would be to waste not only the stakeout, but the entire summer's work. Worse, I would have let down those for whom I sought revenge. And I knew the uncertainty about the murderer's identity and the guilt of having been afraid or unwilling to go there would haunt me for the rest of my life.

I approached my car stealthily, watchful of an ambush, but the muddy ground revealed no footprints nearby. I got right to work on removing the camouflage foliage, then started the car and began easing it out of its hiding place. But the rear wheels immediately began sinking into the sticky clay soil, and I had to stop, gather fir branches for traction, and try again. In a few minutes I was free.

The main logging road was slick, but the roadbed beneath the cap of mud felt firm. I stopped opposite my observation post, climbed the bank, then carted my camping gear back to the car. I made a second trip back to retrieve my sack of garbage.

I glanced at my watch—almost ten. I still had to get back to the main highway and make the four-mile drive to the Champion Springs turnoff. Then it would be about three more miles along a gravel road to the trail head. My quarry might be making better time than I allowed for, so I had no time to waste.

I was soaked to the skin and beginning to shiver, so I took a minute to at least get on a dry shirt and jacket. I thought about changing my socks and pants, but that would mean getting my boots off, then dancing about barefoot in the mud and dark, and so I said fuck it.

The road got sloppier toward the bottom of the mountain, and I almost lost control on a couple of turns before deciding to slow down to a reasonable speed. It made me feel a bit better to catch sight here and there of the S-shaped skid marks made earlier by my quarry on his way up this road.

The feel of the blacktop surface of the main road beneath my wheels was a reassuring one, and the relative ease of driving on it gave me a few minutes to try to figure out what I would do when

270

I got to Champion Springs. First priority would be the identification thing.

But what then? He'd know I had the goods on him, and if we came face to face he would have to try to kill me. If he still had the shotgun with him, and I was pretty sure he did, that could be messy—especially for me.

On the other hand, if I were merely to observe and identify him, what good would that do toward bringing him to justice? I could see myself testifying, "So I'm hanging around the campground at eleven and I see this guy walking along . . ." Big deal.

Then there was the eminently disturbing possibility that he might leave the trail, either bypassing the campground entirely, or else surprising me at my watch post. Would he be crafty enough to do that? Would he consider me smart enough to have figured this all out and be lying in wait for him? I was still thinking about these things when I found myself only a few hundred yards from the campground. I turned the car around and found a place to park it off the road.

There was really no good place to hide it, and that bothered me, but I just didn't feel I had time to screw around looking for something better.

It was now ten forty-five. I hurried up the road on foot, entered the campground, then walked the perimeter road past the camping units. The rainy weather had driven out any remaining campers, and that suited me fine.

At the far end of the campground I found the trail head, marked by a wooden sign on a four-by-four post. My first idea was to check for fresh footprints along the trail leading to the campground, but it was too dark, and I figured I was lucky just to be able to see the trail.

I walked up the trail about fifty or sixty yards and looked back toward the campground. It seemed to me that unless my quarry was extremely familiar with this trail he would have little way of knowing how close to the campground he was. Therefore, I concluded, he would be unlikely to try detouring the campground. If he'd by now figured out I might be laying for him at the trail head, then all he could do would be to approach it cautiously, his shotgun at the ready.

I stood there listening, still unsure what I would do when the time came. I walked a little farther and came upon a huge boulder bordering the trail on my right. I walked around it and discovered that with the help of a sapling growing next to it. I could climb atop the rock and position myself about ten feet above the trail. A big pine tree on the uphill side of the boulder would hide my silhouette somewhat from anyone approaching from that side.

I softly cursed the rain that again began to fall, not because of the physical discomfort—I was beyond that point now—but because its noise would mask the sound of footsteps. Everything depended on my seeing him in time to . . . to what?

The images from my dream flashed in front of my eyes and I could see the hideous face of that creature bent on defiling and destroying beautiful Nora. And it had happened right here. In those few moments of reverie and impending confrontation I lost all sense of objectivity, of justice, of reason of any kind. My memory lapsed; I could not visualize the face of my mother, recall the voice of my father or the words of Mark Twain, writing of forgiveness. Pure hot rage commanded my consciousness now, and primeval instincts took charge. Something clicked in my mind, and suddenly I was an animal, not one in dire need of meat, but one commanded by instinct to viciously strike down its prey simply because that prey was clumsy enough to appear.

And then at the very apex of my transformation into a subhuman creature, the shape of a man loomed on the trail below me. What happened in the next instant, during the next six or more hours, in fact, remains a black hole in my memory, because the next thing I can recall is driving southward in the Sacramento Valley. I was looking at the fuel gauge, and it surprised me to find it reading almost full. I couldn't even remember stopping for gas.

About a month later I called the Cedar Valley ranger station long distance from a telephone booth. It was a Saturday, and Punky Swiftbird answered. He sounded elated to hear from me. I told him I was calling to ask them to hang on to my final paycheck until I had a more permanent address. He said no problem.

"I guess you know what happened after you left here."

"You mean about Adams? Lois told me when I called. It really tore me up."

"No, Harper, I mean about the second body they found at Champion Springs." He told me who it was, and I tried to act surprised.

"My God. Who do they think did it?"

"They can't figure it out. No evidence, I guess. The body was in pretty bad shape. They don't even know for sure what killed him."

"He was right there in the campground?"

"That's the spooky part. His body was in that same garbage vault where they found Nora."

"Anybody have any idea how it happened, how he got there?"

"His pickup was parked by his place back in town, just like always. But one of our government pickups had turned up missing about the time he disappeared. That would have been about a week or so after you left here. Some hunters found the pickup smashed against a boulder off the Oyster Rock road not far from where we found Nora's Jeep that day."

"There was some connection?"

"Well, the sheriffs say they have evidence of his driving it, but if so, nobody knows how he would have got from there over to Champion Springs."

"What do people around town think happened?"

"Well, when the second body was found right there in the same garbage vault, most people figured the guy who did it knew he'd killed Nora and took this way of getting even with him. But nobody knows how he figured it out, or how he got him up there."

"But why would he have killed Nora? He was practically in love with her."

"Nobody seems to have a good answer for that. Some people say it was a lover's quarrel. Lois thinks Nora might have discovered something about him he didn't want known."

"Like he was setting the fires?"

"Yeah. And since you and Nora were together, that could be a problem for him. Maybe that's why he framed you."

"You think he thought I was suspicious of him?"

"Maybe. I caught him coming out of your room one afternoon before this all happened. Said he was looking for you. I didn't think anything of it at the time, but now it makes more sense."

"Was there anything suspicious about how Adams died?"

"The coroner decided it was a heart attack. But his room had been broke into and some stuff stolen, and whatever happened during that incident could have brought about the heart attack. But they never caught anybody."

"Were Adams's notes on his fire investigation found?"

"I know what you're thinking, Harper. It went through my mind too. All they said was his camera and briefcase had been taken but that his wallet was still there, hidden beneath a pillow. Makes you kind of wonder, doesn't it?"

"Sure does. The son of a bitch."

"Harper, I'm sure glad you were no longer around here when they found that second body. A few people might have figured you were involved in it. As far as I'm concerned, you sure would have been justified. And that's just between you and me."

"Thanks for that, Punky, and for everything else you did for me. I'm not sure Don West would have felt the same."

"Don't ask. Anyway, he's being transferred to the Winchester office. We're having his going-away party tonight."

"A promotion?"

"No, a lateral transfer. Something in the lands section, I hear. Word is the forest supervisor wants him in a job without responsibilities for community relations."

"Sounds like a dead-end job. I'll bet he's not very happy about it."

"You could say that. He says he made a big mistake not firing you sooner than he did."

"I'm not surprised. But then he wasn't too good at personnel management either. Anything else happen?"

"Just a couple of messages for you. Vivian wants you to know she delivered the letter, whatever that means. Also, Bob and Sally Boardman would like to see you again and want to know when you'll be back through here. What shall I tell them?"

"Tell them if I ever come back, it'll be only to see them. I no longer have any other reason."

Swiftbird hadn't seemed surprised by what happened, or by who it was that wound up in the garbage vault. In fact, he may have had me figured out the whole way. I drove along, letting things play once again through my mind. Booth and Turpin would have had similar motives for starting the fires. Booth had been forced to resign from the Forest Service because of his affair with the ranger's wife. The event left him embittered and possibly revengeful. Turpin's career was also ruined, he felt, when Bill Marklee was promoted to the prevention specialist job that Turpin dearly wanted. What better way to get even than ignite some fires Marklee couldn't figure out? It was Nora who finally provided the key to the whole thing when she called my attention to the climbing gear in Ned Booth's pickup. That's what prompted me to take a look up in that pine tree. But ironically, Booth had pole spurs, not tree hooks. That backed up his story that he did jobs for the Rural Electrification Corporation; the REC's circuits were almost all metallic and were hung on poles, not trees.

The pole spurs in Booth's pack led me to check out Turpin's telephone gear that same night. He had the tree hooks, all right, but missing from his sack were the come-alongs, crimpers, sleeves, spare insulators, and other supplies used to repair telephone line, none of which would be needed to rig the incendiary device. That stuff was in a carton in his jockey box.

And then there had been the business about the hand axe. Marklee carried one when he climbed during the investigation, but Turpin did not. Turpin had already climbed that tree at the Pegleg fire scene; he'd already axed off the limbs that would have interfered with his climb and didn't wish to bother carrying one up the hill with him. Marklee simply assumed he'd run into limbs to remove as he ascended the trees at the other fire scenes he'd helped Adams investigate.

It was too bad for the murderer when he fell for that misaddressed letter trick. His eagerness to cover his tracks led him back to Champion Springs campground one dark and rainy night where somebody made him pay for what he did to Heath and to

Nora, and maybe to Adams. After all these years, I still wonder what he was thinking about during those last few desperate moments when he realized his life was about to be snuffed out in that stinking garbage pit.

Epilogue

I bent most of my efforts the next few years toward starting a new life, trying to put those horrid scenes behind me forever. But that never has come to be, not even after more than three decades. The nightmares that terrorize me have grown less frequent over time, but they still come often enough to remind me that I shall never escape them, at least not during my lifetime.

At the outset of those terrible events that changed my life, my friends all tried to persuade me that my hatred, my desire for revenge would destroy me. Forgiveness was the answer, they said. That's easy counsel to give others, of course, but the question is, were they right about it? I thought them fools at the time, because destiny had dealt me a situation I had to confront in the only way that then seemed logical and possible.

Now I'm not so sure. What if I had simply accepted my brother's death as a cruel event, an accidental by-product of the arsonist's sick act, and gotten on with my life? I might have enjoyed all these years free of the guilt and uncertainty that still live within me. And more important, Nora might still be alive.

But then, Stan Turpin might still be alive too.